STAR'S REACH

STAR'S REACH

A Novel by
John Michael Greer

Published in 2024 by
Sphinx Books
London

Copyright © 2014, 2024 by John Michael Greer

The right of John Michael Greer to be identified as the author of
this work has been asserted in accordance with §§ 77 and 78 of the
Copyright Design and Patents Act 1988.

British Library Cataloguing in Publication Data

A C.I.P. for this book is available from the British Library

ISBN-13: 978-1-91595-214-1

Typeset by Medlar Publishing Solutions Pvt Ltd, India

www.aeonbooks.co.uk/sphinx

AUTHOR'S NOTE

There's a certain irony in the fact that this tale of the deindustrial future first appeared in serial form as a monthly blog post on the internet, that most baroque and unsustainable of modern industrial society's technosystems. That said, I'm grateful to all those who read, praised, and criticized the story in its original form, and thus contributed mightily to whatever virtues it may have.

My gratitude and thanks are also due to Harry Lerwill, Dana Driscoll, and Sara Greer for their help revising and editing the manuscript.

CHAPTER 1

THE PLACE OF BEGINNINGS
AND ENDINGS

One wet day on the road that runs alongside the Hiyo River toward Sisnaddi, Plummer told me that every story in the world is just a scrap of the only story there really is, one big and nameless tale that winds from the beginning of things all the way to the end and sweeps up everything worth telling in between. Everybody has some part in that story, he said, even if it's just a matter of watching smoke from a battle over the next hill or listening to news that's whispered in the night. Some people wander further into the story and then wander right back out of it again, after they've carried a message or a load of firewood that settles the fate of a country or a dream. Sometimes, though, somebody no different from any of these others stumbles and falls into the deep places of the only story there is, and gets picked up and spun around like a leaf in a flood until finally the waters either drown him for good or toss him up gasping and alive on the bank.

Plummer said all of that between one mouthful of cheap Tucki whiskey and the next, as we sat and waited out the rain under the shelter of a ragged gray ruin left over from the old world. I nodded and said nothing and decided he was drunk. Now, though, I'm not so sure. Yesterday I got to the one place on Mam Gaia's round belly I'd given up expecting ever to come, and nearly got reborn doing it. As the five of us who

1

made it here sat in the darkness and waited for nightfall and wondered if we would live to see morning, the thought came to me more than once that this journey I'm trying to write out just now is part of something a mother of a lot bigger than the travels of one stray ruinman from Shanuga—bigger, for that matter, than the different roads that led each of us here, bigger than Shanuga or Meriga itself.

For all I know, Plummer may be right. If he is, I know to the day when his one story caught me up and set me on the road to Star's Reach. It was the morning of the sixth of Semba in the thirty-seventh year of Sheren's time as Presden, four hundred years and some more after the old world ended and ours began. That was the day I turned twenty. It was the day I became a ruinman, and I nearly got myself reborn then, too.

I was in the Shanuga ruins that morning, down in the underplaces of a big building that must have soared way up above its neighbors before storms and clumsy scavengers brought it down. Now most of it lay sprawled over two blocks of smaller ruins, filling up one of the old streets in between. Streaks of rust ran down the concrete and showed where rain liked to pool and flow in the wet season, but there was good metal in the ruin as well, and maybe reason to hope that valuables might have been left in the buildings that got buried in the rubble when the old tower went down.

Still, that was work for other ruinmen. When the guild misters held a lodge after the rains and pulled shards from a pot to settle who got what part of the dry season's diggings, Mister Garman drew the piece that stood for the underplaces of the tower. Gray Garman, we called him—we in this case meaning his prentices; he was tall and lean and dark, with a head of tight curled gray hair and a short gray beard and a frown, more often than not, that twisted his mouth to one side and made him look as though he was thinking about something dead.

He hadn't been frowning the morning he told us what the draw had given us, and for good reason. The underplaces of the old towers are dangerous, worse even than the upper floors of a tower that hasn't quite gotten around to falling over or pancaking, but there's no place you're more likely to find the sort of salvage that can pay for a dozen sparse seasons in a single day. Once the rains stopped and the ground dried out enough, then, we went to work on it, clearing rubble out of the old stairwells and shoring up places where cracks ran through the concrete and might bring all of it down on our heads. As it turned out, though, Garman might as well have frowned. Whether the tower was abandoned and stripped before the old world ended or cleared by scavengers in the drought years afterwards, we never did figure out, but room after room was as empty of salvage as it could be.

We spent most of two months making sure we'd been through all of it, every closet and corridor, and finally Garman decided it was time to start cracking the concrete. By this time some of the other misters and their prentices had much better finds, and made sure we knew about it. Mister Calwel, who was as close to an enemy as Garman had, found a parking garage that fell in with half a dozen cars still in it, and got to haggle with the metal merchants over that while we were coming back with empty hands.

Garman told us first thing that morning, the morning I turned twenty, that we'd go to work breaking the building down the following day. I didn't mind the extra time off, since there's no harder work in the ruinman's craft than pounding concrete with hammers to get the metal inside it, and the girders, rebar, and iron pipe you get from it don't bring that much money Still, I had another reason to want a day's delay. All the time we spent searching the building, I'd been chased by the feeling that we'd missed something, and I wanted another look at it before we went to work with the hammers.

I told Garman as much, not long after he'd announced the day off. I expected him to frown and tell me not to waste my time. He frowned, sure enough, but said nothing for a long moment and then nodded once. "Well," he said. "Let me know, Trey."

"I'll do that, Sir and Mister," I told him, and went to get my tools. That year I was his senior prentice, and so had tools of my own: pry bar, grapplehook, hammer and chisels, thin-blade knife and wide-blade knife, a couple of electric lamps, and a bag of special things for papers and the like, since Gray Garman did jobs for the scholars in Melumi now and then and knew what they wanted. With a belt full of tools, a steel hat on my head, and ruinman's leathers already caked with a dry season's dust, I felt ready for anything, and I went from our camp by the river to the stairwell we'd cleared.

One of Garman's other prentices, a boy of thirteen or so named Berry, waved to me as I got to the stairwell; he was up above in the tangled wreck of the tower, pulling wire out of a conduit—that was one of the ways prentices could make a few spare marks in off hours, salvaging wire to sell the copper. I did the same thing the day before and had a big tangle of heavy copper wire in my pocket, nicely stripped of its insulation and ready to sell when the metal merchants next came by. I waved back and started down.

Down below the air was cold and still and damp. I tapped the switch on the electric lantern and tried to get my thoughts clear, emptying out the chattering mind the way the priestesses teach. What had we missed? I let the question sink into silence, waited for a moment, and then headed deeper in, following nothing I could name.

Two levels down and over toward the river side was a big square room with a couple of closets on one side. We'd shored the ceiling here with timbers, because that side of the build-ing had taken more damage than the others, and a bit of light filtered down through the holes where old ventilation ducts used to run. The closets were empty, like everything else down there, and we'd added to the empty look by taking off the metal doors and their frames and hauling them away to sell.

For all I could see, the room and its closets had nothing more to offer than the rest of the ruin, but something just wouldn't let me pass them by.

So I went around the room a senamee at a time, checking the walls and the floor for any sign of an opening that had been sealed up or hidden. When I found nothing, I went to the closets. The first had nothing better to offer, but as I crossed to the second I felt the little prickle of knowledge that said I'd been right. There on the floor, where the door frame had covered it, a seam split the concrete; the closet's floor had been poured at a different time than the room's, and though it was hard to tell in the dim light from the lantern, the floor of the closet looked more recent: a little coarser and visibly more cracked.

If Mam Gaia had given me the brains she gave geese, I would have stopped then, gone back up to the surface and found a half dozen prentices to help. Instead, I went into the closet, set the lantern down in the doorway, and started to crouch down so I could get a better look at the floor. I was maybe halfway there when the floor creaked, lurched beneath my feet, and fell away.

I jumped for the door the moment the floor shifted, but it dropped too fast, and the best I could do was catch myself on a couple of pieces of broken rebar below the doorway as a crash and a great choking cloud of dust came up from below. The lantern teetered and then fell, just missing my head; I got a brief glimpse of a little square room below me, and then the lantern struck a piece of fallen concrete. I heard glass break and the light went out, and then the rest of it rolled onto the floor. Light flared again, brief and blue-white, like lightning, and the lightning-smell the scholars call ozone tinged the air.

That was when I knew just how close I was to getting reborn.

The ancients did a thing, clever and nasty, with certain places here and there in the ruins. They took power cores, which are big cylinders that turn out a steady trickle of electricity—nobody knows exactly how they work, but if you cut one open your radiation detectors go crazy and everyone nearby is going to be dead by day's end, so it was something nuclear—and wired them up to banks of metal plates that are shielded from one another so they hold a charge. Wires from those plates go to thin metal strips in the floor of the entrances to the places I mentioned. You can't see the strips unless you know what to look for, and if you step on the wrong two of them at the same time, the charge goes through you and you fry.

There are one or two of these places in most of the old cities, and sometimes many more. The scholars say they were built as shelters for soldiers and rulers in the last days of the old world, and they may be right, for certainly it's common enough to find the bones of people who hid there, in among old machines and cabinets full of papers. There are tools that ruinmen use to drain the charge out of such a trap, but I didn't have any of them with me. The one thing I knew for certain was that if I lost my grip and fell, my chance of landing on concrete wasn't good, and if I touched the floor, my chance of taking another breath afterwards was small enough not to notice. I truly expected to die.

I hung there in the darkness for what seemed like a long time and tried to think of some way to save my life. The doorway was out of reach, and trying to haul myself up to it brought down more pieces of crumbling concrete; no escape that way. Shouting for help was pretty clearly a waste of time, since there was nobody closer than Berry up above. Trying to wrestle my backup lamp out of the bottom of bag on my hip would give me a better look at what was going to get me reborn, but it might make me lose my grip and fall. So I clung to the rebar, mind racing, while the scents of dust and lightning rose up from underneath me.

It must have been less than a minute, though it felt like an hour, before I thought of the tangle of wire in my pocket. The thought of letting go of one the pieces of rebar that held me up was not exactly comforting, but no other plan came to mind. I tightened my right hand on the longer piece of rebar, reached down with the other, pulled the wire from the pocket of my coat and threw it toward where I thought I remembered the floor had been completely bare, then caught the rebar again before my right hand could slip.

Lightning flared again, and went still. After a moment a dull red glow and a hot-metal smell began to fill the room: the wire, heating up to cherry color from the current flowing through it. The light from the wire, dim as it was, gave me a gift I hadn't expected: I could see, below me and a little to one side, a big piece of concrete that had landed flat on the floor. I gauged the distance, swung myself over that way and dropped.

A moment falling through near-darkness, and then my feet hit; I breathed out all at once and landed as soft as I could. The concrete shifted beneath my feet, but I kept my balance, and once the dust settled I was able to dig through the bag on my belt and pull out the backup lamp. Ruinmen always carry an extra way of making a light, and this was why; the lamp's pale light blended with the glow from the copper wire burning out halfway across the room to give me a good look at the place that had almost killed me.

The room was much bigger than the closet above it, the walls rough, as though the concrete had been poured in a hurry. An iron ladder went down one wall from the broken ceiling to within a few feet of the floor; a hatch must have been sealed up above sometime after the shelter was built. There would be another entrance somewhere, but finding that could wait. Over to one side, a metal door led out of the room, and a tiny red light glowed next to it, the only warning the ancients gave of the death they'd woven into the floor. There would be a switch on the other side of the door that would turn off the current, if I could reach it.

I crouched, held the lamp close to the floor and made out the pattern of conductive strips on it. I'd crossed a floor of the same kind before more than once barefoot for practice, with Mister Garman watching, and the charge on the plates drained until a false step would bring a painful shock instead of sudden death. I'd never tried to cross such a floor in a ruin no one had cleared yet, and I was far from sure the copper wire discharged everything the trap had to offer. Still, unless I wanted to wait until someone came looking for me, I didn't have a lot of other choices. After a moment, I stood up, pointed the lamp at the floor, and started toward the door.

To this day I don't know if I did the thing right, or if the charge was simply low enough by then that my boots offered me enough protection against it. One way or another, though, I reached the door, and thank the four winds, it was unlocked. I had to lean against it to force it open; hinges that had been still for better than six lifetimes screeched their complaint but moved anyway. I reached through, fumbled for the switch on the other side, flipped it. The little light next to the door went green, and something hard and cold as old metal unknotted in me.

A murmur of sound from above caught my attention. After a moment, it turned into the drumming of feet. A familiar voice boomed: "Trey?"

"Down here, Mister," I shouted back up. "Floor in the closet gave way, but I'm fine."

"How far down?"

I glanced up. "About four meedas. There's at least one more room down here."

"Good." Then, muffled: "Conn, Berry, get me that rope. Two more lamps, too."

It was Gray Garman, of course. It didn't occur to me until then that the crash of the closet floor must have echoed all through the old ruin, loud enough to tell the people up on the surface that something was wrong and send them running for help. I was glad of that, since the thought of finding a way up out of the hidden room had begun to weigh on me.

A moment later a rope came snaking down from above and Garman came down it hand over hand. Once he'd reached the floor, he glanced at me, at the green light, at the floor. "Room was trapped?"

"Good and proper," I said. "Gave me a bit of trouble."

"Well." He was looking at me then with his frown. "It's not prentice work to get past one of those. Give me your pry bar."

I stared at him blankly for a moment and then handed him the tool from my belt. He hefted it, then with a flick of his wrist caught me with the sharp edge on the bent end just below one cheekbone, hard enough to draw blood. I managed not to flinch. Then he was holding the bar out to me, saying, "Take it, ruinman."

I took it, dazed, while the prentices whooped—three of them had followed Garman down the rope, and a fourth was on the way. "Well, Mister Trey," Garman said then with a faint smile at the formal courtesy, "did you check out the room back there?" A motion of his head pointed at the door behind me and the room beyond.

"Didn't have a chance, Mister Garman. I was heading that way when you showed up."

"Let's see what they left for us," he said, and motioned for me to take the lead.

By then my mind was trying to grapple with what had just happened. Going from prentice to ruinman, said the guild rules, took some proof of skill that none of the misters could quarrel with. Some prentices did it by plain hard work, and some by a chance find they followed up the right way, but you could also do it by landing yourself in deep trouble in the ruins and getting out alive. The thought dazzled me: after ten years as Garman's prentice, I was a mister and a ruinman myself, and I was about to be the very first through a door that, beyond the last shadow of a doubt, nobody had opened since the old world stumbled to its end.

Hinges yelled as I shouldered the door open and raised my lamp. Garman and the others pressed close behind me. The light showed a metal frame that once held two beds, one atop the other, against the wall to the right; shreds of a curtain failed to hide the toilet next to it. Shelves along the far wall would have held food and water once, and there were two long things, guns almost certainly. Over to the left, not quite against the wall, was a table with dusty shapes on it I didn't recognize at first.

We were most of the way to the table before I realized we weren't alone in the room. The other person there was a long way past greeting us, though. He was sitting at the table with his head and shoulders slumped forward; bits of bone showed through what was left of the stiff heavy clothing the old world put on its soldiers. A sheet of cracked and yellowed paper was under the bones of one of his hands, and right next to that was a box with dials and buttons, probably a radio. I stared at him for a long moment, then made the blessing sign, even though he'd been there long enough that even his ghost must have been dead by then.

I glanced around the room again. You could see the last weeks or months of the man's life written there plain enough. He must have hidden there in the last years of the old world, and sat by the radio day by day while the food and water dwindled, waiting for some message that came too late if it came at all. There must have been thousands of stories like that, since ruinmen find such things pretty often.

"Well," said Garman. He'd already examined the guns, and went to the radio. "The guns are in fine condition. This—" He motioned toward the box on the table. "—won't work any more, but we'll get plenty for it. Conn?"

Conn was his senior prentice now, and had been searching the shelves. "A couple of small machines—I'm not sure what they are—and bullets for the guns."

"Good. I know gunsmiths who'd sell their eyeballs to get those. Now let's see what this has to say—" He moved the bones of the dead man's hand away from the yellow paper, and I raised the lamp as the others crowded around. This is what it said.

```
TOP SECRET/STAR'S REACH
PAGE 01 OF 01 R 111630Z NOV 34
FM: GEN BURKERT DRCETI
TO: CETI PROJECT STAFF ORNL
1.  (TS/SR) PROJ DIR LUKACS REPORTS EVAC
    COMPLETE FROM NRAO AND LANGLEY. ALL
    RECORDS AND STAFF SAFE. WRTF OPERA-
    TIONAL AND CETI INCOMING.
2.  (TS/SR)  POTUS/DNS/DCI  ADVISED  THAT
    PROJECT ONGOING DESPITE CRISIS.
3.  (TS/SR) TRANSPORT FOR ORNL PROJECT STAFF
    TO WRTF TO FOLLOW ASAP. INSTRUCTIONS
    VIA FEMA/GWEN WHEN SITUATION PERMITS.
CLASS BURKERT DRCETI RSN 1.5E X4
TOP SECRET/SPECIAL ACCESS REQUIRED
```

We all looked up from the paper and at each other. "Mother of Life," said Garman. "Well." He said no more, nor needed to. The words hung in the dry air. I can still hear them in my mind, wrapped up in the silence of that place of beginnings and endings.

That was five years ago. Today the promise of the words on that brittle yellow paper became real, for me and for the others who came with me—Thu, Tashel Ban, Berry, Eleen, and old Anna, for whom all this is the closing of a circle and not the opening of a door. It's been a long road and I won't pretend it was an easy one, but we finally reached the place where, if the stories are true, the last big secret of the old world lies waiting.

As I write these words, we've settled for the night in what were probably living quarters two levels below the surface. The rooms in this part of the ruin are bare concrete and not much else, but they're dry and not too dusty, and there's plenty of space for the supplies we brought here. One lantern lights up the room where I sit; we turned off the others to save battery power. Eleen sleeps with her head in my lap, brown hair fallen all anyhow under my hand. The others are asleep too, except for Thu, who never sleeps.

We dodged a miserable death getting in through the door, and killed to do it. I don't doubt we'll have plenty of other chances to die before we find what we came for, if we find it at all. Still, it's a grand thing to have finally gotten to Star's Reach.

CHAPTER 2

STORIES TO THE DARK

I must have been eight years old when I first heard of Star's Reach, since my father told me the story, and that happened not long before he was called up to fight the coastal allegiancies and never came back from the war. It was a night a couple of weeks after the rains, I remember that, and we were out on the porch of the little two-room shack where we lived then, my father, my mother and me, enjoying the cool air after a hot damp day and a dinner of rice and greens and a rabbit my mother snared that morning. My mother had her spindle with her, as she usually did, and her arm rose and fell as she drew cotton out into yarn for weaving; my father sat back in his chair and puffed at a clay pipe; I lay on my belly right on the edge of the porch and stared off across the garden in front of our house toward the great dark shadow of the forest and the not-so-dark sky above it, blazing with stars. Fireflies danced between me and the forest, and I made believe that some of the stars had come down to play in the still air.

My mother's voice, high and soft, and my father's, measured and rumbling, wove in and out of each other behind me. I had other things to mind just then, notably the fireflies, and so didn't hear a word of what they were saying until my mother let out a sharp little yelp. That made me roll over and sit up, facing them.

"No," she was saying. "Maddy's boy?"

"The one," said my father. "Came back to their farm yester-day evening sicker'n a dog. They had a doctor come out, and then a priestess, but he was already too far gone."

"Do they know…"

"He'd been out to the ruins. He was babbling about Star's Reach before he died."

A long moment of silence went past. "Then it was his own fault," my mother said, in a hard brittle voice that wasn't like her at all. "People who go messing around in those places deserve what they get."

My father said nothing. After a while I asked, "Pappy, what's Star's Reach?"

"Never you mind," my mother told me in the same brittle voice, but my father said, "He'll hear it soon or late, Gwen. Might as well be the true story, and not whatever lies sent young Calley off to die."

She let out a sharp sigh, but did not argue. My father took a long slow draw from his pipe, let the smoke trickle out, and said, "The stars are suns like ours, just a lot farther away. They teach you that at school yet, boy?"

"Yep," I told him; the priestess who taught us at the temple down in the village had said something about it that very week.

"Good. Those suns have worlds turning around 'em, the way Mam Gaia turns around our sun, and in the old days they thought there were people on some of those other worlds. Not people like us. A-lee-in, they used to call 'em: that means different."

"Different how?" I wanted to know.

"That's just it. Nobody knew. You know the spyglass Cullen has?" I did, and wanted one of my own desperately just then. "In the old days they made spyglasses big as this farm and chucked 'em up in the sky so they could see the stars better, and even through those, the other worlds were smaller'n a pinprick. They're that far away. But the people who live on those worlds, if there are any, aren't Mam Gaia's children. Maybe they've got purple skin, and eyes like bugs, and big claws to git you with." His hands turned into claws and lunged toward me, and I squealed with laughter and rolled back out of reach.

"Back in the old days they tried all kinds of ways to figure out if there were people on those other worlds," my father went on. "Finally, so the story goes, somebody figured that they probably used radios, same as we do, and started listening. Of course the other worlds are so far away the signal's less'n a whisper by the time it gets to us."

"Like the Sisnaddi station," I said. We had a little crystal radio, and sometimes at night, if you jiggled the thing just right, you could just hear the big station at Sisnaddi playing patriotic music and talking about the news.

"Like that, but so much fainter you can't imagine it. So they built antennas big as towns and radios bigger'n this house, and when those didn't do the job, they built even bigger ones. Finally, just about the time the old world ended, they built the biggest antennas and radios of all, at a place called Star's Reach, and the story is that they did it. They got a message by radio from one of those other worlds, circling one of the suns out there." His gesture swept across the stars.

He said nothing for a long moment, and finally I asked, "What did it say?"

"Nobody knows." He took another draw from the pipe, breathed out a plume of smoke that scented the night around him. "They got the message, the story says, and it got passed around to all the scholars they had in those days, who could figure things out like that, but nobody could work out what it meant. Then the old world ended and the lights went out forever and that was the end of it.

"But that wasn't really the end of it." His voice went low, and dead serious. "Because ever since the old world ended, people have gotten so caught up in that story that they've gone off into the ruins looking for Star's Reach, hoping they can find the message and figure out what it means. And it kills them, the way it killed Calley. He must have gotten too close to something nuclear, and it poisoned his bones and his blood. There's plenty of that, and plenty of other poisons that choke you or blind you or get in through your skin and leave you twisting like a half-dry earthworm before you die, and plenty of pits you can fall into and old rotten towers to fall on you and squash you like a bug.

"And here's the thing. Nobody's ever found Star's Reach, or anything to show that Star's Reach was ever a real place. It might just be a story. They used to tell lots of make-believe stories, in the old days, about all those other worlds and what might be out there. The whole business about Star's Reach might be one of those, and Calley and all the others who went looking for it and died were chasing something that was never real at all."

"Wicked," said my mother then. I turned to face her. None of us were more than shadows in the dim light just then, but even now I'm half sure I could see her shoulders and her face drawn up in hard unfamiliar lines. "That's what they are, the ones who try to dig up the secrets of the old world. What's dead is dead, for good reason, and there's nothing good to be gotten from dabbling in the corpse."

"I don't see you turn up your nose at metal from the ruins," my father reminded her.

"If the priestesses hadn't blessed it first I'd do without," she said. "But I'm not talking about the ruinmen. They're doing Mam Gaia's work, tearing down what's left of the old world and selling us the metal so we can leave the trees to grow and the land to heal. It's the people who won't let the old world stay dead, those are the ones I mean. They deserve what they get."

My father didn't answer. After a while, I lay down on the porch again and tried to lose myself in the darting of the fire-flies and the slow wheeling of the sky. It was no use; my father's story would not leave my mind. A message from another world seemed just then to be written out across the night sky, blazing in starry letters I couldn't quite read. The fireflies had changed as well; they had stopped being stars, wandering or not; their pale gleam made me think of the way that the eyes of ghosts are supposed to glow, and then they were the eyes of the ghosts of all the people like Calley who died looking for Star's Reach, looking up at the a-lee-in letters they could no more read than I. I shivered, though the night was warm enough, and tried to forget what my father had said.

I kept thinking about Star's Reach for a couple of days after that, before something else pushed it out of my mind. Still, I remembered all of it the next time somebody mentioned Star's Reach to me. That happened not long after I became a ruin-man's prentice, when I was ten, and still learning how to take apart a ruin for its metal without getting reborn in the process. Like the other first year prentices, I didn't go into the ruins much; my place was in camp, where I helped with cooking and cleaning part of the time, and part of the time got taught by a senior prentice how to handle tools and tie knots and do all the other things ruinmen need to be able to do. It was as dull as it sounds, especially with the gray broken shapes of the ruins rising up toward the sky so close to camp that you could just about hit the nearest concrete with a thrown pebble.

One evening right after dinner Conn and I were doing the dishes. We were the same age and prenticed with Gray Garman the same year, and we both came from farm families in the hills west of Shanuga where Tenisi and Joja run with the part of Cairline that belongs to us and not the coastal allegiancies, so it was probably a safe bet that we'd end up either good friends or blood enemies. Fortunately we got along well. Conn had a big family on a farm up somewhere near Chicamog, and I didn't have any family left at all by that time, so I liked to listen to him talk about his brothers and sisters and cousins and imagine that I had a big family too.

Earlier that day he got a letter from his family—well, it was actually from the priestess at the temple near where his family lived, since nobody in the family knew how to write, but she took down they wanted to say and then wrote it out for them. Back then, Coll was just learning to read and hadn't gotten good at it yet, so he brought me each letter he got, and when we had spare time I'd pick through the words one by one and tell him what they said. Every so often, when he'd sold enough wire and other metal scrap to pay the postman's fee, he'd have me write out a letter to his family and send it to Chicamog for the priestess to read to everyone.

Most times the letters he got were just the usual sort of thing you'd expect from a poor farm family up in the hills. The time I'm thinking of, though, there was real news: one of his brothers was in the army, and came home on leave telling stories of some jennel from the presden's court who thought he knew where Star's Reach was. He brought scholars with him to Orrij, up north of us, where there used to be a place for scholars before the old world ended.

"I hope they find it," Conn said as he washed a plate. "Wouldn't that be something?"

"I want to read a message from the a-lee-ins," I said.

"What's a-lee-ins?"

"Creatures out there." I waved a hand at the sky, as though I knew what I was talking about. "Not people like us. Not Mam Gaia's children at all."

He considered that. "I bet they have three eyes."

"I bet they have claws like a crawfish."

"I bet they have three legs and seven arms."

"I bet they have bright blue skin."

"I bet they have their faces on their backsides," Conn said then, grinning. I aimed a swat at him, which he ducked, and we both laughed and went on to talk about something else.

We heard later that the jennel and the scholars didn't find anything, and I learned a lot later that they hadn't been the first to look there, either. Still, when we were done washing the dishes and getting the kitchen ready for the breakfast crew, we walked back across the open space in the middle of the camp to the tent where all the first year prentices slept. The fireflies were coming out beneath the stars, and all at once I remembered lying there on the porch of the little shack, when the fireflies looked like the eyes of ghosts.

I thought about both those nights and the pale ghost-eyes looking up at the stars that morning deep down in the Shanuga ruins, as we stood staring at a piece of paper that everyone from the scholars at Melumi to the jennels of the presden's court to backwoods farm boys like Calley sunna Maddy had been chasing after for more years than I could count. In the flickering light of Gray Garman's lantern, I suppose we all must have looked a little like ghosts ourselves.

"Well," said Garman again, and the moment passed. "Mister Trey, you got some resin?"

The scholars at Melumi brew a resin that can be sprayed out of a bulb onto old paper, to keep it from going to bits. Garman taught me years ago always to carry some when searching a ruin, in case something written turned up that was worth selling. I pulled a bulb out of the sack at my belt and squirted the resin in a fine mist all over the paper. Stink of the solvent wrestled with the dust and concrete smells of a fresh ruin, and lost. I turned the paper over once the resin was dull and dry, and was most of the way through spraying the other side—an even coat, not too much, just the way I'd been taught—when I noticed the writing there.

It was one word only, in the pale gray writing they made sometimes in the old days: CURTIS. I glanced up at Garman, saw no more understanding in his face than must have showed in mine. For lack of anything useful to say, I finished spraying the paper and put the bulb away.

"You got a choice, Mister Trey," Garman said then. "One find from this room is yours by right, but this—" His gesture indicated the paper. "—is two. You can have it, or you can have the finder's rights to what's on it, but damn if I'm giving you both."

The paper would be worth hundreds of marks, maybe more, to the scholars at Melumi, enough to set me up as a ruinman with prentices of my own. Finder's rights might be worth much more or much less; they meant that if anyone followed the paper's lead to a site, I had rights to a share of it. Among the better sort of ruinmen, it also meant that other misters would give me first shot at finding whatever the paper might lead toward, and start looking for it only when it was pretty much clear that I had failed. I knew which one I ought to choose, and I knew which one I wanted to choose, and damn if I could decide between them right then. "That I'm going to have to think about," I told him.

He smiled a little tight smile and cuffed me on the shoulder. "You take your time. Mam Kelsey up top can make an honest copy, and that'll be needed one way or the other." To the prentices: "First of you to find a way out of here other'n that rope gets a mark."

That sent them scurrying, and soon enough Berry won the mark by finding a half-hidden door into a part of the ruin we'd explored days before. From the other side, you couldn't see it at all; that was common enough for the old shelters. Prentices around the campfire at night used to wonder aloud what scared the people of the old world so much that they hid so many doors and laid so many traps. They may be asking the same question around their fires tonight, and I'm not yet sure that I could give them an answer.

CHAPTER 3

THE MISTERS' LODGE

Four days have gone by now since we got to Star's Reach, and I'm finally beginning to get some sense of the shape of it all. There's a lot of it, at least ten levels going down, and each level the size of a big city nowadays or a midsized farm town in the old world. As far as we can tell, it's empty, which answers a question I wondered about on the way here. After Anna joined us in Cansiddi, it occurred to me more than once that we might just find people still living here, with all the good and bad chances that might bring. Everywhere we've searched so far is silent, though, and the only tracks in the dust are ours.

The first level, just below the surface, has skylights in the ceilings, though there are places where the roof's cracked and sand's gotten in. The second and third levels are easier going, with light wells from the surface to bring in the day-light and no sand to speak of. Below that the darkness closes in. Anna says that there were hundreds of power cores down deep in the underplaces, and those may still be working, but we haven't been able to get any of the lights to work but ours. Since the lamps we brought with us run on sunpower, they have to spend a good part of each day at the bottom of a light well charging. So I have plenty of time to write.

I have plenty of paper, too. Two days ago we found a couple of boxes of blank notebooks in an otherwise empty storeroom, sealed in plastic with the air pumped out and nitrogen pumped in, and I took one notebook for myself. So far those are the only paper we've found anywhere in Star's Reach. Eleen is fretting about that; there's always the chance that the people who were here after the old world ended, Anna's people, might have destroyed all their papers before whatever happened to them got around to happening.

Still, as evening tosses blue shadows into the light well and Berry and Thu clatter the pots over in the corner of the room we've set aside for a kitchen, I have a hard time worrying about what will come of this journey of ours. I think of other times over the years that the path to Star's Reach looked as though it had come to a dead stop, no way onward, and then picked up again once I'd seen through a misunderstanding or dodged a danger. If it's true that they listened to a message from a distant world here, and anything is left of it, I think we'll find it.

I don't remember just now if I felt the same way when Mister Garman and his prentices and I left the place in the Shanuga ruins where we'd found the letter that led me here. We were pretty far down and the way back up wasn't straight by any means, so it took us a while to climb up out of the underplaces of the building. By the time we saw daylight it was close to noon and getting hot enough to hurt. Big heaps of cloud were rising over the hills around the ruins, and big bright birds came flapping past out of the forest that wraps the ruins on three sides. I drew in a deep breath to remind myself that I was still alive.

Word must have gotten around that something was up, since a mob of prentices and a good handful of misters were waiting for us down in the old street. "Found something," Garman told them. "A little more than you'd expect." He held up the paper, then waved off the prentices so the other misters could get close and read it. That was worth seeing. Mister Calwel spat out a bit of language so hot I half expected my ears to catch fire, and Mister Jonus, the senior mister there that season and a man who never seemed surprised by anything, blinked and read the paper again and said, "Garman, now that's a find."

"Found by Mister Trey here," said Garman, "who'll get either the paper or the finder's rights once he makes up his mind." He gave me a look and nudged me with an elbow, and I think it was then that the other misters noticed the blood on my face. All of them, even Calwel, came up to shake my hand and let me know that if I took the finder's rights they'd offer a good price for them. I grinned and told them they could go ahead and jump off the next tower they happened to climb, and they laughed.

They didn't have to acknowledge me. They could have called me out if they wanted to. Ruinmen go to the circle now and then, with hands or knives or pry bars, and during my prentice years I saw more than one fight end with a mister carried away dead. Still, either they had no quarrel with my advancement to mistership or they didn't fancy the risk of going to the circle with me. Prentices fight more often than misters, though it almost always stops at first blood, and I won't claim I never lost those fights but I will say it didn't happen much. That wasn't just a matter of talent, either. Gray Garman hired a fighting master to teach his prentices the tricks of staying alive in the circle, which is more than most of the misters did.

Once the misters all had their look at the paper, the prentices crowded around to read it, and most of them weren't half so quiet as the misters had been. Some of them whooped and some of them used language I won't write down, and there were only a couple of them who stopped and stared with big round eyes; I think those were the ones that really caught what it was that we'd found. Soon enough Garman waved them off, and he and I crossed the ruins to the tent where Mam Kelsey spent the digging seasons.

Most ruinmen hire failed scholars from Melumi to puzzle out old writing and make copies of any papers that get found, and when the ruin's of any size the misters go in together to pay one to stay out there at the site through the digging season. The Shanuga ruins were big and rich enough for that, so we had a failed scholar there every season since I first became a prentice. The last four years I was there, that was Mam Kelsey. She was a lean thing with hair the same gray color as the robe of her guild, and eyes so bad she had to wear glasses thick as old bottles to see more than a few senamees past her nose.

Her tent was over to one side of the camp, not far from the river. When the ruinmen had no work for her she would sit on a little folding chair behind a little folding table that always looked ready to collapse beneath notes for the book she was writing to get back into the Versty. When we had work for her, she would push the notes aside, pull her glasses just that extra little bit down her nose, and do whatever needed to be done without saying any more words than she had to. I used to feel sorry for her now and then, but the misters paid her a good wage and she could still call herself a scholar without shame. Later on, I met one failed scholar who worked as a cook in a roadhouse and another who was a harlot, and neither of them would admit to most folk they'd ever been to Melumi at all.

The prentices used to talk about her book sometimes around campfires at night. Nobody knew what it was about, and I don't think more than one or two of us had any notion why she spent all her time on it. Melumi was six hundred kloms northwest of us by the shortest road. Some of the misters had been there, but unless they felt like talking, all we had to go on was the stories that traveling folk told, and that wasn't much. So we wondered, and made things up, silly or scary as the mood struck us. I don't recall any of the prentices suggesting that the book might be about Star's Reach, but that must have been the only thing nobody thought to mention.

One day during the first season Mam Kelsey was at the Shanuga ruins, though, a few of us managed to get a look at her book. It was a hot sluggish day toward the end of summer, and most of us had been set loose for the afternoon, because part of the old tower Gray Garman was salvaging had gotten unstable and needed to be blasted down. That's work for misters and their senior prentices, and it's dangerous, since the big kegs of powder we get from the gunsmiths don't always go off right. So the rest of us were left to sit around in camp or scavenge wire in safe areas while Garman and his two oldest prentices set the charges.

Three of us were playing toss-the-bones over on the side of camp by Mam Kelsey's tent. There was me and Conn, and another boy name of Shem sunna Janny, who died the next year when a couple of floors in a building we were stripping flapjacked on top of him. We'd gotten halfway through the game when we saw one of Mister Jonus' prentices pelting across the field toward Mam Kelsey's tent at a run. We couldn't hear what he said to her when he got there, but it wasn't hard to guess: Jonus' people must have found something written in the part of the ruins he was working, and needed her help to figure out what it meant. After a moment, she pushed her notes aside, got up, and followed the prentice back across the field toward the ruins.

I think all three of us thought of her book at the same moment. We looked at each other, and grinned, and once she was out of sight got up and pocketed the knucklebones we'd been playng with and went oh so casually over to her tent.

I was the only one of us who could read, and I won't say I was that good at it, even with the practice I got reading Conn the letters from his family. Still, the other two pushed me over to the book, saying "What does it say?" almost at the same moment, so the words tumbled over each other. The book was open, lying there on Mam Kelsey's table. I know I looked at it, and I know I tried to read it aloud, but that's about as much as I recall of it at this point.

There were a lot of long words, I remember that, and I slid to a halt after beating them up so bad that their own mothers wouldn't have known them. I don't imagine Conn or Shar got any more out of what I'd read than I did, but we'd looked at the book, which was the point of the exercise. After a moment Conn said, "I bet she'll be back soon," and we hurried back over to where we'd been playing and started the game where we'd left off. It wasn't more than a few minutes later that we heard the big rolling boom of the blast, and only a few minutes after that people came running from the ruins to get us. The keg of powder had gone off too soon. Gray Garman was unhurt, and we managed to dig one of his prentices out from the rubble with no worse than a broken leg, but we never found the other one. The priestess said the words for him and recited the litany on top of a mess of broken concrete, and we had to call that good.

I'm pretty sure that Mam Kelsey found out that we stole a look at her book, probably from someone else in camp who caught sight of us over at her tent. She never said a word about it, but I always got the sense when she looked my way that something in the back of her mind was whispering, "That's the boy who looked at my book." The day that Garman and I came to her tent with the dead man's letter in our hands was no different. She glanced up at us, seemed to take note of me, pushed her notes aside, pulled her glasses down her nose a bit, and took the brown resin-stiff paper from Garman's hands. She read it, then stopped and read it again, much more slowly.

"Honest copy, Mam Kelsey," Garman said to her. "Front and back both."

She nodded, took a piece of paper from the black leather case by her chair, dipped a pen and copied the paper letter by letter. When she was done, she signed the copy, pressed her seal into the paper good and hard, and then got out a bulb of resin and sprayed the copy front and back so it couldn't be changed without a mark you could see. She blew on the copy until it was dry, then handed it to Garman. He thanked her, and she nodded, waited politely for a moment, and then spread her notes back out on the table and got back to work. I was impressed. I'm sure Mam Kelsey understood at least as much as any of us what that piece of paper meant, but even so she never said a word.

By the time she finished copying the letter, work had come to a halt all over the ruin. That happens most times a big find turns up, since most misters are smart enough to take their prentices off the job when they can't concentrate enough to be safe. That was the one break we usually got from work between the time the ruins dried out enough to dig and the time the rains came back, too, so it gave the prentices another good reason to keep an eye open for signs that might lead to something.

There were a few misters in the Shanuga guild who balked now and then at letting their prentices go when a find turned up, but even Mister Calwel knew better than to hold them back this time, since nobody had an eye open for anything but Star's Reach. It didn't matter that none of us could make head or tail of the message in the letter, or had the least notion what a potus or a nrao might be. That would be tomorrow's problem, for as many tomorrows as it took to send somebody to Melumi and ask the scholars. For the moment, as Garman and I walked back into camp from Mam Kelsey's tent, we passed clusters of prentices talking low and fast, and every last one of them was talking about Star's Reach.

Most of them jumped up and came over to ask for another look at the letter. Even the ones who were bitter rivals of mine the day before called me "Mister Trey" and were as polite as you could ask. Garman, who had both the copy and the original, let them read the copy. He gave me a sidelong glance every time he handed it over, and I knew he was wondering when I'd tell him whether I wanted the letter itself or the finder's rights. I couldn't have told him if I wanted to. I knew which one I should choose if I had any brains at all, and I knew which one every senamee of me wanted to choose, and unfortunately they weren't the same one.

So we went across the camp to the big tent in the middle of everything that was the misters' lodge seven months of the year. Before we got there, the other misters had already hauled one of the big wooden chairs outside the entrance to the lodge and left it there for me to haul back inside. Of course they'd tied a bunch of scrap iron to the thing so it weighed close to fifty keelos, just to add to the welcome. Still, I counted myself lucky. A couple of years before there had been one prentice just turned mister that a lot of people disliked, and whoever loaded up his chair drove a stake into the ground and chained the chair to the stake, then draped a bunch more chain all around it so it took him a dozen tries and some of the hottest language I've ever heard before he figured out why the thing just wouldn't budge.

I had an easier time than that, but the chair was still a mother to lift, and a mother with babies to carry into the lodge. Most of the other misters were already in the tent, sitting in their chairs or gathered in twos and threes around the walls, so I had an audience while I staggered a quarter of the way around the lodge to the open place they'd left for me, and set down the chair with a crash like a building falling over. The misters laughed and applauded, and then the circle got quiet as I sat down for the first time in a mister's chair.

"Well," said Mister Jonus then, taking his seat. As the senior mister at the ruin, he had first and last voice any time the misters made a decision in lodge. "Unless anyone objects, we've got a new mister among us."

No one objected. Garman gave me one of his rare smiles and went to his chair. Jonus nodded once, and that was settled.

The rest of the meeting was pretty dull; misters' lodges usually are, though I didn't know that yet. A couple of younger misters who were working claims next to each other on the west side of the ruins had gotten into a quarrel about who had the right to a little building right on the line between them, and had the common sense to bring it to the lodge instead of going to the circle to settle it with knives. A couple of senior misters working the underplaces close to the river warned of water getting into the deep parts of the ruin. Jonus passed the bucket for money to pay Mam Kelsey's wages, and I panicked a bit before I remembered that she wouldn't cost me anything yet since I didn't have a claim of my own. The bucket went round a second time for money for ruinmen who couldn't work any more, and I found a few coins for that, and then the meeting was over.

By the time we filed out of the tent, Jonus first as the oldest mister and me dead last as the youngest, the sun was well west of noon and the clouds had started to break up after dropping a little rain somewhere else. By then the prentices had gone from talking low to arguing at the top of their lungs, and somebody had dragged out a barrel of the small beer the misters let prentices drink in the ruins. You couldn't get away with giving beer to boys of ten back in town, but nobody came out to the ruins but ruinmen, their prentices and failed scholars, and the few priestesses who were willing to get that close to the leavings of the old world, and so nobody made a fuss about it. It's true enough that they had little reason to worry, for you had to drink one mighty lot of the stuff to get noticeably tip-overish from it.

Still, the prentices did their level best to get lively with what they had, and once the rest of the misters headed off to their tents or wherever, I was surrounded by a fair-sized mob. Until a few hours before I'd been their equal, and they weren't ready to let me forget that just yet. So I got dragged over to the barrel and handed a big wooden mug of beer, and had to repeat the story of how I'd blundered my way into the hidden room in the underplaces, and nearly gotten reborn, and got past that to find something that everybody in Meriga had been looking for one way or another since about an hour and a half after the last of the old towers went dark and the last airplanes fell out of the sky. Then I had to repeat it again, and again, with more beer, as more prentices joined the crowd and more barrels followed them.

Then somebody who hadn't seen it wanted to know what the letter said. I remembered about half of it, and some of the others remembered more, but neither the beer nor the excitement helped us get it straight, and the potuses and the nraos got mixed up with a lot of nonsense, and none of us could say any of the odd words without sounding like we were talking backwards. Before long we were all laughing too hard to stand up. Conn topped it off by guessing what a potus might be, and I'd be lying if I said his guess was anything clean. Before long we were discussing the difference between an ornl and a ceti, or some equally clear and important point, while clutching our sides and rolling on the ground.

Things went on like that for quite a while. Some of the younger prentices finally got bullied into fixing food for everyone before the misters got too tired of waiting, and I got handed a big bowl of bean soup and a wedge of hard bread almost as large. That might have helped steady me a little, except that it came with another big wooden mug of beer, and there were more after that.

Night got close and dark around us, and we got quieter, though it took a while. Most of the younger prentices went off to their tents, and one or two of them got noisily sick on the way. A little later, the prentices who worked for other misters asked blessings on our dreams and headed off to their parts of the camp; I'm pretty sure some of them got sick, too, from the way they were weaving as they walked, but if so they weren't so loud about it. Then it was just me and Mister Garman's prentices in a circle lit by little lamps, with the stars peeking down through great torn gaps in the clouds above us and the stink of spilled beer around us, talking about other times and the ones who'd been there with us and weren't with us now, the ones who quit their prenticeships and the ones who got reborn.

Finally we ran out of things to say. A gap like the ones in the clouds was opening between me and the others, and it wouldn't close again, I knew, even if they all lived to become misters themselves. I'd seen the same thing happen from the other side often enough, but even so it wasn't easy to sit there in the pale lamplight and know that something that had been the nearest thing to a family I had after my father and mother died was gone now.

When the silences had gotten long enough to be uncomfortable, I tried to stand up. That wasn't the best move, it turned out, for it landed me on the ground with a thump. You have to drink a mighty lot of small beer to get tip-overish, as I said, but I must have drunk a mighty lot that day and then a bit. I tried to stand up again, without much more luck.

The others laughed and teased me, which broke the silence for the moment. Berry, who was the only one of the younger prentices still there, came over and helped me stand up. I wished the rest of them good dreams and, leaning on Berry, managed to walk the thirty meedas or so to my tent without ever quite falling over.

When we got to the tent, he more or less poured me into a sitting position on my cot and then stood there facing me for a long moment. "I'm the one who went and got Mister Garman when the floor fell in," he told me then, saying it in the way that lets you know a favor is going to be asked before too much longer.

"I'm grateful," I managed in response.

"You're going to take finder's rights to the letter." Then, all in a rush: "You get to take one of Gray Garman's prentices as your first prentice. I want you to pick me."

I stared at him for a moment, trying to get my brain to work. "I haven't settled what I'm going to choose," I protested, but he just grinned, and said, "You're not gutless enough to turn down finder's rights to Star's Reach."

He was right, of course, though he could have said *not smart enough* just as truly. "If I do," I tried again, "I'm not going to have more than half a dozen marks to my name. How do you think I'm going to feed a prentice? I'll have to hire out at other mister's sites, for certain."

"Then you can hire me out too." The grin faltered. "Trey—Mister Trey—for a chance at Star's Reach I'll eat dirt and run naked and sleep under a bush for the rest of my life. Anyone would. I bet you have twenty prentices sitting in front of this tent when you get up tomorrow." The grin was gone, and he swallowed visibly. "But I want you to pick me. I—I know I'm not even your best choice. But I had to ask."

I sat there looking at him for what seemed like a long while, thinking about the one time I'd wanted something that bad, and asked for it, and gotten it. Anyone else would probably have turned him down flat, or put off the decision until morning and turned him down that way, and I tried to talk myself into doing either one, and failed. "You'll do," I said.

Berry's face lit up like a lamp. "You mean it?"

"I mean it. I'll tell Garman first thing tomorrow."

He put out his hand, and I clasped it, sealing the deal. He grinned, then, and said, "Just like the Robot's Hand. Mister Trey, you have the best dreams anyone ever had. I'll be here with my things first thing tomorrow."

A moment later he was gone. I went to the door of the tent, thinking about the Robot's Hand, and then fell to my knees and got very sick with as little noise as I could manage.

CHAPTER *4*

SHAKING THE ROBOT'S HAND

Something woke up in the deep places of Star's Reach during the night, for no reason we can tell.

I blinked awake all at once out of some dream about of the Tenisi hills of my childhood, knowing something was wrong but not knowing what. The room was dark except for a little glow from the lamp in the corner where Thu keeps watch. Thu wasn't there; he stood in the doorway looking out into the corridor beyond, a black shape against not-quite-darkness.

A moment later I knew what brought him there. A faint vibration came up through the concrete around us, deep and steady. I recognized it at once as old world machinery. You don't find that in working order often in ruins, but it does happen, and when it does it usually means the worst kind of trouble.

I was on my feet before I quite realized it. Thu glanced back at me and made a quick silent gesture: come.

I got my feet into my boots, threw on my ruinman's jacket, got my toolbelt around my waist. A moment later I was standing beside him at the doorway. He pointed to the stair, but I was already looking at it, and the dim light that came up through it.

"I'll wake the others," I said in less than a whisper. He nodded, never looking away from the stair's mouth.

A few moments later we were all awake. "The light and the sound came at the same moment," Thu told us, his voice low. "Nothing else. No sound or sign of anyone."

"Could the machines have turned themselves on?" Tashel Ban asked.

All of us looked at Anna. She tilted her head, thinking. "It's possible," she said after a moment. "There were certainly machineries that worked by themselves, but I wasn't allowed down into the lower levels—none of the children were."

"Someone must go," said Thu. He meant he should, and I had been about to say the same thing about me, so I just grinned. He gave me a look and nodded once, and the two of us went to the door together. The first time Thu and I met, he did his level best to kill me, and there's nobody on Mam Gaia's round belly I trust more.

Five levels down and one room over from the stair was most of a wall covered with lights and screens. A couple of days earlier, when we'd searched those rooms, they were dark and dead, but now the lights were on and the screens lit up. Our earlier footprints were the only ones in the dust on the floor, so Thu went back up the stair to tell the others while I looked at the blank glowing screens and thought about the robot's hand.

Eleen and Tashel Ban both told me, when I asked them last night, that the way to write a story like mine is to start at the beginning and go on step by step until you get to the end. She's a scholar from Melumi and he's more or less what they have in Nuwinga in place of scholars from Melumi, and they both know a lot more about writing than I do, but try as I might this thing I'm writing won't follow their advice. If Plummer was right, and my story is part of his one story, it got started a long time before I did, and there's no way to keep the earlier parts of it out of the part I meant to tell.

So I'm going to have to take some pages here to write about the Robot's Hand, even though that part of the story happened to me more than ten years before Gray Garman and I found the letter in the Shanuga underplaces. If other people ever read this, they might be able to understand the rest of the story I want to tell without knowing about the Hand, but they won't understand me or Berry or the ruinmen, and I'm not sure at all that they'll be able to figure out why Berry and I turned our backs on the life we'd been living among the Shanuga ruinmen and went looking for a place nobody had been able to find for more than four hundred years. To explain the Hand, though, I'm going to have to go a bit further back, to a gray rainy morning when I was nine years old and the world I thought I knew had just fallen apart around me.

That was after my father was called up to fight the coastal allegiancies and never came back from the war. My mother waited out the rest of that year hoping the news was wrong, but the men who straggled back from the Cairline coast had little hope to offer. He'd been in the front ranks at Durrem, they said, when the Jinya cavalry broke through our lines, and those who didn't run fast got reborn in a hurry. My father wasn't the kind of man to turn and run.

When the rains came and went without word, and everyone knew that there wasn't any use in hoping further, my mother sent for a priestess to say the litany for him, and then set about selling our farm. If ours had been a bigger family she might have been able to keep it, but it was just the two of us, and I wasn't old enough for the heavy work. With the war and all, there were enough empty farms that she couldn't get much for it, but she got enough to get us to her family in Shanuga and maybe enough to find me a place as a prentice there.

So we gave away everything we couldn't take and hadn't been bought by the farm's new owners, loaded up the rest in a couple of packs, and started walking one cool wet morning down out of the hills toward Shanuga. I don't remember much of anything about the journey, though it took us three days and I'd never been anything like that far from home. I'd cried when we first heard my father wasn't coming home, and cried again when it became pretty much clear that was true, and then again when my mother told me we had to leave the farm, but somehow none of that was quite real to me until I shouldered the pack and followed her out through a gate I'd known since I was born, and that I suddenly knew I'd never see any more. There were no tears bitter enough for that, and I simply trudged along in the mud behind my mother, thinking of nothing, feeling nothing but a huge cold empty space where my life had been.

We got down to Shanuga toward evening three days later. There are bigger cities in Meriga, and I knew that even then, but I'd never seen any settlement bigger than the couple of market towns you could reach from our farm in a day's walk, and they had maybe two hundred people each. Shanuga has twenty thousand. It has buildings seven and eight stories tall, with windows of glass salvaged from the ruins, and wind turbines turning slow and silent on top of them; it has walls around it, big and gray and sturdy, with gates going through here and there.

I learned later, after I became a ruinman's prentice, that the walls were made of chunks of old freeways, cut up more or less square and mortared together. That's what gets used for city walls all over Meriga, since there are plenty of freeways to tear down and not much point in using them when the fastest thing we've got to move on them is an oxcart or a messenger's horse. I didn't know that then; all I knew was that the walls were the biggest things made by people that I'd ever seen.

The guards at the city gates watch the people passing by through narrow windows. They looked down at my mother and me, saw a couple of harmless poor folk from the hills heading into the city like a hundred others must have done that day, and probably forgot all about us in the time it takes to blink. Me, I was staring openmouthed at everything around us, and my mother had to speak to me twice to get me to pay attention and follow her into the shadow of the narrow streets.

She'd been to Shanuga to visit her family a few times since she married my father, and so the city wasn't anything like as unfamiliar to her as it was to me.

Her older sister had a tavern inside the walls of the city. I don't remember it well; I lived there for only a few weeks and visited only a couple of times after my mother died, which wasn't that many months after I prenticed with Gray Garman. Most of what I remember is the narrow stairway in back going up and up and up, five floors to the little room they could spare for my mother and me. One floor down was where Aunt Kell lived, with two daughters and whoever she had as her good time boy that week; two and three floors down were rooms that people could hire for the night, or longer if they wanted; four floors down, on the street level, was the public room, and below that was a basement full of barrels of beer, some aging, some brewing, some with a spigot stuck in them and a mark drawn with charcoal to tell the barmaids whether it was good enough to drink sober or bad enough not to give to anyone who still had wits enough to notice.

My mother went to work right away, cooking and cleaning for the tavern guests. There wasn't much I could do just then, so I mostly stayed out of the way. Once the rains stopped for good, I knew, the crafts would be taking prentices, and my mother and Aunt Kell meant to find me a place with one; that seemed like a good idea to me, too, though I hadn't yet gotten past the shock of having my life tossed into the compost by some Jinya cavalryman I'd never know. Still, as the rains finished and the first bits of clear weather started to show up, it happened more than once that I came down for a meal with my mother and Aunt Kell and her daughters and her good time boy, and Aunt Kell and my mother would stop talking and look at me, and then there would be one of those busy silences where it seemed like all the words that weren't being said kept chattering to themselves off where you can't hear them.

It was the night after one of those times that I dreamed my first dream about Deesee. Now of course I learned growing up to pay attention to my dreams and watch for the ones Mam Gaia sends, but up to then I'd never dreamed anything that would make a priestess pay the least attention. This one was different. I don't think it came from Mam Gaia, though; damn if I know who or what sent it to me, but if it hadn't come to me I can tell you for certain that I wouldn't be writing these words by lamplight in Star's Reach now.

Like so many dreams, it didn't so much start as unroll from something else too dim to recall. The first thing I remember was that I was walking down a city street so wide you could have built a block of Shanuga houses in the middle of it with room to pass on both sides. There were buildings to either side of the street, too, high and pale, with windows lined up in ranks like soldiers in a parade, except all the same size and all the same color. I was the only person I could see anywhere in the city, but not the only thing living; there were schools of fish swimming here and there between the high pale buildings, and when I breathed out my breath turned into bubbles and went rising up toward the silvery sky maybe fifty meedas above me.

None of that seemed strange to me, and I kept on walking. I was supposed to meet somebody in the drowned city, and I turned a corner to get to where I knew I was supposed to go. Ahead of me was what looked like a big grassy meadow with trees, except the grass and the trees were all seaweed that moved back and forth as the water took it. That meant I was getting close, and I hurried a bit more as I walked.

Finally I reached the seaweed meadow, and looked up and to my right, and that was when I figured out where I was.

People call it the Spire nowadays; it had a longer name in ancient times, but I don't remember it just now. Until the night that it fell, you could see it for kloms along the Lannic coast, rising up pale and stark from the sea, a square shaft of white stone with a pointed top. I had never seen it back when I had this first dream, nor for many years later, but I knew what it was and what it looked like; back when my father was alive, I played with other boys whose families kept pictures of it in their homes. There was an old story that as long as it stood there, sparkling in the mist off beyond the breakers, the drowned city beneath it might still someday rise up from the sea, and the old world and all its treasures would come back again. I never met anyone who admitted they believed the story, but I never met anyone but a priestess who insisted it was just a story, either.

But that was what I was looking at: the Spire, or the lowest part of it, rising up from its hill to pierce what I'd thought was the sky, and I knew then was the surface of the sea. The one I was supposed to meet would be waiting there, I knew, and I started up the hill toward the base of the Spire. Just then the world began to shake all around me, and the Spire shuddered and swayed; and all of a sudden I was in my bed in the little room on the fifth floor of Aunt Kell's tavern, being shaken awake by one of Aunt Kell's daughters so I'd be up in time for breakfast.

I thought about that dream all day, while sitting up in the little room and watching the clouds clear and the last few flurries of rain blow past. I thought about Deesee, the dead drowned city where the presdens of Meriga used to live before the lights went off and the seas rose up and the old world toppled into ruin like so many of the old towers I've helped salvage since I became a ruinman's prentice. I thought about the old world itself, and all the scraps and pieces of itself that lie scattered all over Mam Gaia's round belly, so that you can hardly dig in the ground anywhere in Meriga and not find something made back then. Finally, after a good long while, I thought I knew what the dream was trying to tell me.

We ate dinner early in the tavern, so that everyone got fed and the dishes cleaned up before the evening got too lively downstairs. It wasn't that many hours after breakfast, then, that I came down for dinner, and again my mother and Aunt Kell suddenly stopped talking and looked at me. I knew what they were talking about, and right then I knew what I had to say.

"Momma, I want to prentice with a ruinman, if one'll take me." That's what I put into the silence they'd made. "Aunt Kell, do you know any?"

Aunt Kell glanced at my mother, then back at me. "Happens I do," she said.

"Would you write a letter to him, if Momma gives her leave?"

Aunt Kell looked at my mother again, and my mother looked at her. "It's an honest trade," Aunt Kell said, "and if he makes mister he'll never want for money."

"And it's Mam Gaia's work," my mother said. Then, to me: "Trey, if that's what you wish, you've got my leave."

I whooped and grinned, but there was something in her voice that left me feeling cold as metal, somewhere down deep where I couldn't quite figure it out. There's a kind of peace that you see when somebody's gotten past something and can go on with life, and then there's a kind of peace you see when somebody's gotten past something and just wants to be done with living; I didn't know that difference yet, but I think I must have sensed it. My mother smiled, but there was next to nothing behind the smile: a little relief, maybe, that she had done the last thing she needed to do and could let herself fall into the hollow place where her heart had been.

Thinking of it now, I'm not even sure how much of that I sensed then, how much of it I put into the memory after she caught a coughing disease six months later and died, and how much of it got tangled up after that, when I thought about what had happened and tried to piece together the pattern of my life. Memory's a tricky thing; I think I remember that first dream of Deesee as though I was still having it right now, but sometimes I wonder how much of that memory comes from later dreams, or from what I saw from the Lannic shore when I went to the place by Deesee where every question has an answer, and saw the Spire rising out of the sea beyond the breakers, a few hours before it fell. If my life got caught up in the one big story old Plummer talked about, that day on the road to Sisnaddi, how much of what happened before then got rewritten by the storyteller so it would fit the tale he wanted to tell?

Still, there's no doubt about what happened next. A few days after I had the dream, when the rains finally stopped for good, Aunt Kell wrote a letter to the ruinman she knew and had one of her daughters run it over. I never did hear whether the ruinman wrote back or just sent word, but seemingly he had room for a new prentice and was willing to have a look at me. My mother got me dressed up and combed my hair till it hurt, and then the two of us walked the dozen blocks or so from Aunt Kell's house to the street with no name where the ruinmen live.

Everybody in Shanuga knows where that street is, and most of them would shave between their legs with a broken rock before they'd go there. It's on the south end of town, just outside the walls through a gate most other people won't use, and the street turns into a muddy road after a bit and heads straight toward where the old ruins loom up out of the river mists, tall and pale and stark like bones against the round green shapes of the hills beyond. The ruinmen's houses are like every other house in Shanuga, narrow and close together as though they were drunk and leaning on each other's shoulders to keep from falling over, and they have signs hanging in front of them like the shops of any of the other guilds in town.

Just before the houses end and the street turns into a road, though, the ruinmen's guild hall stands there, and it looks like a bad dream. Other guilds have halls that look like houses, only twice or three times as wide and a couple of stories taller. The ruinmen are, well, ruinmen, and don't do anything the same way as anybody else. Their guild hall in Shanuga is a big gray round thing made of metal that stands way up in the air like a ball perched on a stick. I learned later that the ruinmen a century ago took one of the huge water tanks the ancients put up on the hills here and there, hauled it down to the edge of town, put it up on its base and used scrap steel from the ruins to reinforce it and put floors into it. It really is one of the scariest things in town, unless you're a ruinman, in which case it's your second home.

We didn't go there, though I stared at the thing looming up above the end of the street all the way from the gate to the front door of the house where we were headed. My mother knocked on the door; a prentice answered; they exchanged a few words, and then he let my mother and me in and left us in a couple of chairs in the little front parlor.

A little while later Mister Garman came down the stairs from above. He wasn't Gray Garman yet, or at least there wasn't more than a little bit of gray in his hair back then, but he had the same frown as always and the same habit of saying little and listening a lot. I know he had some questions for my mother, and a few for me, but I honestly don't remember a word of what was said. For all that I'd been jumping up and down at the thought of becoming a ruinman's prentice, I was as scared at that moment as I've ever been since. Mister Garman was big and muscled and scarred, and I guessed even then that trying to wheedle or coax him the way I could my mother or Aunt Kell was a waste of breath.

Finally Mister Garman was satisfied, and sent the prentice for the papers. My mother couldn't read or write, but she was used to making her mark on papers and taking it on faith that they said what they were supposed to say; I could just about spell my own name and the easier words of the litanies, so I wasn't much help figuring out the papers, but I signed my own name on the line where it was supposed to go, and that made me one of Garman's prentices until I made mister, got reborn, or quit and walked away, whichever happened first.

My mother hugged me and left. Mister Garman told the prentice to take care of me, and went somewhere else, and the prentice—his name was Jo; he got reborn when a floor dropped out from underneath him two years later—took me upstairs to the big room where the prentices slept, showed me the pallet where I'd be sleeping and the chest where I got to put my things, and then led me back down two flights to the workshop where the rest of the prentices were busy getting tools ready for the season that was about to begin. I got introduced to all of them, and then right away got put to work rubbing oil into somebody's leather coat, with an older prentice keeping an eye on me to make sure I didn't skimp on the rubbing.

That's how I spent the rest of the day, except for a spare little meal of bread and thin soup around noon and another meal, even scantier, come sunset. I worried a bit about whether I'd get enough to eat as a prentice, but I didn't have a lot of other choices just then, and I knew it; my name was already on the papers, and it wasn't as though I had anywhere else to go. Then it was up to the sleeping room. I thought it was early for sleep, and of course it was, but everyone but me knew what was about to happen.

As soon as the door closed I realized that everyone was looking at me. "Trey," said the senior prentice, a big redhead nineteen years old named Bil, "You ever had anybody in your family who was a ruinman or a ruinman's prentice?"

"No," I admitted.

Bill considered me for a moment. "Then you didn't know that putting your name on a bit of paper isn't all there is to becoming a prentice here." He waited for an answer. Finally I said, "What do I have to do?"

He leaned toward me, and in a loud whisper said, "We've got a robot in the cellar. If you're going to be a prentice here, you've got to meet the robot."

For all I know, it's only in Meriga and Nuwinga that people like to scare each other silly by telling robot stories late at night, and if anybody ever reads these words, it's as likely they'll come to Star's Reach from Genda, or Meyco, or the Neeonjin country past the dead lands on the far side of the mountains, as from our little piece of Mam Gaia's belly. My father could tell a robot story in a way that would make the chairs shiver. He had a way of making robot sounds, too, so when the robot finally showed up, you didn't have to imagine the clanking and buzzing it made as it headed toward whoever was about to be buttered all over the walls.

So the half of me that believed what Bil was saying was terrified, and the half of me that figured he was telling a story was fascinated. "Okay," I said, and my voice shook enough to make the story sound pretty convincing, even to me.

"Good," said Bil. In a quieter whisper: "We've got to go all the way down the stairs, and not wake Mister Garman. Not a sound."

A moment later we were all trooping down the stairs, barefoot and silent, down floor by floor until we finally got to the cold damp silence of the cellar. Nobody brought a light, so it was blacker than black. Bil took my arm and led me somewhere, then had me sit down on something flat that I guessed was a wooden box. "Wait here," he whispered. "The robot's on its way."

I sat there for a while, and had just about decided that the joke was to leave me in the cellar and slip back upstairs to sleep, when I heard something somewhere in the darkness ahead of me: a faint cold clank, like metal landing on stone.

"You hear it?" Bil was still close by, though I hadn't known it.

"Yes," I said, and this time my voice was shaking for real.

Another clank followed, a little louder. Then there was a long silence, and then more clanks, a slow steady beat of them, as though something was walking on metal feet: something that was getting closer to me in the cellar. After a bit I could hear a faint buzzing and beeping that would be the machinery inside it.

"Here it comes," Bil hissed at me. I didn't answer, because I'd seen two tiny red lights ahead of me. They turned this way and that, as if they were looking for me. I knew that that was exactly what they were doing; I knew they were the robot's eyes.

The clanking and buzzing got louder, and louder, and the little red dots of its eyes got closer and loomed up above me. I could just about see a darker shape against the darkness, and imagined its glinting metal and wires.

"Put out your hand," Bill whispered to me then. "You've got to shake the robot's hand."

I don't think more than a tiny sliver of me still thought that it was all just a joke by then, but there was still only one thing I could do. I bit my lip and drew in a breath and put out my hand, and felt cold metal touch it, then suddenly clamp hard around it and move it up and down in quick mechanical jerks.

Then, blinding, light: a dozen electric lamps turned on all at once, and along with it laughter and whoops that rang off the cellar walls. It took a moment before I could see anything, and only then did I see the robot: another of the senior prentices, of course, with a glove covered with pieces of metal on his right hand, and a hat on top of his head with two little red lamps on it. All the other prentices were gathered around him, and some of them had noisemakers in their hands: pieces of metal to tap on the stone floor, little toothed wheels that made a buzzing sound when you turned them, and reed whistles to make the beeps.

"You see that?" Bil said to the others. "He reached right out. Come on."

Still laughing and whooping, the whole lot of them more than half dragged me back up the stairs to the dining room on the fourth floor. Mister Garman was sitting in a big chair at the head of the table, dressed in the formal clothes of a guild mister, and straight in a line down the table in front of him was as much food as I'd ever seen in one place.

The prentices lined up on the other side of the room, and got as silent as they could. Bil pushed me a step out in front, and then said in a voice that could have passed for a jennel of the presden's court in Sisnaddi, "Sir and Mister, the newest apprentice, Trey sunna Gwen."

"Has he shaken the robot's hand?" Mister Garman asked in the same oh-so-formal tone.

"He has, Sir and Mister." Then, grinning: "Put his hand right out. *And* we didn't have to drag him down the stairs."

"Then let the feasting begin," said Mister Garman. He got up from his chair, with the closest thing to a genuine smile on his face that I ever remember seeing there, and walked to the door. He turned to me and said, "You'll do well, Trey." Then, to the others: "Don't make him do all the cleaning—but this room and the kitchen had better be spotless tomorrow morning."

The moment he left the room, everyone made for the food, but there was more than enough to go around, meat pies and sweetcakes and just about anything else good you care to think about, and birch punch to drink, which I'd never had before. I gathered from the talk that the scant meals and the hard work were parts of whatever test I'd taken and passed, for some of the prentices laughed about how they'd all but had to be dragged down to the cellar, and others how they'd just about decided to give up and go back to their families, and there were a few who mentioned boys who did just that, up and quit after two bleak meals and a lot of hard work, or who bolted out the door into the night because they were too afraid of meeting the robot.

I didn't mention that I'd had my share of hard work and scant meals as a farmer's only child up in the hills, though that was mostly because I was too well fed and comfortable by the time the point seemed worth making. Still, I did my share of the cleaning when it came to that, and the dining room and kitchen were close to spotless when we got up the next morning.

It's a funny thing, the robot's hand. Every ruinman's prentice, not just Garman's, gets to shake the robot's hand, and ever after that there's a line between you and everyone who hasn't gone to meet the robot. The old world is a little less distant, maybe, and the things that people outside the ruinmen's guild think and say seem a little less important. Certainly, as I lay in bed and tried to quiet my mind enough to sleep, the night after I found the dead man's letter in the Shanuga underplaces and got started on the road to Star's Reach, the robot's hand was what kept coming to mind; I imagined myself going down some other stair, in some vast ruin I could barely imagine, and shaking a hand that didn't have another prentice on the other side of it.

Maybe that's what the ancients who built Star's Reach were trying to do, in their own way. I know it's one of the things that sends ruinmen down into the underplaces of the old world's dead cities, when the pay's so often poor these days and so many of us get reborn in the doing of it. To touch something that thinks but isn't human, or isn't the kind of human we are nowadays: it's a heady thing, and it makes my head spin to think that I'm as close to doing that as I write these words as anyone has been since the old world ended.

CHAPTER 5

THE ROAD TO MELUMI

The morning after the day I found the letter came way too early. I dragged myself off of my cot about the time first light came up in the east, found some cold water to wash with, and made myself about as presentable as somebody who hasn't had time to sleep off one mother of a lot of beer is likely to get. The face that looked back at me from the little tin mirror over the washbasin wasn't much different from the one that blinked back the morning before, barring the cut on my cheek, but I felt different. At the time, I thought that was a matter of becoming a ruinman and a mister of the guild, or maybe squeaking past getting reborn by a senamee or two. Looking back, though, I think it was probably the beer.

Finally I got dressed in ruinman's leathers and left my tent, and damn if Berry wasn't right: there must have been twenty prentices waiting for me with hopeful looks. Some were just about as old as I was, and some were so young they must have signed on with their misters just before that season, but it took all of one look to tell me that every one of them was hoping I'd pick him and nobody else to be my first prentice. I had just about enough wits in my head to raise a hand before they all started talking at once. "Already chose my prentice," I told them. "Sorry." A couple of the youngest ones burst into tears, and all of them gave me the kind of look that makes you feel like you just stomped their puppy or something.

That didn't trouble me much, to be honest, and I waited until they were leaving and walked a bit unsteadily over to Gray Garman's tent. I'm sure the man slept sometime, but in all the years I worked for him I could count the times I saw him sleeping or washing up or anything on the fingers of one foot. This morning was no different. He had his tent flap open, and waved me in when I stopped just outside. Berry was there already, clean and bright-eyed and doing his level best not to jump out of his skin with excitement, but Garman just looked me up and down the way he always did, waved me to a chair, and said, "You decided?"

He meant the letter or the finder's rights to Star's Reach: one a big chunk of easy money but nothing more, the other nothing more than a hope, maybe, but a hope of finding the thing every ruinman dreams of finding. I sat down on the chair, looked at him, and said, "I keep on telling myself that I ought to have some brains."

For once, Garman laughed. It was as dry as an old granny's whatnot and as short as a dumb ruinman's life, but it was still a laugh. If he'd suddenly sprouted feathers I don't think I'd have been more surprised. "If I was twenty years younger," he said, "I'd be telling myself that." Then: "Berry says you picked him."

"That's right."

Garman nodded once. "Good choice. He'll be of use." Berry lit up like a lamp; Garman didn't say that sort of thing lightly. "The original's going to Shanuga today for auction," Garman went on, "but a copy needs to go to Melumi right quick; Mam Kelsey's talked with them by radio and they want it. You headed that way?"

I hadn't even begun to make plans yet, but it suddenly seemed like the best possible idea, not least because I guessed what Garman had in mind. "I was thinking that," I lied.

"Good." He pulled two copies of the letter off a table next to his chair, handed them to me. "One for you and one for the scholars. And here—" He tossed me a leather bag that landed in my hand with a clink. "Ought to be about a fifth of what they'll pay. That'll keep the two of you in food on the way."

A fifth of the price was courier's wages, but from the hard plump shape of the bag, he'd rounded up a good bit. I pretended not to notice, and thanked him.

"Don't mention it." He leaned forward, then, and gave me one of his looks. "Now listen. You two go fast, keep mum, and stay off the main roads. Some people might kill to get this before the Versty does." He handed me another sheet of paper. "This might help."

I read the paper. It was a letter from him to some mister in the Cago ruins, up north on the lakes, saying the Shanuga ruins didn't have room for a new mister and asking the Cago ruinmen to find a place for me. "If anyone asks, that's why we're traveling."

"That's right." Then: "And it's close enough to true, anyway."

I knew what he was talking about, of course. The Shanuga ruins still had a lot of metal in them, but raw metal doesn't pay a ruinman much, and the good finds—old machines and rare metals and documents—had been getting scarcer since before I was born. I'd already heard of towns where they'd closed the guild; they only allowed a certain number of misters, and a prentice couldn't make mister unless somebody had just died or he was ready to go somewhere else. It hadn't yet occurred to me that there might not always be somewhere else to go. That came to mind later, after I'd traveled a bit and learned just how close the ruinmen's guilds had gotten to digging themselves out of business.

After that we had some papers to sign for Berry, so the laws would treat him as my prentice and not Garman's. Garman put his name on the lines and I put mine, and then Berry surprised the stuffing out of me by reading the papers and signing his own name nice and neat in the right place. Then we said our goodbyes and Garman cuffed me on the shoulder, one mister to another, and Berry and I left the tent and went to get some food before we started.

The camp was mostly awake by then. Off in the middle distance I could hear Mister Calwel's voice, high and sharp, yelling at his prentices. Chickens clucked and scratched in the grass, and one of their wild cousins crowed off in the forest somewhere. I was about to get in line at the cook's tent when Berry cleared his throat and gave me a look that he must have learnt from Garman, reminding me that I was a mister now and it was prentice duty to go fetch food for me. So I sat down at an empty table and watched the mists burn off the river for a bit, until he came back with bread and chicory-brew and two big bowls of soup. I don't think either of us said a word until most of that was gone.

"Have you been to Melumi before?" Berry asked then.

"Not me." I considered him. "You?"

He grinned. "No, but I always wanted to. You think they can figure out the letter?"

It's a funny thing, how once you make a decision, it's easy to think up reasons for it. I nodded, as though the trip to Melumi had been my idea all along. "They ought to be able to tell us what a potus is, and the rest of those words. I figure it's the best first step."

And of course it was, and I'd agreed to do courier duty for Garman as well, but right then the thought of going to Melumi didn't need anything practical to recommend it to me. That's common enough; I've met farmer folk who couldn't read their own names if you helped spell it out for them, who day-dreamed about going to Melumi just to look through glass at the books and the scholars, and ask some question that didn't matter to anyone so that a scholar in a gray robe could look up the answer and tell them.

Ask most people and they'll tell you that the scholars know everything. Ask people who read and write, and know a little bit about the world, and they'll tell you that the scholars know most everything that matters. They're as wrong as the first bunch, but compared to what most of us know nowadays, they might as well be right. Meriga's come down a long ways since the days when Deesee was above water, and there are countries in the world that are bigger and richer, but the Versty at Melumi, with its shelves and shelves and shelves of books from the old world, is one thing we can still be proud of.

Berry was still grinning. "I'm ready."

"I bet." We finished up the food, and then he ran to get his things and I went to my tent and started packing. Not that I had that much to pack; prentices don't have much chance to load themselves down, and the only thing I'd had time to collect in the day I'd been a mister was a hangover. So one leather pack was enough for clothes and tools and all, with a little bag of keepsakes down in the bottom of the pack: a ring that had been my mother's; a bit of wood carved to look like a horse's head that I got from Toby, who was my best friend among the prentices for most of four years and got reborn when a building fell on him; the little star of yellow metal the government gave my mother after my father died in the war; and a butterfly of the same yellow metal that was a parting gift from Tam—and I'm going to have to write about her one of these days, since she's part of my story and part of what got me to this bare concrete room here under the desert at Star's Reach.

By the time I'd gotten everything packed, Berry showed up with his pack over one shoulder. He was just about hopping, he was so excited, and I couldn't fault him for that. Me, I was stuck halfway between being just as excited, and worried that I'd just pitched myself into something way too deep and dangerous for me. Gray Garman's words about people who might kill to get the letter I carried were on my mind; so was the fact that I had no notion what I might do if we got to Melumi and the scholars couldn't tell me what the letter meant.

Still, I swung my pack up onto my back, got it settled, and tried to chase the worries out of my head. I tied the tent door open to let Garman's prentices know I was gone, and Berry and I turned our backs on the ruins and started walking. The day was turning clear and, thank the four winds, not too hot for a change; a couple of buzzards circled way up in the sky, which is supposed to be a good sign for travelers, though nobody's ever told me why.

Just north of camp we went over to the riverbank and walked along it until a ferryman got close enough that we could wave him in. I handed over a few bits, Berry and I climbed into his little boat, and we sat and watched green water roll past as he puffed and hauled on the oars and got us to the other side. We got off the boat there and scrambled up the bank, and a few minutes later we were walking north on the road to Melumi.

One of the roads to Melumi, I suppose I should say, because there's more than one. From Shanuga, you can go on the main road east of the river up to Noksul, or you can go west of the river on what's not much more than a farm track most of the same way, and then cross the ridges at the first good place you can find and head west to Nashul or north into Tucki. Berry and I took that second route, partly because Gray Garman said we ought to stay off of the main roads, and partly because Noksul's a soldier's town. That's where my father went when he was called up for the war; it's where the Army of Tenisi is, when it's not playing tag in the mountains with raiders from the coastal allegiancies; and a town full of soldiers is not a place where you want to take something people might kill to get their hands on.

I was nervous about that last bit. As soon as we found the dead man's letter in the Shanuga ruins, I knew that even a copy of it would be worth a mother of a lot of money, and I realized not that much later that a lot of people would want it for reasons that didn't have a thing to do with how many marks they could get for it, but it took Gray Garman's words to make it sink in that one ruinman and his prentice might be fair game if the wrong people figured out what we were carrying. With luck and Mam Gaia's blessing we could get ahead of the news and stay there, but we'd need both the luck and the blessing. The radio message to Melumi about our find would have come to many ears, even if it was in code, and of course one rider on a fast horse could spread the news way ahead of us.

We talked about that a little, while we walked; talked about the route we'd settled on, too, straight up through Tucki to Luwul and from there straight to Melumi; but mostly talked about nothing in particular, when we talked at all. More often we just walked. The day was clear and cool, the sort of dry season weather you long for when the rains set in and it's one big sea of mud from wherever you are to wherever you wish you could get to; the sky was blue with a few puffy white clouds in it, and the road was from the old world. It was rutted and cracked and big chunks of the old paving were gone, but it still ran mostly straight and level, and here and there you'd walk on big gray slabs of concrete, like pictures in a storybook about the old world, except the paint that made a line down the middle of the road got weathered away long ago.

All that country was full of farms. With Shanuga so close, there's plenty of money to be made selling garden stuff and eggs and the like to the city markets, and the land's rich enough that you can do that and still grow plenty for a family on a pretty modest plot. Ox carts rolling into the city came by so often that Berry and I took to walking along one side of the road to stay out of their way. Other than that we mostly saw people working in the fields, and most of them took one look at our ruinmen's gear and looked away.

We walked north until it was nearly full dark, and found a farm where the people were willing to give us a meal on the kitchen steps and a place to sleep in the barn for a couple of bits.

Berry dropped off to sleep as soon as we finished getting settled in the hayloft. I envied him that, as I lay there staring into the darkness, thinking about Star's Reach and how on Mam Gaia's round belly I was going to figure out where it was if the scholars at Melumi couldn't help me.

Still, I managed to get to sleep after a while, and then the noises of farmhands going about the first chores in the gray morning woke me up. Berry and I washed our hands and faces at the pump in the farmyard, got some breakfast from the farm folk, and started north before the sun was fairly up over the mountains off east of us.

That second day might as well have been the first, except that the farms were bigger, and grew less garden stuff and more corn. The day after that was sister to the first two, except that the fields started spreading themselves out and left patches of empty land between them. We passed places where low gray ragged shapes heaved up through the grass: foundations from the old world that nobody had gotten around to digging out and breaking up for building material. A good bit of the poorer ground had been left in pasture, too, and herds of loms watched Berry and me incuriously as we walked by.

The loms reminded me of the hill country where I'd grown up. My father and most everyone else had some for wool, and for hauling loads to and from market; I'd been carried on a lom's back often enough when I was too young to walk far, and fell in love a bit with the smell of their long straight wool and the way their heads swivel around on top of their long, long necks, as they taste the wind and listen and look.

They didn't have loms in Meriga in the old world. I heard that from some traveling folk once, though I'm still not sure whether to believe it or not; farmers in Tenisi have been raising loms as long as anyone remembers. What I heard, though, is that in the old world, people got wool from a different kind of animal. They called it a cheap, and the people who told me the story swore that that was because it didn't cost as much as a lom does. Cheap weren't as big as loms, and they had short necks and wool that curled.

When the old world was dying, though, a disease came through and killed most of the cheap, and the scholars they had back then couldn't figure out how to get rid of the disease, so most of the new cheap that got born every year died of it. That meant you couldn't make a living raising cheap, so the farmers just got rid of the last of them and took to raising loms instead, and that's why we don't have cheap any more. Of course the same sort of thing happened to a lot of other things back then, and it nearly happened to people, too. We were lucky, I guess, that nobody had to make a living raising us.

We managed to find a farmhouse to stay at that night, but the next morning, even the pastures and the loms got scarce, and from noon on there were no more farmhouses in sight. We talked a little about that, Berry and I, the morning we left the Shanuga ruins, and brought blankets and fire gear and the like with us for sleeping rough; we both knew perfectly well that there'd be plenty of that on the way to Star's Reach. Still, I was nervous. You might think that somebody who'd go crawling down a hole in the ground that nobody had been down for four hundred years wouldn't blink at the thought of sleeping under a tree, but the fact was that I'd never actually spent a night out in the forest.

That's what it came to, though. By the time the sun got near the top of the ridge to the west of us, we hadn't seen another human being aside from each other in many hours, and there weren't even any loms in sight. So we kept on going until the sun was down, and then left the road and worked our way about halfway from the road to the river. We found a bit of an old ruin there, a couple of low walls that came together in a corner and went up about as high as Berry was tall. The point of the corner faced toward the road, too, so we could build a small fire and not be seen if anyone was looking.

So I gathered some dry wood and Berry got water from the river, and by the time it was all the way dark we had a nice little camp in the corner of the ruin. We didn't have a lot of food, just a bit of bread the farm wife had given us that morning and a couple of cakes of dried soup Berry begged from the kitchen at Mister Garman's camp back at the Shanuga ruins, but we'd eaten well enough until then. Once we got a fire started, Berry tossed one of the cakes of soup into a tin pail of water on top, and it turned into something not half bad in short order.

So we ate some of the bread and drank the soup, and the night got darker. Wind made noise in the branches above us, and other things made their own little noises lower down. I tried not to show it, but I was on edge, and when a wild dog barked somewhere off in the middle distance, Berry and I both just about jumped out of our skins.

"Nervous?" I asked him.

"Yes." Then: "I've never spent a night out in the forest."

"Me neither."

Even in the dim flickering light from what was left of the fire, I could see his eyebrows go up. "I heard you were a farm boy from the hill country."

"True enough. Doesn't mean we slept under trees, you know."

That got me a quick glance, to make sure I wasn't angry, which I wasn't. "I was born in Nashul," he said after a moment. "Inside the walls."

I let out a whistle. "No kidding. How'd you end up a ruinman's prentice?"

"I—I'm a tween, you know."

"I didn't."

"Is that—" He didn't finish the sentence, not that he needed to.

I didn't give him time, either. "Garman ever give you trouble over that?"

"Not once."

"That's good enough for me."

His face said "thank you" better than words could have. I put a couple of sticks onto the fire, so neither of us had to say anything for a moment.

I don't think they had tweens in the old world, either, or if they did I've never read anything about them. The priestesses say that they're one of the things that happened to us because of all the poisons the people of the old world dumped everywhere they could think of. Some of those were fast poisons, and that's part of why so many people died during the years just after the old world ended, and some of them were slow poisons, and that's part of why there still aren't a twentieth as many people as there were back then. Some of them, though, were the kind of poison that gets inside you and messes things up, not for you, but for your children and their children, and of course that's another part of the reason why there are so few people nowadays compared to how many there were back then.

It's because of that third kind of poison, the priestesses say, that so many women can't have babies and so many men can't father them, and that's also why so many of the babies that do get born are sick from birth and die young. Still, you also get babies who are born different rather than sick. You get green children, for one. When they're young, there's something in their skin that feeds the little green one-celled plants the priestesses talk about so much, and so they turn a nice grass green a few weeks after they're born and stay that way until they get into their teen years, and then the little plants go away and their skin turns brown again. Up in Mishga and Skonsa and Aiwa you get a lot of people with a coat of hair all over them like bears; down in the border country near Meyco you get a lot of women with four breasts instead of two, and men with four nipples: there's a lot of that sort of thing.

Then there are tweens. There are more of them than the others, and they're called tweens because they're not really men or women but something in between. The two of them I've ever seen with their clothes off had something like a set of each kind between their legs, and little breasts you'd never notice under a shirt. The priestesses say that tweens count as men, meaning they can't be priestesses or belong to Circle; most other people aren't too sure what to make of them, and there are places where they're not welcome. Even before Berry and I traveled together, that last thing seemed stupid to me, but then people do nearly as many stupid things nowadays as they did back in the old world.

I got the fire fed, and saw that Berry was watching me. "You know," he said, "I should probably tell you my story—about where I came from and how I got to be Garman's prentice." He looked down. "Since I'm your prentice now, and there are some things you ought to know."

"Fair enough," I said. "I'm listening."

He drew in a breath, just a bit raggedly, and began.

CHAPTER 6

THE GRAY TOWERS

I've been trying for two days now to figure out the best way to write about what Berry told me that night in the forest, and tore half a dozen pages out of the notebook before I realized I'd better work it out before I wrote another word. Part of the problem is that I don't know who's going to read this, if anyone ever does. For all I know we might die here at Star's Reach, and Meriga could have a fourth civil war once Sheren dies and there's no heir to step up and become Presden, and the next people to come this way might be from the Neeonjin country, or someplace even farther away that nobody on this side of the world has heard about for four hundred years. What can I write that they'll understand?

Take Nashul, where Berry said he'd been born and grew up. I've never been there, but they say it looks a lot like Shanuga, only bigger—the same gray walls made of old world concrete and mortar, the same tall narrow houses and winding narrow streets inside the walls, the same places outside the walls for things nobody wants to think about, and a ruinmen's hall out there somewhere that looks like somebody took a bad dream and tried to build it out of salvaged metal. Most cities in Meriga look like that if they're big enough to have walls at all, so unless you're a ruinman and know how towns used to look in the old world, or work in another trade that knows the same things, it might never occur to you that towns haven't always been that way.

It's just too easy, though, for me to picture somebody who's walked all the way over the mountains and the dead lands from the Neeonjin country, with straw sandals on his feet and a couple of swords at his belt, like the Neeonjin man in a picture book I had when I was little. He turns on a light and sits down here at this steel desk, and opens this notebook all anyhow, and the first thing he reads is me going on about the walled cities we've got here in Meriga. The priestesses say that there are places on Mam Gaia's round belly where there aren't any cities at all, either because there aren't enough people or because there are laws against it. If they don't have towns in the Neeonjin country or the ones they have don't look like ours, whoever reads this will probably decide I was drunk or dreaming when I wrote, and use the rest of the notebook to light a fire to cook his dinner.

Here in Meriga, though, cities have gray walls and narrow streets and everything else I mentioned earlier. Nashul's like that, and Nashul's what Berry started talking about first, that night in the forest where the two of us sat and tried to pretend we weren't scared of what might be moving around out there in the darkness.

"I was born in Nashul inside the walls, as I said," he told me. He was facing our little fire, turned half away from me, with his arms folded around his knees. "Born up high, like they say, but raised down low. My mother's mother was a big name in Circle, big enough that whether my mother got into Circle mattered a lot to the family. So my mother went playing, once she got to the age that girls do that."

There's another thing: Circle. You find Circle everywhere in Meriga and Nuwinga; they've got it in Genda and the coastal allegiancies, too, except it's not quite the same, and nothing like as powerful; down in Meyco they don't have it at all, and I don't suppose anybody knows what mothers do or don't do in the Neeonjin country or the Arab countries across the sea, or anywhere else further off. Ask anybody who's in Circle and they'll tell you that it's as old as people are on Mam Gaia, that women already got together in Circle in the days when everyone lived in caves and made tools out of rocks, the way the priestesses said we all did a long time ago, long before the old world got started. Maybe that's so, but I never saw a word about Circle in old books, not even when I was in Sisnaddi for most of a year searching the archives in what I thought was the last chance I had to find Star's Reach.

Now if I could sit down with that Neeonjin traveler over a meal and a couple of beers, I could tell him about Circle, or as much about it as a man is ever going to know. I'd tell him what I learned from Plummer, and talk about how back in the days after the old world died and ours was born, maybe one woman in a dozen was able to have healthy babies, and the ones who could banded together to help each other, when there was no other help from anywhere else. I'd tell him how those circles of women spread and linked up with each other, and linked up with the priestesses, too, until pretty soon every town and city had Circle, and if you wanted to make something happen, even if you were the presden, you pretty much had to hope that Circle wasn't against it. There's a reason why most of the presdens Meriga's had for the last two hundred years have been women.

"And you were what happened," I said.

"Pretty much."

I let out a whistle. "That must have caused a flutter or two."

"That's what they told me." With a little laugh: "They were all set to bring my mother into Circle as soon as I was born. They'd already made all the plans for the ceremony, and then I came out tween and the whole thing had to be hushed up in a hurry. They'd probably just have pressed a pillow over my face and solved the problem that way, except my mother's family were Old Believers and she wouldn't let the birth women do that."

Then there are the Old Believers. I'd never yet met one of them, that night when Berry told me his story, though I've met them since. They don't worship Mam Gaia and they don't watch their dreams for messages from her; they've got a god of their own who's dead, except he's not really dead, and they talk to him instead of listening for what he has to say. They say that in the old world most everyone believed the way they do, and one of them I met in Memfis told me that what happened to the old world was their god's doing, not Mam Gaia's or just what happens when you do enough dumb things for long enough and the consequences finally gang up and clobber you.

But the Old Believers won't kill newborns, even those that are born horribly sick and won't live for more than a couple of hours anyway, and there's all kinds of other things they won't do, and some things that we won't do don't bother them a bit. There are a few Old Believer families who are big names in Circle or in the army, but they mostly keep to themselves, in their own villages and their own cramped little quarters in cities, where they make and sell things that the priestesses say are wrong but people want anyway.

"So I got sent outside the walls," said Berry. "They found a woman who'd had a dead child and was willing to nurse me instead, and paid her to go live off by herself in a little house off by itself. So that's where I grew up, and that's most of what I remember of Nashul."

He stopped for a bit, so I asked, "She was the one who taught you to read?"

That got me a quick glance. "Nah, I had a teacher who visited three times a week for a while. When she stopped coming, I was old enough to go to school with the priestesses. I was seven by then, and Ranna—that's the name of the woman who took care of me—she told me that my mother had a healthy baby and had gotten into Circle after all, and so I'd better get used to living like everyone else."

It took me a moment to catch what Berry meant. "If she hadn't—"

"There'd be no reason to pretend I didn't exist." A shrug. "So she had her healthy baby and for all I know she's a big name in Circle now."

"Ouch."

He went on as though he hadn't heard. "So I went to school with the priestesses for a while, and then it came time for me to prentice with somebody, and I got told that I could go into any trade I wanted, but it wasn't going to be in Nashul. So I said I wanted to be a ruinman, and about six weeks later some men came and got me and everything I had and put it all in a wagon and drove halfway across Tenisi to Gray Garman's house on the ruinmen's street in Shanuga."

I waited until I was pretty sure he was finished, and said, "I remember when you showed up and we had you shake the robot's hand."

That got me another glance, and then a sudden grin. "When we all went back upstairs and met Mister Garman, that was the first time I can think of when I really felt that somebody was happy to have me around." Then: "Garman knew I was a tween, and a couple of prentices found out—when you sleep in a tent with somebody, it's not too easy to keep your middle covered up all the time. But nobody made any kind of fuss about it. I was just another prentice."

"And now you've got a mister dumb enough he thinks he can find Star's Reach."

"And still pinching myself sometimes to make sure I'm not just dreaming that." Then, suddenly serious: "But if you ever wondered why I can read and do numbers and talk like a jennel, when I'm Berry sunna nobody, Mister Trey, now you know."

I nodded. "Fair enough. I'm glad you can read; that could be a mother of a lot of help."

He grinned again. "I'm hoping."

We talked about some other things after that, though I don't remember a word of it, and finally got sleepy enough that the night around our little camp didn't seem half so threatening. So we wrapped up in our blankets, and I went to sleep thinking about Berry's story, and Tam, who I haven't written about yet and need to.

That might have had something to do with the dream I had that night. I was in Deesee again, walking down the wide empty streets with the fish swimming down them and the surface of the water all silver and rolling fifty meedas overhead. This time Tam was with me; she had her blue dress on, the one I tore once when we were playing, and her hair was tied up in a scarf, the way she used to wear it when she wanted to annoy her family. We walked down the street and turned to see the Spire soaring up from its low hill. Tam tried to say something to me, but all that came out of her mouth was bubbles of air that drifted up between us, so she pressed her body up against mine.

Right then I woke up. The first gray light of dawn was starting to filter down through the forest. Berry was sound asleep and still wrapped up in his blanket, but he'd moved up against me, no doubt for the warmth. I lay there and thought about Tam, wondering what she'd made of her life since she had her baby and got into Circle. After a bit, I got up, and Berry woke up; we washed up by the riverbank and got something to eat, then shouldered our packs and found our way back to the road.

The old dream about Deesee kept on coming back to me, night after night, while Berry and I walked north out of Tenisi and started across Tucki. That was about the only interesting thing that happened for most of two weeks, though. The road we followed ran west and then north through forest, for the most part, with villages or scattered farms here and there when the soil was good or somebody's great-grandparents just up and decided that this was where they were going to build their house.

It's a funny thing, but the further we traveled from cities and the poorer the folk we met, the better the welcome we got.

Close to Shanuga, as I wrote earlier, we were lucky to get a place to sleep in a hayloft and a cold meal on the back steps, but as we got deep into Tucki, as often as not we ate at the table with the family and slept on a pallet in a room of our own. Nobody seemed to care that we were ruinmen. In fact, it was pretty much the opposite; half the time, when we stayed the night at some farmhouse, sooner or later the farm folk would mention some scrap of ruin over on one corner of the property and ask if I thought there was anything in it that might hurt anyone. It happened fairly often that Berry and I went out the next morning at first light and followed somebody over to an old gray lump of concrete wet with dew, poked around it, scanned it for radiation and poisons, and left the people there feeling a good bit easier.

Mind you, I could have skipped the morning walk and told every one of them what I'd find. Outside of the old cities, if you find a small ruin out by itself, just a bit of concrete sticking up out of the grass like a rotten tooth in a green gum, you can bet it's nothing more than the foundation of a house or a shop from the old world, and anything dangerous got washed away a long time ago. It's the big ruins that can still kill you, and nobody farms too close to those—the priestesses wouldn't stand for it, the jennel or cunnel who has land in the area would put a stop to it, and I don't think anybody's dumb enough to try it in the first place. So the ruins we checked on that trip north were no threat to anybody. I could have told the farmers as much without looking, but it made them feel better to have Berry and me out there in our ruinmen's leathers sweeping the ground with radiation counters, and it seemed like a fair return for their hospitality.

So we made our way north. Now and then we spent a day or two in country that didn't have a single house anywhere in sight, and Berry and I got used pretty quickly to sleeping in the forest. Sometimes the cracked gray road beneath our feet was the only sign that any human being had ever come that way since Mam Gaia shaped that part of her belly; sometimes we passed through what was left of some town the people of the old world put someplace that didn't have good soil or running water or any of the other things people nowadays need and they seemingly didn't. We must have walked through half a dozen places full of low gray shapes of concrete mostly overgrown with vines and the like, with mounds here and there where something big had tumbled down a couple of hundred years back. Most of the mounds showed traces of digging, and there was plenty of broken concrete that had been cracked open for the metal, showing that we weren't the first ruinmen to come that way.

There came a stretch of the journey where we didn't see a trace of anything human for most of two days. We didn't think much of it until late on the afternoon of the second day, when we crested a rise and found ourselves face to face with a couple of huge gray shapes, cracked and crumbling at the top, that rose out of the forest in the middle distance like giant ghosts.

I knew from one look at Berry's face that I didn't have to tell him what they were. Without a word, I got out my radiation counter and scanned the road at our feet.

"Nobody said that there was a nuke this way," Berry said then.

"Might be an empty," I reminded him. "I'm getting nothing but background."

He gave me a dubious look, but followed when I started down the road.

I didn't blame him for the look. There are safe ruins like the ones the farmers had in their fields, and there are dangerous ruins like the one in Shanuga where I nearly got reborn, and then there are nukes. You find them here and there all over Meriga, and most of them are dead zones with fences all around a couple of kloms out from the ruins and nobody living anywhere nearby, especially downstream. The priestesses put prayer flags on the fences, partly to ask Mam Gaia to heal the land there, partly because anybody who goes past the fence and messes with what's inside is going to be too busy getting reborn to have a lot of time for prayers.

I learned about nukes from Gray Garman, of course. Every ruinman's prentice learns about them from his mister, since the only thing the priestesses will tell you about them is that they're evil and if you go there you're going to get reborn in a hurry. That's true enough as far as it goes, but a ruinman needs to know more.

What Garman taught me was that there are two things to worry about when you're dealing with a nuke. The first is the reactor building itself. For some reason the ancients didn't take the time to shut everything down properly when the old world ended, so the old fuel rods and everything are still there, but the machines that used to keep them cool and safe haven't been working for more than four hundred years. Nobody knows what's inside nowadays, because the radiation has you doubling over and vomiting before you get much past the door of the building, and you don't last long after that.

But that's not the worst of it. The worst of it is the used fuel rods. Those are in what used to be pools of water, sometimes inside the reactor buildings, sometimes in buildings of their own nearby. I read once in Sisnaddi, when I was searching the archives there, that people spent years back in the old world bickering about what they were going to do with the fuel rods and all the other dangerous stuff that came out of the nukes, and they ended up never doing much of anything at all with them except leaving them in the pools of water.

Of course once the old world ended and there wasn't anybody to make sure the pumps kept water flowing into the pools, things started going bad in a hurry. The fuel rods got red hot, and a lot of them caught fire, or melted their way down to groundwater and leached out into the ground, or simply turned into dust that blew here and there on the wind, and a mother of a lot of land around the old nukes ended up contaminated enough to kill you quick or slow. You can't see the contamination, or taste it. Unless you've got a radiation counter, you don't have any way of knowing it's killing you until you take sick and the doctor tells you that all she can do is send for the priestesses.

I had a radiation counter, and I wasn't about to let something like that happen to me or Berry from being too brave to use it. As we went down the road, I kept the thing in my hand and listened to it click. It didn't show anything above normal, and as we kept walking and the counter kept clicking mildly to itself, both of us got a little more confident. It didn't hurt that the road didn't seem to be heading straight at the cooling towers, either.

So we kept on walking, and the towers seemed to drift slowly to one side as we went. Finally we got alongside them; the counter still wasn't showing anything but normal, but just then we noticed two things. The first was a cleared trail heading straight toward the towers from the road, with a pair of saplings tied together in an X marking the place where it hit the road—one of the old ruinmen's signs. The second was a thin line of smoke rising from someplace close to the nearer tower.

Berry looked at me, and I looked at him. "You sure that counter's working?" he asked.

"Checked it in Shanuga," I reminded him.

"Maybe you're right, then, Mister Trey."

He meant what I'd said earlier about the nuke being an empty. That was something else Garman taught me, though I heard about it later, and in more detail, too, from Plummer one time when we were traveling down the Misipi on the *Jennel Mornay*. During the years just before the old world ended, the ancients tried to make up for everything else they were running out of by building lots of nukes. Most of those never got finished, and so now and then, when you see the big round towers rising up out of the forest, there's nothing there but a bunch of old concrete. Most people won't go near them anyway, just in case, but some ruinmen make a living out of breaking down the empties for the metal that's in them—sometimes a sparse living, if all they find is rebar and girders in concrete; sometimes a pretty good living, if all the wiring and pipes got put in, and if you're very lucky some of the machines that they used to run the nukes.

We looked at each other again, and I shrugged, and we turned off the road and went down the trail past the crossed saplings.

Sure enough, the radiation counter never did pick up anything more than background, and the trail didn't lead us up to a fence strung with prayer flags. Instead, we clambered down a dirt trail and came out of the forest under the shadow of one of the towers, and found ourselves just about face to face with a ruinman and his prentice loading chunks of old pipe onto a wagon. They looked at us and we looked at them, and then I greeted them with the old words that ruinmen use so other ruinmen know they're members of the guild. That was all it took; the other ruinman gave us a nod and an assessing look. "You fellows looking for work?"

"On our way to a job in Cago," I said.

"Well, drat." He was getting on in years, with gray all through his hair and beard and a couple of nasty scars along his face. "We've got us a nice clean ruin here and not half enough hands to make the most of it. Name's Cob."

"Trey," I said, and shook his hand. "My prentice here's Berry."

"Sam." A motion of his head indicated his prentice, a boy about Berry's age. "Surely you're at least looking for someplace to spend the night."

"Crossed our minds."

He grinned. "Consider it done. Where you fellows from?"

So I told him, and we got to talking, and pretty soon Berry and I were helping him and Sam load the last of the pipe into the wagon, because that's what you do if you're a ruinman and you're staying at somebody else's site. By the time we were done,

Cob had explained that he'd be taking the wagon down to Lebna, the nearest town, when morning came around, and offered Berry and me a ride that far. Of course we agreed, and helped him with a couple of other bits of lifting and hauling while the daylight was still good, because again, that's what you do.

Later on, the lot of us ate stew and pan bread in a room Cob and Sam had cleared in the main building of the nuke. We were close enough to where the containment vessel would have gone that we'd all have been dead in minutes if it wasn't an empty, but that didn't bother me any. Berry and I told as much of the news from Shanuga as we could without mentioning Star's Reach, and Cob had plenty of news about Tucki and some from Sisnaddi itself, which after all is just across the river from Tucki. They'd been driving the wagon down to Lebna every week or so to sell metal, buy supplies, and listen to the gossip, so some of it was pretty recent, too.

I don't remember most of it. I was tired, and being around another ruinman made me a bit homesick for the Shanuga ruins and the people I knew, but one thing I do remember. "They say Sheren's taken sick," Cob said. "Mam Gaia bless her, she's been presden what, near forty years now? I'd always figured she'd outlast me, and I hope she does. There's going to be a mother of a mess when she goes, they say."

I wasn't at all sure what he meant by that. "Been a while since we had an election," I said, guessing that might be it.

"And it might be longer before we have another one. There's some who'd rather cast their vote with guns." He shook his head. "Damn fools. Like they'd gain anything by that."

I couldn't think of anything to say to that. A moment later, though, I happened to look Berry's way, and he was staring into the fire with an expression I'd never seen on him before, eyes wide and mouth shut tight and every line of his face holding something in. He noticed me looking at him, then, and put on a different expression, fast, but I'd seen the earlier one, and wondered about that for the rest of the evening.

CHAPTER 7

THE WAY OF RUINS

One of the things that makes this story hard to tell in a straight line is that so much of it has to do with ruins, and ruins have their own way of doing things. They all have stories to tell, but they don't tell them from beginning to end, the way that Eleen and Tashel Ban say I ought to tell the story I'm trying to write here. Ruins know how to wait, seeing as they've had plenty of practice at it. They say a word here and a word there, and it's a pretty safe bet that you won't figure out what they mean by those words the first time you hear them.

If you're a ruinman's prentice, you either learn that quick or you get reborn, because more often than not, if a ruin's going to kill somebody, it starts saying that to the ruinmen in its own roundabout way days or weeks before anything happens. I wrote something a while back about Shem sunna Janny, who became a prentice the same year Conn and I did, and who looked at Mam Kelsey's book with me. He wasn't stupid, but he never did figure out how to listen to a ruin, and so he was pulling wire out of a conduit one morning in a building we'd started taking down when something inside gave way all at once, and a couple of floors came crashing down on top of him.

The ruin had been saying that it was going to kill someone since we started work on it that year. When the wind blew, it creaked and shifted, and when we chopped pieces of it loose and dropped them into a clear space below, it creaked and shifted some more. Now of course plenty of ruins creak and shift, and there are some that don't and still end up dropping on somebody, but that's the way of ruins; you have to listen to them talk, and then sometimes you can figure out enough to keep from getting reborn. The other prentices stayed away from the ruin that flapjacked on Janny when they didn't have to go there, even though it had plenty of wire and other things prentices can salvage. Janny didn't, and that was why we had to haul more concrete than I like to think about to get to his body so a priestess could say the litany for him and we could leave him out underneath the sky for the wild things to bring back into the circle.

That's the way ruins are. They tell you what you need to know, but you can't ever count on having an easy time figuring out what they're saying. The ruin in Shanuga where I found the dead man's letter and nearly got reborn was like that. It told me everything I needed to walk straight here to Star's Reach, but I didn't figure out what it was trying to tell me until I'd been to Melumi and Troy, and traveled down the Misipi in a steamboat, and gone digging in the Arksa jungle, and spent my time in Sisnaddi half buried in the old archives, and went looking for the place where every question has an answer near drowned Deesee, and all the rest of it.

It took me all of that to figure out that a single word I'd noticed and then half forgotten was the one thing I needed to understand. Every ruin I've ever gotten to know has been like that, and Star's Reach is like that doubled, tripled, and with whiskey poured on top.

If I had any doubts that Star's Reach was like that, they got neatly laid to rest earlier today. We've been searching the whole underground complex here level by level and room by room, looking for the place old Anna remembers, where her mother and father and the other people who used to live and work here had their living quarters, their books and records, and the old computers they'd kept running or cobbled together out of old parts. As far as we can tell, the door where we first got into Star's Reach let us into a part of the complex that no one lived in for most of four hundred years. That's why the lights don't work; the current got shut off a long time ago, and the switches that did the shutting are someplace we haven't found so far.

We haven't found the place where Anna was born and her parents lived, not yet, but we found something else almost as important. There's a big corridor on fourth level, wide as a road, that runs most of the way from one end of the complex to the other. All the stairways either open onto it or connect to corridors that do, and the boxes the ancients used to go up and down from floor to floor when they didn't want to use the stairs—there's a word for those, but I forget what it is—those are all close to that corridor too. It's close to five kloms long, and it's big and dark and full of echoes, especially when the only people in it are two ruinmen with a little electric lamp, and the layer of dust on the floor pretty clearly hasn't been bothered in a good long time.

The first time Berry and I found that corridor, we walked all the way to the end of it, and didn't notice much of anything except the doors and corridors that opened off it. We must have walked down it again half a dozen times, doing a rough search of the fourth level and looking for signs that people had been there recently. It wasn't until Berry and I were coming back from the last of those that he noticed that a long blank wall toward the middle of the complex, had a little black screen on the middle of the wall, just sitting there doing nothing in particular.

He stopped and looked at it, and called me back to it, and it wasn't until then that we noticed that the long blank wall had seams in it. I guessed what it was, about half a minute after Berry did, and so he ran to get old Anna while I looked over the fingerprint lock. Those are common enough in old ruins, but I'd never heard of anybody who managed to open one except with pry bars and saws, or maybe a keg of gunpowder.

Berry brought everyone else with him, too, which I'd expected, but Anna was ahead of the others. She walked up to the screen, studied it for a few moments, and gave me one of her sidelong looks. "Do you want me to open it?" she asked, as though there was any question.

I nodded. "If you think it'll recognize you."

That got me a smile that didn't have the least bit of humor in it. "Of course it will," she said. "All the children had their prints entered as soon as they were born." She put one of her fingers flat against the screen and rolled it back and forth a bit, and damn if the screen didn't suddenly light up and turn from black to green.

Then the rumbling started. I thought for just a moment that it might be an earthquake, and it certainly shook the corridor like one, but it was just old gears that hadn't moved for something like a century. All of us but Anna watched with our mouths hanging open as a section of the blank wall slid back a good half meeda, split in the middle, and slid away to either side. Inside was pitch black, and then we raised our lamps and walked forward into one of the secret places of Star's Reach.

The ancients had a lot of places like the one we entered, and no one, not even Plummer, has ever been able to tell me why. They're like mazes, with flimsy shoulder-high walls of some kind of plastic foam and fabric, all rotted by the time we get to them, held up with metal posts; in every nook of the maze there's a desk, and usually a chair, and if you're lucky there's an old computer sitting on or under each desk, or at least some pieces of one that can be stripped for metal and parts. Sometimes there are other things too. Ruinmen love finding places like that, because you can break up the flimsy walls and take apart the desks and chairs and things without any risk of bringing the ceiling down on you, and the metal's worth quite a bit even if there aren't any computers left. What made so many of the ancients spend their days in places like that is another question, and one I can't begin to answer.

I didn't have to wonder what the people who used to work at Star's Reach were doing in their maze, though. It was a big one, bigger than any I'd ever seen in Shanuga; a lot of the computers had obviously been stripped for parts a long time back, but the hulks were still there and so were the wires, linking each one to the others, and to dusty shapes on a table along one wall. "Printers," Tashel Ban said; he went down the row of them, pushing something on them, and little red lights started blinking on the sides of a couple of them. Above the printers were shelves, and on the shelves were books of a sort; they were each a good six or eight senamees thick, with covers on both ends, but the paper in the middle had been punched and fastened together with a bit of flimsy metal instead of being properly bound. That's what we found out when Eleen pulled one down and opened it.

"What is it?" I asked.

She couldn't say a word, just looked at me as though somebody had walked up behind her and hit her over the head, so I went and looked over her shoulder. I'd guessed by then what the books had to be, but seeing what was on the page was something else again—

```
DATE RECD 04232112
  197606348  671934867  130486713  496710396
  713673104  975132348  240618946  720394352
  797062309  475102346  713949751  309486723
  094896713  049571304  986703047  246097240
  956872349  587134967  130476139  587620958
  670479587  624390567  249567495  876340958
```

—and so on for page after page after page. Every page had DATE RECD and a number on the top, and I could guess well enough what that meant.

By the time I was up to noticing much of anything beside the page, everyone else but Anna had gathered around, and they were staring at the numbers pretty much the way Eleen and I were doing. After a long moment, Tashel Ban turned and walked down the row of shelves and printers, pulled down another book, and opened it. "Same thing," he said. "There must be a couple of hundred of them."

That's how we found one of the things we came to Star's Reach to find, the reason Star's Reach itself was built: the messages from some other world around some other star that came to the old world, our old world, right when it was falling apart. We might have found them days earlier or days later, but that's the way of ruins; they choose their own time to tell you things.

We searched the rest of the room, but there wasn't much else there, just the maze with its desks and stripped computers, and the long table with the printers and the books above it. Then we went back and checked every single one of the books—there were two hundred twelve of them—to make sure they were all just the same strings of numbers, and none of the people who sat at those computers had managed to turn the numbers into words and read the messages. Anna says that she thinks they managed it, at least partway. That's what her mother and father and the rest of them were doing, up to the time that they left Star's Reach for good, but if that happened none of it got left there in the room we had found.

Eventually we finished searching and came back to the room where we're staying. Eleen took the very first book off the shelf and brought it with her. She says she wants to try to figure out if there's a pattern in the numbers, and I'm sure she'll give that a try, but I think one of us would have brought one of the books back with us even if she hadn't come up with that reason. You don't come this close to the old world's biggest secret and then just leave it sitting on a shelf, even if you can't figure out a blessed thing of what it means.

Still, as I sit here at the desk in the corner of our room and smell dinner cooking, what keeps coming to mind are some of the other times that ruins have handed me a secret, and for some reason the one that I remember best just now is a place that isn't a ruin yet, but might just become one in a hurry once Sheren dies: the archives in Sisnaddi, where I spent most of a year. They're in the bottom couple of floors of a big building close to the Presden's palace, and it's pretty dark because there isn't enough electricity for more than a few lamps, so it was easy enough, when I was there, to think that I was in a ruin.

I suppose I was, in a way. Everything they had in the archives, I found out one day, was what got gathered up from Deesee and hauled inland to Sisnaddi when the ice broke up in a place called Greenlun and slid into the sea, and the seas rose fast and hard everywhere around the world. It was done in such a rush that everything got jumbled together, and the archivists were still trying to sort things out when they weren't looking things up for jennels and cunnels at the presden's court who wanted some bit of fancy stuff from the past to pad out a proclamation or the like. A lot of the books went to Melumi, but the records of the old presdens and their courts—or as much as they could get out of Deesee as the sea came rushing in—all stayed in Sisnaddi in the archives, shelves after shelves of big books and binders reaching off into the darkness.

I learned that story, and a lot more, because I'd already learned the way of ruins, and didn't try to make the archives or the archivists give me what I wanted right away. After I'd been at the archives for a few weeks, one of the archivists let me know in that quiet, offhand way of theirs about the little corner by two tall windows where people gathered for lunch every day. Every day there'd be a big pot of soup or something brought over from the kitchens of the presden's court, and after a big formal dinner there might be other things, pastries or cabbage rolls or what have you. One time we got a suckling pig without a single slice cut out of it, and we all feasted like dons in Meyco.

There, sitting with the archivists and the handful of other people who were searching for something, was where I learned most of what I found in the archives. When there didn't seem to be any way forward after all, and I went to Deesee and finally found out the one thing I needed to know, it's because I spent all those noon hours eating soup with the archivists that I was able to go to them and tell them what I'd learned, and walk out of there with the secret of Star's Reach not three hours later.

That's the way ruins are, and that was just as true of the ruin I should be writing about at this point in my story, the old empty nuke south of Lebna in Tucki, where Berry and I spent the night with Cob and his prentice Sam. For some reason I didn't sleep well that night, and so at one point when I woke in the darkness I happened to hear Berry and Sam talking in quiet voices off in the next room. I couldn't make out a word of what they were saying, and didn't particularly try; there was another secret there, and you could say it was hidden in that ruin, but it wasn't one that was meant for me. So I rolled over and tried to get back to sleep. After a while I dozed off, and dreamed about Deesee, and Tam, and the ruins at Shanuga, and voices out of the night sky whispering words that nobody here on Mam Gaia's round belly would ever understand.

CHAPTER 8

THE MEDICINE SELLER

The next morning we all got up a little before the sun did, and I lent Cob a hand with the last pieces of metal that had to be loaded on the wagon while Sam and Berry got breakfast ready. It was a bright, clear day, good for travel. After we ate—it was good everyday ruinman's fare, bread and bean soup and big mugs of chicory brew—Berry and I climbed on board the wagon and found places for our packs in among the metal, while Cob gave Sam instructions for the day and then swung up onto the seat in front and took the reins.

"Be a bit rough at first here," Cob said over his shoulder as the horses started up the trail toward the road. "Hope you don't mind." He wasn't lying, either. The wagon lurched and jolted its way up to the road, and Berry and I hung on as best we could. Finally we got onto the old road, and from then on it was pretty smooth going as wagons go. They say that the old roads used to be so smooth you could ride down one of them in one of their cars, faster than a horse can gallop, and you'd hardly notice any bumps at all. I'm not sure I believe that; I've helped dig plenty of cars out of old ruins, and they all had handles on the inside for you to grab, and belts to keep you from being thrown out of your seat. Still, that's what people say.

These days, of course, if a road's still good enough to drive a wagon on it, that means either you're very lucky or you're on a road that's been fixed up for the army not too long ago. We were lucky, or rather Cob was, because he had to get the metal from the old empty nuke out to buyers, and it would have been a mother with babies to get done if there hadn't been the road. As it was, Berry and I had to jump off a couple of times and help get the wagon across some difficult place or other.

Finally, though, we started passing farms, a few at first and then a lot of them, and the road got better in the rough sort of way that happens when country folk do it themselves. Some of the people in the fields waved to Cob, and he waved back, which surprised me; around Shanuga nobody but another ruinman will greet a ruinman, or give him the time of day. Then the fields gave way to houses and shops around a big central market square, and we were in Lebna.

Cob drove the wagon straight to one corner of the market. There were a bunch of men sitting there playing cards, but they put the cards away and got up as soon as they saw Cob coming. Two of them were blacksmiths by the leather aprons they wore; I couldn't place the rest, but I guessed they were craftworkers of some sort, looking for metal for their trades.

"Well now," one of the blacksmiths said to Cob. "Got yourself some help, I see."

He meant Berry and me, of course. "Nah," Cob told him, "just a couple of ruinmen from Shanuga heading north."

The whole bunch of them got very quiet, and I knew that word must have gotten out. The blacksmith who'd spoken turned to me, and said exactly what I thought he was about to say. "From Shanuga, eh? They say the ruinmen down there found something out o' the usual."

"News to me," I told him. "What was it?"

"Some kind o' paper about Star's Reach."

I used some hot language, then: "Come on."

"That's what they say."

"Nothing like that turned up when I was there, but it's been most of a month. Some folks have all the luck, I guess."

I could see that the blacksmith didn't believe a word of it, but he nodded after a moment, and went to look at Cob's metal. Berry and I said our goodbyes to Cob and left him to his customers. There was a fair crowd there for the market, and plenty of sellers pitching everything from vegetables and ironwork to bolts of cloth and bottles of whiskey, but we pushed through the crowd and got out of there just as fast as we could without seeming to hurry.

Lebna wasn't that big of a town in the old days, and it's a lot smaller now than it was; I spotted plenty of old concrete foundations in the pastures and open country we passed through on the way in. Still, the houses seemed to go on forever as Berry and I took a dirt road north out of town. It didn't help that my mind was running full out the whole way. Word of the discovery couldn't have gotten to Lebna without running down the Hiyo valley first. That meant that Luwul, where we'd hoped to cross the Hiyo River, would be full of the news, and so a likely place for trouble. We could go west or east and miss it, but I had no way of knowing which would be best, or whether either one might land us in an even worse place. That's what ran through my mind, over and over again, while we kept walking and I tried not to imagine watchful eyes peeking out at us between the curtains of the houses we passed.

Finally we got into the farm country north of town, the houses got sparse, and loms out in the pastures turned their heads on their long necks to watch us go by. Forest lined the edge of the distant fields like a green haze, and the green hills beyond that rose up one crest after another toward the sky's edge. Once we got in among the trees, I knew, we'd have an easier time dodging anyone who wanted to follow us, but the forest was still quite a ways off, and the road we were on wound from side to side as though it wasn't in any hurry to get where I wanted to go.

"Do you think—" Berry started, and then stopped; he'd seen the man up ahead just a moment after I did.

A farmer, for certain, or at least he looked like one; shirt and trousers of homespun, bare feet, straw hat, and a lazy look that could have had anything at all behind it. He could have been standing just like that, leaning up against a fence post, in the Tenisi hills where I was born. What got my hackles up, though, is that he just happened to be standing right where the road split into two, one branch going a little west of north, the other a little bit east.

"Afternoon," I said to him as we came up to the fork.

"Afternoon," he replied.

"D'you happen to know which road goes to Luwul?"

He nodded to the left hand fork. "That's the one."

"Thanks."

"Sure thing. You two have a good day, now."

We passed him by, and headed along the road to the left. Pretty soon it veered further left, then swung straight again on the far side of a clump of trees. I glanced back to make sure we were out of sight of the ford, and then around to make sure nobody else was watching. "Now," I said to Berry, "we figure out how to cut back across to the other road without being spotted."

That's what we did, too. A little further on a creek cut across the road; it had willows growing along the bank, all thick with leaves, and there weren't any farmhouses or people in sight beyond it. As soon as we were past it, we ducked into the field and hurried across, staying close to the willows. It got mud on our boots, but a quarter of an hour later we were on the other road. Mam Gaia's blessing was with us; there was nobody else on the road just then, and the forest was close by.

As soon as we got under the trees, I said, "Now we find a place to hole up for the rest of the day, someplace where we can see the road and not get seen."

Berry took this in. "You think somebody's going to come after us."

"Those people at the Lebna market guessed who we are. Bet you a mark to a mud-turtle, too, that that farmer wasn't just standing there to hold up the fencepost."

He thought about that, then grinned. "If you're right, he'll send them down the road to Luwul. Still, I'm not convinced we've got anyone after us at all, Mister Trey."

"Well, we'll see," I said.

Rumble from up ahead warned us, and we ducked off the road and hid in the bushes until the wagon rolled past. By the time it was gone, both of us had spotted a bit of gray concrete ruin on a low hill not far from the road, and once it was safe to move, we scrambled through the underbrush and climbed up to it. It wasn't much, part of two walls rising out of four hundred years of dirt and fallen leaves, but there wasn't any sign that other people were in the habit of going there, and it had a good view of the road down below. I went to take a look, saw the wagon rolling out of sight toward Lebna and a couple of farm folk heading toward a distant house.

"Look at that," Berry said from the other side of the ruin. I went over and looked where he was pointing, and damn if the other road wasn't right out in plain sight away in the middle distance. Something was moving along the other road, the one to Luwul the farmer sent us down. Trees got in the way, and then all of a sudden they came out into a clear patch: five riders on horses, riding hard. Farmers don't ride that way, and I didn't know of any reason why soldiers would be in the middle of Tucki when the nearest fighting was off in the mountains where Meriga runs cheek by jowl with the coastal allegiancies. That didn't leave a lot of options.

"There's your answer," I said to Berry. We watched them until they were out of sight.

We kept watch turn and turn about all the rest of that day, and got what sleep we could. Once the sun was down, we used the last bit of light in the sky to get back down to the road, and then got moving quick and quiet. We'd talked it over, and neither of us could think of a better plan than traveling by night and not by day, and staying off the road when there was anybody else likely to be on it. By the time we got going on the road, the moon was up; it wasn't much past the new, a thin crescent up against the first stars, but it gave us a little help finding our way.

I'd spent more than a little of the day we hid in the ruin wondering what to do if we came to another fork in the road, but as it turned out I needn't have worried; a few muddy tracks veered off one way and the other, but even by the little light the moon gave us, it didn't take much more than a look to tell which way the main road went. Once we went past a farmhouse where one flickering light still showed in a window. Another time a dog somewhere off in the distance started barking, and that had my hackles up, because wild dogs are not something you really want to risk facing out in the open. Still, it must have been a farm dog yapping at the night wind; there was never more than the one dog barking, and the sound came from the same place, ahead of us, beside us, behind us, until we couldn't hear it any more.

That was a long night, as long as the first one Berry and I spent out in the forest, and Berry and I didn't say more than a handful of words to each other from dusk to dawn. Partly we both wanted to hear hoofbeats or footsteps as soon as we could, but there was more to it than that. In the old world they used to shine bright lights all night long, so that people didn't have to see the stars and feel small by comparison. Nowadays nobody has enough electricity to do that, and the priestesses would forbid such a thing even if we did; they say that we need to be reminded now and then of just how small and unimportant people are, and how big the universe is, so we don't make the same mistakes the ancients did. If they're right, Berry and I got a good double helping of Mam Gaia's favorite lesson that night.

The sky was clear, and we were a long way from the nearest city; the moon was thin enough that it didn't drown out more than a few small stars, so we got to see the Milky Way just as bright as it gets, and more stars than anyone this side of the old world could ever count. The moon crept across the sky, and all the true stars moved with it; a couple of false stars, the ones the ancients put up in the sky, cut across the sky following their own angled paths; and once one of them fell out of the sky in a sudden line of light that ended somewhere off to the east.

When I was small and my father was still alive, the priestess who ran the little temple down in the village where I got my schooling used to say that when the very last false star finally dropped back to Mam Gaia, that would be the sign that people had worked off the debt we owed to the rest of life for what the old world did. That's not anywhere in the holy books, but even now that I know that, and know what the false stars are and why they got put up there in the first place, I still feel a little better whenever I watch one burn up in the air.

Anna was the one who told me about the false stars. That happened much later in my story, just a few months ago, after the whole band of us left Cansiddi and crossed the Suri River and left settled country behind for Mam Gaia alone knew what. We were maybe a week out of Cansiddi on the night I'm thinking of, and none of us really knew Anna very well yet, since Cansiddi was where she joined us; but that night I couldn't sleep, and she was sitting up by the fire, and right about the time we got to talking, one of the false stars fell out of the sky, good and bright, off to the west of us.

"What is it your priestesses call them?" she asked me, meaning by that, or so I guessed, that they weren't her priestesses.

"False stars."

"That's hardly a proper name for a satellite. They're nothing like stars, you know."

"I don't," I told her. "Where I grew up, we didn't learn a lot about them."

Anna nodded, after a moment, and gave me one of her sidelong glances. "No, I imagine not." Then, when I thought she wasn't going to say anything else: "They're just machines, put up above the air so they can do their job better. The ancients put thousands of them up there for one reason or another. There were still a few in working order when I was a girl."

"What sort of things did they do?"

She didn't usually talk much, but for some reason this night was different. "Some of them looked down at the earth and sent back pictures. Some of them listened for radio signals from the ground and sent them down somewhere else. A lot of them were put there to learn something about space, or the sun, or the stars, and send that back down to people on the ground. And then there were some that were part of the Star's Reach project: long gone by my grandparents' time, for they weren't needed by then."

I was looking up at the sky as she talked, and another false star came past, this one still following its path across the sky. I pointed to it. "There's one."

"Probably," she said, with a thin smile I couldn't read at all. "It might be something else." She wouldn't say anything else, so I never did find out what else it might have been.

Still, the night when Berry and I walked under the stars toward Melumi, I didn't spend much time thinking about the false stars, and by the time the first whisper of gray showed up over the hills to the east I was tired enough that I wasn't thinking about much of anything. We were well away from farmland at that point; the road wound through low hills thick with trees, and so we started looking for a place to spend the daylight hours as soon as we could see anything at all. Being ruinmen, of course the first thing we looked for was a glimpse of old concrete, partly because a sturdy ruin offers a bit of shelter and more than a bit of concealment, and partly because most people nowadays won't go anywhere near a ruin unless they have to.

We both spotted the same rough gray shape at about the same moment, maybe half an hour before sunrise, when everything was getting light enough that I was starting to worry about being seen. It was maybe half a klom from the road, partway up a shallow slope; that was enough for us, and after a brief muttered conversation we left the road and picked our way through the forest, trying to leave as little trace and make as little sound as possible in case somebody came along the road just then. That took some time, and so it was nearly full light when we reached the ruin and ducked in through an empty doorway half full of earth and leaf-litter. We were both inside before we found out that we weren't alone in the ruin.

Something rustled and moved in the dim light, and something else flashed like steel. I grabbed my pry bar and jumped to one side, a trick I'd learned in the fighting circle. Berry flattened himself against the nearest wall and drew his own bar. For a moment, while I tried to get the shadows behind the knife facing me to turn into a human shape, nobody moved.

"Well, now," said a voice with just a bit of waver in it. "And what do two ruinmen want with an old man minding his own business?"

I found my own voice after a moment. "Nothing at all. We were looking for shelter."

"At sunrise, in the middle of the Tucki woods?"

"I could ask you the same thing," I pointed out.

He allowed a dry laugh. "I suppose you could." Another long moment passed as he sized us up, and we tried to do the same with him. Then: "If you'll put those very threatening pieces of iron away, this—" The knife blade twitched in his hand. "—will also go away. It occurs to me that we may have interests in common."

I guessed at what he meant. "Like not being seen."

"Among other things."

I lowered my pry bar; he lowered his knife; we both put our weapons away; out of the corner of my eye I saw Berry do the same thing, though his face was still tense with mistrust.

"I may have the advantage of knowing something about you," the old man said then. The sun was coming up and putting light in through holes in the ruin, and so I could just about see him by that point, a lean figure with a mostly bald head and eyeglasses round as moons. "Or I think I might. There's certainly been quite a bit of talk about a ruinman and his prentice going to Melumi with a very important letter." He waved a hand. "No, you don't have to tell me if that's you or not. Do you have anything in the way of food, by the way? I can contribute some very respectable ham and part of a loaf of bread. Also whiskey, if that's of interest."

It wasn't, but the food was, and we'd been given some things by Cob the day before, so we managed to have a creditable meal there inside the ruin.

"My name's Plummer," the old man said as we ate, answering a question I hadn't quite asked. "Or one of my names. In my line of work, a man sometimes needs more than one."

"Must be some line of work."

By way of answer he pulled a glass bottle out of his pack and set it on the concrete between us. I didn't have the least idea what it was, but Berry did. "Medicine?"

"Exactly," Plummer said. "I make it and sell it. Entirely natural ingredients, of course, but these days half the people in Meriga think that anything other than plain dried herbs is an affront to Mam Gaia, and now and then some of them are rather too fond of expressing that opinion with sticks and stones."

"Which is why you're hiding here," Berry said.

"A regrettable fact." Plummer shook his head. "I had to leave Dannul in something of a hurry several days ago. Two of the farmers there took exception to my presence at the market, and went to gather their friends and a selection of weapons.

I had reason to think they might try to follow me past Lebna. So you find me here."

I thought about that while I chewed on a piece of ham. "This is pretty far past Lebna," I said when I'd swallowed. "Did you know there was a safe place here?"

Plummer gave me a long careful glance through those glasses of his. "I can answer that question," he said finally, "but there's an inconvenient detail attached. If you communicate that answer to someone who shouldn't know it, someone will cut your throat. I don't mean that as a threat, not at all; merely an observation of fact."

It took me a moment to realize what he was saying. "Ruinman's bond."

He smiled. "Good. You take my meaning."

So Berry and I bound ourselves by the old words of the bond, and Plummer nodded once, as though that settled everything. "This is one of, shall we say, several places of the same kind," he said then. "They change from time to time, for safety, but they can be recognized by those who know how. There are two more on this road between here and Luwul."

Berry and I glanced at each other. "This road goes to Luwul?"

"You were told otherwise, I gather."

I told Plummer about the farmer at the fork in the road, and he let out a little sharp laugh. "Had you taken the other road, it would have led you in a circle back to Lebna. No, we are three days from Luwul by the road down there." His gesture pointed back to the road Berry and I had followed all night. "I cannot recommend going back to Lebna. If you happen to be minded to go through Luwul, though, and don't object to company, I can point out the safe places on the way."

Looking back on it, it's clear enough that Plummer had planned on making that offer as soon as he'd sized us up. I didn't guess that at the time, though; I didn't know him yet, though that would change. Still, I was wary. "And you wouldn't mind company, I would guess."

Again, the long careful glance. "There are men, I'm sorry to say, who would beat and rob a solitary old man without a qualm," he said. "Most of them would think twice about it, however, if the old man was accompanied by two sturdy young ruinmen equipped with those iron bars of yours. So if you happen to be going my way ..."

I glanced at Berry again; his look said "Whatever you decide, Mister Trey" as clearly as if he'd spoken it out loud. "We'll go your way," I said then. "For now."

"Excellent." Plummer gestured at the remains of the meal. "More ham? It really is quite good, I think."

CHAPTER 9

JENNEL COBEY'S LETTER

That's how I met Plummer. Of all the people who didn't join me on the journey to Star's Reach, he's the one who put the most into the story I'm trying to tell in this notebook, and to this day I'm not sure why. I'm not sure of a lot of things about Plummer. Most people you meet, you get to know them and a lot of the things about them that seemed funny or puzzling early on look like plain common sense as soon as you've been around them a while, but Plummer isn't like that. The more I learned about him, the more puzzled I got.

All that came later, though, and I didn't guess any of it when I first met Plummer there in the ruin beside the road to Luwul. About the time we finished eating that first meal with him, the sun came up, and he settled down in a corner of the ruin and wrapped himself in an old shabby coat and went right to sleep. Berry and I weren't anything like so confident of him as he seemed to be of us, and so we kept watches, turn and turn again, while the sun was up.

Still, nothing happened. We were far enough off the road that if anybody went riding past, looking for us or otherwise, neither of us saw or heard it. Mam Gaia took her sweet time turning that part of her belly away from the sun, but finally dusk came rising up out of the east and the first stars came out, and Plummer woke up.

He'd hardly moved the whole time, but all of a sudden he was dead awake. "I suppose wishing you a good morning is a little untimely," he said. "I trust you both managed to find some sleep, though."

"Enough to get by," I said. I'd taken the last watch and so was wide awake; Berry was still rubbing his eyes and blinking.

"Good. The next safe place I know of is perhaps twenty kil—kloms away from here; there should be food, and friends, but of course it will be necessary for us to get there."

The comment about friends got my hackles up a bit, since we still didn't have any way of knowing whether Plummer could be trusted. Still, we'd stayed with him and shared his food, and unless we hit him over the head and left him there in the ruin there wasn't an easy way to go somewhere besides where he was going. So Berry and I looked at each other and didn't say anything. As soon as we'd all had a little food, we shouldered our bags, and the three of us made our way through the dusk back down to the road to Luwul.

I'd worried as well that Plummer might talk on the way, and make it harder to listen for the people who might be following us, but once we left the ruin he didn't say a word more than he had to. If you've ever watched an old fox come up to the edge of a road, listen and sniff until he was sure it was safe for him to cross, and then trot across it, no faster than he had to but no slower either, that was Plummer. Even in the faint light I could see his eyeglasses glint as he looked here and there or canted his head to catch a sound.

That night didn't seem quite as long as the one before, though it was still a long slow journey down empty roads. For the first half of it we might as well have been a hundred kloms from any-place; the road wound its way through forest, and even with the moon up we didn't have a lot of light to go by. Later on, past midnight by where the moon was, we got back into farm country and had an easier time of it. Nothing but us moved anywhere on the road, and the scattered farmhouses we could see were dark as old ruins; even the wind hushed, the way it does sometimes in the hours before dawn, so that every sound our feet made on the road, no matter how quiet, seemed to hang there for a moment.

About the time the first bit of gray showed up off to the east of us, we got to a place where a narrow little farm track headed off to one side of the road. Plummer looked at it, tilted his head, then motioned down the track and said in a low voice, "This way. They are expecting me." It took a moment for that to sink in, and when it did I looked around and tried to see whatever sign must have been left for him.

I know what it was now, or at least I think I can guess, but right then I couldn't see a thing. I nodded anyway, and Berry and I followed him down the track.

We were both more than half expecting him to lead us to another ruin, even though that didn't square with what he'd said about food and friends. The track led right up to a little farmhouse well back from the road, though, rather than a ruin. Plummer motioned for us to wait by the gate, saying, "They will need to know that I'm not alone, or—well, not to worry about that. A moment, please."

He disappeared into the night, and a few minutes later I heard a door open and close. Berry gave me a worried look, and I could tell his hand wasn't too far from his pry bar. I was too busy thinking to do the same thing, though I could have gotten mine out in a hurry if I'd had to. What Plummer had said about friends, and safe places, and throats being cut if the wrong things got said to the wrong people had me wondering just what Berry and I had stumbled across, and whether we'd been meant to stumble across it, and why. Certainly Plummer had figured out who we were quickly enough.

After a few minutes, the door opened and closed again, and a bit after that Plummer came out of the darkness. "All's well," he said. "If you'd care to come this way?"

So we followed him, to a meal and a place to sleep or a club across the back of the head, I didn't know which. It probably would have served me right to get the latter, but that's not what happened. Instead, Plummer led us into the farmhouse, through one door into a dark place, and then through another into a big comfortable room that didn't have any windows to let the light of a lamp out into the night. There was a table in the middle of the room and some solid wooden benches, and a couple old enough to make Plummer look young, who were putting food on the table. The woman, who was plump and sturdy and had her white hair tied back with a scrap of rag, nodded and smiled at us and went back out through another door into what I guessed was the kitchen; the man, who was lean and bent and walked with a limp, put the platter he was carrying down on the table and then shook our hands, saying, "Pleased to meet you. Nobody uses names here; I hope you don't mind."

"Not a bit," I said. "I hope it's not a problem if I say thank you."

"Of course not." Pointing to a third door: "Washroom's there if you need it."

I did. When I got back there was a meal on the table and everyone else was sitting down to it, so I joined them, and noticed only after plates were being filled that nobody had called for Mam Gaia's blessing first. I stuck that bit of knowledge away with the rest of what I'd noticed about Plummer, and wondered what it meant, with the very small part of my mind that wasn't thinking about pork sausage, potatoes, squash, and the unmistakable smell of pie coming in through the kitchen door.

There was talk around the table, the sort of thing you'd hear in any household, but it had a very odd feeling to it. I got the same feeling later on when I was searching the archives in Sisnaddi, and eating lunch every day with the archivists. Until I got to know them and learned something about their lives and their work, it was as if most of the conversation was happening somewhere I couldn't hear, and the part of it that

I could hear had big holes in it full of things I didn't understand, people I'd never met, and words I didn't know. The archivists didn't mean to hide anything, they'd just been working and sharing meals together for so long that it never occurred to them that everybody else in the world didn't spend their time talking about how to keep old high-acid paper from turning back into the wood pulp it was made of, say, or the games the jennels and cunnels of the presden's court played for blood and money and power that sometimes made the archivists work extra hours for a week or two.

There in the room without windows, though, I was sharing food with people who knew how to hide things, and had plenty of practice doing it. That's the sense I had, clear as midnight stars, by the time we finally finished up the meal and the old woman showed Berry and me to the little room on the second floor where we slept through the next day. It wasn't just that Plummer and the old couple were used to talking to each other and not to Berry or me; I guessed that Plummer and the old couple knew each other only just a little, if at all. It was that they had something to hide and were used to hiding it in the most graceful way, and so they talked back and forth about whatever it was in a way that they understood and Berry and I didn't. It didn't occur to me then that they might have wanted me to notice that, and to wonder about it.

At any rate, Berry and I went right to sleep. We didn't bother to keep watch, since we wouldn't have much of a chance to get away if Plummer and the old couple did plan on handing us over to somebody, and it had been quite a few days since we'd had a chance to sleep on real pallets with blankets and all. I slept hard, and if I dreamed about the ruins of Deesee that night I didn't remember it when sunset came and the old woman knocked on the door to wake us up.

The old couple gave Plummer a sack of food for the road and wished us all a safe journey, and as soon as it was good and dark the three of us slipped back to the road and headed north toward Luwul. When we were out of sight of the house, Plummer turned to me and said, "By morning there will be no one in that house, and no sign that anyone has been there in weeks. In case you were wondering." The moon gleamed on his eyeglasses, so I couldn't see his eyes; I think he wanted me to ask a question, but I didn't know what question to ask, so I let it be.

That night we had to leave the road twice, once early on when a wagon came rumbling by and once later, a little before midnight, when the sound of hooves off behind us warned of horsemen coming our way. There were three of them, riding fast, but they didn't keep us from getting to the next safe place Plummer had in mind. That was another ruin, most of a klom away from the road in a little patch of forest between two farms. Like the one where we'd met Plummer, it had a roof to keep out weather, and Plummer showed us where somebody had stacked dry firewood; it was in a place you couldn't see unless you knew where to look, with a bit of oiled cloth over it to keep the damp off during the rainy season. We didn't need a fire; it was a fine clear day, pleasantly cool except around midday, the kind of weather most of Meriga gets more often than not in winter. I nodded and thanked Plummer, and wondered why he'd showed the wood to me.

So we hid there through the day, made a good meal of the old couple's food before getting some sleep, ate another as the sun went down, and got ready for our last day on the road with Plummer. "By morning we will reach Luwul," he said as we filled our packs, "and there our paths part for the time being. The ruinmen's hall is on this side of the city, just outside the gates, which should be convenient for you. By the time you get there, however, I will be gone."

I thought he was joking, and laughed. Still, that's the way it happened. We spent the night walking through farm country; the road went nearly due north by the stars, and we all kept an eye out for watchers and an ear listening for any sign of pursuit, but the only thing we saw was the slow turning of the stars and the only thing we heard was, toward dawn, the first roost-ers making noise and clattering and voices here and there as farm hands headed out for the earliest chores. The east turned gray, and then the rest of the sky did, and about the time the first glow of sunlight hit a few scattered clouds high up above us and the sky went blue, and the farms gave way to market gardens and then to rows of houses, I glanced toward Plummer and suddenly realized that he wasn't there.

Berry hadn't seen him leave either. We stood there like a couple of fools in the middle of the road, looking at each other, and then laughed and shrugged and kept going. The first wagons were rumbling in from the market gardens to the city, but we'd already seen the ruinmen's hall rising up over the roofs into the morning sky, and we decided to finish the trip as quick as possible and let the stout door of the ruinmen's hall be our answer to anybody who was after us.

I'm not sure what it is about ruinmen's halls. Other guilds either buy a couple of houses and tear out the walls between them, if they're poor, or build something for themselves toward the center of town if they're rich. Nobody wants the ruinmen in town, of course, which is why our halls are always out-side the gates, but you might think ruinmen would build the same sort of halls as the others. Not a chance; it's always some improbable chunk of salvage from the old world, tipped up on end so it rises up above everything else and can't be ignored.

Luwul's was no exception. Some bright boys a long time ago, back when metal was cheap, hauled half a dozen old airplanes from wherever they got left when the fuel ran out, cut off the wings and the tails, and propped them up on end in a circle as though they were all about to fly off together to the moon. That gave them six tall towers, and they used the wings and other salvaged metal to make walls to fill the spaces between the towers, and put in floors every three meedas or so; the rooms for traveling ruinmen were right there in the bodies of the planes, so you could look out the little oval window next to your pallet and see the walls and roofs of Luwul against the sky, if you were on one side, or the farms south of town stretching away toward the hills if you were on the other.

We saw the towers from a couple of kloms away, so we didn't have any trouble finding the hall, and we didn't have any trouble on the way there, either. We got to the guild hall just as the sun came up. The houses of the misters around the hall were empty and silent—everyone would be living in tents at whatever ruin they were working that season—but the hall itself, like every ruinmen's hall everywhere, was always open and always had people in it.

The door was big and made of riveted metal, and it boomed when I knocked on it. After a moment it opened, and an old man in ruinman's leathers stood there. He had a wooden leg, which explained why he wasn't out at the ruins, and he gave me the same sort of dubious look I imagine doorkeepers at ruinmen's halls must always give people who come knocking at sunrise.

"Trey sunna Gwen, a Mister from Shanuga," I said. "This is my prentice Berry."

The man's face changed suddenly; he grabbed my arm and all but pulled me inside, and motioned Berry to follow. As soon as we were in, he shut the door hard, and dropped the bar back into place. "Mister Trey," he said then. "We've heard about what you're carrying. I'll have someone go get the misters; there's trouble you need to know about."

It wasn't half an hour later that Berry and I were sitting in the big main room of the Luwul ruinmen's hall with a couple of the senior misters. We'd had a chance to wash up and get some food, but they still had dirt from the Luwul ruins on their leathers; they'd come back as fast as they could once word of our arrival got to them. I wasn't sure yet why one of the prentices at the hall had gone sprinting out to the ruins as soon as we'd gotten settled in at the hall, but it was pretty clear that we'd stumbled into a mother of a mess.

"Word got here about two weeks ago," said Mister Bron. He was one of the senior misters in the Luwul guild, a big burly man with one eye gone and a scar from whatever did it that ran halfway down his face. "Upriver from Duca with the boatmen, and then downriver from Sisnaddi the same way. We didn't think too much of it, rumors being rumors, until we got a letter from Jennel Cobey Taggart."

"Who's he?" I asked. "I don't think I've heard of him."

"No?" Bron's eye turned to look at me. "Shanuga's further out of the way than I thought. He's a big name these days. The Taggarts are an old Tucki family, cousins of the presden's or something like that, and they've had a house here in Luwul since I don't know when. Jennel Cobey's usually either in Sisnaddi or out on the borders with the armies, but the letter came from here and had his private seal on it, and it asked about you. By name."

I blinked. "That's a surprise."

Bron laughed, a short deep laugh that seemed to come from somewhere down past the floor. "True enough."

"What did it say?"

"Mostly that the jennel wants to talk to you as soon as you get to Luwul. I'll let you see it, if you like." He motioned to one of the prentices who were hanging back, listening but trying not to look like that was what they were doing. "Frey, get the letter from Marsh, will you?"

The prentice hurried off. Berry gave me a worried look, though it wasn't half so worried as I was feeling right then. "What do you figure he means by that?" I asked.

"That's what we don't know," said Bron.

I thought about that for a long moment. People don't trouble the guilds often, and they trouble ruinmen even less than they do the other guilds. Annoy the gunsmiths or the doctors or the radiomen, and they turn away your business from then on, which can be bad enough; annoy the ruinmen, though, and you might just find out what kind of nasty things hang around in old ruins. I heard of two people who thought they could rob ruinmen and get away with it, and both of them had their hair fall out, took sick, and died a couple of months later. Not that anything ever got proved, you understand. Still, not even ruinmen could get away with doing that to a jennel, and especially to a jennel who had connections at the presden's court.

I knew that part of what Bron was telling me was that if this Jennel Cobey sent for me, I didn't have much choice in the matter. Even if Berry and I left the guild hall and tried to make a run for it out of Luwul, once it came out that we'd stopped at the hall, there would be six kinds of trouble to pay for; ruinmen are supposed to protect each other no matter what, but "no matter what" in this case could be soldiers battering down the doors of the guild hall and sticking the misters' heads on spikes over Luwul's gates. There are times when you can ask for people to make good on their promises, and there are times when you know better.

The prentice came back with the jennel's letter, then, and Bron told him to go wash up and get a clean shirt on. I didn't listen too closely, because the letter took some reading; it was written in the long curving letters the presden's court uses these days, and used all the old names of towns, which I didn't know too well then. I made sure Berry could see it, in case he had to help me with it, and started reading. This is what it said:

> To the misters of the Ruinmens' Guild of Louisville, my greet-ings. A ruinman of Chattanooga, Trey son of Gwen, is traveling through this part of the country on his way to the scholars at Bloomington. If he comes to your guildhall, I will consider it a personal favor if you contact my people here in town at once. I want to talk with him.
>
> —*General Cobey Taggert*

I looked up from the letter.

"You'd better send somebody to the jennel's house," I told him.

He nodded. "I don't know anything else we can do."

"As for the letter, I've got two copies, one for Melumi and one that's mine. I'd like to leave one here."

Bron nodded again. "I see. Good. Yes, and we can get it to Melumi, in case." *In case you don't come back* was what he was too polite to say, of course.

So the prentice Bron sent to wash up went trotting off to Jennel Cobey's house as fast as he could. I got out one of the two copies of the dead man's letter I had with me, and handed it to Bron, then took the other one and handed it to Berry. He gave me a startled look, and gulped, but took it. We sat there and talked a bit about the ruins in Luwul and Shanuga, the way you find something to talk about when the thing everybody is thinking about is the thing nobody wants to mention, and Bron mentioned in passing that he had room for an extra prentice or two in his end of the ruins, which was his way of saying that Berry would have someplace to go if something happened to me.

By the time the prentice came back I was almost relieved. "Mister Trey," he told me, "The jennel sent two of his servants and wants you to go with them." I got up, shook Bron's hand and Berry's as well, and went down the stairs to the guildhall door.

I was half expecting soldiers, but the two men waiting outside the door were ordinary servants in the sleeveless shirts and knee-length trousers people wear in the Hiyo valley, and they had three horses with them. "Trey sunna Gwen?" one of them asked.

"That's me."

They both bowed, just a little, and the one who'd spoken motioned at one of the horses and said, "If you'll come with us, Sir and Mister."

That's the proper title for a guild mister, but nobody on Mam Gaia's round belly had ever used it for me before then. I was pleased, in an odd sort of way. The horse was another matter, for I'd never ridden one and only had the sketchiest idea how. Horses aren't common nowadays; they like a drier climate than Meriga has now, and the old world left us with some diseases that kill two foals out of three every year, so if you're not a cavalryman in the army or a servant or soldier of a jennel, or just plain rich, you don't usually get much of a chance to ride one.

I certainly wasn't going to miss the chance this time, especially not if my head was going to be on a spike sometime soon. I walked over to the side of the horse, grabbed whatever you call the thing on the front of the saddle that you're supposed to grab, got one foot into the stirrup and swung myself up. I had no idea what I'd do if the horse objected to the proceedings, but it just shifted its feet a bit and let me mount. Once I got myself settled, it swung its head around to glance at me with one eye, as though it wanted to ask if I was done yet.

The two servants popped up into their saddles with a mother of a lot more grace than I must have had, grabbed the reins and started down the street. I wasn't sure what to do, but my horse started off right away without bothering for me to guide it. I picked up the reins, too, and the horse gave me a second glance; I think it was wondering if I was going to do something stupid. I wasn't. I figured the horse was probably smarter than I was, and let it do whatever it was going to do.

That's how I rode through the streets of Luwul that morning: sitting in the saddle holding the reins as though I knew what I was doing, without the smallest baby kitten of an idea where we were going or what was going to happen to me when we got there. Luwul's a bigger town than Shanuga, but it's still got the big gray town walls made of old concrete chunks mortared together, the gate with a pair of tired guards looking down from their windows, the narrow muddy streets inside with tall narrow buildings rising up on either side, pigs and dogs and people all busy with their own affairs in the streets and the dim little alleys, smoke and smells and a hundred different noises all tumbling over each other in the sultry air.

I got to see plenty of Luwul, too, for the ruinmen's hall was outside the south side of the walls and Jennel Cobey's house was on the river, which runs along the northern edge of town. Plenty of Luwul got to see me, too; a lot of people in the streets looked up at me as I rode past them on the horse and then turned to watch me go. I wondered whether they'd heard about the letter from Shanuga, or if the thought of a ruinman on a horse was just strange enough to catch their interest.

Still, as we got close to the jennel's house, the people thinned out. The houses got bigger, and more of them were made of stone, with big gates and courtyards, and towers up above where men with guns could keep watch over the street and the river if they had to.

Jennel Cobey's house was one of those, as big as any and bigger than most. We rode up to his gate, where a couple of his soldiers glanced at us and hauled the gate open, and then into his courtyard, where the servants swung down from their horses and waited patiently while I did the same thing. "This way, Sir and Mister," said the same one who had spoken to me earlier, and motioned toward a door. I followed him through the door, up a stair, and along a corridor with tall windows along the one side looking out toward the river, and paintings on the other side of faces of men I didn't recognize. The second servant was right behind me; I never heard him say a word then or later, but I could feel his gaze on my back the whole time.

Finally we stopped at a door. "Please to wait here, Sir and Mister," said the servant who did all the talking, and went inside. I could hear his voice, though not the words, and then another voice; and then the servant came back through the door. "If you'll follow me, Sir and Mister." I followed him into the room, and that's how I met Cobey Taggart.

Thinking back on that first meeting now, after everything that's happened, it's hard for me to be sure how much of what I think I remember got changed around to fit what happened afterwards. For most of five years, I would have said that Cobey was one of the best friends I had on Mam Gaia's round belly, and I still thought that right up until the moment at the door to Star's Reach when I realized that one of us was going to kill the other. I traveled with him, shared hopes and finds with him, told him some of my secrets and guessed at a few of his, saw how he lived and watched him die. It's hard to set that aside and reach back to the memory of our first meeting, untouched by anything else, but I'll try.

He was younger than I expected, not ten years older than I was, with a mop of sand-colored hair and a narrow beard along the edge of his jaw, the sort of thing that was fashionable that year at the presden's court. He was dressed all in green, the way jennels usually are, but the only sign of rank he had anywhere on him was the bone-handled gun that showed at his hip.

"Trey sunna Gwen," the servant said, and ducked back out through the door; I heard it click behind me. "Sir and Jennel," I said; if he was going to have his servants use my title, damn if I wasn't going to use his.

"Mister Trey," he said, and crossed the room to shake my hand. That startled me, though I tried not to show it. "Thank you for coming. I suspect you're wondering why I sent for you."

"That I am, Sir and Jennel."

That got a sudden bright smile, which startled me even more than the handshake. "The simplest explanation is right over here. If you'll follow?"

He set off across the room. It was a big room, nearly as big as the main room of the ruinmen's hall I'd just left, with tall narrow windows along two sides and bookshelves along a third. Heavy timbers framed the ceiling above, and the carpet that covered the floor was nice enough that I was sorry to be walking on it with dusty boots. In the corner where the walls with the windows met, there was a table, and on the table was a flat box as big as a sheet of paper.

He got to the table first, and lifted the lid off the box. "I think you'll recognize this."

I did, too. I bent over to give it a close look, and he motioned to me to pick it up, then stood back, watching me, as I examined front and back, the bits of gray dust stuck to it, the hint of fingerprints where I must have held the thing before the resin I'd sprayed on it had time to dry. The single word on the back was there, too, in the pale gray writing nobody nowadays knows how to make. I set the thing back in its box and turned to face the jennel, wondering how he'd gotten the letter I'd found beneath the dead man's hand in the Shanuga ruins.

CHAPTER 10

DELL'S BARGAIN

Looking back over what I wrote last night, I realized that I've gone and talked about all kinds of things that people won't know about unless they grew up in Meriga or spent a good long time there. Jennels, for instance. They don't have those in Nuwinga or Genda, and Mam Gaia only knows whether they've got anything of the kind over in the Neeonjin country way off past the mountains and the dead lands of the west. In Meyco they've got dons, who are like jennels with attitude, but then Meyco's an empire and that comes with extra bragging rights.

Anyway, Meriga has jennels. We've got a couple of hundred of them, maybe, and a couple of thousand cunnels, who would have been jennels if somebody back along the line of their grandfathers had been firstborn sons and not second or third or whatever. Most of the jennels are heads of families that have been famous names in Meriga since the old world ended; they own a lot of land and a lot of other things, they have soldiers and servants, and when the presden names somebody to take one of her armies off to the borders to fight, it pretty much has to be one of the jennels.

One of the archivists at Sisnaddi told me that that's all the jennels used to be, leaders of the Merigan armies back before the old world ended, and all the rest of it came later.

That would explain why they don't have them in Genda or Nuwinga, since I don't think either of those countries had a big army back then. Meriga did, which is why ruinmen here know the look of the stiff heavy clothing soldiers wore in Meriga before the old world ended; you find a lot of bones in what's left of that clothing, tucked away here and there in the old ruins.

The man looking over my shoulder as I examined the letter I'd found down deep in the ruins at Shanuga wasn't wearing that kind of clothing, of course, but some of his grandfathers' grandfathers back more than four hundred years had worn it. The plain green clothes he was wearing might as well have been the same thing; you only see that on jennels, and then only on jennels who know that they don't need to announce who they are to everybody, just as the really big names in Circle aren't the women in the fancy gowns and pearls but the ones in the plain dresses and the plain red hats, who don't talk much and don't have to.

Jennel Cobey didn't have to talk much, either. He stood there while I examined the letter I'd found down inside the Shanuga ruins, watching me as though he had all the time in the world.

"I'm curious how you came by this, Sir and Jennel," I said finally.

He laughed; it was a louder laugh than I expected, and it sent echoes scurrying all over the room like mice. "I imagine so. Still, no mystery there; one of my people in Noksul heard about the letter as soon as word got out and contacted me by radio, and so I was able to get someone to Shanuga in time for the auction. That was good and lively; your Mister Garman did very well out of it."

"I'm glad to hear that."

"The man I sent to Shanuga mentioned that you had the finder's rights for it."

"That's right."

He was still watching me, of course. "I hope you won't feel insulted, Sir and Mister, if I say that you've taken on quite a task there."

He meant, of course, that I was a brand new mister who probably didn't even look my twenty years just at that moment. "If you'd had a chance at something like that, Sir and Jennel," I said, "would you have turned it down?"

A moment later I knew I might just have said the worst possible thing, since of course he did have a chance at something like that, and could take it by nothing more difficult than having one of his people cut my throat. He smiled, though, a broad smile as though what I'd said came close to making him laugh. "Of course not," he said. "Good. I think we have the basis for an understanding, then."

He reached for the letter, and I handed it to him. "You want to find Star's Reach," he went on then. "So do I, badly. Still, finding it and digging down to it are your line of business, not mine. If I recall correctly, your guild sometimes does contract digs."

"Sometimes," I said.

"And in this case?"

I considered that long and hard. In a contract dig, the ruinmen are paid out of somebody else's pocket, instead of getting by each season on whatever they made on finds from the season before. That's not something most ruinmen will do unless the dig's really worth it, because whoever pays the costs gets their money back before anyone else gets paid, and after that a share of the profits goes to the contract holder as well. On the other hand, a dig at Star's Reach would cover almost any contract I could imagine with plenty to spare; having someone else foot the bill for the digging would make it one mother of a lot easier for a brand new mister and his prentice to get a good crew together, too, and do the thing the way it ought to be done.

"In this case, Sir and Jennel," I said, "it's a possibility."

He nodded, then: "If you're worried about your profits, don't be. I'm perfectly willing to see the salvage go to the ruinmen

and whatever records are there go to Melumi. That's your business and theirs." Seeing my expression: "You're wondering
why. I don't need the money. Partly I want to find Star's Reach
for the same reason everyone else in Meriga dreams of finding
it; partly—" He leaned a senamee or so toward me. "Partly,
whoever finds Star's Reach is going to become the most famous
person in Meriga as fast as word can spread. That could be a
real advantage to me in Sisnaddi."

"Fair enough," I said, though I didn't have the least idea just
then why it would be an advantage to him, or to anyone else.

"Then would it be fair to say that we have a bargain?"

I agreed, and we shook hands. "By the way," he said then,
"do you have any idea yet where Star's Reach is?"

"Not yet, Sir and Jennel. That's why I'm headed to Melumi."

"Sensible. That was my destination as well. Would you
be willing to ride with my party? I think I can promise you
a faster trip and better accommodations than you'd have on
your own."

I agreed to that gratefully enough, and he said, "Good.
We were planning on leaving tomorrow, if that's suitable.
I'll have a horse sent—do you have prentices?"

"Just one."

"Two horses, then, to the guild hall tomorrow morning."
He said a few more pleasantries, which I don't remember just
now, and then without ever having to say a word about it he
dismissed me and I turned to find his servant waiting for me
just inside the door.

All the way back to the ruinmen's guild hall, I thought about
what had just happened. Just about every ruinman I'd ever
met would have called that the best bit of luck I could have
had, and more than half of me thought the same thing, but the
rest of me wasn't so sure, because the bargain I'd made with
Jennel Cobey felt a little too much like a Dell's bargain.

That's something else I ought to explain, because I know
for a fact that people from outside of Meriga don't say that or

know what it means; I used the phrase once in front of Tashel Ban, and he gave me the look he always gives when whatever somebody says doesn't make the least bit of sense to him. Dell—well, you don't mention him around the priestesses, because they don't believe in him and don't like it when other people do, either.

Dell's not a human being, though he looks like one. He looks like a tall man with light-colored skin, like people from Genda have, and he wears fancy clothing from the old world, with one of those funny strips of bright cloth tied around his neck and hanging down onto his shirt. Nobody knows where he lives, but if you want to find him, they say, all you have to do is go right at midnight when the moon's down, to a place where two roads cross, going with one eye closed and one hand inside your clothes and hopping on one foot, and call him. Sometimes he shows up even if you don't call him, if you want something badly enough, or that's what people say, but if you go to the crossroads that way and call him three times, before you finish calling him the third time, he's there waiting for you.

I never knew anyone who called him, but the story goes that you can call him if you want something so bad that you think nothing else matters. If you do that, and tell him what you want, he'll get it for you, but you have to promise to give him something else in trade for it. You don't get to pick the something else, he does, and he doesn't have to tell you what it will be when you make the bargain; sometime later, maybe years later, he just shows up and takes it, and you know just as well as I do that it's going to be the one thing in the world you care about more than the thing you got from him.

That's a Dell's bargain, and that's what it felt like I had just made with Jennel Cobey. Now of course I hadn't promised to give him anything but whatever fame he got from being the one who paid for the contract dig at Star's Reach, but since he was a jennel he could pretty much show up and take anything he fancied whenever he wanted, the way Dell does.

Still, I couldn't think of any way I could have said no to him and been sure of leaving with an uncut throat, and there were plenty of good practical reasons to have said yes. That's what I told myself, at least, as I balanced unsteadily on the horse and Jennel Cobey's servants took me back through Luwul's streets to the ruinmen's guild hall.

Back at the hall, Mister Bron was glad to see me still breathing, and said so. Berry acted as calm and cool as though nobody'd ever said a word about heads on spikes. Bron and his prentices headed back to work at the ruins, though, and once Berry and I went to the room they'd given me up in the guild hall to get some rest and wait for the next meal, he threw his arms around me and clung there, shaking like a leaf in a good strong wind. I got him calmed down after a bit, and we sat and talked, or rather I talked about what had happened at the jennel's house and he took it in with one hand curled around his chin and an expression on his face I couldn't read at all.

When I mentioned what Jennel Cobey had said about the advantages of being the most famous person in Meriga, though, Berry nodded. "He's right, you know. They say that the presden's sick again, and if—well, when—she dies, it's anyone's guess who becomes presden."

"Since there's no heir."

He nodded. "The jennels could have a lot to say about who gets chosen, and I'm sure they've all got their favorite choice in mind. If everybody thinks of Cobey Taggert as the jennel who found Star's Reach, his choice would be hard to ignore."

That made sense to me. "You know a fair amount about politics."

Berry looked away. "A bit. My teacher in Nashul used to talk about it all the time. Her mother was some kind of big name in Circle, though she never had children herself, and so she used to follow the news whenever we'd hear anything." He didn't seem comfortable talking about it, though, so I let it drop and we talked about something else until the dinner bell.

CHAPTER 11

WHAT THE WIND SAID

This morning I was putting my tools in order for the day's work and thinking about the last part of the journey to Melumi when I heard running in the corridor outside the room where we've had our camp since we arrived here. It turned out to be Tashel Ban, and that made me sit up, because people from Nuwinga don't usually move any faster than they have to.

"What's up?" I asked him.

"Found a door." He was panting hard. "In the computer room. Stairs and—a smell."

I knew right away what he meant, as much from the look on his face as anything. Ruinmen get used to the smell of people who've been dead a long time, but most other people don't, and it's probably a good thing. As often as not, when you find dead people from the old world, what killed them hasn't gone away.

So I loaded the last of my tools into my belt and put it on, and by the time I'd turned around to see where Berry was he had his belt and his leathers on as well, and was turning on a lamp to light the way there. Tashel Ban gasped his thanks, still panting, and stepped out of the way, and Berry and I headed down the corridor. We didn't run. Ruinmen don't run when they're in a ruin, or at least those who do don't live long enough to bother noticing; but I won't say we dawdled much.

There were lamps burning in the computer room, and the light splashed out through the open door—we'd jammed it open, so Anna didn't have to come and open it again any time we wanted to go in. Tashel Ban and Eleen had been working on what was left of the old computers, with as much help as Anna could give them, while the rest of us kept searching for the place where the last people at Star's Reach lived and did their work. Eleen and Anna were both there in the big room, but I didn't need to do much more than follow their glances to find the door Tashel Ban had mentioned. There was a big metal bookcase pulled away from its place against the wall, and the door was behind it, half open.

"We pulled down some of the books," Eleen explained, "and the shelf moved. It's not fastened to the wall; I don't think it used to be there when there were people here."

"So you looked behind it."

"So we looked behind it." With a worried look: "And figured out right away that it was work for you and Berry, not for us."

"You didn't go up there?"

"Not after smelling the air."

I smelled the same thing as soon as I came into the room: like dust, but not quite, and with just a hint of something rotten. "Good," I said, and glanced at Berry, who was already tying on a cloth dust mask. "Let's see what's up there."

I could have said a lot more, and so could Eleen, but there's an odd thing that happens with us, and I think it happens with a lot of people in the crafts, ruinmen and scholars and radiomen and all. There are plenty of times when Eleen and I are two people who are trying to figure out whether they love each other or not, but when there's work to be done she's a scholar and I'm a ruinman and we stop being much of anything else. So I put my mask on and pulled out my radiation counter, Berry raised his lamp, and we started up the stair.

The steps looked like they'd been cut out of the concrete long after Star's Reach was built, but we still made good and sure the steps weren't trapped, and we sniffed the air for the sour lightning-smell that tells you there's electricity close by. There wasn't, and the counter clicked slow and soft, nothing more than background radiation, which was comforting in its way. The stair ran more or less straight, and we'd climbed up more than a level, probably close to two, before we saw the dim gray light up at the top of it.

The stair climbed four levels in all, right up to the topmost level of the complex, and then opened out into a room, a large one. The light came from big skylights of glass block set into the ceiling. We looked around, and that's when we saw the bodies.

There must have been fifty of them, all laid out neatly in a row with their heads close to one wall. They weren't as far gone as the bodies you normally find in ruins, just shriveled up after spending the last however many years in dry desert air, and their clothes looked brittle but they weren't quite gone to shreds yet. What I noticed first, though, was that they all had cups next to them; it was pretty clear that they'd all drunk something, lay back on the floor, and died.

Berry gave me a look with wide eyes, but neither of us said anything, or had to. You find things like that in old ruins often enough.

We searched the rest of the room, found two doors opening off it, and went down the corridors to look into the rooms beyond them. No question, we'd found the place where Anna's people lived; there were long rows of bedrooms and a big kitchen, a couple of rooms where a few hundred people could gather and a lot more that would fit ten or twenty, and a big space under skylights where withered sticks in tubs of dry dirt showed where they'd grown vegetables. The room we found first had computers in it, a bunch of them on a long desk up against one wall, and other machines I didn't recognize. It also had something else, something we didn't notice until we were almost finished: a heap of black ashes, over near one corner of the room, that looked like it had probably been paper before somebody lit a fire.

I sent Berry down to get the others. By then everyone else was in the room below, and their footfalls came echoing up the stairs. Eleen got to the top first, and let out a little cry when she saw the bodies; Tashel Ban muttered some hot language under his breath; Anna drew in a sharp breath and then turned sharply away so that none of us could see her face. Thu, who came up last except for Berry, was the only one who didn't make a sound; he glanced at the bodies, then at me, nodded once and that was it.

We did a little more searching and found another stairway, going up, that led to a door onto the surface. Once we found that, Thu and I hauled a couple of empty shelves from the room below and used them to carry the bodies outside half a dozen at a time. The desert was as quiet as it ever gets, and a wind was gusting up out of the south, pushing big heaps of white cloud with it. We laid the bodies out decently beneath the sky so they could go back into the circle. We don't have a priestess here and Anna, who's the oldest woman present, doesn't know the litany, so Eleen said the words for the last people of Star's Reach, while the wind blew across the bodies and sent shreds of their clothing fluttering off across the sand.

Afterwards, when Anna could talk again, we sat with her in the room where her people lived and died, and Eleen asked her about her last hours there.

"I recall very little," Anna said. "It was a long time ago, remember, and I was very young. We left at night, I know that; it was dark outside, and my mother and I went with maybe two dozen others down into the lower levels and then out to one of the main doors—probably the one we entered originally. We sat outside, waiting for my father and a few more people. It was a long time before they arrived, and then we started walking in the dark. But I don't remember much of what happened before that, not to anyone but me and my mother and father."

She leaned forward, then, and stared at nothing any of the rest of us could see for a long while. Then: "There was shouting. Before my mother came and started gathering up our things, and telling me we had to leave. There was shouting, and angry voices that went on and on; I could hear them down the corridor as I played in our room. That wasn't normal, and I wondered what it meant." Then, blinking and looking at us: "That's all."

Tashel Ban came back then from the heap of ashes. "Paper," he said, "and quite a bit of it. Unless something turns up elsewhere, that may be their records."

"The computers might have something," Eleen said without too much hope.

We spent the rest of the afternoon searching the rooms we'd found, or rather Berry, Thu and I did, with what help Anna could give us. That wasn't much, though none of us could blame her. Not long after we started searching, we found the room that had belonged to her family, with things nobody had taken the time to pack scattered around. Among them was a little stick-figure drawing that looked like it was supposed to be two adults and a child, with her name written in a child's block letters down at the bottom. She turned sharply away and left the room, and I heard her dry hard sobs from one of the other rooms. After a while she came back to help us search, but her thoughts were somewhere else.

Tashel Ban and Eleen were working on the computers all the while. We'd been searching the rooms for a few minutes when Eleen let out a whoop like nothing I'd ever heard from her. It turned out that this part of Star's Reach still had power coming to it from power cores down below, and at least one of the computers would still run. After that they were silent for a long while, except for muttered words now and again as they worked.

Meanwhile we found everything we were going to find in the other rooms, which was quite a bit as far as salvage, but next to nothing that could help us in our quest. Anna's family and the ones that left with them took what they could carry, but the dead left everything behind, clothes in the closets, pots and knives in the kitchen, tools next to the place where they'd grown their vegetables, and everything else you might expect people to have where they and their ancestors lived for all those years.

There were books here and there, sometimes one or two, sometimes a shelf of them, and we checked those to make sure they weren't messages from some other world. One room had most of a wall covered with shelves, and most of those were full of books with brown brittle pages and cracked paper covers that used to have bright colors on them; all of them came from before the end of the old world, though, and the papers and records we wanted to find weren't anywhere among them.

By the time we'd finished searching I was about as discouraged as a man can get. It didn't matter just then that I'd done the thing that every ruinman in Meriga had been dreaming of doing for four hundred years, and found the biggest and most famous ruin of them all; it didn't matter that I could pretty much count on being welcomed to the ruinmen's guild anywhere I wanted to settle, and being rich as a jennel besides. I wanted to know what the people from that other world had been trying to say to us right when the old world ended, and it seemed unfair after coming all that way and getting so close, to have those messages turn out to be long strings of numbers nobody could read, and a heap of black ashes nobody would ever read again.

I wandered into the place where Anna's people used to grow their vegetables with those thoughts in my head. The skylights of glass block overhead let in evening light, and just then something, probably a big ball of tumbleweed, went rolling past in the wind. I thought about the wind up above, blowing over what was left of Anna's people on its way across the desert, and all at once I realized that the wind was saying something.

They found something, it said. *They found something in that message from the stars, and drank poison and died. Are you sure you want to find it too?*

I left the dead sticks in their tubs and went back out to the main room. The others had gathered there already, following some call I hadn't heard.

"They tried to erase all the computer files," Eleen said, "but they didn't take the time to do it the right way. It's as though they had a library, and instead of burning the books, they just tore all the covers off the books and mixed them together so you can't tell which book is which, or even where one ends and another begins."

"But the pages are still there?" Berry asked.

"The pages are still there." Eleen rubbed her eyes. "Tashel Ban's going to try to get one of the printers to work; we've got plenty of paper in the storerooms and two cartridges that were stored in nitrogen and still ought to work. If we can get a printer going, we're going to print out everything that might be a document, and try to piece them together and make sense of them."

The wind was on the other side of the glass blocks and a mother of a lot of concrete and steel, but damn if I didn't hear its voice, saying the same thing it said to me in the place with the dead plants. Still, I knew what my answer had to be, and I knew it was the same answer every one of us would give. Whatever it was that Anna's people found, we couldn't stop without finding it ourselves.

CHAPTER 12

WHEN THE RAINS COME

It's been three days now since we found the place where the last people at Star's Reach died. Since most of our work will be there from now on, and there's no point walking half the length of the ruin every day, we moved all our supplies and gear from the rooms where we've stayed since we first got here. More to the point, all of us but Eleen and Tashel Ban hauled bundles and boxes and kegs halfway across Star's Reach. Eleen and Tashel Ban worked on the computer; they're still working, and whether they manage to get it to talk to them will settle whether or not we came all this way for nothing.

So the rest of us shouldered the bundles and boxes and kegs, and tried to make as little noise as we could when we went through the big room where they were working. Late this morning we got everything hauled and stowed away, and after Thu and I cooked up a meal for everyone—it would have been my turn and Eleen's, but we shuffled the schedule—Berry looked at me across the table, and I looked at him, and we decided that we had something better to do than wait there while Eleen and Tashel Ban worked and muttered.

We spent the rest of the day tracing cables. That's something ruinmen do whenever they find bundles of cables running through a ruin, or the marks that show where cables used to run. If you know how to trace them and luck's with you, they'll

lead you to metal worth salvaging and sometimes to things
that are worth quite a bit more.

We didn't have salvage in mind, of course, but there were
cables in bundles running from half a dozen rooms in the place
we'd found, over to a closet and then down through the floor,
and that was a temptation not many ruinmen can resist.
Me, I mostly just wanted to do something other than wait
and think; Berry, once we were away from the others, said he
thought they might lead to other places where records might
have been kept, which made sense.

Still, there's another point to tracing cables, which is that it's
a game. When I was growing up in the Tenisi hills, there was
a game all the children knew how to play with stones. You set
fourteen of them out in a triangle, leaving one empty place,
and then move one stone over another to the empty space.
Any stone you leap over gets taken out, and you can't move a
stone except by leaping over another next to it. If you end up
with just one stone left, you win, and if you have more than
one left, you lose. On winter nights, we used to play it by the
hour. Tracing cables is like that, and the prentices I knew in
Shanuga used to play it the same way.

I'm good at it, and Berry's better than I am; I won't say it was
easy, but we won the game. It took us all afternoon to do it, and
we nearly lost the trace when the cables dropped two levels
inside a solid wall, but toward evening we scrambled down
a narrow staircase eight levels down and found the machines
at the other end. There was a whole bank of them, big con-
soles with screens and buttons and lights, and three of them
were lit up like the one we found earlier: lit up and waiting, for
what we still don't know. Half the floor of the room was steel
grate, and we could see further down the big gray cylinders
full of something or other nuclear, turning out a steady trickle
of electricity as they'd done for more than four hundred years.
There were a lot of them, more than I'd ever seen or heard of
in a single place.

We searched the room, scanned it for radiation, shone a light through the doors that opened out from it into other parts of the eighth level, and then started back up the stairs. We got back just about the time the evening meal was ready; we were winded from the climb but exhilarated, and ready to tell our good news to anyone who would listen.

As it happened, though, it was the only good news anyone had. Eleen and Tashel Ban hadn't had anything like the luck we had, and whatever was in the computer was still tangled up around itself and impossible to read, maybe for now, maybe forever.

"There's still some chance," Tashel Ban said, gesturing with a piece of bread. He was sitting back in one of the big padded chairs we'd dragged into what we were already calling the common room, as though Star's Reach was a tavern. "The data's in there, no question of that. The question is getting it out in some form we can read."

"Were there machines to do that?" Berry asked. I gave him a startled look; the idea hadn't occurred to me, and it sounded like a good one.

"There were programs," Tashel Ban said after a moment. "I don't think anybody knows how they worked. There are maybe fifty people this side of the oceans nowadays that can make a computer do anything at all, even when it's in good order, and maybe five who can fix one that's not working if the problem's a simple one."

"This is not simple, I gather," said Thu.

"I wish I could tell you." Another gesture with the bread, short and sharp, put a period on the end of his words. "Maybe something simple, maybe not."

"If there was a program that could read the files," Berry said then, "there in the computer, do you think you could find it?"

I think all of us stared at him then. "I might," Tashel Ban said after a long moment. "Maybe." He didn't say another word during the meal, either, just stared at his soup as though it was a computer screen and he could make the beans and salt pork spell out messages from the stars by thinking at them hard enough. Eleen mostly just looked tired. Once we'd finished the meal, they went back to work, and I went to the room where we'd found the shelf full of old books and pulled one out at random.

Its pages were brown and brittle and the cheap paper cover was going to bits, but we'd brought enough resin from Melumi to preserve a building full of books, and so I took it with me into the sleeping room Eleen and I are sharing, got a bulb from my pack, used a sharp knife to cut the pages loose from what was left of the binding, and squirted every page with resin on both sides. That's the way you save a book, if you're a ruinman and can't be sure of getting the thing to a scholar before it crumbles away to nothing, and I told myself that that's what I was doing. Now of course what I was actually doing was trying to keep my mind off the chance that we might have come all this way to Star's Reach and gotten this close to the messages from the stars and still managed to fail, but saving an old book seemed like as good a thing to do as any.

So I sprayed every page front and back, and read it in the process, but I'd be lying if I said I understood everything in it. It was all about people from other worlds who were coming to ours in ships that looked like a couple of plates stuck together edge to edge, and how the government was pretending that wasn't happening, but any day now something would happen that the government couldn't hide and there we'd be, and the aliens—I finally found out how that word is spelled, after all these years—would save us or something.

Any day now, I thought. I looked back at the page right at the beginning where it says when a book got made, and saw that it was already more than fifty years old when the old world ended. What do you do when any day now was five hundred years ago?

By the time I'd finished the book and wrapped up the pages for safekeeping, it was late, but I didn't feel a bit of sleep in me. I pulled out the notebook where I'm writing this, but couldn't think of what to say. I could hear the clatter of the computer keyboard from the common room. Then, after what seemed like a long while, silence.

Then footsteps whispered down the corridor, coming to our room. Eleen came in a moment later. "Trey? I'm glad you're awake."

"Any luck?"

"Maybe." She sat down next to me on our bed. "Maybe. Berry might just be right." She leaned against me; I could feel the tiredness in her. Then: "What did you find?"

She meant the book I'd sprayed and wrapped, which was sitting on the bare metal table here in our room. "Not too sure," I said. "One of the old books. Somebody saying there were aliens visiting our world back in the old days."

"Flying saucers," she said.

"Something like that."

A little, tired laugh. "Funny. They've got all the records about that at Melumi. The old Merigan government made the whole thing up, so they could hide tests of airplanes and things they didn't want other countries to know about. Every few years they'd fake another round of reports, and they always looked like whatever stopped being secret five or ten years later: round silver balls when they were testing balloons, black triangles when that's what the planes looked like, that sort of thing. They kept it going right up until the old world ended."

"Well, nobody told whoever wrote this book."

"Funny," she said again. "I wonder why it's here." The last couple of words weren't much more than a mumble, and I just about had to undress her and help her into bed, she was that close to falling asleep.

Afterwards, when I'd written about the last few days, I sat there at this desk for a while and looked at her. I thought about the long road we'd traveled to get here, and of course I ended up remembering how Eleen and I first met. That was what I was going to write about next, before Tashel Ban came running to tell us about the door and the smell, and so I might as well write about it now.

It happened back when Berry and I got to Melumi the first time, riding along with Jennel Cobey and getting a glimpse of what it's like to live when you don't ever have to worry about where your next meal is coming from. I got my first taste of that the morning after I'd met the jennel, when a couple of his servants showed up at the door of the Luwul ruinmen's hall with horses for themselves and one each for me and Berry, and led us jingling and clattering through the streets of Luwul to the ferry across the Hiyo River. We met the jennel and the rest of his party there, a couple of dozen servants and soldiers on horseback, and a bunch of horses with nothing on their backs but packs and bundles.

The jennel greeted me in what certainly sounded like fine spirits, then caught sight of Berry. For just a moment he looked about as startled as a man can look, and then smoothed the look off his face as though it had never been there, nodded politely and said a few words to me that didn't mean a thing. I've never known anybody but Plummer who caught on as quickly as Jennel Cobey did, and I used to think that he might have guessed at a glance that Berry was a tween. These days I'd guess differently, but that belongs later in this story.

So we crossed the river and rode north through Inyana with the jennel. He had people riding ahead of him, so every night we stopped someplace where there were beds and hot meals for the jennel and his advisers and officers and friends, which meant us among others. A couple of days when we were riding, he sent a servant to bring me up near the head of the line with him, and he asked about the ruinmen and Star's Reach; a couple of evenings when he wasn't yet busy with the harlot or two that his servants found for him pretty much every stop along the way, he sent for me to join him at dinner. The rest of the time, Berry and I rode well back in the line, had our meals with the servants and soldiers, and had a quiet room to ourselves wherever we stayed. It was pleasant enough, the way a dream can be pleasant, and felt almost as unreal.

We got to Melumi late one afternoon most of two weeks after we'd left Luwul. There were big heaps of cloud looming up dark in the sky behind us, warning of the approaching rains, and a rising wind set the tree branches dancing and the grass bending low. We'd been riding all day through Inyana farmland, and finally came to a town no different from any of the others we'd passed, except this one was Melumi and had the big brick buildings of the Versty back behind it and women in gray scholar's robes everywhere.

The Versty used to be bigger than it is nowadays. I learned that later, but when I first saw it I don't think I would have believed it if somebody told me. There were six huge buildings of red salvaged brick: the library, the school, the offices, and the three buildings—dorms, they call them, though I don't know why—where scholars, students, and visitors sleep and eat. We rode into the big square in the middle of it all, and while the servants and soldiers went to the dorm for visitors, the jennel and Berry and I got down off our horses, and went inside the offices.

The jennel's people had ridden ahead, of course, so the scholars were waiting for us. There were three of them, all with gray hair pulled back tight around their faces and lips pulled back tight across their teeth. There was a Versty official too, someone of high enough rank to chat comfortably with a jennel, and half a dozen junior scholars or senior students a little older or younger than I was, but it was the three scholars who mattered and just then they were the only ones I noticed. We exchanged a few words and then I handed the copy of the letter over to them, and Jennel Cobey startled the stuffing out of me by handing them the original as well.

We could have given them each a pound of gold or a dead rat, and I don't think their faces would have moved any more than they did. One of them turned to one of the girls and held out her hand, without a word, and the girl handed her a hand lens; the scholar sat down and went over the original so slowly I think she must have looked at every fiber in the paper. The other two took the copy and read it, word by word, glancing at each other now and then; one would make a little nod or shake of the head to the other, and then they'd go on reading. The three of them were at it for more than a quarter hour, and then all of a sudden they turned to the official. Two of them nodded and the other, the one who'd used the lens, said, "Authentic."

The official beamed, and handed the original back to the jennel. "Well. Not that we had any doubts, of course." Cobey allowed a broad smile, but didn't say anything.

"Can you tell us what it means?" I asked then.

All at once three pairs of cold clear scholar's eyes were looking at me, with exactly the same expression they would have turned on the dead rat. After a moment, one of them turned to one of the junior scholars, and said, "Eleen, you'll prepare a translation."

That's when I noticed Eleen: thin and bony, with lighter skin and redder hair than you usually see this side of Genda. She made a little curtsey to the scholar and glanced at me briefly with no particular interest, and then took the copy and left the room. I glanced after her, then turned back to the scholars and didn't give her a second thought.

That was how I first met her, and that's also how I first saw Melumi. I got to know both a good deal better in the next few months, because the rains arrived. Nobody travels during the rainy months. Once the rains start, most roads end up waist deep in water or worse, riverboats tie up at the nearest town and get covered with tarps to keep from getting flooded and sunk, and everybody who goes outside gets used to being soaked right to the skin. If you're traveling and the rains catch you, you stay wherever you are, with whoever else happens to be there, and you do what you need to do to get along; if that means a baby gets started or somebody's life gets turned upside down, well, that's what happens.

Still, I was glad I could get to Melumi before the rains came down, so that Berry and I could spend a couple of months learning everything that was known about Star's Reach. I admit that was maybe half an excuse for wanting to spend some time at Melumi, but there was some reason to it, and maybe some hope. If the scholars at Melumi could figure out all the strange words on the letter I'd found, one of them might point us in a direction nobody had looked before and then, just maybe, we'd be on our way to Star's Reach.

The first part of the plan worked fine. We got settled into a couple of rooms in the dorm they have for guests and visitors. I still had most of the money Gray Garman gave me back in Shanuga, so the cost of staying in the guests' dorm until the rains ended wasn't going to be a problem. It turned out to be even less of a problem than I thought, because when I went to talk to the old woman who ran the dorm about paying, she told me that Jennel Cobey was covering it. I still tried to be careful with what I had left, since I knew it might have to see us through a mother of a lot of travel before our search was over.

We were at the dorm maybe two days, and the sky was getting full of dark heavy clouds, when a messenger came from the library to tell us that the translation was finished. Berry and I followed the messenger back across the big open square at the center of the Versty, ducking past scholars in gray robes and visitors staring goggle-eyed at the big brick buildings, and ended up in a little room with a table and some chairs and not much else in it. The messenger—she was a young thing, not much more than fifteen, with black hair pulled back tight from her face and eyes that looked a little frightened all the time—motioned for us to sit down and then left, closing the

door behind her. A few minutes later the door opened again
and Eleen came in.

I recognized her from our arrival at Melumi, and said
something polite, I don't remember what. She replied with
something just as memorable, and then sat down across the
table from us and handed us a sheet of paper. This is what
it said:

TOP SECRET/STAR'S REACH

This was the highest level of secrecy; only people who
were allowed to know about Star's Reach could see it.

PAGE 01 OF 01 R 111630Z NOV 54

There is only this one page. It was sent on the eleventh of November 2054 in the old calendar, late in the
afternoon.

FM: GEN BURKERT DRCETI

It was sent by a Jennel Burkert, who was in charge of
(something about) talking with beings who live on other
worlds.

TO: CETI PROJECT STAFF ORNL

It was sent to the people who were trying to talk
with beings who live on other worlds, at the Oak Ridge
National Laboratory, which was near Orrij in Tenisi.

1.(TS/SR) PROJ DIR LUKACS REPORTS EVAC COM-
PLETE FROM NRAO AND LANGLEY. ALL RECORDS
AND STAFF SAFE. WRTF OPERATIONAL AND CETI
INCOMING.

The TS/SR means the same thing as the Top Secret/
Star's Reach at the beginning. Someone named Lukacz,
who was in charge of the project, said that everything
and everyone had been gotten out of the National Radio

Astronomy Observatory, which was in the mountains on the border between Jinya and Meriga, and Langley, which was close to Deesee and is now underwater. (Something) was working and talk from beings who live on other worlds was coming in.

2.(TS/SR) POTUS/DNS/DCI ADVISED THAT PROJ-ECT ONGOING DESPITE CRISIS.

The presden and the two jennels who commanded Meriga's spies had been told that even though there was trouble, the work hadn't stopped.

3.(TS/SR) TRANSPORT FOR ORNL PROJECT STAFF TO WRTF TO FOLLOW ASAP. INSTRUCTIONS VIA FEMA/GWEN WHEN SITUATION PERMITS.

Someone was trying to get everyone working on that project out of the place near Orrij and take them to (something). As soon as possible, they would be told what to do by a special radio system the presden used when there was trouble.

CLASS BURKERT DRCETI RSN 1.5E X4

Jennel Burkert ordered the message to be kept secret because it had scientific knowledge in it that nobody else was supposed to know. It was not going to be made public even after ten years because it showed how the presden planned to deal with certain kinds of trouble.

TOP SECRET/SPECIAL ACCESS REQUIRED

Means the same as the first line. This had to be put on everything that was this secret.

I read through it twice, and then handed it to Berry. "Thank you," I said to Eleen. "This is going to be helpful. Well, except—"

She folded her hands in front of her and waited without saying a word.

"The thing called WRTF." Berry had already finished with the paper by then, and he handed it back to me. I took it, and tapped where the letter said ORNL PROJECT STAFF TO WRTF. "That's where the people who were working on this thing were going, weren't they? That might be Star's Reach, the place I'm trying to find."

She tilted her head to one side, considering. "Possible," she said after a moment. "It's not in the books of acronyms, though."

Back then I had no idea what an acronym was, but I wasn't going to tell her that. "Is there any other way to find out what it means?"

"Maybe. It could take weeks or months, and there would be a fee, of course."

That set me back for a moment, and then I remembered what Jennel Cobey had said. "The jennel will pay for that," I told her.

Her eyebrows went up, and I could just about see her move me from a box in her mind marked "scruffy young ruinman" to another, not too far away from it, marked "scruffy young ruinman who knows somebody rich and powerful." After a moment: "Then I can certainly do that." She stood up. "Is there anything else?"

"Well, yes. We want to spend the rains reading as much as we can about Star's Reach. Is there somebody I can talk to about doing that?"

That got another pair of raised eyebrows, and I went into a third box, this one marked "scruffy young ruinman who maybe isn't as dumb as he looks." "I can make the arrangements," she said. "It will take a day or two to find you a cubicle."

"That'll be fine," I told her. "And there's one more thing besides that."

She folded her hands again and waited.

"The word on the back." I'd remembered it the day before, sitting in our room in the guests' dorm and staring at nothing much while evening closed in. "The one in gray writing."

"The word in pencil," Eleen said. "Curtis. It's a name, a common one back then. Probably the name of the person who received the message."

I thought of the dusty room deep in the Shanuga ruins where I'd found the letter, and the dead man in the heavy clothing of an old world soldier who was sprawled on the table next to it. Curtis, I thought, imagining someone calling him that when he was still alive. It all seemed to make sense, and because it seemed to make sense I didn't ask the question that might have gotten me to Star's Reach years sooner than I did.

She asked if there was anything else, then, and when I said there wasn't, smiled and nodded and left the room. Before I could do much more than draw in a breath the messenger took us out of the library. Berry and I followed her, went back to the guests' dorm, and managed not to say anything to each other until we were safely in my room with the door shut.

There were two chairs and a table in every room in the dorm, all of them exactly the same, and all probably salvaged from the same ruin. I put the translated letter down on the table. Berry settled into one of the chairs and leaned forward. "WRTF," he said, spelling out the letters. "I figured that out about half a minute before you said it, Mister Trey."

"That that's what we have to know?"

He nodded. "That WRTF might be Star's Reach."

"What else could it be?"

He glanced up at me. "Someplace they were going first, before heading to Star's Reach."

"Oh." He was right, of course. "Well, we'll hope it turns out to be Star's Reach."

He grinned. "Even if it isn't, if we know where they went from Tenisi, that's a clue, and there might be other clues there."

That cheered me up a bit. I sat down next to him and we spent a couple of hours going over the letter and trying to figure out if it was telling us anything we weren't hearing. Later that day I took the translated letter up the stairs to the top floor of the guests' dorm, which is where rich and important guests got to stay, and spent an hour or so talking it over with Jennel Cobey.

He read the thing over, tapped one finger on the letters WRTF, and said, "That's the key. We'll have to ask the scholars to find out what it means."

"Already done, Sir and Jennel," I said. "The scholar I talked to said it would take a while—weeks or months."

He nodded once, as though that settled something. "With the rains so close, that's hardly a problem." To one of his servants: "Creel, have somebody take care of the fees." Then he turned back to me and started peppering me with questions about the letter and the ruins it mentioned; I was glad that Berry and I had been over it earlier, because I would have been pretty fairly lost otherwise. Still, when I went back down to my room I was about as pleased as I could be, and Star's Reach felt almost close enough to touch.

The next day I had other things to think about, because the rains started. There were a few spatters on the windows when I first got up, and more a bit later on, and then about an hour before noon the skies opened up and the rain came down in great gray sheets. Any other plans Berry and I might have had went to wherever it is that might-have-beens spend their days, since the first day of the rains isn't a day to get anything done. We dropped what we were doing and headed outside into the warm wet air and the warm streaming water.

There's about three hundred years of history behind that. After the old world ended but before the seas finished rising, there was a long time when most of Meriga was as dry as an old bone. There were plenty of places where it didn't rain a drop for years on end, and even the places that did get rain got just a bit of it, now and then, so farmers never knew when they put seeds in the ground whether they were going to get a harvest or not. It was a hard and hungry time, and a lot of people died. After that, Mam Gaia decided that we'd had enough punishment, or that's what the priestesses say; the ice down in Nardiga melted, the seas rose a lot more, and the rains came sweeping in for the first time, the way they do every year now. Everybody danced and partied in the falling rain, so the story goes, and everybody still dances and parties the day the rains come, all over Meriga.

Everyone from the Versty was heading into the town, and we followed them. I don't have the least idea what Berry did, since I did what most people do when the rains come; I let myself get lost in the crowd and end up wherever I happened to end up. In my case it was a string of bars along a narrow little street off one side of the Melumi town square, getting thoroughly drunk on cheap whiskey and dancing in the rain with local girls who felt like being a little daring, or maybe just this once didn't care that I was a ruinman.

Somewhere in the middle of all that, a half dozen or so of the young scholars from the Versty came into whatever bar I was in, and one of them was Eleen. We danced, and then spun away with other partners, and then ended up dancing together again. She was about as drunk as I was, and not as good at keeping her feet, so when that dance ended we stumbled our way over to a booth over to the side, and one thing led to another. One thing fairly often leads to another on the first day of the rains, but to this day I'm not exactly sure how we ended up at a rooming house a couple of doors away, in a narrow little upstairs room with a narrow little bed, going at it like a couple of cats in heat and then curling up around each other, wet and drunk and happy.

The next morning I held her hair out of the way while she threw up into the chamberpot, helped her get close enough to presentable to pass muster at the scholars' dorm, and got her back there. I wasn't in the world's best shape myself, but we'd matched each other drink for drink there for a while, and there's a lot less of her to handle the whiskey. Me, I dragged myself back to my room in the guests' dorm, slept for most of the day, and woke up thinking that the thing with Eleen was just one of those things that happens when the rains come, over and mostly forgotten once the whiskey wears off. I was wrong, but I wouldn't find that out for a couple of years, and both of us had a long hard road to travel first.

CHAPTER 13

THE YELLOW BUTTERFLY

I came in here to write about two hours ago, after one of those uncomfortable meals where nobody has anything to say but nobody wants silence, either, so each of us tried to say nothing in as many words as possible, and failed. Berry and I spent all day tracing cables, more to have something to do than for any better reason, and we found two more rooms full of machinery with lights on and electricity humming to itself in the air; we got back upstairs to find Eleen and Tashel Ban still hunched over their work, and the last meal of the day mostly ready.

So we ate, and tried to find something to say, and then I came here to the room Eleen and I are sharing and sat down to write. All I did for what seemed like a long time was look at the blank paper and think about what we were doing here, and whether we'd come all this way to read messages from another world or just to dig up Meriga's last really big heap of scrap metal. Finally, I picked up the pen and got ready to write, and damn if it wasn't then that I heard footsteps in the hall outside.

It was Eleen, and if an alien from some other world had suddenly popped out of the computer and shaken her hand I don't think her face would have been more surprised or more delighted. "Trey," she said, and tried to say something else, and couldn't; and then just said, "You've got to come."

So I came. Tashel Ban was tapping on the other doors, letting people know, so by the time we got back to the computer everyone else was either heading that way or already there. "You found something," Berry said, which was what I was thinking too.

"If I ever ignore one of your suggestions," Tashel Ban told him, "you have my permission to hit me with a stick."

Berry blinked, then: "The program?"

"That's the one. We were able to find close to a hundred program files, and one of them turned out to be a recovery program. So we've got our first readable text."

"What does it say?" This from Thu.

"Have a look." Tashel Ban waved a hand at the computer screen.

We all crowded around the screen. This is what it said:

```
28 Mar 2109
    To: Executive Committee Members
    From: Donna Kitzhaber VC Security
    Foley and Benedetti got back from Kansas
City last night. A full report will fol-
low after debriefing; the short version is
that right now there's no central govern-
ment to receive our report, much less do
anything about it. Our logistics team in
KC can't get any details about the prog-
ress of the fighting in the southeast or the
Japanese refugee situation on the Pacific
coast, other than that both are bad and
ongoing; the team's running short of almost
everything and they want to return here
while the roads are still open. We're going
to have to figure out soon how much of an
operation we can keep going here without
outside help, whether there's a point to
```

doing so, and what if anything we're going
to tell the CETI team and the support staff.
                                         —DK

I'd be willing to bet that every one of us read it through twice, except for Anna, who glanced over it, nodded, and said, "I knew a family named Kitzhaber."

"Friends of your parents?" Tashel Ban asked her.

"I think so. I used to play with their daughter, before we left." She didn't say anything else. I don't know if it's just that she's old and doesn't remember things that well, or if she still has all her memories and just doesn't talk about them; I'm starting to think the second is more likely than the first, but that's a guess at best.

"So what does it mean?" I asked Eleen.

"2109 in the old calendar is just over three hundred fifty years ago," she said. "The Second Civil War was going on then, so it's no wonder they couldn't find a government."

"That's the one with the three presdens?" Tashel Ban asked.

"Exactly. The rest, well, we'll see what else we can get out of the computer."

"I wonder what the report was," Berry said then. "The one the letter mentions."

Tashel Ban glanced at him, nodded after a moment. "I was wondering that myself. We may just try to find it next."

"Not tonight, I hope," I said. I was thinking about the haggard look on Eleen's face.

"No," said Tashel Ban. "No, not tonight."

It wasn't too much later that I got Eleen tucked into our bed and sleeping, but I had too many thoughts and memories running through my head to sleep, so after her breathing settled and slowed I crawled out from under the blankets and sat down at the table again.

When I wrote about how I met Eleen, that got me thinking again about Tam, and a part of the story of how I got here to

Star's Reach that I meant to write earlier and didn't. It's even more out of place here than it was when I was explaining how I became a ruinman and how Berry and I left Shanuga, but it's got to go in somewhere, and it might as well go here.

There's another reason Tam's story might as well go here, too, because I met Tam pretty much the same way I met Eleen, at the start of the rains. I was sixteen then, and one of Gray Garman's senior prentices. We'd just finished hauling everything back from the Shanuga ruins at the end of the season, racing the rain clouds as they marched up from the south. That was hard work, and there was plenty more of the same just ahead, getting the tools and gear cleaned and repaired for next season and getting them packed away where they belonged.

Still, the end of a season's always a glad time unless the season's been a mother of a mess, and this one had been pretty good. We'd only had three prentices get reborn that year, and two of them brought it on themselves by getting cocky and taking stupid risks. The building we stripped had plenty of metal, enough to pay for a couple of bad seasons; it also had a bunch of old broken computer gear in a room we had to dig our way into, three levels down into the underplaces where looters hadn't been. Best of all, I'd found a couple of metal chairs buried in rubble, and small finds like that are a prentice's to keep or sell if he wants to. I sold them to the metal merchants, and ended up with a nice bit of money in my pocket.

So I was feeling pleased with myself that day, as we sorted out the shovels and picks—this one's fine, that one needs filing, that other one needs a trip to the blacksmith—and the clouds we could see through the windows turned from white to gray to dark gray to that inky blue-black that means Mam Gaia's about to cut loose on you good and proper. It took an effort to pay attention to the tools, and when the thunder finally rolled and a first flurry of fat raindrops spattered against the windows, we gave up trying and pounded down the stairs to the street.

The younger prentices stayed there in the ruinmen's quarter, splashing each other with water and getting into half-playful fights with the other misters' prentices. The half dozen of us who counted as senior prentices, though, headed toward the town gate and the buildings just outside it. We couldn't go in, not without some good reason the guards would believe, but there were taverns where a boy of sixteen could get small beer if he was polite to the tavernkeeper, and shops where you could buy any number of little useless things, and prentices from some of the other crafts that were outside the walls; and there were also girls.

That's one of the things about being a ruinman's prentice. Most of the crafts only take boys as prentices—well, boys and tweens, who count as boys according to Circle and the priestesses. With girls, there's always the chance they can have healthy babies, in which case they go into Circle and whatever time the mister's put into their training goes dancing down the four free winds. There are a fair number of guilds that will take women who've had their twenty without a baby, but the ruinmen aren't one of them.

What that means is that if you're a ruinman's prentice, eight or nine months of the year you're someplace where the only woman you're likely to see is one failed scholar three or four times your age, and unless you happen to fancy men rather than women, you're pretty much out of luck. When I was ten and I was first working at the ruins, that didn't matter to me a bit, but by the time I was sixteen it was starting to feel like an inconvenience.

So when the senior prentices go to the buildings piled up around the little southern gate of Shanuga by the ruinmen's hall, a good many of them have girls on their mind. You can find girls there, too, and not just the kind who can be hired for the afternoon for a dozen marks or so. There are trades besides ours that have their place outside the walls for the same reason we do, because people think they're dirty or shameful or toxic; some of those are family trades, and the girls from those families won't get into Circle no matter how many babies they have, so when they get old enough, if they're interested in boys, they make friends with prentices from the ruinmen, the chemists, the burners, and so on. You also get girls who aren't born healthy but whose families for one reason or another won't let the birth women put a pillow over their faces when they're born. There are trades that take them young and train them, the way the guilds take and train prentices, and those are outside the walls too.

Now and then, though, you also find girls from good families who come there because they want to feel like they're being wild and taking risks, and that's more or less what happened on the day I was talking about. Conn and I were inside one of the taverns with a couple of glasses of small beer we'd whee-dled from a friendly barkeeper, having spent a good two hours splashing and shouting and getting into a friendly fistfight or two with a couple of prentices from the burners—there's an old rivalry there, since they burn the bodies of dead people and we handle a lot of bodies from the old world.

There we were, and the rest of the tavern was full of wet happy people, but it was a bit quiet for the day the rains come, and after a while I saw why. There were two girls sitting at a little table up against the wall in a quiet corner. One looked excited and embarrassed and the other just looked embarrassed, and from the clothes they were wearing nobody in the tavern had any reason to doubt that their mothers could buy the tavern and everyone in it with spare change from their pockets and not notice the difference.

I turned my chair so I could look at them, and after a while Conn noticed where all my attention was. "You're not," he said with a big grin, all but daring me.

"You watch me," I told him, and got up.

So I walked up to the two of them and asked if they'd like a beer. The one who was just embarrassed, a little dab of a thing with a good bit of brown in her hair, gave me a look like I'd offered to cut her throat, but the other one, the excited one, smiled and said "Sure." I managed to wheedle three more glasses out of the barkeeper, which took some doing; carried them back over and asked, "Mind if I sit?"

They didn't, or at least the one I was interested in didn't. Her name was Tam, short for Tamber, and the other one's name was Shen; they'd been good friends since, oh, always, and was I really a ruinman's prentice? So I sat, and we talked, and talked, and talked some more. It was starting to get dark outside by the time Shen insisted that they had to get back home, and would Tam *please* listen and come? So they left, and I left a little later, feeling pretty thoroughly dazzled by my luck.

Conn followed me—he'd been doing something else in the tavern the whole time, probably toss-the-bones, and probably winning, as he usually did—and proceeded to push me into the deepest puddle he could find. I'd have put it down to jealousy, except that he's always fancied men rather than women, so I suppose it was just the beer. So we had another fistfight, one of the kind where both parties are laughing too hard to do much damage to anybody but themselves, and stumbled back up the stairs of Mister Garman's house late enough that we got a week's worth of the grubbiest cleaning chores Gray Garman could find for us.

I figured that was the last I'd see of Tam, but it didn't work out that way. A week later, I think it was, I was back at that same tavern, and damn if she didn't walk in the door, spot me, and come right over to the table where I was sitting. She was alone this time, and we talked again for what must have been a couple of hours; she had someplace she had to be at sunset, and I made good and sure she left the tavern in plenty of time, because I'd started to get hopeful and didn't want to make it any harder for her to get outside the gate again. That time, before she left, we'd already settled when and where we'd meet next.

I think it was the fourth time we met, or it may have been the fifth, before one of us worked up the courage to suggest going somewhere less crowded than a tavern, and I honestly can't remember which of us made the suggestion first. There were places outside the gate where you could take a girl, or a girl could take you, and a mark or two would buy a bed that wasn't too dirty and a couple of hours of privacy. That's what we did, and things proceeded from there. Afterwards, though, she nuzzled her face into my shoulder and suddenly started to cry, and after she'd finished crying I asked why; we talked, and I began to figure out what she was doing in a cheap rented bed with a ruinman's prentice.

She was from one of Shanuga's important families, as I'd guessed, with a mother who was a big name in Circle, and grandmothers and great-aunts who wore the red hats that only Circle elders get to wear. Of course they'd expected her to follow after them, and let her know once she'd gotten old enough that she needed to get a baby started, and she'd gone out and found a likely boy and done the thing, except that there wasn't a baby. Of course that meant she had to keep at it, and she'd done that until every boy in Shanuga's wealthy families got to thinking of her as free for the taking, and there still wasn't a baby on the way.

That was when she realized that she wasn't going to follow her mother into Circle. She told them so, and there was a big fight with the grandmothers and great-aunts and everybody involved, and at the end of it all Tam's mother told her that if she didn't have enough sense and pride to do the right thing by her family, then she might as well go off to the ruinmen. "She used to scare my brothers when they were little and mis- behaved," she told me, laughing through the tears, "by telling them she was going to send them to be ruinmen's prentices. I couldn't believe that she'd say that to me, and I couldn't help it. I laughed at her." Then, three days later, the rains came and she teased and bullied Shen into coming with her to the nameless street where the ruinmen live, where she met me.

"I can't exactly get you into the ruinmen's guild, you know," I told her.

That got another laugh. "I know that. Still—Trey, I've got just over three years before my twenty, and then I'll have to find a life for myself, you know. I need to know what it's like out here, outside the gate where you live. And—" She pressed her face into my shoulder again and said something that I couldn't figure out at all; so I eased her back from me a bit and she said it again, and we did some kissing and then pretty soon we were going at it again.

"I want to be a butterfly," she said later. I made a wing-flapping motion with my hands, and she laughed. "No, I mean it. You know how butterflies start out as little green worms, and spend all their time on one tree, until finally they turn into a whatsit and then hatch out and go fluttering off into the world?"

I'd learned that much from the priestesses. "Yes."

"When I have my twenty, I'll hatch out, and then I want to fly."

It was late by the time she left to go back into the city, and later still before I got back to Mister Garman's house, but nobody made a point of it this time and I made sure to get my share of the work done and then a bit for the next few days. I had a lot of thinking to do. Even then I wasn't quite slow enough to think that Tam had met me and fallen giddy in love, and that was all there was to it. Partly, I guessed, she was getting back at her mother and grandmothers and great-aunts by doing something that would make them yell like panthers if they ever found out, and partly she was right about finding something else to do with her life.

Once she had her twenty—her twentieth birthday, that is—if there hadn't yet been a baby or any sign of one on the way, the door to Circle would swing gently shut and her family would close up around itself with her on the outside. That's the way Circle works, and if you want to know why, I'm not the person to ask. One of the old women in red hats might be able to tell you, but probably won't, because Circle has its secrets and holds onto them good and tight.

Still, after thinking all that through a couple of times on a couple of nights where I didn't get much sleep, I decided that none of it mattered, because whether or not she was in love, I was, and I'd just take my chances. We'd arranged to meet again a week later, and a day or so before then I went up to one of the little shops outside the gate where they sell little trinkets and things. I knew what I wanted to find, and found it after most of an hour of looking through little bins and cases of bright bits of cheap metal, the sort of thing that boys give to girls and girls to boys.

There's an alley back behind the tavern where we first met, and the grubby little place with rooms and beds for rent has a door that opens onto it. That's where we met, with rain pelting down from a sky the color of cold iron, and we laughed and kissed, scampered inside and hurried up the stairs to the room I'd already rented; we'd settled on that as much to have a quiet place to talk as for the obvious reason. We were both soaked, as everybody is during the rains, and so of course we had to get our wet clothes off and hanging on the pegs next to the door; she sat on the bed, brown and plump and glowing in the dim light, and smiled up at me.

"Close your eyes," I told her, "and hold out a hand." I put what I'd found into her palm. "Go ahead and look."

She looked at her hand and then at me, and her eyes were round and wet. "Trey," she said. "Oh, Trey."

There wasn't much I could say in response, and we didn't do much talking for a while after that. Later, when she was lying on her back and I was propped up on one elbow, looking at her, I took the gift and perched it on her nose: a little butterfly of yellow metal. "That's your butterfly," I said, "and it'll take you someplace you can't even imagine."

She laughed, moved the butterfly to her lips and kissed it, and then set it on the bedside stand and pulled me down to her.

All that first rainy season we got together once or maybe twice a week, and when the rains stopped and it was time to head back out to the Shanuga ruins we said our goodbyes with plenty of tears and laughter. I missed her like anything the first month or so, but I was one of Gray Garman's senior prentices by that time, as I said, and so I didn't have any great amount of time to sit and fret.

For all that, I didn't know what to expect when the clouds piled up again over Shanuga at the end of that dry season and we hauled our gear back to the house on the street with no name and got ready for the rains. Half of me was sure she'd come to the tavern where we used to meet once the rains came pouring down, and half of me was sure that I'd never see her again, and between the one and the other, I must have been a mother of a mess to deal with those last few days of work.

When the rains finally came, I made myself stay away from the tavern for an hour or so, just to try to prove to myself that I wasn't as tied in knots about it all as I knew I was, and then headed for it when I couldn't stand not knowing any longer. I turned the corner and just about bumped into Tam and Shen as they splashed across from the street outside the gate. We stood there laughing and kissing in the pouring rain while Shen blushed and tried to find something else to look at, and about the time she gave up Tam and I drew back out of one more long kiss and headed into the tavern with Shen right behind us.

Over three glasses of small beer we talked and caught up on eight months away from each other, and I did my level best to make room for Shen in the conversation, but it wasn't easy; all I wanted to do was look at Tam and hear her voice and, well, I could go on but don't really need to. They'd both filled out more than a bit, Tam more than Shen, and weren't half so coltish as they'd looked the year before, so there was plenty for me to look at, too. Finally they went back inside the walls and I went out into the rain, feeling quite a bit giddier than the beer would explain, and got into a good rousing fight with some burners' prentices, but we'd made plans to meet again within a few days, and it was straight to the little rented rooms that time.

Not much had changed in her life, though her family had finally gotten around to noticing that she'd done her best to get a baby started, and gone from being angry at her to being sad and pitying, which irritated her even more. All through the rains that year, when we weren't busy with each other's bodies, she asked me questions about the ruinmen and what I knew about the people and the trades outside the walls, or spun fine stories about what she might do after she had her twenty, when her life would be her own to make. Me, I had my own ideas about that; I knew that some of the misters in the ruinmen's guild had women they lived with, with everything to make a marriage except the blessing from the priestesses you don't get without children, and I'd begun to think about becoming a guild mister someday and sharing that life with Tam.

Her stories weren't anything like so ordinary. She liked to daydream about adventures, going to Genda or Nuwinga, sailing on the sea, and yes, one time she told a story about the two of us finding Star's Reach and learning what it was that the people from other worlds wanted to say to us, although for the life of me I don't remember what she decided that was. I thought they were fine stories, and I was still young and silly enough that it didn't occur to me that there wasn't a bit of reality in any of them. I knew, because she'd told me, that she wanted a baby, wanted the place in Circle that would have been hers if she could have a healthy child, but it hadn't occurred to me that her stories were one of the ways she was consoling herself for the life she wasn't going to get, though I knew perfectly well that I was one of the others.

But the rains ended, as of course they had to sooner or later, and we said our goodbyes with more tears and more laughter, and I went off to the Shanuga ruins again and spent eight more months digging and hauling metal and tracing cables. We worked hard that season, harder than usual, for

Gray Garman's luck landed us with a big heavy windowless building of concrete and steel, and we tore it right down to its roots to get the metal that ran all through it. Night after night I went to bed aching in every muscle, but we all ended the season with plenty of money, and when the clouds piled up and we hauled our tools back home I couldn't have been happier.

So when the rains came, I went to the tavern sooner rather than later, and waited for Tam. I was still waiting a couple of hours later, and finally I couldn't stand it and went outside and there was Shen, all by herself, huddled and miserable in the rain, trying to work up the courage to come inside.

I knew right away that something was up, but I took her into the tavern and got her a beer. She wouldn't meet my eyes at all, just looked at the table and sipped the beer, and finally said, "Trey, Tam's about to have a baby."

I stared at her for a long time, tried to say something, and had it come out sounding a lot like a pipe gurgling. I guessed right away what had happened, of course, and Shen confirmed it: "They think it'll come in a week or two."

"Did she—" I wanted to ask if she'd had any other lovers, and couldn't, but Shen caught what I was trying to say, and finally met my eyes. "Just you."

Of course I understood what kind of a mess Tam was in. If word ever got out that the baby was fathered by a ruinman's prentice, the old women in red hats would get together and quietly agree that Tam wasn't going to get into Circle no matter how many healthy babies she had, and there would be sixteen kinds of trouble for her from every side as well. So I swallowed and nodded, and promised I'd say nothing to anybody. Shen told me a few more things, none of which I remember now, and then scurried back to the gate with a promise that she'd come in two weeks if there was news.

Those were the longest two weeks I've ever had. When they were over, Shen showed up looking even more huddled and miserable than before. I met her outside the tavern, and was startled out of my skin when she looked up at me with red wet eyes and asked if we could go someplace private instead of the tavern. That pretty much meant one of the little rented rooms, so there we went. Since there was nowhere else to sit we sat down on the narrow little bed, and then all at once Shen burst into tears. I put an arm around her to comfort her, and she tensed for just a moment and then went limp against me, clinging to me while she cried.

It took a while before she could say much of anything, but finally she told me that Tam had had her baby, and it was a fine healthy little boy. So Tam was in Circle, paraded through the streets to the Circle hall with her mother and all the other women in the family beaming and laughing along with her. Whenever she mentioned Circle she started crying again, and I held her and stroked her hair and only then realized what she was trying not to say.

"You could follow her," I said.

She looked up at me then. In a whisper: "I've never had my blood come. And I've been trying to start a baby since before Tam."

So I held her and stroked her hair some more. I don't think either of us was expecting what happened next; still, we both had an empty place in our lives where Tam used to be, and as Plummer said to me more than once, human beings don't have to make sense. Still, when we were done, Shen kissed me and thanked me, and then got a little bag out from somewhere in the wet heap of her clothes.

"She wanted you to have this," she said. "She told me to tell you—to say that now you're going to have to be the one that sprouts wings and goes into the world."

I knew what it was before Shen was done talking, but of course I had to open the bag and look at the little yellow butterfly, and I did some crying of my own then. Still, I kept it, and that's why it's sitting on the table next to me right now.

Shen and I got together a couple more times after that, mostly because there wasn't anybody else either of us could confide in, and then she went to the priestesses and became a postulant. I think she'd hoped that I might give her a baby the way I'd given one to Tam, but that didn't happen, and with the door to Circle good and closed the priesshood was probably the best choice she had. I got a letter from her a few months later, when she'd been accepted at the mother house in Nashul, and another a year after that, when she'd been sent to her first posting up in Misota. She sounded happy in the letters; I hope she's still happy, wherever she is now.

I wonder if either of them, Tam or Shen, will ever hear about me and about how I found Star's Reach, and guess that the yellow metal butterfly came with me and is sitting here on the table beside me while I write. I wonder about the child I've got in Shanuga, who I'll never know and whose name I went out of my way not to learn; I can't think that Tam will ever be fool enough to let him know who fathered him, but I still think about him. And I wonder why I'm fool enough to sit here late at night, looking at a little butterfly of yellow metal, when I could be sleeping next to Eleen.

A few rooms away from me, there's a computer full of messages from some other world, and if I were looking at all this from some distant star I'm sure I wouldn't notice the three little lives that got tangled up together for a couple of years, and the fourth that got started as a result. Still, Plummer was right when he told me that human beings don't have to make sense.

CHAPTER 14

WHISPER FROM THE SKY

We were just finishing up breakfast this morning when something started howling down below in the belly of Star's Reach, like a machine doing its best to sound like an animal and not quite failing. Thu and I were both on our feet so fast that the chairs we were sitting on went clattering across the floor, and then a moment later Tashel Ban jumped up, sending a third chair flying, and ran for the computer. I followed him. Something I couldn't read was flashing across the screen when I got there; a moment later, as the others followed, Tashel Ban started pounding at the keyboard, and the howling suddenly stopped.

His fingers kept going at the keyboard for a while, and then he sat back and let out the little grunt that means he's got something fixed. "What was that about?" I asked.

He glanced back over his shoulder at me. "We're getting a message."

I heard Eleen draw in a quick sharp breath behind me, but it took me a moment to figure out what he meant. "From the aliens?"

"That's what it looks like." He tapped a few more keys, and the screen went blank for a moment, and then things started appearing on it, one letter or number at a time.

```
DATE RECD   03192471
512160734   212396027   883760386   957860278
679386673   028671846   671690739   126820368
387316713   698036416   290569348   949037662
486768902   689037693   602690736   235567987
690842093   093701746
```

It went on like that for a long time, starting at the top and then marching down the screen, while we all crowded around and watched, and didn't make a sound.

I've noticed that there's a difference, at least for me, between what I think is real and what I know is real, and sometimes something slides from one to the other fast enough that you can feel the world flowing around it, like water in a river around the hull of a ferry as it crosses from shore to shore. That happened the first time I went with Mister Garman and the other prentices to the ruins south of Shanuga, right at the beginning of my prenticeship, when the gray skeletons of the old buildings turned from dim shapes at a distance to real concrete and rusted metal that could make me rich if I was lucky or kill me if I got stupid. It happened the first time I was with a girl, and the afternoon not two years ago that I got to the top of the dune behind the beach by drowned Deesee, looked off across the blue rumpled sheet of the sea, and saw the Spire rising up out of the water, white and stark and only a few hours from its fall, though I didn't know that yet.

It happened, too, when we arrived at Star's Reach. We broke camp at first light and started up the road, knowing that if the maps and the records from the Sisnaddi archives were right we'd get to the site toward the end of that day. We were well into the desert by that time, with high thin clouds sweeping by overhead , flat gray sandy emptiness all around us, and the track of an old road leading us north of the old highway to the place we were going. When we got to what was left of an old metal fence, toward late afternoon, we all looked at each other, but there are plenty of old fences here and there in the desert and we all knew it.

When we got to the remains of the second fence, with barbed wire on top of it and a gatehouse for armed guards, I started to let myself wonder if we might have found the place. It was about a quarter hour later, though, when we got close enough to see the low blunt shapes of the antenna housings sticking up out of the sand like teeth, line on line of them off into the distance, and found a door half buried in sand in a hollow too regular to be Mam Gaia's work, that Star's Reach stopped being a dream and turned into a place, a real place, right in front of me.

And of course that's what happened, at least for me, as we stood there around the computer and watched the numbers march down the screen, as close as nobody's business to the pages and pages of numbers we'd found in the computer room on fourth level. I'd been thinking all along about people, alien people, out there somewhere on another world circling another star, but there was a mother of a lot of difference between that and actually seeing a message that some alien had sent to us, tapping it out with its claws or whatever on something that probably didn't look anything like a keyboard, and maybe looking up at the sky with six eyes and wondering what kind of weird creatures were listening in from the distant planet we call Mam Gaia. Even now, as I write this, the thought makes my head spin, and right there, trying to listen to a whisper from the sky that none of us could read yet, was like it must have been the day that people here on Mam Gaia's round belly figured out that the world wasn't safe and steady as they'd always thought, but whirled through space around the great burning fire of the sun.

The message went on for a while, and then stopped, and the computer printed out:

```
MESSAGE REPEATS—KEEP PRINTING? Y/N
```

Tashel Ban hit a key, and the words vanished; the numbers stayed there on the screen, like ghosts.

"Of course," Eleen said. "They'll have sent it multiple times so it gets through."

"I wonder how long it's been since the last one arrived," Tashel Ban said. "It shouldn't be too hard to find that out."

There wasn't much else to do but wonder, though, so while Eleen copied down the numbers in a notebook, Thu and I went back to the table and cleaned up the breakfast dishes. Later on, while Eleen kept doing something at the computer, Tashel Ban showed Berry and me his way of tracing cables: not just following the wires, but tracking the signal going through them with a device he had. It had earphones and a little box with dials on it, and let him hear the signal in any wire he could get the box up against.

The message from the aliens was still coming through, and so we were able to trace the signal down to the room full of machines on the eighth level, and then up again, all the way to first level and through the roof to the antennas. I knew, and so did Berry and Tashel Ban, that there wasn't anything to see, but we climbed the stair and went outside anyway. The sky above us was mostly clear, with long curling mare's tails of cloud drifting by high overhead. I watched them go past, and wondered what the alien out there who was trying to talk to us could see if it looked up at its sky.

We went back down, Tashel Ban got back to work, and since I had nothing useful to do, I took another book down from the shelf of old brown brittle books about aliens, and got to work on it with the resin. It was a lot like the first one, all about aliens coming to visit us in machines that looked like two plates stuck together edge to edge, and a lot of angry words about how the government was hiding it all from people. I thought about what Eleen had said about that, how it was all something the government cooked up to hide things they were doing, and wondered what it had been like for the people back in the old world who thought the aliens were right there over their heads but the presden and his jennels wouldn't admit it.

That kept me busy until dinner, and since Eleen and Tashel Ban went right back to work on the computer, I came back to the room Eleen and I are sharing and started writing. If we hadn't had a message from the aliens come through, I would have started right in on the story of how Berry and I spent our time at Melumi and then headed off to Troy. That's the next part of my story, but since we got the message from the aliens, it seems like something that happened to somebody else a long time ago, or something that happened to that six-eyed alien I imagined beneath its strange sky, tapping out a message to us with its claws and wondering about us the way we're wondering about it.

It was a couple of days after the rains started, back there at Melumi, that a messenger came from the library to tell us that they'd found a cubicle for us and we could start reading about Star's Reach. If it hadn't been right after the beginning of the rains, I'd probably have spent the time before the messenger came pacing around the dorm at Melumi and making life miserable for Berry, but I had one mother of a hangover to get through, and it did a fair job of keeping my mind off Star's Reach for a little while. Still, by the time the messenger came, I was eager to start, and Berry and I went splashing across the brick square at the center of the Versty just as soon as we could.

The messenger led us in through the big double doors of the library and told us to wait there in the big empty room just inside. Before we could ask much of anything she was gone through one of the little doors on the far wall, and so Berry and I stood there and waited, steam rising from us in the warm damp air, looking up at the windows to either side. I don't know what they were made of. They looked like somebody had taken pieces of colored glass or something and fit them together into a picture, all red and yellow and green and blue with clear bits here and there to set the other colors off. It was really something to look at, and so that's what we did.

Click of the door told me that somebody had come for us. I turned, and saw Eleen standing there. I'd been wondering, since the hangover stopped making thinking hard, just how she'd react when we next met, after the way we spent the first day of the rains. I guessed that she would look embarrassed but say nothing about what happened. I was right, too; her skin was light enough that you could see the blush, but all she said was, "If you'll follow me."

So we followed her, through the door and down a long hallway lined with doors and finally to a big room lit with watery light from tall windows along one side. The wall under the windows was divided up by short walls that jutted out a little way into the room, and between each pair of walls was a table and a couple of chairs. On the other side of the room from the tables and chairs was a long counter, and beyond that was the library itself, shelves and shelves and shelves full of more books than I'd ever imagined in one place.

Eleen led us to the cubicle third from the far end, and waved us to the chairs. "This is yours," she said. "When you're ready for books, go to the counter and ask the librarians; they'll get them for you. I've talked to them about what you're looking for, so they should have something ready."

"Thank you!" I said. She smiled and nodded, and turned to go.

"Good luck finding that acronym," Berry said then.

That got him a startled look over her shoulder. "Thank you," she said, and left the room.

We went to the counter right away, and one of the librarians, a plump old woman with glasses so thick they made her eyes look huge, came over. "You're the ruinmen looking for Star's Reach," she said, as though it wasn't a question she needed to ask.

"Yes."

"Ah. Just a moment." She went over to another part of the counter, reached underneath it, and pulled out close to a dozen books in a teetering stack. Berry and I both thanked her, took the stack back to the cubicle, sat down, stared at each other for a long moment, and then started looking at the books.

We figured out right away that Eleen hadn't made things easy for us. I wanted to read about Star's Reach, and so she had the librarians find books that had something to say about Star's Reach, but what they had to say wasn't in any particular order and a lot of the words were longer than I was used to reading back then. After a bit, Berry whispered a suggestion and I nodded, and he went to the counter, talked to the librarian for a bit, and then left the room and came back maybe a quarter hour later with a couple of notebooks and pens. We spent the rest of the day copying out everything we could find on Star's Reach into those notebooks; the light through the windows got too faint to read before we were done, and so we gave the books back to the librarian and did what we could to keep the notebooks dry while we crossed the brick square to the guests' dorm in time for dinner. Afterwards, back in our room, the two of us went over what we'd found, Berry helped with the words I didn't know, and we tried to figure out anything we could about Star's Reach.

That's how we spent the next day, and the day after that, and pretty much all the days we were in Melumi while the rain pounded down and life did what life in Meriga usually does during the rains, which is to say, not very much. Now and then there were breaks in the routine, when Jennel Cobey had us come up to his room and tell him what we'd found so far, or when the library was closed for some Versty function and nobody but the scholars went there, but the rest of the time, Berry and I were copying things out of old books in the daytime and trying to figure out what it all meant at night.

By the time the clouds started to thin and the rain went from pouring down every single day to skipping a day now and then, we'd filled a couple of notebooks each, but I don't think either of us knew much more than we did when we started. I won't say that it was wasted time; the librarians found us a couple of books about how people in the old world went looking for life on other worlds, which were at least interesting, and they also brought us any number of things written by scholars at Melumi who read every scrap of paper left from the old world that mentioned Star's Reach or anything like it, and that saved us a bunch of searching but didn't tell us anything we didn't already know.

Everyone pretty much agreed that if the Star's Reach project actually existed, which nobody knew for certain, it started out using the big radio telescope in the hills between Meriga and Jinya, the one the letter I found called NRAO, and the people who were trying to figure out what the aliens were saying were at the place near Orrij in Tenisi the letter also mentioned. Most of the scholars insisted that the whole thing had been shut down when the Second Civil War broke out, or maybe when all the ice on Greenlun slid off into the sea and Deesee and the other cities of the coast went under water; some of them thought that all the people and equipment might have gone somewhere else, but they didn't have the least idea where.

One evening toward the end of our stay in Melumi, Berry and I got to the end of a couple of hours of trying to make some kind of sense of the latest things we'd copied, and both realized at right around the same moment that we hadn't gotten anywhere. I got up and went to the window. The clouds were breaking apart off to the west, and stray beams of orange sunlight were slanting down over the Versty and the town off past it, reminding me that we didn't have that much longer before we'd have to choose a direction to go. Berry stayed at the table, propping his chin in his hands.

"I hope she finds something about WRTF," he said after a long moment.

I turned around. "So do I." Then: "If she doesn't, we can go to Orrij and the radio telescope place, and see if the records have anything."

It was a long shot, and we both knew it. The jennel and the scholars who went to Orrij looking for Star's Reach, back when I was a first year prentice, weren't the first people to go searching through what's left there. The ruins near Orrij had been stripped of salvage not long after the old world ended, and though there were some papers and other things there for scholars and the like, there wasn't much. As for the NRAO, it was right in the middle of the fighting in a couple of campaigns in one of the civil wars, I forget which, and ruinmen had been there, too, long before I was born. There might still be something about WRTF in one place or the other, but more likely there'd be nothing at all.

Still, Berry nodded. "Worth a try, Mister Trey."

I think it was two days later that we got something better, and it wasn't in anything the librarians brought us. Berry and I were in our cubicle as usual; the only sounds in the whole library, it seemed just then, were the rain drumming on the windows above us, the scratch of pens on paper, and every so often a rustle and tap as one of us handed a book to the other and tapped a finger on a passage worth a second look. That's why I noticed, long before anybody came into sight, footsteps in the corridor coming toward us fast.

It was Eleen. She caught sight of us, and motioned for us to come with her. A few minutes later all three of us were in one of the little rooms off the corridor, and she was handing me a small piece of paper. On it were these words:

```
White River Transport Facility
```

I realized what the words meant before I'd even finished reading them. "You found it."

"Maybe," she said. "I know where it is, too, or nearly. There was a White River in most of the old states, but this one's in Mishga, the old state of Michigan, near Muskegon—that's Skeega nowadays."

I nodded, and tried to stay calm while I wrote down the name of the town in my notebook. "Somewhere near Skeega."

"That's what the book said." She drew in an uneven breath. "We're not quite finished searching, but this is the only WRTF that's been found so far."

I thanked her, and she nodded and left the little room. Neither Berry nor I had any patience left for the books then; we went back to the guest's dorm, across a brick square that was only a little wet with drizzle, and went straight to our room to talk. Jennel Cobey would hear the news soon enough; until then, this was ruinmen's business.

"Transport facility," Berry said as soon as the door was shut.

"Meaning they may have gone somewhere else from there."

"That's my thought. I hope there are records."

I grinned. "Best in the world. Skeega's right across Mishga from Troy." Berry's eyes went wide, as I expected, and before he could say anything I went on: "So we'll have to stop at Troy on the way."

He let out a whoop, and at his age I would have done the same thing. Troy's where the ruinmen started, and if there's a ruinman in Meriga who hasn't been there and doesn't want to go, I'll eat my boots for breakfast. Back five hundred years or so it was a big city full of factories and towers, but even before the old world ended it fell on hard times, most of the people left, and most of the factories and towers and houses and all fell into ruin. The story has it that people started making their livings by stripping the ruins for raw materials and selling them, and as time went on and the people who were doing that figured out that they'd all be better off if they worked together, the first ruinmen's guild got started. All but one of the ruins in Troy were stripped down to bare ground so long ago nobody alive remembers it, and there are only a few ruinmen there now, but the guild hall is still there and they've got records of most of the digs in Mishga and the parts of Meriga that are close by. Melumi is where the scholars and most of the other people in Meriga keep their memories, but Troy is where we keep ours.

Now of course Berry and I both knew that our chances of finding out where the people in the Star's Reach project went from Skeega weren't that much better than our chances of figuring out the same thing by digging through the records in Orrij and NRAO, but at least we had another chance at it, and the chance to visit Troy into the bargain. The watery sunlight that came in through the window now and then, reminding us both of the approaching end of the rains, seemed much more promising than it had a few days before, and I began to hope—well, not that I would actually find Star's Reach, but that the search wouldn't come to a dead halt quite as soon as I thought. There was a much longer and stranger road ahead of me than I had any idea just then, but of course I didn't know that yet.

Over the next couple of days there at Melumi, as the rains finally stopped and the sun got a chance at last to take a good look down through the clouds and find out what had gotten itself washed away this time, it didn't feel like a long strange road ahead at all; it felt as though Star's Reach was right around the next corner. Berry and I still went over to the library most days, since there wasn't much else for us to do until the roads dried out enough to be fit for travel, but I'm pretty sure he spent a lot of time staring past the books and thinking about Troy, Skeega, and the transport base we hoped to find there, and I know I did.

We spent a couple of evenings with Jennel Cobey talking over what we'd found and what our plans were. He'd mentioned early on that he and his men would be riding to Sisnaddi as soon as the roads allowed, because of something political, but he wanted to know everything we'd found out about the base near Skeega. I told him, too; that was part of our Dell's bargain, and I guessed—and guessed right, as it turned out—that he was going to toss some money our way to make the trip easier.

Finally we had two weeks of clear weather, and one of the jennel's riders came galloping back to the Versty late one afternoon to say that the roads were open and people were starting to move again. Berry and I had dinner with the jennel that evening, since we both planned on leaving first thing in the morning and of course we'd be taking different roads. "This is all very promising," Cobey said as we finished up the meal. "I know it may turn out to be a dead end, but if you find anything..."

"We'll let you know soonest, Sir and Jennel," I said.

"Thank you, Sir and Mister." The titles had become a bit of a running joke between us. He leaned back in his chair, glanced from me to Berry and back again. "I wish I could come with you. Digging for clues to Star's Reach sounds a great deal more useful just now than tackling another round of political nonsense, but..." He shrugged. "Unfortunately, it can't be helped." Then, to one of his servants: "Creel, this glass is getting empty. You'll fix that, I trust."

By the time Berry and I got downstairs to our room in the guest's dorm, quite a few empty glasses had gotten filled, and I was a bit less steady on my feet than I like. Still, we had packing to do, and got to work trying to fit too much gear and clothes into a couple of packs that didn't have room for it all. We'd been at it for maybe half an hour, and I was starting to wonder if clothes breed when they're left in a chest for too long, when somebody knocked at the door.

It was a messenger from the Versty, the same thin scared-looking girl who'd come to bring us to the library when Eleen finished with the dead man's letter, back before the rains began. "Mister Trey," she said with a nervous little curtsey, "if you'll come with me. They've found something."

That startled me. I turned to Berry and said, "I'll be back as quick as I can."

He looked as surprised as I probably did, but nodded and said, "I can finish up here, Mister Trey."

So I followed the messenger down the stairs, across the brick courtyard, and into the library. That late in the evening, it was dark inside, with an electric light here and there glowing pale the way fireflies do before night finishes settling in. One of the little rooms off the corridor had the door half open and a light on inside, and that's where the messenger took me; it was empty when I got there, but not much more than a minute after the messenger left me there, the door swung wide again and Eleen came in.

"You're leaving tomorrow," she said: a question, though it didn't sound like one.

I nodded. "That's the plan."

"Then we were doubly lucky. One of the scholars happened across a stack of old government records from just before the end of the old world, and there was a reference in it." She handed me a slip of paper. This is what it said:

```
Walnut Ridge Telecommunications Facility
```

"It's west of Memfis," she said, "in Arksa." Then: "The records we found mention radio gear, a lot of it, being shipped there about two years before the date on the letter."

I stared at her. "Radio gear. So that might be Star's Reach."

"It might, or it might not. But I thought you'd want to know."

I glanced down at the slip of paper again, trying to fit a second WRTF into the plans Berry and I had made. "Yes. And thank you. You've been a good bit of help in all this, and I'm starting to think we may actually find the thing."

She smiled, then all at once startled the hay out of me by throwing her arms around me and kissing me good and hard. "That was for luck," she said then, "and this—" She kissed me again.

If she'd stayed up close against me much longer I might have tried to take things a good bit further than a kiss, but she pulled away then, and hurried out of the room without saying another word. I listened to her footsteps as they whispered down the corridor into silence, then looked at the slip of paper one more time, and walked slowly out of the library.

The stars were coming out as I crossed the brick courtyard, and I wondered if someday I'd have the chance to hear whatever it was that someone out there among them was trying to say to us. That's happened now, and Eleen and Tashel Ban are trying to figure out if there's a way to turn the rows of numbers into whatever the aliens are trying to say with them. I wonder how many more things that I never expected to see might just end up becoming real before we leave Star's Reach.

CHAPTER 15

THE VIEW FROM TROY TOWER

Berry and I talked things over that night and decided to go on to Troy and Skeega first anyway, since we were closer, and for all we knew there was just as much chance of finding the way to Star's Reach there as in Arksa. The next morning, we opened our eyes about the time the stars were shutting theirs, shouldered our packs, and headed north out of Melumi about the time the sun came up. We'd said our goodbyes the night before and didn't have a bill to pay at the guest dorm, so there wasn't anything between us and Troy but a long walk.

We had a fair bit of money this time, though, partly from what Gray Garman gave me back in Shanuga that I hadn't had to spend yet, and partly from a plump little sack of coins Jennel Cobey had one of his people run down to us before we left. Since the letter was safe in the jennel's hands and the copy was safe in Melumi, I figured nobody would be following us and we didn't need to run and hide the way we'd done on the road north from Shanuga. I was wrong, but I didn't know that yet, and so we went by the main road north to Naplis and then northeast by Fowain and Leedo to Troy. Most nights we stayed at taverns or farmhouses that put out a sign to let travelers know they could get a bed and a breakfast, and there are ruinmen's guild halls at Naplis, Fowain and Leedo, so all in all we had an easy time of it.

We also had a chance to see a bit of the fellowship you get on the main roads all over Meriga, which we missed on the backroads we'd used to get to Melumi in the first place. There are plenty of people who live on the road. More than half the people in Meriga are farm folk who hardly ever go more than a few kloms from where they were born, and most of the rest work in crafts that don't cover a lot more ground than that, but Plummer told me once that maybe one person in twenty makes a living by traveling, and most of them take to the road just as soon as the mud isn't too bad and stay on it until the rains come down. Before we'd gone more than a day or two, certainly, we had plenty of company on the road—farmers and traders with oxcarts loaded with goods, pilgrims on their way to one or another of the famous shrines, messengers on horseback with ribbons tied around their right arms to show which jennel or cunnel they served, players with their instruments and actors with their costumes and props on the way from one town to another, drifters and grifters and people who had no particular reason to be on the road but just couldn't stand the thought of staying put one more day.

For all that they're on the road for every reason you can think of and some you probably can't, travelers on the main roads more often than not treat each other like ruinmen treat each other, which is to say, pretty well. Oh, there are exceptions now and then, but if an oxcart gets a wheel stuck in the mud you can bet that anybody who's nearby will come help give it a shove. If the sun goes down and there isn't an inn or a farmhouse in sight, in the same way, whoever finds a good place to camp first builds a fire and waves to anyone else nearby to come on over, and before long there'll be twenty or thirty people sharing whatever food or drink they happen to have with them, and keeping watch by turns through the night.

Not that there's much to worry about on the roads nowadays. There are plenty of stories about the bad times after the Third Civil War, when gangs of soldiers who got turned loose after the fighting used to wait near the roads and kill anyone they could catch, but one of the presdens in my great-grandfathers' time, I think it was, made it her job to hunt them all down. There were troops of cavalry galloping all over Meriga until the roads were safe again. These days the worst thing that's likely to happen to you is getting cheated by a dishonest innkeeper or beaten up in a tavern fight. There are some pretty doubtful characters on the roads, people you wouldn't want to trust around your henhouse or your pretty daughter, but I only saw one time that somebody on the road stole something from somebody else who was traveling, and the thief got stripped naked and tossed into a patch of poison ivy for his pains. That was a couple of years later, though, and halfway across Meriga.

From Melumi to Naplis, Berry and I mostly walked alongside farm carts hauling grain from last season's harvest to the Naplis grain markets, and the farmers were good honest folk, about as likely to steal something as they were to sprout wings. After Naplis, we got onto the main road from Sanloo up to Troy and the Genda border, and that meant a livelier crowd, but I can't say they were less honest, and they were a good bit more friendly. Farm folk are no more comfortable around ruinmen than most people are, but plenty of road folk get the same treatment, and to them, ruinmen are just like anyone else.

A day out of Naplis, we ended up walking with an elwus named Cash and his motor, a quick little man named Morey. Cash was a quiet, lanky sort with mud-colored hair, though you wouldn't know that when he put on his white elwus costume and his black wig and glasses and went up on stage, wiggling and singing songs and cracking jokes in that funny voice all the elwuses use. Berry and I got to see his act maybe twenty times, since that's about how many farm towns we went through between Naplis and Leedo, and putting on a show at every farm town is how elwuses make a living.

Cash was good, better than most of the elwuses we used to see in the Tenisi hill country where I grew up. He'd dance around and make like he was singing into the short black stick elwuses carry in one hand while Morey pedaled away at the mechanical box that played the music. Cash would always finish the show by saying, "And Ah'd like to thank Morey, mah motor," and Morey would always say "Pro-motor," drawing out the "pro." I think it was a joke of theirs, though I never did learn the point of it.

They were good company on the road; they knew which inns were honest and which farmhouses had the best breakfasts, and you knew you could trust them. After a drink or two, Cash used to tell stories about his travels, and Berry and I would tell ruinmen's stories, and Morey would sit back and sip his whiskey and say nothing at all. They were Old Believers, the first two I'd ever met; I never did learn why they didn't stay in one of the villages or the cramped little quarters in cities where most Old Believers live, but they both wore the Old Believer sign around their necks, like a letter T with a line going up a bit from the middle of the top. They went off by themselves to talk to their god for a little while each morning, and Berry and I knew better than to wish blessings on their dreams.

Now and then as we walked together, we'd fall in with a bunch of players or actors who were going from farm town to farm town the way Cash and Morey were, though the next morning either they'd take a different route or we would. It happened once, at a little town called Poyen about halfway between Fowain and Leedo, that we arrived by one road just as a bunch of players showed up by another. It turned out they knew a bunch of elwus-tunes, so for once Cash got to do his singing and dancing with a band and a couple of other singers to back him, and it was quite a show. The farm folk loved it, and tossed a lot more money into Morey's hat than usual, but split two ways it wasn't as much as Cash or the players would have made on their own, so the next morning they left on their road and we left on ours, and it was back to Morey and the mechanical box.

When we got to Leedo, though, their road led east along the lakeshore and ours led north to Troy, so we said our goodbyes. I hated to see them go, but the way things turned out, it was probably just as well.

North of Leedo the main road runs a ways inland from the lakeshore, past farms and little towns with big magnolia trees growing here and there. Berry and I got to a town one afternoon fairly late, and were just starting to talk about finding someplace there to stay the night, when we came up to a crowd around the town hall. Somebody turned and looked at us, and called out, "Hey! A ruinman!"

The whole crowd went silent and turned to look at us. For a moment I was wondering whether Berry and I were going to have to dodge a riot, but nobody moved. Then somebody went into the town hall, and somebody else came out of it. The crowd let him past, and he walked right up to us: a soldier with a ribbon on his sleeve. "Sir and Mister?" he said. "Cunnel Darr wants to talk to you."

We followed him through the crowd and into the town hall, which was big and plain and echoed like the inside of a drum. It took a bit for my eyes to get used to the dim light, and so I ended up bowing to somebody I couldn't see while the soldier said, "Sir and Cunnel."

"Good," said the cunnel. I straightened up from the bow, and more or less saw him, a gray hard-faced man in green clothing. "Your name, ruinman?"

"Trey sunna Gwen, Sir and Cunnel," I told him. "Mister of the Shanuga ruinmen's guild."

One of the old man's eyebrows went up. "Well." Then: "You've come at a useful time. This man—" He motioned to one side with his head. "—was caught drilling a gas well."

"Sir and Cunnel!" shouted the man, who was bald and burly and had shackles on his hands and feet. "I swear to you it's not anything of the—" The cunnel moved one hand in a short sharp gesture, like a knife cutting meat, and one of the soldiers next to the shackled man cuffed him into silence.

"A gas well," the cunnel repeated, "or something that looks very much like one. I suppose you can tell one way or the other, ruinman."

Of course I could, and I said so. Toward the end of the old world, when people were trying anything they could think of to keep their machines running, underground gas was one of the things a lot of them tried. Some of it went into pipes that ran across the countryside, and it's a lucky ruinman who finds what's left of one of those, since the metal and the machinery are usually worth plenty. Some of it went into tanks on trucks, and those are worth finding, too, but some of it, especially toward the end, went straight from the ground into machinery in a building built right there on the spot. If the pipes are still there and the gas hasn't all leaked away, one of those can blow you from here to the other side of Mam Gaia's round belly if you get careless or just plain unlucky, so any ruinman with a brain in his head knows how to test for gas and how to deal with a gas well that's still got gas in it.

That's how Berry and I ended up following the cunnel and his soldiers, a priestess, the prisoner, and most of the people who were milling around the town hall when we got there, out of town a mile or so to a rundown barn not far from a glass-blower's shop at the end of a road. Inside the barn, next to a heap of gear of the sort you'd use to drill a well for water, an iron pipe with a heavy valve on the top of it stuck out of the ground.

The cunnel waved me over toward the pipe, and I nodded, got what I needed from my pack, and tested it. It's an easy thing if you know where the gas might be. There are little strips of paper the chemists make that turn blue if you get them wet and put them where there's gas, and I had a little bottle of the strips; I took one out, spat on it, used it to make sure the thing wasn't leaking gas with the valve closed, and then nudged the valve just a bit, to get the little faint hiss that tells you you're not far from risking your life. As soon as it hissed I tapped it shut, and by the time the hiss stopped the paper was bright blue.

"Sir and Cunnel," I said, "it's gas, all right."

"It was an accident!" the prisoner shouted then. "We didn't know we were going to hit gas. I was drilling for water—"

The cunnel gestured again, and a soldier cuffed the man across the face. "Of course," said the cunnel in a bored voice. "Everyone drills for water inside a barn, and then just happens to forget that a well that finds gas has to be reported to the local magistrate. On pain of death. You do know that, of course."

The prisoner fell to his knees. "Please, Sir and Cunnel, you must—"

Again the gesture and the cuff across the face. "Must," said the cunnel, "is not a word I am used to hearing." He turned to the crowd. "Does anyone have any doubt of his guilt?"

It wasn't a pointless question. If even one person had said yes the cunnel would have had to call up a jury on the spot and hold a trial; that's the law in Meriga; but nobody said a word. After a moment, the old man nodded once and said, "You know the penalty. Get some shovels, now." He turned to me then and said, "Thank you, ruinman."

It was as clear a dismissal as I've ever heard. "Sir and Cunnel," I said, bowing, and left the barn as quickly as I could, so fast that Berry had to trot to keep up. Behind me I could hear the shovels biting into the ground, the priestess chanting a litany, and the man sobbing as they dug a pit to bury him alive.

I heard the details later, after we got to Troy. The man was a glassblower, and one of his prentices had gone to the cunnel with word of the secret gas well. Maybe he was tired of paying for compost-gas, or maybe the farms in that part of Mishga don't have enough pigs and loms to keep a local digester fed with manure, and the man was having trouble getting enough gas for his work. The story I heard didn't say, but it was probably one or the other; it usually is when they catch someone in one of the crafts using fossil fuels, which happens somewhere in Meriga every few years or so.

Sometimes it's not for craft work, and the people involved have their own reasons, but those don't matter; if they get caught, they get buried alive. I know the reasons for that as well as anyone, but knowing it isn't the same thing as remembering the way the glassblower's voice sobbed and babbled as the scrape of the shovels and the slow patient drone of the litany marked the last minutes he'd ever have on the outside of Mam Gaia's round belly.

About the time we got far enough away that we couldn't hear any of those, Berry and I looked at each other, and decided that we weren't going to stay the night in that town after all. We kept walking until the sun went down, and just about the time we were about to start looking for a camping place, Berry spotted a bright flash through the pines up ahead. We hurried up the road by the day's last light and found a dozen travelers sitting around a fire and starting to share out dinner. They welcomed us cheerily enough, and we sat around the fire with a couple of traders up from Naplis and a troupe of actors who saw what was going on in the town we'd just passed and decided, sensibly enough, that there'd be no one interested in their play that day. We had a pleasant night and a good breakfast the next morning, and started toward Troy as soon as it was light enough to see the road.

It took us another day to get there. The road was busy; there's a ferry across from Genda at Troy, and a lot of trade crosses there, and so Berry and I had plenty of company on the way. The day was clear and cool, with a few stray clouds and a sharp wind blowing out of the west, and the road veered down slowly toward the water. Before long we got close enough to see the white sails of the lake schooners heading up to Troy or down to Leedo and the ports further east. From where we were, in among farm wagons and a herd of loms on their way to market, the thought of sitting on board a schooner and letting the wind do all the work was pleasant enough, but thinking that didn't keep us from making good time.

There's a place where the road to Troy tops a low hill, and I heard later that people who travel that road a good deal get used to travelers stopping dead in their tracks right at the crest. That's certainly what Berry and I did, at least until a lom bumped into me from behind and reminded me that getting out of the way was probably a good idea. I did, and so did Berry, and then we stood there for a long moment and stared at the distant gray shape, taller than anything else in Meriga, that jutted up above the trees off in the distance.

That was Troy Tower. It used to have another name, back in the old world, but I don't think even the ruinmen who tend it remember what that was. There used to be a couple of dozen like it, too, just in Troy, and dozens more in every city in Meriga, and the drowned cities of the coast used to be one of them right next to another for kloms on end, or that's what people say. Now there's just one of them, and it belongs to the ruinmen.

Troy is where the first ruinmen's guild got started, as I wrote a while back. All the other towers and factories and buildings in Troy and around it got stripped right down to bare dirt by those first ruinmen, but they left Troy Tower alone at first, and later on started using it as a guildhall and a place for records and the like. Nowadays there aren't many ruinmen there, just the few who keep the Tower standing and take care of what's in it, but as I wrote earlier, it's still a place that every ruinman wants to visit if he hasn't been there already.

Pilgrims come there all through the dry season, too. Troy Tower isn't a holy place, pretty much the opposite in fact, but the pilgrims come and look at it and say their prayers and plant a tree somewhere in the space where Troy used to be, back in the old world, before the ruinmen rooted every scrap of the city out of the ground. There's something in one of the priest-esses' litanies about how we water the trees with our tears, and some of the pilgrims do just that, though I don't know that it does the trees any more good than plain water.

The pilgrims haul plenty of that up from the shore, too. There are racks of wooden buckets down near the water north of the town, and all through the dry season, so I was told, you can pretty much count on seeing pilgrims: fetching buckets, filling them, and going around to water any young tree that doesn't look as though its roots got wet that day, murmuring a prayer for blessings or forgiveness or something all the while. How many of them get their prayers answered I'm not about to try to guess, but there are certainly a lot of healthy young trees around Troy, and that's something.

We certainly saw a lot of trees, at any rate, as Berry and I got moving again and followed the road right up to Troy. It's not a big city these days. Maybe a few thousand people live inside the walls, and there's maybe a hundred soldiers in the fort next to the ferry, which faces across the water toward the bigger Gendan fort on the other side. We didn't have any reason to go inside the walls, and so we turned off the road right outside the gate and found the path that went straight to Troy Tower.

From the hill on the road the Tower looks too big to be real. From right up underneath, it looks even bigger, but it's as real as a building can get, all gray and brown stone and windows, soaring up to bump against the bottom of the clouds. When we got there, Berry and I both stood there staring up for what seemed like a long time, and then walked up to the door at the foot of it.

There was a big archway there, and back in the old world there had been a row of doors beneath it, but most of them had been walled up, and the one that was still open was a plain wooden door with a little window in it, like the ones you'd find down at Troy town in buildings two stories tall and twenty years old. I almost laughed when I saw the door. Imagine a horse with an ant's feet or a jennel wearing the kind of straw hat poor farmers teach their children how to weave, and that's about how that little piece of our world looked, there at the foot of the old world's last big tower.

We knocked on the door and waited, wondering about the people wearing feathers who were carved into the stone here and there. After a little while, the door opened and an old man in ruinman's clothes looked out. He brightened up when he saw us, and after we'd given him the words and signs ruinmen use to test each other, he wanted to know all about who we were and where we'd come from. Once I said my name, of course, he knew exactly who we were and what we were there for, but we could have been on our way to crack concrete in Cago for all he seemed to care. His name was Jorey; he showed us around, introduced us to the dozen or so old ruinmen who lived there, and found us a room.

The guild hall and sleeping rooms were all on the first six floors, it turned out. The records were above that, and then above that it was empty all the way up to the top. At the top, Jorey said, there was a place where you could see everything for kloms around, and the elevator would get there if the wind turbines had charged the batteries enough. That sounded worth seeing, so after we'd stowed our gear in our room on the third floor and had a meal, I asked about the elevator.

It was the only one of a whole row of elevators that was still working. The wind had been blowing pretty well, Jorey told us, well enough that it would get the two of us to the top, but he wasn't prepared to bet on a third. So he showed us how the thing worked, and we went inside, pushed the button, and waited. A moment later the thing lurched and started up; Berry looked as calm as though he'd been standing on solid ground, and though I didn't feel half so confident—the jerks and rattles as the elevator climbed were enough to frighten anybody—I wasn't going to let on that I was nervous.

Finally, after I don't know how long, the elevator sighed to a stop and let us out. There was almost nothing on that level. The ruinmen had stripped away everything that wasn't actually holding the tower up to lighten the burden on the girders further down, so we stepped out onto a bare metal floor that boomed like a drum beneath our feet, and the only thing there, except for bare metal walls, was a stair going up. We went up, and came out into a little room of glass and iron beams at the very top of Troy.

From there, you could see just how huge the city used to be. Even though every other building was gone, the pattern of the old streets was still there, reaching out to the edge of sight in every direction but south, where the water broke the pattern. On the far side of the water was Genda, and the streets started right back up there too, wherever the Gendan town and fort didn't cover them. I stood there and tried to imagine what it had been like in the days when Troy Tower was just one of the towers at the center of town, and the Troy within the walls now was a little corner of town beside the water, next to a ferry that they probably didn't need in those days. The Shanuga ruins were big, or I'd thought so, and I'd climbed up on some of the tallest ruins still standing to get a look at them more than once, but Troy was bigger than big. Like the tower, it was so big it was hard for me to remember that it was real.

Troy was an important town in the old world. It wasn't as big as Cago, which is the biggest ruin above water anywhere in Meriga, or the drowned cities of the coast, which would be one big ruin reaching from halfway up Nuwinga all the way down to Deesee if the seas hadn't risen, but it's where the ancients built their cars, and built them by the million. There was even a war fought over it, or so I heard once from a storyteller in Ilanoy. An army from somewhere else in Meriga spent ten years trying to capture it, and they finally did, by some trick or other. The man who thought up the trick was called Dizzy, if I remember right, and after the war was over it took him ten more years to get back to his home in some town up in Nyork, I forget which one.

Later on, when we were digging in the wrong place in Arksa and spending the rains in Memfis, I heard some other stories about Dizzy. They said that he played one of the brass horns the players use down in Memfis and Sanloo, and that he was one of the best ever, right up there with another player called Sashmo. Some of the players knew tunes he'd come up with, and even though I don't know the first thing about that kind of music, I could tell they were good. I figure Dizzy must have been to Memfis before the war, and learned to play the horn there.

One time when Plummer and I were traveling together, I said something about Dizzy, and Plummer told me that there were two different people with the same name. Maybe so, but I still wonder sometimes. After spending so much time on the roads myself, walking alongside elwuses and traders and puppet-actors and all, it's just too easy to imagine Dizzy wandering the same way I did, stopping at every village to play his horn and catch coins in an old battered hat as he made his long slow way back home.

I didn't know about Dizzy yet when Berry and I stood there at the top of Troy Tower and watched afternoon turn to evening, and I don't know that I'd have thought of him if I had known. All I could think of was how big Troy used to be and how little it was now. Berry went around the room a bit at a time, leaning on the rail and staring outward with an expression on his face I couldn't read at all. Me, I just stared. I don't think either of us said five words to the other all the time we were up there, but finally the sun got close to setting and we looked at each other and decided to go back down. So we went down the stair to the little room with the metal floor and got onto the elevator, and it clanked and rattled downward and finally let us out on the fourth floor where we'd started. We had dinner with the other ruinmen, and made an early night of it.

The next morning we got up about the time the sun did, got some breakfast, and I asked Jorey about the records. "Skeega?" he said. "Yes, those'll be here. Every ruin that used to be in Mishga, plus most of the states all around. If there isn't a guild-hall any more, the records are here." He turned to one of the other old ruinmen. "Shor, where's the records from Skeega?"

"Ninth floor," said Shor, without even looking up from his breakfast. "Northeast part, over against the light well." I'd already learned that each floor in Troy Tower was shaped like a letter H, so the rooms in the middle could get some light and air, so I knew what he meant.

"Ninth floor," Jorey repeated. "You'll have some company there, I think. Isn't that fellow from Nuwinga working on that floor?"

"That's right," said Shor, and went back to work on his breakfast.

That had my curiosity up, no question. Nuwinga used to be part of Meriga back before the Second Civil War, and these days it's about as close as Meriga has to a friend among countries, but I'd never met anyone from there. Nuwingans are great sailors but they don't travel by land a lot, and Shanuga's kind of hard to reach by ship.

So I had more than one thing in mind as we trudged up the stairs to the ninth floor—it had to be the stairs, because the wind had died down overnight and there wasn't enough electricity to work the elevator. The ninth floor, it turned out, was about a dozen big rooms that were full of old metal cabinets, and the cabinets were full of papers and records and journals from something like three hundred years of digs all over one side of Mishga. We didn't have too much trouble finding the papers from Skeega, but when we found them it turned out they weren't arranged in any order we could figure out, just lined up in the cabinets, drawer after drawer and row after row of them.

There was a table and some chairs over against one wall, so we had a place to work, and I knew enough about how ruinmen keep their records that it wasn't too hard for me to sort out what was worth looking at from the rest, and show Berry how to do the same thing. That was about the only thing going for us that first day, though. If the man from Nuwinga was anywhere around, he didn't show himself or make a noise, and we went through more paper than I want to think about, looking for the letters WRTF or the words they might stand for, and finding nothing.

We stopped for lunch around noon, then went right back up and kept at it until the sun got low enough that we didn't have enough light to work by. The next morning we went up again, and settled in for another day of turning pages. Before long we were both so deep in the work that I don't think either of us heard the man from Nuwinga until he said, "I hope you won't mind an interruption."

Berry and I both looked up from the papers we were reading. He was standing by the door, a short stocky man in clothes that weren't quite the same as anything you'd usually see in Meriga, though it would take some telling to say just how. He had a square craggy face and big hands, and he talked about half as fast as people talk in Tenisi.

"Not a bit," I said. "What do you have in mind?"

"If you happen across something that has to do with radios, could you let me know? I'm in the room across the way."

Berry and I looked at each other, and then I said, "We'll do that. We're looking for something that has to do with radios ourselves, actually. I'm Trey sunna Gwen."

The man gave me a blank, owlish look for a moment, and then his eyebrows went up. "You'd be the ruinman who found the letter about Star's Reach."

"That's the one."

He thought about that, then: "We should talk about that some evening. There's not much about radios that I don't know. The name's Tashel Ban, by the way." Then: "Well, we all have work to do." He turned and went out the door.

That's how I met Tashel Ban. I didn't know a thing about him other than what he'd said, of course, and it hadn't yet occurred to me that it would take more than a ruinman's skills to make sense of Star's Reach if we found it. If somebody had told me that a few years after that I'd be standing inside Star's Reach next to him, watching him talk a computer into turning a bunch of gibberish into a note that someone here wrote for someone else more than a hundred years ago, I'd have been surprised. If that same someone had told me that the person standing next to me as I watched him tap at the keyboard would be Eleen, the scholar from Melumi I'd bedded half by accident when the rains came, I'd have been startled. If I'd been told that the other people in the room, other than Berry, were the last king of Yami and the last living person born at Star's Reach, well, my mouth would have been open wide enough to catch rabbits, and let's not even talk about what I didn't know about Berry yet. Of course that's the way it turned out, but we all had long journeys of our own to travel before any of that happened.

CHAPTER 16

ON GASOLINE OCEANS

We did it. Well, to be fair, Eleen and Tashel Ban were the ones who did it, they were following a trail marked out by the people here at Star's Reach before us, and what they did mostly depended on some others a very long way away from here who might or might not be people at all; but the thing is, it's done.

I was hauling paper up from a storeroom on the seventh level when it happened. The paper's in big metal bins down there, and you have to open a bin and then go into another room for a while until the inside of the bin airs out; the bins were pumped full of nitrogen to keep the paper from turning brown, and you can pass out if you breathe too much of it all at once. So I came trudging up the stair to the big room where the one working computer is, expecting nothing much, and found everyone clustered around the screen with the kind of look on their faces you see when people are watching somebody getting born or getting reborn.

I put down the paper and went over, and they made room for me. This is what I saw:

```
second planet of the system, about .71 AU from
the star. The planetary mass is 1.3 times
that of Earth, and so Tau Ceti II has both a
```

> higher temperature and higher gravity than
> our world. We are still trying to interpret
> the Cetans' description of the composition
> of their atmosphere, but the most plau-
> sible theory is that it consists mostly
> of methane and hydrogen sulfide, with more
> complex hydrocarbons and noble gases making
> up the rest. Most of Tau Ceti II's surface
> is apparently covered by oceans of liq-
> uid hydrocarbons, scattered with low-lying
> island chains, on which the intelligent
> phase of the Cetan population

I don't know how much time passed before I managed to say, "You found it."

Eleen glanced back over her shoulder at me, beaming. "Yes. This is everything they'd been able to figure out about the aliens by 2240—more than two hundred years ago."

"I think," said Tashel Ban, who was sitting at the keyboard, "that there are other briefing papers, some older, maybe some more recent. The note we found earlier was from 2109 in the old calendar, and there was a briefing paper then, too."

"I wonder what they meant by 'the intelligent phase of the Cetan population,'" Berry said then. His eyes hadn't left the screen for a moment.

"Let's find out," Tashel Ban said, and tapped the key that made the text scroll down.

While it scrolled down, all of me that wasn't struggling with unfamiliar words was caught up imagining a place that nei- ther I nor any other human being is ever going to see, a place with oceans of gasoline and orange skies that smell like rotten eggs, where living things that look like sheets of old world plastic slither over each other in the shallows and now and again crawl up onto the land, bunch together with a couple of hundred others, and turn into a creature with a mind that can send a radio message to us. That's what the Cetans are like, or so the paper said, and it said something else I'm sure I remember right: they have just as much trouble making sense of us and our world as we have understanding them and theirs.

We went through the whole briefing paper a screen at a time, came to the end, and then stood there, stunned, for a long moment. Finally Tashel Ban pushed his chair back from the keyboard, turned to face Thu, and said, "Does anything in here go beyond our agreement?"

Thu considered, and shook his head once. "Nothing."

"Does anyone object if I print out a copy for each of us?"

No one did, and he nodded and went to try to talk the one printer they've managed to get working into making six copies of the paper without jamming.

I haven't mentioned the agreement between Thu and Tashel Ban yet, mostly because that part of my story doesn't come until much later. That happened in Sanloo, where all of us— well, all of us but Anna, who we didn't know about yet—were waiting for Jennel Cobey. We rented rooms in a cheap tavern near the riverfront, one of those rattletrap places that look as though they'd been crammed into not enough space between a couple of other buildings. We had a little common room, some sleeping rooms that were even smaller, three blurry windows that looked out at another tavern across the street, and a single lamp. For most of two weeks that's where we were, with three meals a day you could more or less risk eating, and nerves stretched to the breaking point whenever we thought about what we were about to try to do.

We didn't have anything to do but wait and make plans, we did a lot of talking about what might or might not be at Star's Reach, and Thu and Tashel Ban ended up over and over again on opposite sides of the same quarrel. Tashel Ban thinks that people might be able to have some of what they had in the old world again, without hurting Mam Gaia in the process. Thu is sure that if people decide that they can do that, they'll turn out to be wrong, and damage Mam Gaia the way they did in the old world. They both think there might be something in the messages from the aliens that might make that happen, some secret to making the machines work without the oil and coal and gas the old world used to make them work, but they've got opposite ideas about what that would mean and what we ought to do if it turns out that way.

They were in the middle of one of those arguments, about a week before the jennel finally got there, and their voices and tempers were rising. Right in the middle of it I got out my pry bar and brought it down flat and hard on the middle of the ugly little iron table in the common room. Tashel Ban jumped at the sound; Thu stopped in the middle of a word, and just looked at me.

"You know," I said, "that's probably the tenth time you've both gotten angry about that, when it's still empty breath. I want the two of you to agree right now not to bring it up again until—" I held up one finger. "—we get to Star's Reach, if we do—" I held up a second finger. "—and we find the messages from the aliens, if we do—" I held up a third finger. "—and we figure out how to read them, if we can—" A fourth finger. "—and there's something about technology in them, if there is. If either of you can't agree to that, there's the door."

I could get away with that because the papers I'd signed with Jennel Cobey for the contract dig were in my name alone, and either one of them might have tried to push back against me but they weren't fool enough to try that with a jennel. After a moment, Thu said, "And if all those things happen, what then?"

I'd already thought of that. "Then the two of you can settle it in the circle."

The room got about as quiet as an upstairs room in a tavern can get. That was partly because the two of them are probably pretty close to a match—Thu's faster but Tashel Ban's got very good training, on account of who his family is—partly because nobody was fool enough to think that it would stop at first blood if it went to the circle, and partly because it wasn't just their quarrel. Eleen was pretty much on Tashel Ban's side, and Berry was more or less on Thu's, and I was somewhere in the middle trying to decide between them. After what seemed like a long time, though, Tashel Ban glanced at Thu, sizing him up, and said, "I'll agree to that."

"I accept as well," Thu replied, with just a hint of a smile.

They've gotten to know each other quite a bit better since then, on the journey here and since then as well, and they've both been as careful as can be about the agreement. Still, I wonder what will happen if it turns out that the aliens sent us some bit of knowledge that could undo the end of the old world. The Cetans, I ought to call them, since that's the name the people who were here before us gave them. The Cetans have a name for themselves, but the briefing paper says they talk with magnetic fields instead of sounds and nobody was able to figure out anything about the bits of their own language they sent us, so I don't imagine I'll ever know what that name is. The Cetans seemingly can't figure out the first thing about our language either, if that helps any.

Tashel Ban is still printing out copies of the briefing paper as I write this. The printer has been jamming on almost every page, and I can hear him swearing even though he's two rooms away. I don't know most of the words; hot language in Nuwinga isn't the same as hot language in Meriga, even though their language otherwise is close enough to ours that you can catch the sense of it most times. I'd probably know more, except that I've never been to Nuwinga and Tashel Ban's usually more careful about his language than he's being tonight. I don't blame him. I imagine all of us want another look at the briefing paper, another glimpse of those gasoline oceans and plastic-sheet creatures, even if the best we can do is to stare at the words and try to picture something human minds aren't made to picture.

Last night, when I wrote down the part of my story where Berry and I got to Troy and met Tashel Ban, I expected to go straight on to the rest of what we did in Troy in the couple of weeks it took us to find out that there hadn't been a thing at Skeega that might lead us to Star's Reach. As I think of it now, though, we didn't do that much. Mostly, we dug through the old papers from the Skeega guild hall, which got torn down and sold for scrap a hundred and fifty years ago when the ruins on that side of Mishga had all been stripped right down to bare soil.

The one thing that happened that deserves a bit more describing was that we got to know Tashel Ban, at least a little. He'd suggested that we talk about Star's Reach, and I thought about it for a while and asked Berry for his thoughts, and decided to go ahead and discuss it, and see if anything would come of it. He was staying there at Troy Tower, the way we were; if you're not a ruinman you usually don't get to do that, but there are exceptions now and then, and people from other countries are one of them, if they're polite and have a good reason to be there.

No other country I've ever heard of has the same kind of ruinmen's guild we have in Meriga, though of course every other country has people who tear down ruins for the metal and other salvage. In Meyco it's the dons who do that, in Genda and Nuwinga it's the government, in the coastal allegiancies it's anybody who has a mind to try it, and if anybody knows how they do things over in the Neeonjin country it's news to me. I guessed, though, that Tashel Ban might be with the Nuwinga government, since they deal with ruinmen in Meriga now and again; I was wrong, but as it turned out, not too far wrong.

Anyway, Berry and I went to talk to him one night after dinner, when the old ruinmen were sipping chicory brew and talking among themselves about digs long before my time and places I'd never been. We came over to where he was sitting, and after a few words, he said something about a bottle of Genda whiskey up in his room, which was true enough but mostly a way to get us someplace private. That's how the three of us ended up sitting on salvaged chairs four floors up in Troy Tower as the sun went down, the fireflies came out, and a last line of pilgrims with lanterns cupped in their hands wove their way through the trees down below, headed off to the big shrine just outside Troy where they'd doubtless spend the night praying.

"That must have been something," Tashel Ban said. We'd been talking about the day I found the dead man's letter in the Shanuga ruins. "Whether or not it gets you to Star's Reach."

I nodded. "Whether or not. I'm certainly going to give it a try."

"All you can do." He leaned forward a little. "I'd be interested in hearing your plans, if you have any, about what you'll do if you manage it."

"I haven't made any yet," I admitted. "Figuring out if I can get there comes first."

"Fair enough." Then, after a long moment. "The thing is, it's more than just another ruin, or it might be. By the time it was built, the ancients were using nuclear power cores, and up to their ears in eye-oh-see planning."

"Eye-oh-see?"

"Interruption of continuity," he said, and that's when I realized he was spelling out letters. "That's the name they used for everything falling to bits, except they thought it would all come back together again later on. The plan was to have everything they thought was really important set up to survive IOC for a good long time. They had IOC facilities in Deesee and the other cities of the coast, though of course that didn't work out very well once the seas rose, and some others in allegiancy territory and other places where it didn't do them much good. Still, Star's Reach was probably planned and built the same way, which means it might not be a ruin."

"Four hundred years is a good long time," I said, and sipped at the whiskey.

"Granted. I don't mean there'll still be people there—but the machinery might still be working. It might still be possible to talk to other worlds, or at least to listen. And the radio gear itself—it's going to be so far beyond anything we've got nowadays that if it's taken apart, even if whoever buys it doesn't just sell it for scrap, it's a good question if anyone will ever be able to get it working again."

That was the first time it had ever occurred to me that there might be more at Star's Reach than cracked concrete and broken machines and maybe a few browned papers to tell us something about what the aliens were trying to say to us. I considered that for a long moment, until Berry broke the silence. "You said you were studying radios, Sir and Mister. Did you mean the kind at Star's Reach?"

He shook his head. "No, but I'd drop anything else for a look at those. And if they're anything short of scrap, you're going to need a master radioman to do much of anything with them, and that's what I am. You're familiar with those?"

"Not at all," I said.

He looked at me for a moment with that owlish look of his, then: "And of course you don't know me from the next fool off the street, either. Do you have time to hear a little story? It's my own, and it might make a bit more sense to you why you'd be better off having me with you if you ever find this thing, and why it matters that it might be more than a ruin."

"I've got plenty of time," I said, and looked at Berry, who just grinned. "Go ahead."

He took a good swallow from his whiskey glass. "To start with," he said, "it might help if I told you my right name is Dashiell Hammett Vandenberg, thirty-first of the name. Not that I go by that outside of Nuwinga, and only there with the right people, if you know what I mean."

Berry's eyebrows had gone way up at the name, and that and what little I'd heard about Nuwinga gave me a pretty good guess. I sipped whiskey and said, "Well enough to wonder what somebody with a name like that is doing digging up radio plans over here in Troy."

He smiled a little lopsided smile. "Three older brothers, and every one of them has pupped his own brats. I don't use that last word lightly." He laughed, and so did Berry and I. "I could have gone to sea, or I could have settled down on our estates near Ammers and done the gentleman farmer, or I could have gone up to Lebnan to mix with the politicians and drink myself to death like my uncle Raymun." A shrug. "None of those appealed much. So I went to Rutlen instead. That's where we have our Versty, the way you have yours down at Melumi."

This time it was my eyebrows that went up. "You're short a couple of things that you'd have to have to get into Melumi."

"True. In Rutlen, though, they let men in to study, if they're of good enough family and pay more than I want to think about."

I nodded and took another sip. Outside the window of the little room where we were sitting, the night was closing in.

"The thing is," said Tashel Ban, "the Vandenbergs have a habit of pupping oddities now and then. My great-great-aunt Aggie was a sea captain, one of the best, and sailors who wouldn't take ship if there was any other woman on board would kill for a berth on the *Flying Gull*—that was her ship."

"I've heard of it," said Berry.

That got him a glance. "A lot of people have. Broke up on the rocks on Genda's north coast long before I came along, though of course the family has another by the same name now. But Agatha was one of our oddities. We had another who crossed over to the Arab countries, took up their religion, and tried to bring it back with him." A little sharp shake of the man's head; I gathered that the project didn't go well. "We had another who took it in his head to go west to the Neeonjin country—I don't think anyone knows to this day what happened to him.

"And then there's me. I took an interest in radio, though that's not the sort of thing a gentleman's son does in Nuwinga. Here in Meriga, you've got a radioman's guild, as I recall."

I didn't know much about them, since that wasn't one of the guilds that has its guildhalls out with the ruinmen, the burners, and the other crafts nobody wants inside the walls. In Shanuga the radiomen's hall is right in the middle of town, tall and narrow like a rich family's house, and it's got a forest of antennas up above the roof so the radiomen can talk to people all over Meriga. Still, guilds are guilds; the radiomen have their misters and prentices, and they're just as closemouthed about their guild secrets as we are about ours.

I nodded, and Tashel Ban went on. "We don't in Nuwinga, or not quite. With us it's a government thing. You pass tests and get licenses; there are different tests and different licenses, and the top of them all is master radioman. Last I heard there are a hundred twenty-six people in Nuwinga who've passed that test, and I'm one of them." He sipped some whiskey. "And I passed it when I was fifteen years old."

"So you're good," I said.

"Yes, but that's not the point. What do you do when you've decided to put your life into radio work, and you get the thing most radiomen spend their lives trying to get before you're old enough to grow a beard?"

That interested me. "You tell me."

"I haven't the least idea what anybody else would do," Tashel Ban admitted. "Me, I decided that I was going to find out things that not even the master radiomen know, things that got lost when the old world went down. There's a lot that nobody knows about radio any more, and I don't just mean how they made chips—you know about those?"

I did. When you're stripping an old building that wasn't looted after the old world ended, you're likely to find electronics of one kind or another, computers or radios or other things that nobody even has a name for these days. Unless they were old when the old world ended, or made in the troubled years right before the fuel ran out and the seas rose, what's inside is mostly pieces of stiff plastic studded with little electronic things, and about half of them look like square black centipedes with lots of metal legs. Those are chips. Most of them don't work any more, and some of the ones that work are so complicated that not even the radiomen can figure out what to do with them, but if you get some that work you're in luck, because nobody can make them any more and the radiomen and a couple of other guilds will pay good money for them. "I've salvaged a fair number of them," I said.

"So I'd guess. But there were ways of doing things, back before chips were invented, that could probably be done today if anybody knew how. Not just vacuum tubes—we make those, and I think you make them here in Meriga too, though there again there are a lot of tricks that we still haven't figured out yet. There are layers up in the air that bounce radio waves back to the ground, and the ancients used to use those to talk to people on the other side of Mam Gaia; the layers aren't the same as they were in the old world, and nobody's sure why. We can get fair range these days, but if we could figure out how to do as well as the ancients did we could stay in touch with ships no matter how far away they sail; we could find out what's happening in places nobody from Nuwinga or Meriga have been for four hundred years—plenty of other things, too."

"I wonder, Sir and Mister," said Berry then, "if it might turn out better for everyone if some of those things stay lost."

Tashel Ban turned and gave him a good long look. "That's something I think about," he said. "Along with the other master radiomen. Where do you cross the line between the technologies that help people and don't hurt Mam Gaia, and the technologies that might lead us back down the road to the same mistakes the old world made? I don't know the answer. I do know that radio's a way to help people talk to each other when they can't get close enough for voices to carry, and getting people to talk is a good thing much more often than not. So I'm guessing that figuring out more ways for people to talk by radio isn't going to cross that line."

Maybe it was the whiskey, but my mind jumped all at once from there to the thing I was looking for. "And if we're talking about the distance between one star and another, do you think it's the same?"

Tashel Ban was silent for a while. "I think so," he said finally. "The same, and even more so. If it's true—if they actually did get radio messages from somebody living on a world around some other star, whether they figured out how to read the messages or not—just knowing that there's someone else out there, that we're not all alone in all of the universe, sitting here in the middle of a great big dead emptiness where nobody anywhere else will ever think a thought or follow a dream or figure out something about the way the universe works, that's something. And if there's anything more, there again, it's hard to think of a way that talking can hurt us."

He downed another swallow of the whiskey. "But I'd give anything you care to name to be there when Star's Reach gets found, if it does. It's been more than thirty years now since I passed my master radioman's test, and I've found a few things and learned a few things since then, but I'd like to do something on the grand scale, and helping find Star's Reach would count. If you'll have me, that is. I know this is a ruinman's thing, and it's also yours, if I hear right."

I nodded. "I'm not going to make any promises," I said, "but I'll keep that in mind."

He considered that, nodded. "Fair enough."

"The one thing I'm not sure of is how to find you, if it turns out all this leads anywhere."

He gave me one of his owlish looks again. "That's not hard. Get a letter to the Nuwingan embassy in Sisnaddi and they'll have it to me soon enough; they know where I am." Then, with another lopsided smile: "I mentioned my uncle Raymun, didn't I? The one who drank himself to death? He was presden of Nuwinga when he did most of the drinking. Our presdens don't all come from one family the way yours does, but the job doesn't stray too far, and I've had better than a dozen ancestors in the Gray House."

We talked for a while longer, though I don't remember about what, since I'd had a fair bit of Gendan whiskey by then, and then we stumbled back to our room—well, I stumbled, at least, since Berry hadn't had more than a few sips of the whiskey. When we got back to our room and the door was closed, I sat down on my bed and asked Berry, "What do you think of him?"

He was a prentice and I was a mister of the ruinmen's guild, but by then he didn't bother with the sir-and-mister business unless there was someone around who needed to be impressed by it, and I'd have laughed if he did it any other time. "I'm not sure," he said. "He's likable enough, and I think he can be trusted, but I'd worry about what would happen if there's a lot of the wrong kind of technology at Star's Reach. He might not just stand by while we scrapped it."

"If we get there," I reminded him.

He grinned. "If we get there. I have to keep telling myself that."

That night seems long ago and far away now, as I sit here in Star's Reach and write these words that maybe nobody will ever read, and look up now and again to see Eleen asleep in our bed, after another hard day trying to get an old computer to give us the secrets of a world so far away it takes light more than ten years to get here from there. Once Tashel Ban gets finished making the printouts, I know I won't just read mine once; I might just keep reading it over and over again, until the hazy orange skies and brown oceans and the Cetans themselves are as real to me as Mam Gaia and her human children on this side of the sky.

It rains gasoline on Tau Ceti II. The Cetans need to keep themselves from drying out, but they can't go back into the ocean without breaking up into the couple of hundred plastic-sheet things that are their ocean phase, so they build pools and channels to catch the rain so they can splash around in it most of the time. That's the first thing they ever built, they say, the way that huts to keep the rain off were the first thing humans ever built, and before then they lived in hollow places where the rain gathers the way we used to live in caves. When we were going over the briefing paper, I stopped at the bit where it talked about that, and just stared at the words for a long moment. It's a funny thing, that something that reminds me just how different we are from the Cetans makes me think of them as people like us.

We went from caves to huts to Troy Tower and Star's Reach. They went from hollows in the rock to pools and channels to—what? We don't know. The people here at Star's Reach two hundred years ago didn't know, though they'd seen something in one of the messages from Tau Ceti II that made them think the Cetans built something or other like our buildings. They certainly know how to build a radio as big as the one here at Star's Reach, which is no small job.

It's occurred to me now and again that they may be smarter than we are, enough smarter to have missed making the mistakes that sent the old world to its end. Mind you, it's also occurred to me now and again that they may be sitting in their pools of gasoline and wondering if we're smarter than they are, and missed some troubled time in their history that we probably can't even imagine. It's the kind of thing that I used to wonder about when I was younger, and used to stare up at the stars and think about what might be out there; it's almost frightening that now we're starting to find out.

CHAPTER 17

WHAT'S ALWAYS REAL

It's been close to a week now since I last wrote down any of my story, and there's a good reason for that. Sometime toward afternoon on the day after I wrote that last bit, Berry came around. I was in the room with the bookshelf, spraying resin on page after page of yet another alien-book, so I was glad for the interruption. "Tashel Ban and Eleen want everyone in the computer room," he said, and hurried on, so I got to my feet and went to see what it was.

"This isn't something I expected," Tashel Ban said once we were all there. "Though I'm not sure why I didn't. Once the people here and the Cetans worked out enough of the details about each other's senses, it was an obvious thing to do."

"What Tashel Ban is trying to say," Eleen broke in, "is that both sides spent around fifty years figuring out how to send pictures to each other—pictures of their world that we could see, and pictures of ours that they could—" She stopped, laughed. "We don't even have a word for it. Whatever replaces seeing for creatures that sense magnetic fields instead of light."

"The point, though," said Tashel Ban then, "is that both sides managed it."

The whole room got very quiet.

"We've got fifteen huge files—picture files—that came from a Cetan message," he went on. "We just have to find the program that will turn them into pictures."

"Pictures of Tau Ceti II." It probably ought to have been a question, but Thu didn't say it that way.

"Maybe pictures of Cetans," said Eleen, and everyone got quiet again.

So for the last week, that's what Tashel Ban and Eleen did, finding everything that might be a program, figuring out how to get it running, and then trying to use it on the picture files. I should say, the two of them and Berry; he's been helping them out with the computer work over the last month or so, since there hasn't been much else to do. The rest of us, me and Thu and Anna, agreed to take over the cooking and washing until they got the pictures done, and for a couple of days after that if we had to bully them into taking some time off. They ought to be looking for any sign of dangerous technologies, so we can settle the question that's kept us silent here while the food gets closer and closer to running short, but nobody argued the point; for a look at Tau Ceti II, I'll put up with a few more sparse meals, and I know I'm not the only one.

Still, cooking and cleaning don't take that much time, so I ended up back in the room with the alien-books. I made myself finish the one I was spraying when Berry came, but once it was dry and bundled up, pulling down another one and starting the whole thing over again was more than I could face. So I muttered some hot language, stared at the bookshelf for a while, and then walked over and took the last book off the top shelf. I'd left it for last, since it's about three fingers thick and all the paper's gone brown as Misipi water and frail as a bug's wing. What I didn't know until I cut the binding loose and went to work on it was that it wasn't an alien-book like the others; it was a story.

More exactly, it was a mother of a story, a mother with babies and then some. I forgot that I was supposed to be spraying the pages so many times that I finally just gave up and read the whole thing through to the end, then read it again when I went back through to spray the pages I hadn't done yet. Once I was done I showed it to Eleen, and her eyes went round; she'd heard of it, most scholars in her field have, but everybody thought all the copies had gotten lost around the time the old world ended. That happened to a fair number of books, and especially stories like this one. They were a kind of make-believe story set off in space, and not many people wanted to read that sort of thing when the old world was ending around them.

Nowadays I think a lot of people would like it. For all that it's set in space, you can just change some words here and there, and anybody in Meriga with the brains Mam Gaia gave geese would be able to figure out what's going on. The hero's the son of a jennel, or close enough that the difference doesn't matter, and there's a quarrel going back a long way between his father and one of the other jennels. So the other jennel, who's got the morals of a Jinya pirate, works up a plot to get the presden to send our hero and his father and mother and their servants off to the deserts out west—well, of course it's some other planet, but it might as well have been Cansiddi—where they can be ambushed and killed by the other jennel's men and the presden's soldiers. Our hero and his mother get away into the desert, though, and meet up with the desert tribes, and the story goes on from there. Of course the desert tribes here in Meriga ride horses instead of big worms, but it's a make-believe story and you've got to make allowances for that.

Eleen's reading it now. She probably ought to be sleeping instead, but in a little while she'll doze off over the book and then I'll get her tucked in and sleeping. I'd meant to write about how Berry and I left Troy and went to Skeega, and how we found out we were still being hunted, but just now my head is still too full of sandstorms and knife duels for that.

This afternoon I finished reading the story the second time through, got all the pages coated with resin front and back, and tied them up in a bundle once they were dry. All the alien-books I'd treated and read were back in the room where I'd found them, bundled and stacked in a spare box I'd found; so they'll be in good order when it's time to pack them for the trip to Melumi. I didn't put the story I'd just finished in the box, since Eleen wanted to read it, but I wandered into the room anyway and looked at the shelves full of books that were left, reading what I could off the spines. I thought I might be able to find another story, or at least something besides another alien-book. Before I got very far, though, I heard somebody moving in the hallway behind me, and looked back over my shoulder.

It was Anna. I said something friendly, I forget what, but she just looked at me for a long time, and then came a step or two into the room. "You've been preserving those," she said.

I nodded.

"Have you read any of them?"

"All I've treated so far." I gestured at the box.

"What do you think of them?"

I wasn't at all sure what to say to that, and her face gave me no clue; the wrinkles around her eyes might as well have been a mask. "I don't know what to think," I said finally.

She tilted her head and gave me one of her sidewise glances. "Good," she said. "That's a useful habit." Then, after a moment: "May I tell you a secret? You'll need to promise not to tell it to anyone else, though."

That was tempting enough that I nodded. "Ruinman's bond."

Anna smiled her thin tight smile. "The secret is this: those books are the reason Star's Reach is here. Well, part of the reason, but a very important part."

I thought about that for a moment. "Care to tell me what the reason is?"

Her smile tightened even more. "Keep reading, and you'll find it," she said. A moment later she was gone, and I heard her footsteps whisper away down the hall.

I stood there for a while, I could hear Tashel Ban pounding at the computer keyboard—he always sounds as though he's attacking the keys, where Eleen types soft and quick so you can hardly hear her at all—and someone, probably Berry, busy in the kitchen. I tried to pay attention to the book, but mostly I sat there and sprayed pages with resin and thought about Anna.

She was the last one to join us on the journey out to Star's Reach, and we didn't even know she existed until we got to Cansiddi. That seems like a long time ago now, though it wasn't much more than a month and a half.

We left Sanloo the day after Jennel Cobey and his man Banyon showed up, heading pretty close to due west on the army road from the Misipi to the Suri River. That road reminds you every step of the way that you're nearing the borders of the part of Meriga people can live in. You come up out of the Misipi valley where it's all green and full of trees, like most of Meriga is, and as you go the land gets dry. Day by day, as we walked west and the pack horses trudged along with us, the land dried out, the wind picked up, and the trees got further and further apart, with stretches of tall grass between them. It was as if we were walking back in time, going back to before the rains came rolling in and saved Meriga from the long drought.

Finally the trees go away for good, and then a while after that, you come to Cansiddi. There's a big fort there full of soldiers, since the desert tribes like to cross the Suri and go raiding for horses when they can, and the Meycans have outposts off to the southwest, far but not far enough. Other than the fort, the stores and taverns and harlots and all that cater to the soldiers, and some merchants who aren't supposed to trade with the desert tribes but do anyway, there's not much to Cansiddi. It's just gray walls and low brown buildings and dust and the Suri River itself, which is a mass of brown water and floating junk when the rains come and a long streak of mud and pools and mosquitoes the rest of the year. When I was reading about the town on that desert world in the story I mentioned, Cansiddi really did come to mind.

I'd have worried about getting through Cansiddi in one piece if we hadn't had a jennel with us. As it was, all the soldiers took one look at Jennel Cobey and jumped as though Tashel Ban had wired their whatnots to a battery and thrown the switch. We went to the fort and talked to the cunnel there—well, mostly the jennel talked—and then we rented rooms in one of the two decent places in town. Other than a visit to the ruinmen's guild hall Berry and I made the next day, we stayed right there at the tavern while Cobey's man Banyon made arrangements with the tribes so we could cross part of the desert and not get our throats cut. There we were, even more keyed up than we were in Sanloo, and one evening I went down to get a glass of whiskey from the bar when I heard something like an argument out by the front door.

Even though it was one of the two best places in town, they had fights in the bar pretty much every night we were there, and I don't mean people yelling at each other for a bit. They hauled a corpse out the first night we were there, after some soldiers got into it over a card game and were too drunk to take it to the circle the way they should have. So I didn't pay much attention to the voices I heard out front, until I got close enough to realize that it was one of the big toughs they keep to guard the door telling someone else that they weren't going to bother the jennel or the ruinman or any of those people. That meant us, and I was bored and curious enough to go over and see who it was.

I crossed the bar from the stair to a place where I thought I could see the front door without being spotted, ducking around the tables and a few puddles of beer the barmaids hadn't mopped up yet. About the time I got close enough to see that the other person was an old woman with a spray of white hair like feathers on the head of an eagle, though, she looked past the tough and in a voice I could have heard half a klom away said, "Ruinman, you're trying to get to Star's Reach. I was born there."

The tough stopped in the middle of a sentence, and then started laughing, a big rumbling good-natured laugh, the kind you don't expect to hear from somebody who makes his living knocking spare teeth out of unruly drunks. I walked over to the door, looked at her, and said, "Prove it."

"I can't, of course," she said. "But there are locks there that only open to a fingerprint." She held up one finger. "If they still work, they'll recognize this."

That caught my attention right away. The ancients had locks like that, and you find them in ruins now and again; of course there's no way to get them open except with a pry bar or a barrel of gunpowder, because whatever fingers were supposed to open them have been topsoil for more than four hundred years. The thing is, next to nobody outside the ruinmen's guild knows about them, the same way that next to nobody but ruinmen know about the kind of trap that almost killed me in the Shanuga ruins. She might have found out about them some other way, but it made her story a little less unbelievable than I thought it was at first.

The tough turned to me. "Sir and Mister," he said, "This woman, she's old Anna, who does laundry and sewing for some of the officers up at the fort. If she's from Star's Reach, I'm the presden's one and only virgin daughter."

That got me laughing, too. "Tell you what," I said. "Upstairs there's a scholar from Melumi who knows everything anybody knows about Star's Reach. If this Anna's lying, we'll know right away, and you can chuck her out the door once we chuck her down the stair." I turned to Anna, who looked at me with her head tilted just a little and a look on her face that might have meant anything. "And if you are lying, you probably want to turn right around and leave now."

"I'll gladly talk to your scholar," she said, without a bit of hesitation in her voice. The tough shrugged and stepped out of the way, I motioned with my head, and Anna and I crossed the bar and went up to our rooms.

Everybody was there in the common room we'd rented except Banyon, who was still out settling things with the tribespeople, and every eye in the place turned toward us the moment they realized there was somebody else with me. "This is Anna," I said by way of explanation. "She's made a pretty remarkable claim."

"What the ruinman means," she said at once, "is that I was born at Star's Reach. I hear you're trying to get there."

That got a moment's dead silence. Jennel Cobey glanced from me to Anna to Eleen and back to me; the others looked at each other; Eleen looked straight at Anna and said, "That's quite a remarkable claim. Would you care to say more about it?"

"My mother," said Anna, "was a linguistic analyst, and my father was a software engineer. Both of them were E-6 technical specialists."

Eleen's eyebrows went up, so I knew the words meant something. "And you?"

"I was five years old when we left. We and a few dozen others were the last ones alive; that's what my parents told me."

"Can you lead us there?" This from the jennel.

"I don't know," Anna said. "It was a long time ago." Then she explained about the fingerprint locks, and I explained that that was why I'd brought her up, and then everybody started talking at once, asking questions and then not waiting for the answers, until finally I held up both hands and we got down to some serious talk.

That was how Anna joined us. There was still a lot we didn't know about her then, and I think there's still a lot we don't know about her even now. Or maybe just one thing: she knows something we don't, or thinks she does, about Star's Reach, why it's here and why we're here. Maybe it's in the alien-books, but if it is, I haven't found it yet.

The thing that makes me wonder about that is that the alien-books are basically all the same. Start reading and before long you can count on finding something about aliens kidnapping people and doing things to them, or about a place called Roswell, or another place called Area 51, or—well, there are about a dozen things in all. It's always those same things, and how the government's trying to hide them, and sometime soon the government will fess up or the aliens will land and then we'll all know the truth. There's never anything about gasoline oceans and rotten-egg skies, or creatures with a free-swimming ocean phase and an intelligent communal phase on land, and nothing we've learned about the Cetans makes me think they fly around in spaceships shaped like dishes, or that they got off their world at all, the way a few of us did for a little while back before the old world ended.

I didn't particularly want to keep reading about those things, but I didn't have much else to do just then. I picked one of them and turned to go to the room Eleen and I share, and just then I heard Berry's voice off in the computer room; I couldn't tell what he said, but it was loud enough and excited enough that I got up and headed that way.

By the time I was halfway down the hall he came hurrying to find me. "Found it," he said. "The first picture's loading right now."

So we went and found Thu and Anna, and all four of us hurried back to the computer room and crowded around the screen. It was black when we first got there, with a little line of brownish orange along the top, but the line got wider a bit at a time as we watched, and shapes started to appear. After a while I realized that they were clouds, like Mam Gaia's clouds, but brown and orange and gold instead of white and gray and blue.

Bit by bit the whole screen filled with a picture: a rocky landscape with ocean off in the hazy distance. The ocean was brown except where it caught the light and shone red like fire;

some of the rocks were bluish and others were purplish. Most of them looked like rocks on Mam Gaia, except for the color, but in the front of the picture they were smooth, and there was a golden pool in the middle of the smooth place.

In front of the pool were five blobby pale yellow shapes that didn't look like much of anything, except that they were more or less in the middle of the picture. I guessed the picture was probably a picture of them. I wondered what they were, and then all at once realized that they were Cetans.

I stared at them for I don't know how long. It's one thing to read about alien beings on another world, and I'd done a lot more reading about those than the others who came with me to Star's Reach, what with the alien-books and the stories. It's another to see them, or pictures of them, and know that the blobby shapes in the picture spent years sending messages to our world, and trying to figure out the messages that came back. For me, at least, they stopped being aliens and turned into people, and the fact that they didn't have a blessed thing in common with me or any of Mam Gaia's children other than minds that could look up at the stars and wonder if there was someone to talk to, out there, somehow made me think of them as people even more.

"I can load the next one," said Tashel Ban then, "if everyone's ready."

Everyone was ready. It took a while to load, like the first one, and again the first thing we saw was the sky. This time it was deep orange, and the brown ocean was nowhere in sight. Instead, there was a blue and purple landscape with a building. It was made of stone, or something like stone, and it was purple like a lot of the rocks were, but it wasn't like any building any human being would ever have thought of putting up, not even in the last days of the old world, when they put up some pretty strange things.

You could tell at a glance that it was meant to bring rain in, not to keep it out, and it wasn't divided up into floors with rooms, because—or at least that's my guess—the Cetans don't think that way about buildings any more than they do about numbers. It was a little like a bunch of wobbly-looking plates or shallow bowls piled all anyhow, bigger ones on the bottom and smaller ones further up, except that the sides of most of the plates turned into ramps that led to plates further up or plates further down. There were Cetans all over it, lots of them, piled up all anyhow in heaps in the bowls or moving up and down the ramps.

At first, I couldn't make any sense of the building at all. Still, ruinmen have to learn a lot about how buildings stay up, since part of our job is making them fall down. After a while, looking at the plates or bowls or whatever they were, I could see how each part of the structure carried its own weight and passed it on down to the foundations. After another moment, I could see how the gasoline rain pooled here and flowed there, so the Cetans who used the building, whatever they were doing with it, could keep themselves wet the whole time. Another moment still, and I realized what that meant: on Mam Gaia or Tau Ceti II, take your pick, stone weighs a lot and liquids flow downhill.

That may not sound like too big of a discovery to whoever reads this, if anybody ever does. Still, since Tashel Ban and Eleen first got the computer to give them one of the briefing papers a couple of months ago, I've mostly been thinking about how different the Cetans are from us, how different their world is, and so on. All of us have been thinking about that, and it's all true enough, but a world where stones are heavy and rain puddles and flows is a world that follows the same rules ours does, even if we and the Cetans don't understand those rules in anything like the same way. That was when I understood why, in spite of all the differences between us and them, we could still figure out a way to talk to each other, because some things are always real.

After a bit, Tashel Ban asked if we were ready for the next picture, and we were. Right at the moment I don't remember a lot of details from the rest of it, other than skies that were always brown and orange and gold, and blue and purple rocks, and blobby yellow Cetans. There was one picture of a Cetan being born, if that's what you call what happens when a lot of free-swimming plastic sheet things come crawling up onto a beach and join together to make an intelligent-phase Cetan; there was another of a Cetan dying, if that's anything like what it means when they run out of whatever it is the free-swimming phase gathers in the sea, and turn dark yellow-brown and go back to the sea and separate out into a couple of hundred plastic sheet things again. I hope the people who used to live here at Star's Reach sent them pictures of one of us being born, and one of us dying or dead—and if they did, I wonder what the Cetans thought about those.

Tashel Ban's trying to figure out how to make one of the color printers work; he says that it has an IOC label, so ought to run come drought or drowning rains. If he gets it to work, there'll be copies for everyone. Even if he doesn't, I can look at the pictures later, and I'll do that, since I was thinking too much about what's always real when I should have been looking at Tau Ceti II. One of the pictures was still on the computer screen when I left the room, daring me to think about what it would be like to stand somewhere none of Mam Gaia's children is ever going to stand, watch the gasoline waves roll up onto a purple beach, and talk to a blobby yellow Cetan the way two people from different corners of Meriga talk over a couple of beers when the rains are pouring down and passing the time is the only thing anybody needs to do.

Still, there's something important we can learn from the Cetans. That came to mind later on, when Anna and I were washing up after dinner. We didn't talk much at all; I was too distracted by my thoughts and she was off somewhere by herself, the way she usually is, and glancing at me now and then out of the corners of her eyes, as though she was waiting for me to say something or do something. That reminded me of the way Plummer so often said something and then watched me, waiting for an answer I didn't yet know how to give him, but Plummer always turned toward me and looked straight at me when he did that. With Anna, the look is always sidelong, and if she's waiting for an answer it's not one I have.

The thing that came to mind as I was drying dishes, though, is that maybe the alien-books had it wrong, not just a little wrong but as wrong as you can get. All of them, whether they thought the aliens were going to save us, or teach us something, or conquer us, or eat us for dinner—well, to start with, it's always about us; it's always about how human beings are so important to the aliens that they're going to travel all the way from another star to do something for us, or with us, or to us. But it's more than that.

What the alien-books are saying, at least the ones I've read so far, is that what we think is real isn't real: that the skies are really full of alien spaceships even though we don't think they're there, or that the government is really hiding the aliens or in cahoots with them or something else secret and scary, or that the aliens are going to give us all kinds of wonderful new science and technology that will prove that we don't really have to pay attention to Mam Gaia's limits and laws, or something else like that. The books are always about how the universe isn't what we think it is.

So far, though, the Cetans aren't telling us any of that. If we're important to them, it's the same way that they're important to us, the way that families in some out of the way valley up in the Tenisi hills are important to each other, since there's nobody else you can invite over to talk and share a meal and sip whiskey as the sun goes down. Now of course they can't come visit us, any more than we can go visit them, but it would be a lonelier universe if they weren't out there in their gasoline pools and their buildings made of big stone plates. The thing they're telling us, though, is even more important than that: they're telling us that what's real is always real.

Tashel Ban said that the people who were here before us here had to explain to the Cetans how we see pictures, so they would know to put whatever we were supposed to see somewhere in the middle of the pictures they sent us. It never would have occurred to them to put those five Cetans right in front of the pool, spread apart so we could see them, in the middle of the first picture, since they see—or whatever you call it—in all directions at once. Pictures with edges and something to look at in the middle are a human thing, and whatever Cetan pictures are like is a Cetan thing, but there are things you find in both, like rocks that are heavy and rain that pools and flows, and that just might teach us and the Cetans both that some of what we think is so really is so, all the way from our side of the sky to theirs.

That may not sound like much of a thing to value. Still, thinking back over the long road that got me here, I remember too many times that I thought something was true when it wasn't, and too many others that I thought something wasn't true when it was. For that matter, the priestesses say that the old world died because so many people kept on insisting that things they ought to have known were true weren't true at all, and kept on insisting on it even when Mam Gaia kept slapping them across the face with the truth, over and over again. So if a blobby yellow alien in a pool of gasoline can look at any of the things we think we know and say, "Yes, that's what it looks like to us, too," that's worth something, and if that's all we find here, maybe the long road's still been worth walking.

CHAPTER 18

MULE'S PACE

It took Berry and I a couple of weeks, as I wrote earlier, to finish going through the papers from the Skeega ruinmen. Every couple of days we found something that mentioned the White River Transport Facility, but it wasn't until we'd read most of what they'd left at Troy Tower that we got the records from the seasons when the Skeega ruinmen worked on it.

It was late in the afternoon, and I'd spent nearly the whole day reading the dullest kind of report a ruinman can file with the guild: here's where it was, here's when we worked on it, and all we found was concrete we cracked to get the iron inside. That's what you find more often than not in the ruins of small towns and suburbs, because a lot of people kept living in those straight through the end of the old world; the small towns stayed small towns and bits and pieces of the suburbs turned into small towns themselves, and the people who lived there stripped old buildings for anything they could use long before ruinmen got to work there. So that's what I'd been reading, one report after another from the small towns near Skeega, and then I pulled out another stack and nearly dropped it, because it said WHITE RIVER TRANSPORT FACILITY right across the top.

That was the most exciting thing about that stack of paper, though. The place was a truck depot in the years before the

Second Civil War, when there were lots of little rebellions catching fire here and there all over Meriga and there weren't enough soldiers or fuel to stomp on all of them. That's all it was: lots of trucks, big round fuel tanks to keep them fed, and a bunch of long low bulletproof buildings for the clerks who managed the trucks and the soldiers who guarded the fuel. Most of it got burned by rebels toward the end of the Second Civil War, and it was abandoned and used by squatters afterwards, so the papers that might have sent us on our way were long gone. The ruinmen who dug the place up found a whole mess of buried pipes, and made a lot of money selling the metal, but that didn't do Berry and me any good.

After we'd finished reading all of it, we sat there for a little while, and neither one of us said a thing. "Okay," I said finally. "I guess we go to Memfis, then."

Berry grinned. "I was hoping."

I thought about routes, and added up the money I had. It would be a long walk, unless—

"You know," I said then, "we could go from here to Cago."

His eyebrows went up. "And from Cago?"

"Across to the Misipi, and down by riverboat from there."

That got me an open mouth, and then another grin. "I always wanted to ride a riverboat someday."

"Get ready," I told him. "We can get out of here tomorrow, and get to the Misipi in a couple of weeks."

That's pretty much what we did, too. We said our goodbyes to the old ruinmen who lived at Troy Tower at dinner, shared another glass of Genda whiskey with Tashel Ban that night, got up before the sun did and headed west down the Skeega road.

We weren't quite alone on the road, but it seemed close to that sometimes. The lake schooners go around the north end of Mishga from Troy to Cago, and when the winds are good it's at least as fast as walking there and a lot more comfortable. All the cargo goes by boat, too, because it's cheaper and safer than loading it on a wagon and hoping for the best. So most of what you get on the Mishga roads are farmers heading to market, with a few players or an elwus walking with them just to add a bit of color to it all. That made for less trouble finding places to stay the night, and it was also the reason we figured out that we were being followed.

That happened just west of Ipsee. We took the wrong fork of the road there, and got most of the way to Anarba before we had the chance to ask a local farmer for directions and found out that we'd made a mistake. That meant a couple of hours on rough farm roads going south, but we finally made it back to the straight road to Cago and got to a little town, a place called Leen, just before sunset. Leen has all of one place where travelers can spend the night, a big farmhouse that's probably going to give it up and become a tavern in a few more years. It's already got a big sign out front, and the front room and dining room have been knocked together into a space big enough to feed a pretty large party; it's just a matter of time before the bar goes in and the fields get sold or leased to somebody else.

I hired a room there, we got the road dust off us, and then we went down to the big room out front and saw about some dinner. The place was still enough of a farmhouse to cook up a meal that would make a fieldhand comfortable after a long harvest day, and so the two of us were sitting back and feeling very full when the door banged open and a man came in: just a plain traveler in dusty clothes, with the kind of bland ordinary face you'd have a hard time remembering from one day to the next. The woman who ran the place went over to him, and I could hear about every third word as he hired a room and got a meal ordered. All the while he was talking to her, though, he kept looking past her, across the room, at Berry and me.

That's when I realized that I'd seen his face before, though I couldn't remember where. He might have noticed that I was watching him, because he stopped looking at me, and then a minute or two later he was on his way up the stairs to his room. The woman who ran the farmhouse went back to the kitchen.

I turned to Berry, and his face had that blank look he gets when he doesn't want anyone to know that he's noticed something.

"Sir and Mister," he said very quietly. By that time, as I mentioned earlier, he only used my title for other people's benefit, or for a joke, or when he wanted to say something important.

I figured I knew this time which it was. "The man who just came in."

A quick nod. "He's following us. We passed him on the road to Anarba today."

I considered that for a while, and couldn't think of any good reason why somebody else would make the same double-back we did, and end up at the same place. I nodded and said, "We can talk in a bit," and he nodded back and put his attention into finishing up the last of his dinner.

Once we got up to our room and the door was locked, Berry said, "I don't think he was following us before Troy, but I can't say for sure."

"The roads from Melumi were pretty crowded, but I don't think I saw him," I said.

"If he wasn't—" He didn't go on, but I knew what he was thinking. The roads in Meriga are about as safe these days as they've been since the end of the old world, but every so often you hear of someone with valuables being robbed or worse, and noticing that you're being trailed by some member of a gang who simply makes sure you're where they want you to be is supposed to be one of the few warnings you're likely to get.

All of a sudden, I thought of the riders who had followed us north to Luwul. It didn't seem likely at first that there was a connection, but as I thought about it there in the farmhouse in Leen, the idea was hard to shake.

"Then we'll dodge him the way we dodged the riders," I said.

Berry looked up at me with a grin. "Any idea where we can find Plummer? He'd know what to do."

We both laughed, and didn't think anything more of it.

We might have gone ahead as we did in Tucki and travel by night, but that end of Mishga is too thickly settled for that; we'd have been spotted in no time, and the whole countryside would be talking about the two ruinmen who were hiding in the dark. Instead, we left the farmhouse early the next morning, and got in among farmers from a little town nearby who were on their way to the market at another small town whose name I forget, twenty kloms or so down the road. We stuck with them right to the market town, and didn't leave the town the next morning until we'd found another group of travelers who were going the way we were.

That's more or less how we traveled all the way to Cago. The first few days we didn't see any trace of the man we'd spotted at Leen, and I'd just about begun to wonder whether the whole thing was a mistake, when Berry caught sight of him on the edge of the crowd at the market at Jonsul, and let me know where to look. He was turning away by the time I found him, but it was the same man, I was certain of that.

We caught sight of him again every two or three days from there to Cago. Once we got near the Inyana border, just to be sure, we veered off on a side road when we were sure no one was looking and crossed down to another road running the same way across the very northern edge of Inyana. Sure enough, by the time we got to Sowben, there he was again, watching as we got into town at the end of a long day walking alongside a wagonload of metal from an old airport outside of Elcart that the ruinmen there had sold to a local metal merchant.

By that time we were close enough to Cago that there wasn't much point in making any more detours. Berry and I kept on the Inyana road, staying with the metal merchant's wagon and talking shop with him and his prentices, partly because there's safety in numbers and partly because they were good company and it was pleasant to spend time with people who knew most of the same things we did and shared in another part of the same work. Still, that meant that the man with the bland face had no trouble at all keeping track of us.

We spotted him a couple of times in the days that followed, never more than a glimpse here and there. To this day I don't know if he hadn't realized that we were onto him, or if he knew it, and showed himself to us now and then just to keep us on our toes. We kept waiting for a gang to show up, but none ever did.

Finally one morning we got to the edge of the Cago ruins, and the road veered south a bit to stay clear of them. Cago was a big city in the old world, the biggest still above water anywhere in Meriga, and even though ruinmen had been digging into the ruins there about as long as they'd been busy anywhere but Troy, there are still plenty of buildings standing, most of them close up against the shore of Lake Mishga. It's the only place I know where you can get an idea of what the drowned cities of the coast must have been like before the seas rose, just ruin after ruin as far as your eyes will reach.

Most places in Meriga, the roads stay as far away from the ruins as they can, but south and east of Cago you don't have much choice unless you want to go deep into Ilanoy farm country, so the road runs right up under the ruins. Berry and I and the metal merchant and his prentices had a fine time talking about the buildings we passed and what the local ruinmen found the last season and all. Most of the other people on the road hurried along past us and gave the ruins nervous looks over their shoulders, as though a robot was about to come lurching out from between two heaps of brick that used to be factories and butter us all across the pavement. Most people nowadays are like that; they're glad to buy the metal we salvage and even gladder to have somebody taking the risks you run when you're cleaning up what the old world left behind, but they don't like to think about it much, and when you walk alongside what's left of Cago you pretty much have to think about it.

We walked most of a day alongside those ruins, and weren't to Cago yet by the time the sun went down. We'd just about gotten to a town called Munsa then; the metal merchant had friends in the business a little further on and wanted to get to their place that night, but Berry and I were tired, and so we said our goodbyes and went to find a place to stay in Munsa. There was only one, a big comfortable inn, and it still had rooms to hire, so I handed over some coins and we did the usual, upstairs to our room to wash off the road dust, downstairs to the big room to get a meal. The room was a cramped little place without a window and the food wasn't half so good as you get in Inyana farmhouses along the road, but I didn't mind; I was tired, and wouldn't have minded a bit of bread and bean soup and a place to sleep on the ground.

The common room was mostly empty when we got there. We sat down and called for our dinners, and I was about half-way through mine when all at once Berry nudged me hard in the side with one of his elbows. I tried not to let anything show on my face, which wasn't too easy, since Berry has sharp elbows; still, nobody seemed to have noticed when I looked up from my food and gave the room a lazy glance. I expected to see the man who'd been following us, and didn't. It took a moment before I realized that the only face in the room that was turned toward me was one I recognized.

By then he had seen me as well, and came over to the table where Berry and I were sitting: an old man with just a trace of white hair around his ears and eyeglasses as round as moons. "A very good evening to you both," he said. "I hope you won't mind if I join you?"

"Not at all," I told him. "It's a long way from the road to Luwul, Plummer."

That got me a smile I couldn't read at all. "True indeed," he said, and sat down across the table from me. "A very long way."

I'd half decided not to tell Plummer that Berry and I had someone following us, but we got to talking about the trip west from Troy, and the moment I mentioned the road we'd taken along the northern edge of Inyana he gave me one of his looks and said, "I take it you had unwelcome company."

"More or less," I admitted.

"Riders? I recall some difficulty with them on the road to Luwul."

"No, just one man on foot."

Plummer considered that for a moment. "If you would like to lose him, there might be a way. Still, all in good time. Where are you going next?" I told him, and he nodded once. "If the two of you have any interest in company on the trip, there might indeed be a way. Sanloo's the next place I need to be."

"How's the medicine business?" Berry asked him then.

"Oh, prosperous as always. I'm pleased to report that the good folk of Hiyo and Inyana are less hostile to fine natural elixirs than their Tucki equivalents." He sat back, glanced past me just for a moment, and then smiled. "We should talk about that later, however," he said, and his hand moved: one finger on the edge of the table, and then four. "Tomorrow, perhaps?"

We said our goodnights, and he got up and went to the stairs out front. Berry and I finished our dinners and got up, and I made sure to turn around a little more quickly than usual. Sure enough, somebody was leaving through a door at the back of the common room, and I couldn't be sure but it certainly looked like the man who was following us.

Up in our room, Berry and I looked at each other for a long moment. "The only question I've got," Berry said finally, "is whether Plummer's showed up by chance or not."

"I have no idea," I admitted. "I tend to trust him, though I know that might be a mistake."

"I know." Then: "But it probably wouldn't hurt to have that conversation."

We waited a while, until the hall outside our room was dead silent, and then I went to the door and opened it as casually as

I could, as though I was headed to the washroom. No one was watching. One, four meant room fourteen, and that wasn't too far away from our room; the trick was to make sure nobody realized both of us were going someplace, and that's something every ruinman's prentice knows how to do.

Whenever two or three or half a dozen prentices want to go somewhere in their mister's house where only one was supposed to go, you walk soft and match your footsteps to the others who are with you, so the mister and the senior prentices only hear one set of footsteps. Now of course they did the same thing when they were younger, so it's a bit of a game. If you do it well enough to fool them, you can usually get away with whatever it is, even if they find out about it later on.

This was no game, but Berry and I both knew the way of it, and went down the hall right in step with each other, past Plummer's door as far as the washroom, then went back to the door slow and soft as air so nobody would hear us. I tapped on the door—one, four—and a moment later Plummer opened it, beamed, and waved us silently in.

We made plans in a whisper. Berry went to get our gear, making less noise than your ordinary mouse; Plummer went and got something that I later figured out was clothing, and then we climbed out Plummer's window into the stableyard behind the inn and followed him into the night. After that most of what I remember was hurrying through dark alleys, trying to keep close to Plummer, as he led us on a zigzag path that seemed to go on for kloms and kloms.

Finally we stopped. I could see next to nothing but stars sparkling above us. The moon was down, and a dim light came from a little window in what looked like a low flat-roofed shack just ahead. Plummer whispered to Berry and me to wait, and then went to the shack and tapped on what must have been a door. The light vanished; I heard the door creak open and then shut again. In the silence that followed I heard an odd faint sound that finally turned into the murmur of moving water.

The door creaked again, and then Plummer was motioning us forward. I found my way through it by feel, and let myself be guided to a bench by someone I couldn't see. Berry came through the door, black against the dim starlight, and then whoever it was pulled the door shut again. A moment later, light: a dim lamp in the middle of the ceiling, revealing a tidy little room with a stove in one corner, shelves and cupboards here and there, a table in the middle and a little curtained window in each wall.

"Well," said the fourth person in the little room, a stocky gray-haired man in rough work clothes. "You'll do, no question. You've all eaten? Fair enough. Get some sleep while you can; we'll be going at first light." He made a gesture toward a low door like a hatch. I thanked him—I was pretty tired by then—and stooped to get through the door; on the other side was an even smaller room with four bunks, stacked two to a side, with a straw-filled pallet and a blanket on each. That was enough for me; I found a place for my gear, got settled in one of the bunks, and fell asleep right away.

When I woke up, it took me a long moment to remember why I was sleeping where I was. About the time I got awake enough to figure that out, I noticed that there was a good bit of light coming in around the sides of the door, and remembered what the man had said about starting before the sun was up. The other three bunks were empty, and I wondered for a moment whether Berry and Plummer had somehow managed to leave me behind.

Then I noticed that the room was moving—rolling just a bit from side to side. I rubbed my eyes and laughed, and went to the door. The room on the other side was empty and the door to the outside was open, but that didn't worry me. I could see the green bank of a canal sliding slowly past a few meedas from the door.

Outside the cabin, the sun was splashing its light down on the canalboat, the water of the canal, and the banks and farms to either side. The man who'd welcomed us last night was on the towpath up ahead, next to a gray mule who plodded along the way as patient as only mules can be, and the towrope ran back from the mule's collar to the front end of the boat—the bow, I should say. I learned that word and half a dozen other bits of boat talk over the days that followed.

The cabin I'd taken for a shack the night before was right up near the aft end, a little stable for whichever mule wasn't working was just behind the bow, and between them was the long body of the boat, with hatches here and there that let into the hold. Berry was aft, handling the rudder, when I came out, and Plummer was sitting on the roof of the cabin. Both of them were dressed in the sort of cheap work clothes you expect to see on a boatman.

Plummer slid down from his place with a grace you don't expect from an old man. "Good morning!" he said. "There are clothes a little more suitable than your leathers back in the cabin, and I recommend you try them on. If you're considering food, there's bread and soup in the kitchen—the galley, I should say—and some quite acceptable apples."

I thanked him and said, "Where are we?"

"Our captain," and he motioned with his head at the man beside the mule up ahead of us, "calls it the Calsag channel. If I gather correctly, it runs from Lake Mishga south of Cago out to the main Cago Canal west of here, which will take us to the Ilanoy River and the first steamboat south."

"Good," I said. "Thank you again—this is pretty clever."

"Most people react to being followed by hurrying." Plummer gestured ahead, to where the mule and the captain plodded slowly on. "Most people who follow others, if they lose their target, count on that, and hurry to catch up. Fall behind, and quite often you won't be found."

Even though he was looking away from me, it felt like he was watching me as he said that. I had no idea why, or what he wanted me to say or not say. "You do that a lot?"

"Now and again."

"I guess selling medicine's a risky business."

That got me a quick unreadable look back over his shoulder. "It can be."

The conversation didn't go anywhere else, so I went back inside and had some of the bread and soup and one of the apples, washed up, and got out of my ruinman's leathers into the same kind of coarse cotton clothes Plummer was wearing. Afterwards, I went out again just as we got to a lock. There was a line of canal boats waiting there, so we joined it, and sat there while two boats at a time went up and two more going the other way came down.

The captain came aft as soon as he'd gotten the mules settled in the stalls up front. "Morning," he said. "You ever handle a mule?"

"You find me anybody from the Tenisi hill country who didn't," I told him, "and I'll buy you a drink."

That got me a nod and the kind of ready smile one working man gives to another. "Fair enough. When we get going again, I'd like you to spell me. Your boy hasn't worked with mules, but he's good on the rudder—and so's our other passenger."

I remembered just in time that Plummer's friends didn't use names. "Sure. Anything I ought to know?"

"Just keep Sal on the towpath and we'll be fine."

By the time we were in the lock, I'd gone forward, gotten introduced to Sal the mule, sorted out which of us was boss, and got her harnessed up. Once we were ready to move again, Sal and I headed down the towpath, and pretty quick she settled into the same steady plod as the other mule, whose name was Josey. I got to know both of them pretty well over the days that followed, because that's how I paid my way down the Cago Canal. Night and day, the boat kept moving at mule's pace, a couple of boatlengths behind the boat ahead and in front of the boat behind, and night and day the captain and I spelled each other, four hours on and four hours off.

The only breaks in that slow pace were when we lined up at a lock, or when we pulled into a wide place to load or unload something at one of the little towns that lined the canal. That latter was a break only in a manner of speaking, because it was me and Berry who did the loading and unloading, and none of it was particularly light. We hauled out kegs of nails and wood screws, crates of shovel and hoe and rake heads, all the metal parts and machinery for a wind turbine some farm family had saved up a couple of years of profits to buy, and boxes that had stocky brown jugs of Genda whiskey in them; we replaced it all with barrels of oranges and molasses, bottles of rum, and twenty-keelo sacks of corn and millet from Ilanoy farms. Still, what ruinmen haul on the job is no lighter.

All considered, it was a pretty good time, and the fact that I didn't know the first thing about canal boats before I'd started the trip gave it a bit of interest, too. There aren't a lot of canals down in Tenisi, but they're all over the northern part of Meriga, from Nyork west all the way to the Misipi. I asked Plummer about that once, when we were sitting on the roof of the cabin and Berry and the captain were doing their half of the work.

"The canals? They're quite old," he said. "They came before the old world, or what most people remember as the old world. Most of them were abandoned when fossil fuels came to power everything, and had to be dug out and fitted with locks again afterwards. That started after the Third Civil War, and it's still going on; if I recall correctly, there are two canals being reopened in Hiyo as we speak."

"That was generous of them," I said. "The ancients, I mean."

He glanced at me, took a long swig from his whiskey bottle. "As far as anyone knows, they never thought twice about it. Once they had their cars and planes, they no longer needed the canals, and—" A shrug. "That was that."

"No, I meant it. At least they dug the things out in the first place."

"I suppose that's—" Plummer stopped halfway through the sentence, and a moment later I saw why. There were soldiers, a long line of them, crossing a big stone bridge up ahead of us. We got off the roof—you have to get down most times when a canal boat goes under a bridge—and watched the soldiers march past as we got closer to the bridge.

We were almost under it when the end of the line came past, and there was a captin on horseback right at the back. He glanced at us, looked up and down the boat, then looked straight at me. "You with the hat," he said. (I was wearing one, a cheap straw hat I'd bought for a couple of coins in one of the little towns along the way.) "Care to make a better wage than you're getting now? The jennel's looking for soldiers."

We had enough soldiers in Tenisi that I knew what to say. "Born with a bad foot, Sir and Captin. I can just about keep up with a mule."

He considered that. "Too bad. If you've got friends who might be interested, tell them Jennel Tarl's hiring, a hundred marks for signing even if they've never touched a gun before."

"I'll tell 'em, Sir and Captin," I said, and the man nodded and spurred his horse after the line of marching men.

The damp black shadows under the bridge slid over us then. After we came out the other side, I got back onto the roof and looked over my shoulder. "I wonder what that was about."

"Something we'll see quite often in the next few years, I fear," Plummer said. He drank more whiskey. "An aging presden and no heir is a recipe for trouble, and that means soldiers: for the loyal, the ambitious, those who simply hope to survive. And when she dies…"

He wasn't looking at me that time, either, but I had the same feeling again as though he was watching me, seeing how I would react. I didn't have the least idea what to say, and I didn't really want to say much of anything, either. What Plummer had said a bit earlier about the Third Civil War suddenly made me notice that my time was a lot better than fifty or a hundred years ago or, well, pretty much any time since the old world started to come apart.

Not that long ago, there hadn't been long lines of canal boats moving iron and oranges and grain from one side of Meriga to the other, and for that matter there hadn't been enough iron and oranges and grain, or much of anything else, for a lot of people all through that time. When Sheren died and left the presden's office for others to fight over, I wondered, would it be back to that? I didn't want to think about it just then, but the idea was hard to chase from my mind. As I write all this, here at Star's Reach, it still is.

CHAPTER 19

A DIFFERENT WORLD

"There was a long argument about that in the old world," said Eleen. We were supposed to be eating lunch, but nobody was paying much attention to the bread and soup, and Tashel Ban wasn't even pretending. He was over by the printer, muttering bits of hot language under his breath when the thing tried to jam.

"About numbers?" Berry asked.

"About math." Scholars usually say "mathematics," but Eleen stopped saying that the second or third time one of us gave her a blank look. "One side used to say that math was universal, so every intelligent species in the universe would end up understanding it the same way. The other side said no, mathematics are just the way our brains work, and so every species would have its own math. In the old world, most scholars agreed with the first side, but the other side was right—at least about the Cetans."

"But how did that stop them from figuring out what the Cetans were saying?" I asked.

"Because the first messages we sent them were all about numbers." She rapped on the table: once, twice, three times, five times, seven times. "What do those have in common?"

"They're prime numbers," Berry said at once. Eleen gave him a startled look, and he went on, as though he was embarrassed: "My teacher at Nashul taught us about those."

"Good," Eleen said. "Yes, and that's one of the things they sent the Cetans, because they figured that any intelligent species ought to recognize them—but they didn't. Meanwhile they were sending us the equivalent in their math, expecting us to recognize them, and we didn't. It took a hundred years before anybody on either side realized that the problem was that we think in numbers and they don't."

I tried to get my thoughts to fit around that one. "They don't even count on their fingers?"

"Cetans don't have fingers."

"Well, but—"

"But that's just it. We're born with so many fingers—five, most of us—and we live in a world where things come in nice neat packages you can count: four oranges, ten trees, things like that. They don't. If a Cetan wants to grab something—" Her hand mimed flowing outwards. "—it grows as many fingers as it needs, and when it doesn't need them, they go away. Everything that matters to them is like that. That's why their math starts from flows, not from numbers.

"We've got math that can handle flows. It's called calculus, and there are maybe a few hundred people in Meriga who understand it, but we've got it. They've got math that can handle numbers. It's very advanced math to them—as far as anyone here could figure out, they got there by imagining what happened when a flow got slower and slower, until it approached what we call zero—but they can do it. It took close to a hundred years for both sides to figure out that these complicated relationships they were finding in each other's signals were what the others thought was very simple, basic, easy math."

"Their technology is the same way," Tashel Ban said, coming to the table with a stack of papers in his hands; the printer had finally given up jamming and done its job. "After the math issue got sorted out, the people here tried to explain to the Cetans how we build radios, and asked them how they did it." He handed me my copy, and I glanced at the words on the top of the front page: BRIEFING PAPER 4: OVERVIEW OF CETAN MATHEMATICS AND TECHNOLOGY. "It turns out that they mix up something the consistency of thick paint out of metal salts and start putting it down in layers on a base, sprinkling in other compounds here and there, and letting it dry a bit more or less as they go. When it's done, it's a solid mass that takes in radio waves and electricity, and puts out the magnetic fields they talk with, but nobody here could figure out the details. The interesting thing is that they couldn't make sense of our circuits either—the way we split up current into different resistors, capacitors, tubes, and so on doesn't make any sense to them, and their math can't follow it."

"Can their radios," Thu asked then, "do anything ours cannot?" Everyone else looked at him. He hadn't spoken yet in the discussion, because he didn't need to. Anything we found out about Cetan technology brought us closer to the choice between his alternative and Tashel Ban's. That wasn't a choice any of us wanted to make in a hurry, if we had to make it at all.

Tashel Ban answered after a moment. "Nothing any of the papers has mentioned so far. Electrons and radio waves work there the way they work here—at least, that's the theory, and there's nothing to suggest otherwise. It's just the way they understand radio, and the math behind radio, that doesn't make sense to us."

"Nor should it," Eleen said. "It's a different world."

I read the briefing paper right then, even though my soup was getting cold. At this point I've read enough papers about the Cetans that I can follow them pretty well even when I don't know what they're talking about, and this was no different; I couldn't tell you a thing about most of the technologies the paper mentioned, but there were two things that came through. One was that the Cetans can do pretty much the same sort of things that we can, but trying to figure out how is the sort of thing that makes scholars jump in the river and drown themselves.

The other thing was that the Cetans don't seem to do the things that the old world did and we don't do any more. The scholars who wrote the paper weren't sure whether that's because they hadn't figured out how, or because there's no way to do those on Tau Ceti II, or because Cetans have more common sense than human beings do, but the Cetans don't seem to have cars or airplanes or anything like them. They get their electricity from sunlight and wind and water—well, gasoline, but there it's the same thing—the way we do, and they aren't lobbing any false stars up into the sky or building nukes or anything like that. Why is hard to say, because Eleen's right; it's a different world.

We finally ate lunch, and then the rest of us told Eleen and Tashel Ban that it wasn't going to do anybody any good if they worked themselves to death, and they agreed to take a day or two off. Berry, who's been learning how to run the computer from Tashel Ban, promised that he'd keep an eye on it in case anything happened, and the rest of us bullied the two of them into getting some rest. I don't know whether Tashel Ban slept, since he wasn't the one I was supposed to bully, but Eleen did the sensible thing, settled down on our bed and slept until dinner.

At dinner Tashel Ban and Thu swapped stories about Jinya pirates they'd tangled with, and everyone else ate and drank and hoped that we wouldn't find anything that would force the two of them to take care of their argument the old hard way, knife in hand, in a chalk circle four meedas across. We lounged around for a while, talking about nothing in particular, and then Eleen and I went to the room we share and things pretty much followed from there.

Afterwards we lay curled up around each other, feeling warm and comfortable and not saying much for a while. I was hoping Eleen would fall asleep, because I was pretty sure she still needed more rest, but instead she shifted and said, "All those books about flying saucers."

"What about them?"

"I can't help thinking about the people who spent their lives waiting for the aliens to land, back in the old world. There were millions of them, you know."

I didn't, not until then. "The government had that many people fooled?"

"It was more than that." She settled on her back. "There's a thing called the Big Bang effect."

"That sounds fun," I said, and kissed the nearer of her breasts. She laughed and said, "Not that kind. In the old world, right up until a few years before it ended, scholars believed that the whole universe started out with a big explosion: the Big Bang."

I gave her a puzzled look. "How could that be the beginning? If there's an explosion, you have to have something to explode first."

"I know. That's what they thought, though, and they had reasons for it. Did you ever hear something go by you fast, making noise?" She moved a hand past my head and whistled, and the whistle dropped from high to low as the hand went by.

"Sure."

"That's called the Doppler effect—the way the sound is higher in pitch when it's coming toward you, and lower when it's moving away. The same thing happens with light, and when scholars studied the stars, they found that the light from the stars is redder—lower in pitch—than it would be if they were still. So they figured all the stars are flying apart, like bits of stuff from an explosion. Do you see?"

I nodded. "But..."

"There's more. There was also a theory about the way the universe was put together, written by one of the most famous scholars back then, a man named Einstein. There were many ways to make the math in the theory work out, but the simplest way only works if the universe is getting bigger." I gave her a baffled look, and she went on: "Again, think of an explosion. Something small gets much bigger."

"But..." I tried again.

She put a hand over my mouth. "And some scholars figured out that outer space had just a bit of heat in it, more than they thought it should have, and they decided that the heat was left over from the explosion. So everyone thought, well, the stars are moving away from us, and the theory of relativity works best in an exploding universe, and here's the heat from the explosion—it's got to be true."

She took her hand off my mouth, and I said, "But none of those proves that."

"Of course not." Then, smiling: "Why not?"

"Because something else could have caused each of those things."

"Exactly." She kissed me, then said: "If A causes B, and B shows up, that doesn't prove that A must have happened—not unless you know for certain that A's the only thing that can cause B. People forget that. They forget it all the faster if A can cause B, and C, and D, and all three of those things show up—it's easy to think that A's got to be the cause.

"Then if things come up that don't fit the model, people don't weigh things evenly; they don't say, B and C and D suggest that A happened, but E and F and G and H suggest that it didn't. They take each piece of contrary evidence one at a time: here's E, but E by itself doesn't outweigh B and C and D, and neither does F by itself, and so on. So you can end up with far more evidence against a theory than for it, but nobody notices, because they're taking the evidence for the theory all together, and the evidence against the theory as though each piece stands all by itself. That's what scholars nowadays call the Big Bang effect."

"So how did they figure out that the Big Bang didn't happen?"

"A scholar figured out that there's something else that makes starlight look redder when it comes from further away. It wasn't the Doppler effect after all. Then another scholar took a second look at Einstein's theory, and it turned out that some puzzles that nobody had been able to solve were easy to work out once you realized the universe wasn't getting bigger. The heat had other explanations, too, but nobody had time to figure out which was right, because that's as far as they got when the old world ended."

"There must have been a mother of a lot of embarrassed scholars."

"It was much worse than that." Her face went somber. "The Big Bang had become the foundation of half a dozen sciences. People spent their entire lives working on theories that depended on it—and suddenly there they were. I don't think any of them killed themselves, but there were scholars who kept on insisting that it was all wrong and the Big Bang was real until they went back into Mam Gaia's belly. It was that or admit that they'd wasted their lives."

I realized then where she was going with all this. "And the people who believed in the aliens made the same kind of mistake."

"Yes, but there was even more reason for them to make it. I was taught that the people who believed in flying saucers thought the aliens were about to land and solve all our problems for us. When the old world was ending, most people hoped that something like that would happen—that somebody would somehow fix everything, so that the old world didn't have to end. So every light in the sky, and every story about—what was that place in the desert?"

"Roswell."

"Yes. Every story about Roswell, every faked picture and faked sighting the government put into circulation, and everything else, had to add up to aliens visiting Mam Gaia, or the last scrap of hope they had was gone." She shook her head. "So they waited, and waited, and waited, and the flying saucers never landed. For all I know there are still people waiting for that, the way the Old Believers wait for their god to come back."

I thought I could name at least one who was still waiting for the aliens, but right then Eleen turned to face me and reached for me. "Waiting?" she asked.

"Not any more," I told her, and I didn't, either.

Afterwards, we curled up again, and a little after that she dozed off. I waited until I was sure she was good and sound asleep, then slipped out of bed and got some clothes back on.

The hallway outside the room we share was as hushed as it must have been in the years between when Anna's people left it and when we arrived. I closed the door as quietly as I could and went down to the room where the alien-books were. It was dark and empty. I turned on the light, and noticed that there was a gap in one of the shelves where I'd put the alien-books earlier that day. It was just about wide enough for one large book. I looked at the gap for a moment, and wondered who else was reading about aliens—Anna, or one of the others?

After a bit, I pulled down one of the stories from the top shelf and tried to read it. It was another of those make-believe stories set on other worlds, like the one with the worms I mentioned a while back; this one was about someone who figured out how to predict the future, and the future he saw coming was the fall of an empire like Meyco's, except this one covered the whole Milky Way. It was a good story, too, and I'll go back and read it tomorrow, but just then my mind kept on wandering off and I finally put the book down and just sat there on the floor with my chin in one hand.

I was thinking about Eleen—about how we met, which I've already written about, and how we met again in Sisnaddi after I'd come back from the Lannic shore where I found the one thing I needed to know to find Star's Reach and watched the Spire fall and the rest of it. I came back the way I went, past the burning land to Pisba and then down the Hiyo to Sisnaddi, every step of the way on foot because all the money I had in the world just then was barely enough to keep me fed, never mind pay my fare on a riverboat.

The ruinmen's hall in Sisnaddi is just west of town, a bunch of big shapes like mushrooms that rise up out of the tumble of buildings where the chemists, the burners, and the other guilds nobody lets inside the walls live and do their work. What that meant is that I walked all the way around the city walls to get to the ruinmen's hall, signed myself in, put up with the pitying looks from the old ruinmen there who were sure I was wasting my life chasing Star's Reach, and went to the big west gate just as soon as I'd washed up and gotten something to eat. Not three hours later I was back out the west gate with a scrap of paper in my pocket that told me where Star's Reach was and how I was going to get there.

I could have gone back to the ruinmen's hall and showed it to the old men there, but I knew they wouldn't believe I'd found anything that mattered, so I went to the big tavern right outside the gate with every intention of spending the last of my money getting thoroughly drunk. They probably would have had to carry me back to the ruinmen's hall that night, too, except that I walked in the door and nodded to the barmaid and found myself staring straight at Eleen, who was sitting over by the side of the room at a little table with a glass of cheap whiskey in front of her and a look on her face that told me everything I needed to know right away.

After I got over the surprise of seeing her, I went over and stood in front of the table until she noticed me and looked up. She didn't say anything at all, not at first, just looked at me.

"Mind if I join you?" I asked.

That got me a smile. "Not at all." She waved at the chair across the table from her.

She was still wearing a scholar's gray robe, but the only reason a scholar from Melumi would be in a cheap tavern in Sisnaddi was if she's failed and been sent away. I knew that, and she knew I knew it, and so neither of us had to say anything about it at first, which was probably for the best. "Did you have any luck finding Star's Reach?" she asked.

"Not yet." I wasn't ready to tell her about what I'd just learned. "Both the places you found for me turned up empty—not that that's your fault."

"Thank you for saying that." She tilted her head, considering me. "Are you still looking for it?"

"Not bright enough to quit," I told her.

That got me a laugh, and she reached past her drink with both hands, and took hold of mine. "Good."

So I got a glass of whiskey to match hers; I got a little drunk and she got a little more drunk, and we talked about nothing in particular, and the end of it all was that I didn't get back to the ruinmen's hall that night. We stumbled up the stairs to the sleeping room she'd hired with the last of the money they'd given her when she left Melumi, and spent that evening pretty much the same way we spent this one.

The next morning, I told her about what I'd learned in drowned Deesee and what I'd found in the archives, and said, "I'm going to need a scholar to come there with me, and I'd like it to be you."

She thought about that for a moment. Then, bitterly. "I'm a failed scholar."

"That's what ruinmen always hire."

She blinked, and then straightened a little. "I didn't know that."

"It's not like scholars who are still in the Versty like to camp in the ruins, you know."

She blinked again, and I could just about see her thinking through what it meant to have a place in the world again, not to mention work that could pay her keep and maybe a lot more. "I suppose not." Then: "Trey, if you're willing to take me, I'll go with you, anywhere at all." She put her arms around me. "Among other things, you're good to spend time with, you know."

Of course I kissed her then, and since she wasn't wearing anything and neither was I, things went from there pretty much the way you'd expect.

Later on she talked about why she'd been sent away from Melumi. I'd heard of failed scholars since I was little, and of course there was always one at the Shanuga dig, but it's like so many other things. I'd never really thought about what that meant, or how the failed scholars got sorted out from the others.

By that time we were living together in a little bare room on the fifth floor of a cheap rooming house not far from the ruinmen's hall in Sisnaddi. I'd gotten money from Berry and a good deal more from Jennel Cobey, which was how I could afford the room. That's where we were standing, looking out the room's one little window at the evening sky, and talking about something that led to something that led to her story.

"My parents were farmers too," she said. "They had a big farm outside of Fowain, in Inyana—my oldest sister has it now. Ordinary folk, maybe a little better off than their neighbors; they could afford to send me and both my sisters to school, not just the temple school in the nearest village but a real school in Fowain. My sisters learned to read and write and calculate, and then went back home to farm, but I loved it at the school, and I decided I wanted to become a scholar at Melumi."

"What did your family think about that?"

She shook her head, laughed a tired bitter laugh. "They did their best to talk me out of it. They knew how many girls go to Melumi every year and how few of them stay—I knew that as well as they did, of course, but I was sure I'd be one of the few. So I studied, and studied, and studied, and when I got the letter saying that I'd passed the examination and been admitted to the Versty, I let myself believe that nothing could go wrong.

"So I went to Melumi and began my studies, and found out a little at a time how Melumi actually works. There are a certain number of chairs—they aren't actually chairs, though that's what they call them; they're livings that have been donated by jennels and Circle elders and what have you, and each one will pay for one scholar. If somebody gets reborn while you're there as a student, and you happen to be in the same field of study as the person who dies, and the senior scholars at Melumi decide that you're the best person for the job, you get a chair and then you stay at Melumi for the rest of your life. If nobody in your field dies, or the senior scholars decide that you're not the best student in that field, you get to the end of your time there, and they hand you some money and send you away and that's the end of it."

"I'm guessing that nobody died in your field," I said.

She glanced at me, and then looked away. "Thank you. No, we lost two scholars in history my last year there, and there were three of us who might have been chosen." She leaned on the window, looking out at the evening getting dark. "The senior scholars make the decision in private, and no one ever talks about it afterwards, so I'll never know why Danna and Lurey got chairs and I didn't."

I bent and kissed her neck. "And now you'll be chief scholar at Star's Reach."

She turned, then, and put her arms around me. "I hope so," she said. "Oh, I hope so."

I thought about all that, sitting there on the floor of the room with the alien-books and the stories, and wondered again whether we love each other, or whether we're just two people who needed somebody—I needed a scholar, she needed something to do with her life, both of us needed someone to share a bed with, and then both of us needed to hope that we could actually get to Star's Reach and find out what messages the aliens were sending to us. I've got B and C and D, but do they add to A? I don't know, and what's on the inside of another person's heart—well, it might as well be on a different world.

CHAPTER *20*

IN THE STREAM OF TIME

The funny thing is that the part of my story I want to tell next involved those same words. It happened when we got to Proo, which is where the Cago Canal ends and the Misipi Canal starts up toward Rocalan and the upper Misipi, and it's also where the riverboats that work the Ilanoy River pick up passengers and freight for the run down to Sanloo and Memfis. We had two days in Proo, partly because there were fifty or sixty canal boats waiting to be unloaded there, and we had to wait our turn, and partly because the riverboat Plummer wanted to take hadn't finished its run upriver. So Berry and I slept on the boat, visited the town, drank beer with the other boatmen, hauled and carried cargo once it came our turn, and generally got along fine.

The captain of our boat—no, I never did ask his name, or hear anybody else say it—waved me into the cabin after we'd finished loading up for the trip back to Cago. "You know," he said, "you and your boy did well. There's not much to be made walking a mule, but if you ever need someplace to lie low and stay fed the while, you could do worse." With a motion of his head toward the foredeck: "You run with *him*, you'll need to lie low now and then."

He meant Plummer, of course. I would have given him a handful of marks just then to find out what he knew about

241

Plummer, because I was already pretty sure that there was a lot more to the man than the medicine seller he claimed to be, but something in the captain's face told me that asking any questions was a bad idea and getting any answers wasn't going to happen any time this side of forever. So I laughed and said, "I noticed that." We talked a little more, about nothing in particular, and then I went back on deck and got to talking with some of the other boatmen about nothing in general.

That was the day before the *Jennel Mornay* got to Proo. That was the riverboat Plummer wanted to take, and in case this ever gets read by somebody from the Neeonjin country on the far side of the dead lands, I should probably say that Jennel Mornay was a famous soldier on the presden's side in the Third Civil War. He was a tough old cavalryman with mustaches out to here, who fought his way downriver from Rocalan to Sanloo in the face of everything the Western Allegiancy could throw at him, which was a lot, and when he was done the final battle at Memfis was pretty much a foregone conclusion. I got to know his face on the trip down the river, because they had a big painting of him in the main cabin.

Still, that's getting ahead of my story a bit. That morning, the morning the *Jennel Mornay* came, we said our goodbyes to the canalboat captain and went with Plummer to the Proo levee where the riverboats docked. It wasn't quite packed with people from the water right up to the warehouses, but that's because there was plenty of cargo there too. There were three big packet boats already sitting with their noses to the levee, roustabouts loading and unloading barrels and sacks and crates, and passengers getting on or off their boats. Everybody was talking or yelling, the crew chiefs were blowing on their whistles loud enough to make me wonder why their brains didn't spray out their ears, steam was hissing from the boats, and you could just hear under it all the churn-churn-churn of the big stern wheels keeping the bows up tight against the shore.

Plummer pointed and said something neither Berry nor I could hear, but we both figured out at the same time that "follow me" was part of it. That meant heading through the middle of it all and most of the way out the other side, to the end of the levee where the warehouses were small and rundown and the roustabouts, who were mostly just sitting around, looked like they'd seen a lot of better days. Finally Plummer stopped and so did we; the noise was still loud enough that we could barely hear each other, so we stood there and waited for a while until finally Plummer pointed again.

That's when I first saw the *Jennel Mornay*, and after looking at the packet boats, well, let's just say it was a bit of a disappointment. The plan was the same—one paddlewheel astern, one smokestack around the middle, boxy pilothouse on top of boxy cabin deck on top of boxy freight deck—but it was half the size and twice the age, and showed it. I didn't know yet that most of the river trade runs on smaller boats like the *Jennel Mornay*, and they don't make enough money for the white paint and the big crews and all. If you grow up in the Tenisi hill country and the only riverboats you ever hear about are the big white-painted ones with the fancy carvings all along the roof, let's just say that a boat like the *Jennel Mornay* is not going to impress you, and leave it at that.

Still, we shouldered our bags and got in line dutifully behind Plummer, I paid our fare—you can work for your fare aboard a canal boat, but riverboats burn peanut oil and that doesn't come cheap—and we crossed the landing stage, which I found out a few days later is what they call the ramp that gets swung over from the bow for passengers to board. A rickety stair led up from the freight deck to the cabin deck, where the purser looked at our tickets and waved us over to a couple of cabins over on the port side. They were cramped little rooms and I wouldn't call them clean, but Berry and I slept in much worse on the long road from Shanuga to Cago, so we didn't complain. We got our packs stowed and locked the cabin door and went back out to see whatever there was to see.

There were twenty cabins and maybe thirty people to fill them, and at least as many more who couldn't afford cabin fare and would be sleeping all anyhow down on the freight deck, in among the barrels and sacks and wooden crates the roustabouts were hauling on board to replace what other roustabouts were hauling off. From the walkway that went all around the cabin deck, I could see most of Proo, the little bustling town near the water and the ruins reaching far back into the farm country behind it.

The pilothouse of the nearest of the big white packet boats went up almost twice as far above the water as the *Jennel Mornay*, and it seemed to be looking down with the kind of raised-eyebrow look a red-hatted Circle elder gives a ruinman who's made the mistake of crossing her path. After a few more minutes, the packet boat let out a whistle, the paddlewheel at the stern slowed, stopped, and then started turning the other way, pulling her stern first out into the river. It was a gorgeous sight, everything a Tenisi farm boy could hope for in a riverboat; it's just that this particular Tenisi farm boy was on the wrong boat.

Still, when the last of our cargo was on board and the *Jennel Mornay*'s whistle sounded, it was still a sight to watch as we pulled away from the levee, backed out into the river, turned and started downstream. Ugly little thing though it was, the *Jennel Mornay* handled well, and before long we were churning down the river at a fair pace.

Plummer came out onto the walkway about the time Proo got lost behind a bend of the landscape behind us. "A pleasant day," he said, "made even more pleasant by the number of kloms I would otherwise have had to walk. I hope the two of you find the boat agreeable?"

I wasn't going to tell him that it looked like it got put together out of what was left over when the other boatbuilders had taken their pick. Still, he must have seen it in my face, and laughed his dry little laugh.

"There are advantages," he said, "to a riverboat that doesn't attract rich passengers. Even so, I trust that neither of you play cards or dice."

"Not usually."

"I recommend avoiding it altogether here. I've heard that someone once brought honest dice on board a Misipi riverboat, and the Misipi itself rose up and refused to let the boat pass until they were thrown overboard and replaced by the usual kind."

A man standing against the rail near us heard this, and burst out laughing. "Good," he said. "That's good." Then, turning: "Well, Mam Gaia's bright green underthings! Plummer. Good to see you again."

Plummer beamed. "Likewise. This," he said to Berry and me, "is Slane, an old friend of mine. Slane, Trey and Berry are more recent friends. You're headed to Memfis, I would guess."

"For the moment." He looked me up and down, glanced at Berry, blinked and took a long hard second look. "You?"

"I have business in Sanloo," said Plummer. "These two? Memfis and points west."

By then I'd taken as good a look at Slane as he'd taken at me. He had the sort of clothes that seem expensive but aren't, and the sort of look that seems casual but isn't; if he had dice in his pocket, and I guessed he did, the river probably wouldn't rise up and stop the *Jennel Mornay*.

"Fair enough." To Berry and me: "You two been to Memfis?"

"Not yet," I told him.

He seemed to think that that was funny, and cuffed me on the shoulder. "Good. That's good. You've heard of Dell, haven't you? Memfis is Dell's home town. Fact is, he's a good friend of mine." He laughed again. "You're from, where, Joja or east Tenisi?"

"Shanuga," I said, impressed despite myself.

"I rarely miss a voice. Well, Trey from Shanuga, the Misipi valley's a different world from the rest of Meriga, and Memfis is a different world from the rest of the Misipi valley. It's an easy place to get into trouble. Still, don't you worry; you're a friend of Plummer's, you're a friend of mine—and Dell's." He laughed again, and right then the whistle sounded up above the pilothouse—we were coming up on some little town, I forget the name of it, where the *Jennel Mornay* had a stop to make—and his laugh got caught up in the screech of the whistle and spread from one bank of the river to the other.

I spent a lot of the trip south along the Misipi like that, watching from the rail and talking to Plummer or Shane or both of them as the *Jennel Mornay* stopped at one little town after another. Every few hours through the day, some little town came into sight, the *Jennel Mornay* puffed up to the levee and sat there for a good long while as things got offloaded and a few people clattered down the landing stage, and then bales and barrels and sacks got hauled on board by the roustabouts to go downriver to Sanloo or Memfis and a few more people clattered back up. Once that was done, it was back out into the river, but that still meant that maybe one hour in three went into pulling up to the levee, pulling away from the levee, or sitting there with nobody but the roustabouts doing much of anything at all.

Come evening, whatever little town came next was where we stopped for the night. They say that riverboats used to travel by night a long time ago, but these days there's too much danger from snags and sandbars. A good pilot might risk a night run when the moon's full and there's money to be made, but usually the risk's not worth taking, and so come evening the boats tie up at the nearest town. The ship's officers eat dinner in the main cabin with the passengers who can afford cabin fare, the crew eats down on the main deck with the passengers who can't, and everybody but whoever's on watch goes to sleep until first light tells the engineer it's time to heat up the boiler again.

Thinking back on the trip down the river, it occurs to me that that's one of maybe three times in my life that I haven't had much of anything to do for a good long time. The first time was during the few months between when my mother and I went to Shanuga after my father didn't come back from the war, and when I got taken on as a ruinman's prentice; the second was on the riverboat heading for Memfis; and the third time—well, that's here and now, because even though I'm sitting in the biggest ruin that's left in Meriga, there's not that much for a ruinman to do just at the moment, other than turn the pages of old books about aliens, and wonder what Eleen and Tashel Ban are going to find next, and tell the story of how I got here in the pages of a notebook that nobody's probably ever going to read.

I didn't even have that much to do on the way downriver to Memfis, and Berry was mostly down on the main deck, making friends with the engineer and watching the steam engines run. I'd have done the same thing at his age, and might have done it even at mine if I didn't have as much to think about as I did. Fairly often I'd run into Plummer and we'd talk about this and that, and now and again I'd end up talking to Slane when he wasn't busy rolling dice or playing cards in the main cabin, but I had a lot of time to myself, too, and spent most of it standing on the walkway that ran along the outer edge of the cabin deck, thinking and watching the Ilanoy forests and fields roll by.

That was when I understood, deep down, just how small Meriga is nowadays compared to what it was back in the old world. By that I don't mean just that it lost all the land it did to the Meycans and the Neeonjin and the coastal allegiancies and Nuwinga, or all the dead lands between the Suri River and the Neeonjin country that nobody lives in any more because it's all dust and sand and only gets a few senamees of rain a year when it gets that much. What I mean is that even the land that's still inside Meriga's borders these days fits Meriga the way my father's overalls fit me when I was five years old. There's just not that many people in Meriga, not compared to how many there used to be, and it shows.

I saw that over and over again as the banks of the river rolled past. We'd come to some town with a hundred buildings or so, the sort of lively little market town you find all through Meriga where farmers bring their crops in for sale and buy what they need from the blacksmith, the potter, the leatherworker and the other crafts, and one glance from the walkway around the cabin deck showed the traces of the same town back in the old world, when it was ten or twenty or fifty times bigger. Sometimes, too, we'd pass long stretches of riverbank where there wasn't a town at all any more, and there would be the traces of an old town, all overgrown with trees or sticking out here and there in the middle of a pasture.

The two big towns we passed on the way down to Memfis, Yoree and Sanloo, made the point even harder to miss. Yoree's a town of decent size, and Sanloo's one of the dozen biggest cities in Meriga, but if you look at either one from the river you can see that they're both tiny next to what they used to be. The main ruins in both of them got stripped down to the ground a long time ago, since a prosperous town needs metal and what's close at hand gets dug up first. Still, if you know what to look for, and any ruinman does, the lines of the old streets and what's left of the foundations of old buildings go as far as you can see upriver and down.

Now and then, too, we'd come to a place where the ancients tossed a bridge right across the river; there were big cracked shafts of concrete rising up from the water, and what was left of ramps going up on either side. Sometimes, when the road that used to run to the bridge still gets some use, I'd see a ferryman's house on one side or the other and a square-bowed boat tied up next to it, or scooting across the river like a water bug with the ferryman sculling for all he was worth at the stern. Still, more often than not, what was left of the bridge would just be sitting there in among the trees and the water reeds with nothing else anywhere in sight, cracked and streaked with long red lines of rust, and only there because it wasn't yet worth a ruinman's time to get out there with a raft, crack the concrete open, and haul what was left of the iron to a metal merchant. If the people on the *Jennel Mornay* had been the only people left alive anywhere on Mam Gaia's round belly, I don't think what was left of those bridges or the empty places that used to be towns could have looked any more lonely.

So that's some of what I was thinking about as one day turned into another and the *Jennel Mornay*'s big stern wheel churned the green water into foam. Finally one evening we got to the place where the Ilanoy flows into the Misipi. It was just after dinner, which was soup, brown bread, and the cheap yellow beer they make up and down the Misipi Valley, which I hadn't yet gotten used to back then. We ate it the way all the cabin passengers on the *Jennel Mornay* ate every meal they got, which was sitting at long benches on either side of a long table running down the middle of the main cabin, with the thrum of the steam engines down below making the plates and mugs rattle loud enough that talking wasn't too easy.

About the time I finished my soup, the whistle sounded up above us, three times, long and slow. Slane was eating with us, as he usually did, and looked up suddenly. "When you finish that," he said, "you might just want to step outside. There's something worth seeing."

I'd figured out already that what Slane didn't know about traveling on riverboats wasn't worth worrying about, so I downed the last of my beer and got to my feet. "Which side?"

"Right hand."

I guessed what he was talking about by then, and went outside the way he'd said. Berry was right behind me, since some things are even more interesting than a steam engine. It was as nice an evening as you could ask for, with puffs of clouds scattered over the sky like loms grazing in a field. The Ilanoy was good and wide by then; the land to the left—to port, I ought to say, since it was on a boat—was the same sort of thing we'd been passing for days, bluffs with wetland trees and water reeds all along their feet, but the land to starboard was low, with trees rising up just high enough that I couldn't see past them to whatever was on the other side of them. Then the land to starboard wasn't there any more; the *Jennel Mornay*'s whistle sounded again, three more times, and all of a sudden we were out on the Misipi.

I've never seen another river half so big. It was wider than a lot of lakes, with brown water rolling up out of the southwest just at that point—it bends a lot, and when the Misipi decides to bend, there's not much that can argue with it. The far bank was a low line of green in the middle distance at first, and then we pulled away from the Ilanoy bank toward the deep water more or less in the middle. There were two more river-boats paddling south toward Sanloo within sight of us, and four of them paddling north, maybe headed all the way up to Meyaplis. One of them whistled back to us, but there was more than enough river for everybody, and pretty soon they were out of sight to the north and we were passing others, steaming upstream past us as we steamed down.

After a while Berry said his goodbyes and scampered back down to the main deck, and a couple of other people who'd come out when the whistle sounded went back inside. I walked forward to the front of the cabin deck, where I could see the whole river in front of me and both banks off in the middle distance, and just stood there taking it in. Sanloo was another day or so downriver, Slane had told me earlier, and Memfis not too many days beyond that; I knew I needed to start thinking about what would happen once we got to Memfis—dealing with the local ruinmen's guild, trying to find the Walnut Ridge Telecommunications Facility, and if we were lucky, juggling all the details of running a dig, which I'd never done by myself, much less with one of the most powerful jennels in Meriga looking over my shoulder and paying the bills—but that wasn't what was on my mind just then. So I stood there at the rail and watched the river and the banks move past.

It was getting toward night before we got to the next town, which was Altan, over on the Ilanoy side. There were already lamps being lit there, so I could see it a good ways off, but the sky was still light enough that I could see something else: a line of concrete pilings like broken teeth, rising up out of the Misipi on either side. I blinked, looked again, and said some language hotter than I usually use; it hadn't occurred to me that even the ancients would have put a bridge over a river that big.

"There were once dozens of those, as it happens," Plummer's voice said next to me.

I hadn't heard him walk up, but somehow that didn't surprise me. I glanced at him. "Across the Misipi?"

"Exactly. All of them gone now, to be sure; the last were here and at Rocalan, and they were destroyed during the Third Civil War. A pity; I don't imagine anything of the sort will ever be built again."

"Does anyone even know any more how they were made?"

"There are books on the subject at Melumi and Sisnaddi, and a few other places."

He was watching me with that same odd look, as though he was waiting for me to say something in particular, so I thought for a long moment before answering. It was more than that, though, because Melumi's got the Versty and Sisnaddi's got the government archives, and I'd never heard about any other place with a collection of books worth noticing. He was, I suddenly guessed, trying to tell me something. What?

"If there are books tell how it's done," I asked him, "why won't a bridge like that ever be built again?"

Maybe it was the right thing to say. His voice went quiet, so that I had to strain to hear him. "Building a bridge is a simple thing for a nation that already has factories, machines, plenty of cheap iron ore, plenty of fuel—especially the fuel. And it's an obvious thing if there are tens of thousands or hundreds of thousands of cars, and people who want to drive the cars from one side of a river to the other side and back again every day. If the factories and the machines are gone, and the mines were worked out long before any of us were born, and steel has to be cut by hand out of old buildings by your colleagues, and the fuel and the cars and most of the people are gone as well, then it's neither obvious nor simple. A bridge like that one would cost every mark the government—" He said the word the old-fashioned way, rather than saying it "gummint" the way everyone else does nowadays. "—takes in taxes over ten years, and do no more good for anyone than a ferryman and his boat."

I thought about a conversation we'd had earlier, on the way to Proo. "Well, but don't they spend plenty of money on canals?"

"True. That takes men with shovels and men with trowels, earth and stone and mortar, and all of those can be had for a very modest sum these days. You know the current price of steel, I suspect. How much would it cost to bridge the river here with steel beams?"

I did know the price of steel, and even trying to guess the cost made my head hurt. "Okay," I said. "That makes sense. And I guess there are books in Melumi and Sisnaddi and those other places that tell how to build canals, too."

"Among other things," Plummer said.

Right then I was sure I knew what he was trying to tell me. My thoughts set off running in half a dozen directions at once, but I managed to get them settled enough not to blurt out something like an idiot. "Maybe you can tell me this," I said finally. "If nobody's ever going to build a bridge like that again, what's the point of having books that tell how it's done?"

Plummer didn't say anything for a long time, then: "When I was a boy, which was rather a few years ago now, there was a book I read often, about a boy who made a little boat and put it in the river, hoping that it would travel all the way down to the sea. Did you ever read that?"

I was surprised enough that I turned to face him. The lamps of Altan were spots of light mirrored in his eyeglasses. "I used to love that book!"

"Did you ever make a little boat like the one in the story, and put it in the river?"

"Yes. I used to wonder what happened to it."

"One never knows." He turned away, looking out into the gathering dark on the river. "Knowledge is much the same. It comes down the stream of time to us, and perhaps turns up on the bank, and we can put it back in the water and send it on its way, or leave it on the bank to rot. The difference, of course, is that there is no sea: just a river flowing out of sight, and perhaps the chance that somewhere further downstream the little boat will be of use to someone, for reasons we will doubtless never know."

He looked back toward me, then, and I could just see his smile in the last of the light. "An interesting subject to think about. We'll talk more another time." With that, he turned and went back into the cabin. I stared after him, and waited a long moment before following.

I didn't sleep well that night, because I knew what he was talking about. Ever since I was small I'd heard stories and rumors about people, maybe in Meriga, maybe somewhere else, who had knowledge from the old world that nobody else had any more. Half the robot stories my father used to tell me, and more than half the ones the prentices used to tell each other in Gray Garman's house, had somebody in them who had an old book he wasn't supposed to have, or something like that, and of course one part of the reason that ruinmen live outside the city walls and get uneasy looks from good folk is that people wonder if we know more than we should.

Now of course I knew that the right thing to do was to go talk to a priestess as soon as I had the chance and tell her what Plummer had said to me, and of course I knew that I wasn't going to do anything of the kind. You don't become a ruinman and dream about Deesee and go searching for Star's Reach if you think everything from the old world ought to stay buried, and no doubt Plummer knew that perfectly well. Still, between wondering what Plummer and his nameless friends might be offering me, and wondering what they might ask in return, I had a hard time getting to sleep, and when I finally did, damn if I didn't have a dream about Deesee like the ones I had when I was a boy: the vast empty streets and the water's surface shimmering overhead as I hurried to meet somebody whose name I didn't know at the base of the Spire.

I woke up before the sun came round Mam Gaia's belly to shine on us. Berry was sound asleep and I didn't wake him; I washed up quietly and got dressed and went to see if Plummer was awake yet. I went to the door to his cabin, and found it just a little open; when I nudged it a bit further, I could see at once that the cabin was empty and the bed hadn't been slept in.

I laughed, at myself as much as anything. I knew right away that he'd slipped off the boat as soon as it docked in Altan; I'd have done the same thing in his place, I realized right away, just in case I'd misjudged the person I'd talked to. I wondered how long it would be until he showed up again.

The empty cabin didn't have any answers for me. After a moment I went aft to the kitchen, where they were boiling up a big pot of soup for breakfast, and begged an early cup of chicory brew. We got going about an hour later, and passed Sanloo a little while after that.

From Sanloo south, the Misipi winds its way toward the sea in big sweeping arcs, as though it knows where it's going but isn't in any kind of hurry to get there. The riverboats do the hurrying, or try to, but there's only so fast you can go upstream breasting the current, and on the way downstream you're going to be stopping at every little town anyway, so there's only so much hurrying you can do. That's the way it felt to me, certainly, as the *Jennel Mornay* paddled its way toward Memfis and the last part of our trip down the river went past.

That's not to say there was any lack of things to look at and think about. For one thing, the Misipi has little gray whales in it—little by whale standards, or so I've been told, though the one that came up for air a dozen meedas from the *Jennel Mornay* didn't look that small to me.

Back in the old world, there weren't any whales in the Misipi. There weren't many left anywhere in Mam Gaia's waters, of course, and the Misipi had so many poisons in it toward the end that there wasn't much living in it at all. After the old world ended and the seas rose, some gray whales that managed to hide from the hunters through the last dark days of the old world found their way to the mouth of the Misipi and liked the scenery or something, and they or their children's children got used to fresh water and found places to live upriver, and so there they are. The riverboatmen say it's good luck to see one, and not even a Jinya pirate will hurt one—there are some things the priestesses don't even need to preach about, you just don't do—and so the whales get on pretty well.

It was the third day after we left Altan, I think, that we saw the whale. I was still mulling over what Plummer had said, about knowledge and the places it was kept that he wasn't willing to name; I was wondering when I'd see him again, and whether he'd intended us to meet outside of Cago, and if that was so, why. The brown water splashing around the hull of the *Jennel Mornay* and the green of the riverbanks way off to either side didn't seem particularly interested in giving me any answers just then. I thought about Star's Reach and the hope Berry and I were chasing down the river to Memfis, but there weren't any answers for me there, either.

That evening, about the time the sun went down and the *Jennel Mornay* tied up for the night—it was in a riverside town named Jirido—I got to talking with Slane about Memfis. I don't remember whether he brought it up or I did, but it was probably me. I knew we weren't that far away from it, and I remembered what Slane said about it when we first met. Not that I needed the warning; Memfis has a reputation and then some.

"Not to worry," Slane said. He had a glass of whiskey in one hand, and was leaning up against the rail on the cabin deck with nothing on the other side but dark water and the lights of Jirido. "I promised Plummer I'd make sure you and your boy get to the ruinmen's hall in one piece, and I'll do that."

"Thank you," I said, and he laughed and punched me on the shoulder with his free hand. "You just follow me, you'll stay safe. You been through Cago?"

"Not to speak of. We got a canal boat south of town."

He nodded. "Smart. Cago's only half as big as Memfis, but it's near as rough. Both of 'em have too many people and too much money, but in Cago it's all Genda money and in Memfis it's all from Meyco. You know about the river trade?" I didn't, and he gestured at me with his whiskey. "Well, that's about half of what keeps Meriga plump and happy these days. Genda's got stuff to sell to Meyco and the countries down south, Meyco's got stuff to sell Genda and the countries across the Lannic and the North Ocean, and shipping it up and down the Misipi is a lot safer than sending it around by the Gulf and the Lannic and letting Jinya pirates have a shot at it from one side and Arab pirates from the other. So Cago gets one end of the trade and Memfis gets the other, and a lot of people make money off the deal. Me, for example."

"What do you do?"

"Buy and sell. Bunch of stuff down there on the cargo deck is mine, and it'll be going to Meyco pretty much as soon as we hit Memfis and I find a buyer. Pick up some Meycan goods then, something with a market up north, and it's back up the river." He smiled, or half his mouth did; the other half didn't move much, ever. "Beats the stuffing out of pushing a plow through Aiwa mud, which is what I'd be doing if I'd followed my daddy's footsteps."

"Can't argue there," I said. "I'd have been doing the same thing in Tenisi."

"There you go. But Dell had other ideas for me." He laughed. "Dell and Plummer. Not sure which one's the stranger."

I tried to keep the surprise off my face. I'd gotten used to thinking that nobody anywhere would talk about Plummer. "You've known Plummer a while?"

"Half my life. He got me out of a scrape in Sanloo—I was a dumb kid. We've been friends since then. I see him every couple of years."

"He's got a lot of friends."

"You ever met the ones that don't have names?" He was watching me with that look of his that seemed casual and wasn't.

I don't think he could have said anything else that would have startled me more. "A few of them," I said after a good long moment.

He took a swig of his whiskey. "He ever tell you anything about 'em?"

"Not a word."

"Me neither." Maybe he was dodging the question, but I didn't think so just then. "I just wondered. How'd you meet him?"

So I told Slane the story about how Berry and I met Plummer on the road north to Luwul, and we got to talking about something else from there, I don't remember what. Finally we went back inside, and I headed for my cabin while he headed for another drink.

Berry was sound asleep in his bunk when I came into the cabin, and didn't show any sign of waking up, so I sat on one of the little folding chairs at the little table up against the little window that showed me the night and the river. I thought about Plummer, and about Slane, and about Star's Reach, and after a while when I was sure Berry wasn't going to wake up

I turned on the little lamp over the table and spent a while writing a letter to Jennel Cobey.

I thought he'd probably want to know where we were and how the search for Star's Reach was coming. I didn't yet know that we were going to become friends, or that we were going to travel to Star's Reach together, or that I was going to kill him there. There was a mother of a lot I didn't know yet, and though it was just a few years ago I can't remember that trip down the Misipi without thinking about how foolish I was, and how little I knew about what was going on all around me.

Still, I had a hint, and it came that night. After I'd gotten the letter more or less finished and the ink was dry, I turned out the light and got undressed and went to bed. I thought I'd have trouble sleeping, but the slow rocking of the riverboat and the sound of Berry's quiet breathing and I don't know what else put me to sleep right away, and somewhere toward the end of the night I dreamed about Deesee.

It was like the other dreams I've written about already. I was walking through the streets that were as wide as rivers, between the tall pale buildings with windows that were all the same size and shape and color, with fish swimming past me and my breath going up in bubbles and the surface of the water like a silver sky high above. I knew I had to meet someone at the Spire, and I knew it was important, but I couldn't figure out how to get there. I went down one street after another, turned this way and that, but all I found was more tall pale buildings. Then, when I'd just about given up, I saw a little passage between two of the buildings, and went through it onto green grass, and the Spire stood tall and pale as a ghost, rising up out of a low grassy hill in front of me.

I hurried up the hill and got to the foot of the Spire. The person I was supposed to meet was waiting there for me. He wore the heavy stiff clothes that soldiers wore in the old world, and the funny hat with a flat top and a black bill above the eyes that jennels and cunnels wore back then; his hair was cut short, and his face was long and hard and tense with worry. As soon as he caught sight of me, he hurried across the grass and took hold of both my hands, and said two words, but I couldn't hear them; all that came out of his mouth was bubbles that floated up toward the surface of the water above us.

He said them again, and all of a sudden I realized what they were: he was trying to say "Star's Reach." It was then that I recognized him. I'd seen his face once before, after all, or what was left of it after better than four hundred years buried in the Shanuga ruins. He was the man whose corpse was there with the letter I'd found, the one that sent me on my journey.

I must have screamed then, because all at once it was morning, and Berry was shaking me. "Trey? Are you all right?"

I blinked and stared at him, and then the dream let go of me and I realized where I was. "Just a dream," I said. "Dreaming about a ghost."

He gave me a horrified look, and right away I wished I hadn't said anything. Maybe it's just a Tenisi thing; I've never heard anybody mention it away from Shanuga or the hill country where I grew up, but there it's said that if you dream about a ghost, it means that somebody's going to try to kill you. "Well, not really a ghost," I said after a moment. "That soldier we found down in the ruins with the letter."

Berry nodded, as though that made it less of a bad sign. We got dressed and went to breakfast, and I tried to put the dream out of my mind.

The rest of the trip downriver after that all pretty much runs together in my mind. We went past the place where the Hiyo river flows into the Misipi, where there used to be a fair sized town and isn't one any more because of the flooding every year when the rains come. After that the Misipi got even wider than it was before, and as often as not we could see the sun flashing on lakes and marshes to either side, sometimes a good long distance away. Towns got few and we stopped less often, though Slane told me over dinner one night that there were houses aplenty wherever the ground was high enough that they wouldn't be washed out to sea by floodwaters. It was rich country away from the river, he said, and the farmers grew rice and rubber trees and all kinds of fruit you don't see further north. Come harvest they'd bring their crops down to the Misipi and the *Jennel Mornay* would spend a month or so nosing up to the shore, loading up as much as would fit on the cargo deck, and taking it all down to Memfis or up to Sanloo, depending on where the price was better that week. I sat back and sipped my beer and listened, and found myself thinking about what it would be like to live that kind of life, the way I'd thought about working a canal boat when we'd been on our way from Cago to Proo.

Still, I had a place to find first, if I could. I rewrote my letter to Jennel Cobey that night and sealed it up, so it could be mailed to him as soon as we got to Memfis, and after that all I could do was wait until the *Jennel Mornay* got where it was going.

That happened finally late one afternoon. We'd been warned, so Berry and I were out on the front of the cabin deck along with most of the other cabin passengers. It was as good a day as you could ask for, with clouds drifting past, the sun slanting down, and the Misipi wide and smooth and brown, and there off in the distance was Memfis: a blur along the edge of the sky at first, and then a city so big you could have dropped Shanuga into it a dozen times over and not noticed; and off beyond it, the Misipi spread and opened into a line of silver that was Banroo Bay. We got closer, and the air smelled of salt and tar and a hundred other things I'd never smelled before; and finally the *Jennel Mornay* blew its whistle, right behind us, loud enough to make me put my hands over my ears, and we came up to the Memfis levee.

Slane was as good as his word, too. He had some business to do with a buyer from Meyco, as he'd said, but once that was done he got me and Berry and took us to the Memfis ruinmen's hall, which was just north of town. I lived there off and on for the next two years and a bit, so my memories of that first trip there have a lot of others laid down over the top of them. As best I remember, the trip there was mostly a blur of narrow streets and crowds, and the quarter around the ruinmen's hall was practically big and bustling enough to be a city all its own, with the houses of the ruinmen and the other trades nobody wants inside the city walls all cheek by jowl with each other and with the taverns and shops and markets that sell to them.

The Memfis ruinmen's hall is a huge dome made of triangles, most of them metal but some of them glass to let light get in or let ruinmen look out. When we got there, Slane gave it a long dubious look, then laughed and said, "Damn if I'd stay in a place like that, but it looks about right for you two. You see Plummer any time soon, tell him he owes me a favor."

We promised we would, and thanked him, and said our goodbyes, and he strolled out of my life. For all I know he's still working the riverboats, buying and selling and making a few spare marks now and then with crooked dice, but I've never seen him since. I wonder if he'd be surprised to know that I'm sitting here right now at Star's Reach, as the night settles in, and writing about him.

He got us safely to the ruinmen's hall, as I said, and once Berry and I went in and identified ourselves and got a proper ruinman's welcome, with maybe a bit thrown in because they knew perfectly well who we were and why we were there, I felt safe. I hadn't quite forgotten about the dream, but I didn't think much about what that kind of dream's supposed to mean, and I went about my first couple of days in Memfis as though nothing of the sort had happened. I was wrong, but I didn't find that out for a few weeks.

CHAPTER 21

THE KING OF YAMI

"We may have a problem," said Tashel Ban.

Dinner was on the table, just bread and beans—we've been at Star's Reach long enough that the tastier end of our supplies have started to run short. Still, everyone looked at him. Everyone but Eleen, I ought to say; she sat there, not looking at anyone or anything, the way she does when there's trouble and she can't do anything about it. Tashel Ban had papers in his hands and he was looking at Thu, and that meant a very particular kind of trouble.

Thu said nothing, and after a moment Tashel Ban went on. "We found another paper on Cetan science and technology, probably the last one that the people here had time to put together—it was written about three years before Star's Reach was abandoned. Not much different from the last one, except that it refers to another paper, and we were able to find the other paper.

"You'll remember that the Cetans have their own way of getting electricity from sunlight, unlike anything humans ever tried. That's what the other paper is about. Some of the people here decided to try to figure how that worked from what they'd already learned about Cetan technology. They—" He shrugged. "The compounds the Cetans use aren't stable in an oxygen atmosphere—they catch fire as soon as electricity starts flowing through them—but they were able to figure out the basis for the effect, and find compounds that will work here. So—" He looked straight at Thu. "We have a formula for a Cetan technology that could change the way we get energy here."

Thu considered that for a moment. "Does it differ from the sunpower cells we use?"

"The principle's the same. The details aren't. The solar cells the old world used were made with technologies we don't have any more; the ones we use now are quite a bit less efficient, and they're not cheap to make. This technology is much more efficient and probably much cheaper, once some work gets done on sources for the chemicals."

"Chemicals." Thu repeated the word as though it wasn't something you say around good people. "How toxic?"

"They'd have to be tested. Still, the result seems to be chemically stable, and it's recyclable." He used his hands to show a ball the size of someone's head. "Imagine something that looks like glass, about this big around, with a wire going into the center of it and a net of fine wires all over the outside. Light shines on it and kicks electrons into motion, and they flow out the wire that goes to the center and back in through the net around the outside. The Cetan ones last for about thirty of our years, then have to be melted down and remade. Here, they hadn't figured out how long they would last, but something like that's probably a good guess."

"How much power will come from it?"

"Depends on location and season. My best guess, from the figures in the paper, is that each of them will produce around a hundred watts under average conditions—say, five of them would equal your ordinary farmyard wind turbine."

Thu just looked at him for a long moment, then: "You say they will not be too expensive. As expensive as a wind turbine?"

"Less than that," Tashel Ban answered. "As a guess—and it's no more than a guess—once these were being produced in fair numbers, you could probably buy a five or six hundred watt system for about half as much as a wind turbine would cost you."

Another long silent look from Thu, and then, unexpectedly, he laughed. He doesn't laugh often, but when he does it's a great rolling laugh that fills up whatever space he's in. Tashel Ban looked baffled, probably wondering what the joke was, which was what I was wondering just then, too. The others watched and waited.

"You expect me," Thu said then, "to invoke our bargain and settle our disagreement with knives, because farmers in Meriga will be able to choose between wind and sun to power a few light bulbs and a fan in the summer? No. My requirement—" He tapped a finger on the table, hard enough that it rang. "My requirement is that nothing we find here will give humanity the chance to do again what they did to the earth. Wind turbines have not done that. Solar cells and solar water heaters have not done that. I see no reason to think that this new technology will do that—and I do not grudge the farmers their light bulbs and cool air in the summer."

There's a kind of tension you get in a place where a fight's about to start, and everyone knows it. If the fight isn't going to happen after all, and everyone knows it, the moment when the tension lets go lands like a punch in the stomach. I know I swayed, and I'm pretty sure most of the others did, too. Berry didn't, though. He glanced at me, at Thu, and at Tashel Ban, and then said, "I wonder how hard it would be to figure out whether there's anything later than that paper on the computer."

Tashel Ban thought about that for a moment. "I could probably do it now. We've found enough files with dates that it should be possible to figure out the raw code, and search."

"That might be a good idea," said Berry then. "I've been thinking, and it seems to me that we have to do two things before we can let other people know about any of this."

We were all looking at him then. "First," he went on, "is finding out if the Cetans have sent us anything that might hurt Mam Gaia, or humanity, or Meriga or the other nations. Second is finding out why the people here—" He glanced sideways at Anna, who was watching him sidelong with no expression on her face at all. "—why they died. We could do both by finding what information they left that's later than this."

"True," said Tashel Ban.

"There's another factor," Eleen said then. "The radio."

"Also true," said Tashel Ban, as though the two of them had talked about it before, which no doubt they had. He turned back to Thu. "Before we make a decision about making all this public, we also need to know what's happening in Meriga. If war's broken out—well, then things are going to be rather more difficult." He gestured, palms up. "So I'd like to propose that we assemble the radio receiver. Just the receiver, to listen; we can leave the transmitter for later."

That was another part of the agreement I mentioned a while back, the one I got Thu and Tashel Ban to settle on before we left Cansiddi. Tashel Ban brought his own radio gear with him when he came to join us in Sanloo, a transmitter and a receiver, both of them with the tubes taken out and packed in lom wool to keep them from breaking on the road. They stayed that way after we arrived, because we'd agreed that no word of what we found, if we found anything, was to go out until we all agreed on what to say.

Thu thought a moment, and then said, "That will be acceptable." I glanced around at everyone else and asked, "Anyone disagree?" Nobody did, and so that's what Tashel Ban is doing now, muttering to himself as he makes sure the tubes are still good and figures out how to hook the radio up to one of the antennas outside. Anybody with two bits of common sense would be pretty much frantic to know what's happened in Meriga while we've been gone, since the presden was probably dying when we left and jennels were busy raising armies to fight each other, but what I'm thinking about instead is Thu—how we met, and how he almost killed me.

That happened maybe a month after I got to Memfis. As soon as Berry and I got settled in at the ruinmen's hall there, I went to the misters, explained to them what I was there for, asked about the records of past digs, and told them about the Walnut Ridge Telecommunications Facility and the contract dig I'd agreed to do with Jennel Cobey. They knew a fair amount of that already, of course, since ruinmen carry news with them when they travel, but they didn't know all of it, and it's one of the courtesies that you don't dare skip when you're planning a dig in someone else's region.

Of course I planned on bringing the Memfis misters and prentices into the dig, and paying them with Jennel Cobey's money, and I let them know that. I also mentioned, which they already knew, that I hadn't managed a dig myself before, and would welcome the local guild's help with that. Between the prospect of money up front and the chance to help find the way to Star's Reach, they were pretty pleased with me, and gave me all the help I needed.

It turned out that the ruin of the Walnut Ridge Telecommunications Facility hadn't been worked yet, either. Memfis was a big city in the old world, even bigger than it is now, when it's the largest city in Meriga. Some of the ruins around it are buried deep in river mud and water, and won't be at any risk of being touched by a ruinman's shovel until Mam Gaia decides she wants a different climate again and the sea draws back a good long ways to the south, but there are a lot of ruins less hard to get, and the guild's only been working them since after the Third Civil War. It wasn't too hard to figure out where the place was, and so all I had to do was get the money from Jennel Cobey, hire people, get supplies together, and make a start on the dig.

I sent the jennel a letter right away and started making arrangements. That meant visiting the houses of each of the misters in the Memfis guild, first of all, and making deals over dinner and whiskey; after that was done and I knew how many misters and prentices I'd have to set up with food and tents and the like, it meant visiting the merchants that outfit ruinmen with the things they need, and making deals with them—usually with no dinner and whiskey in sight, since most of them will take a ruinman's money but won't stoop to eat or drink with him. So I went from place to place with somebody's prentice to show me the way and Berry trotting alongside me to prove that I was enough of a mister to have a prentice of my own, and fairly often I got the feeling that somebody was watching me.

Someone was, and I found that out the hard way one night.

Berry and I went to visit a provision merchant that afternoon, and stayed late. The merchant's name was Dalla; she was short and round and pleasant, and got into the provisions trade because she had family in the ruinmen's guild, so we got dinner and whiskey; I don't doubt that she meant to show off the sort of provisions she could get us, too. By the time we settled on a deal, or as much of a deal as I could make before Jennel Cobey got my letter and replied, it was well after dark, and though I wasn't quite tipsy I wasn't far from it. We went down the steps onto the street and the door of the merchant's closed behind us, leaving us in the next thing to perfect darkness, since the moon was down and we were outside the gates of Memfis. We had only a few blocks to walk to get back to the ruinmen's hall, and there was nobody else in sight, so we started off without any particular worries.

Then a shadow came out of a deeper shadow to one side and blocked our way.

I stopped, not too sure of myself. The shadow stood there for a moment, looming over the two of us, and then said in a deep voice, "You have a dead man's letter. I need it. If you give it to me now, you will not become a dead man yourself."

What startled me then wasn't that somebody would be willing to kill me to get my copy of the letter; I'd been waiting for that since Berry and I left Shanuga all those months ago. What startled me is that I had the letter with me, and this person knew it. Now it's true that I'd taken it with me to a couple of other merchants by then, since news about the letter had gotten around and I could usually get a better deal on provisions if I let the merchant see and handle the copy I had. I didn't think of that, though. I could have simply handed over the letter and gotten a new copy from Jennel Cobey, too, but I didn't think of that, either. All I could think of was that somebody was trying to take my one hope of finding Star's Reach away from me.

I pulled my pry bar out of my belt, and the shadow turned into a man and jumped at me.

I don't think I've ever seen anybody else move that fast. I was just barely able to jump out of his way, and flailed at him with the pry bar; that made him duck to one side, and probably kept me from getting spitted, because he had a knife in his hand—I could just about see it as he moved.

I had more reach with the pry bar than he had with the knife, so I dodged past him, as fast as I could, and snapped the pry bar out at the back of his knee, one of those nasty little moves that leaves your enemy down on the pavement where you can kill him or just go away, your choice. It hit—I could feel the shock right up the bar—but I might as well have clobbered a rock. He spun around and came at me again, as though I hadn't hit him at all.

There's a kind of nightmare I've had now and again all my life, where I'm being attacked in total darkness by somebody I can't see, and nothing I do makes any difference. This fight was like that. I think I landed three or four good hard hits with the pry bar, and none of it seemed to do a thing to the man who was trying to kill me. He just kept coming at me, and I kept jumping away and hitting at him. I knew that he would wear me down if the fight kept going much longer but I didn't have a spare moment to think of anything else I could do.

Then he came at me again, and I was just that little bit too slow getting out of his way, and by the time I landed I could feel something wet spreading along my side. The pain flared a moment later: not a deep cut, but bad enough. He moved toward me, slowly, testing. I shifted my grip on the pry bar and got ready to stuff it down his throat.

Then boots pounded on the cobblestones, dozens of them, fast. My attacker turned, stopped, and tried to run, but the moment of hesitation lost him his chance. Dark shapes blurred in a scuffle, and something rose and fell. I knew the shape at a glance: a ruinman's shovel.

Light flared near my face, half blinding me. It was a lantern, and Berry was holding it. It wasn't until then that I realized that I hadn't noticed where he was since the fight started, and guessed that he'd gone for help. "He's hurt!" Berry shouted, and some others in ruinmen's leathers came over, got me down on the street and started doing something with my side.

I couldn't quite see my attacker, just a hand here and a foot there pinned down under a fair-sized mob of burly ruinmen. They'd brought shovels and picks, which only get brought out for fighting when it's a matter for blood.

"Kill him?" someone asked, and I was dizzy enough that for a moment I wondered if he meant me.

"No." One of the guild misters—I recognized him, or almost—shook his head. "He goes back to the hall. If he's somebody's hired knife, we'll find out who, and then ..."

He didn't have to finish. It wouldn't have done me any good if he had, though, because the street was starting to spin around me, and the lantern got very faint and far away, and so did everything else for a good long time.

I woke up eventually, which I hadn't really expected to do, but it was a good long while before I could do much of anything but lay there in my bed in the Memfis guild hall and heal.

The knife cut I took in the fight wasn't deep but it went most of the way through the muscles along my side, and though the ruinmen got someone in to clean it and stitch it up, it's not the kind of thing you can jump up and ignore the next day. So I lay there, and tried not to yelp when the healer came by twice a day to dab it with something that smelled of herbs and cheap alcohol; it kept the cut from festering while it closed up, but damn, it hurt.

The man who'd tried to kill me was in the guild hall, too, down below ground. Most ruinmen's halls have a couple of rooms in the basement where somebody can be locked up—a prentice who tried to cheat his mister, someone who isn't a ruinman but tried to pass himself off as one, that sort of thing. There are places in Memfis where there aren't any basements because the water level's too high, but the ruinmen's hall is up on what used to be a bluff overlooking the river before the seas rose, then became an island, and now is a sort of low ridge, not high enough to count for a hill, between two low flat areas full of warehouses and cheap lodgings that get a couple of sena-mees of water in the streets when the Misipi floods. There's enough room between the top of the ridge and the water level for a basement, but it's damp and smells bad. I can't imagine a better place to take new prentices to shake the robot's hand, but you wouldn't want to store anything there.

But that's where he was, or so Berry told me. He also said that the man hadn't said a word since he was thrown into the room in the basement where they had him; the Memfis ruinmen had tried to get him to talk, to find out who'd paid him if anybody did, but they might as well have tried to get a word out of the stones of the basement walls. So there I was, and there he was, and nothing much changed while my belly healed.

After a while, they let me sit up for a few hours a day, and then for most of the day, and then I got to walk a little; Berry brought me records from the digs out in the part of Arksa where the Walnut Ridge Telecommunications Facility was, and ran messages to the merchants and misters who were negotiating with me about the dig, so I had something to think about besides how close I'd come to ending this story in a puddle of blood on a Memfis street.

Finally, though, I was healed enough to leave the room, eat with everyone else, and start doing more to get the dig going. If was pretty clear by then that the dig wasn't going to start until after the rains came and went again, even if I'd been healed enough to handle heavy work before then, which I probably wasn't. Even then I thought that this was probably a good thing, since it gave me enough time to figure out what I was doing, get as much advice as I could from the other misters, and catch the worst of my mistakes before they cost anything. So I made plans and drew up contracts and waited for word to come from Jennel Cobey.

Still, there was one other thing I wanted to do right away. As soon as I could walk well enough to handle the stairs, I went down to the basement to talk to the man who'd almost killed me. Berry went with me, along with one of the Memfis misters named Ran, a tough white-haired old man as short and solid as a brick, and a couple of his prentices. Just to be safe, the prentices had pry bars at their belts and shouldered a couple of shovels with the blades filed sharp. I didn't go armed, but I pocketed something else I thought would be of more use. So we went down the stairs all the way to the basement, and Ran unlocked the door and turned on a light.

The basement smelled bad, as I wrote a moment ago. The air was damp, and the walls were big rough chunks of concrete split out of some old world structure, bashed into rough blocks, and mortared into place, the sort of thing you find all over Meriga wherever nobody cares what the results are going to look like. Ran led the way down a short passage and turned a corner, and we were in a room of sorts with a few old boxes and barrels in it. Over on the far side was a door made of iron bars, and on the other side of the door was the man I'd come to see.

I hadn't realized until then that it wasn't just the night that made him look dark when he attacked me. He was what they used to call black in the old world, and what we'd call really dark-skinned nowadays, now that everybody in Meriga is some shade of brown. I used to think, when I first heard that people in the old world spent so much time bickering and fighting over skin color, that the people they called white back then actually had skin the color of chalk, and the people they called black had skin the color of soot, and that people looked like that until they finally got around to making babies with each other in the drought years and, thank the four winds, the babies came out brown instead of concrete gray.

Most children in Meriga end up thinking something like that, before somebody gets around to telling them that "white" back then just meant light enough brown that you could see the pink through it, and "black" meant anything much darker than that. This man's skin was a lot darker than that, darker than anybody else I've ever seen in Meriga, the color of really good beer or the kind of leather gear that's stained with nutshells and then rubbed with oil until it glows.

He glanced up at us, noted each of us, and then without a word turned back to whatever patch on the floor he'd been considering when we came in.

"That's him," said Ran. "Maybe you can get him to talk."

"Maybe I can," I said, and faced the man behind the door. "You wanted a dead man's letter from me," I said to him. "I want to know some things from you. I thought maybe we could make a bargain."

He looked up at me, considered. "Let me read the letter," he answered, "and I will answer your questions." He had a deep voice, with just a bit of an accent I couldn't place.

"And if I show you the letter and you won't talk?"

Another glance. "I do not break my word."

The funny thing was that I believed him. People are odd that way; there are men who will kill you in a heartbeat for no reason at all but won't tell a lie, women who will whore their bodies for a handful of coins but won't break a promise; well, we all have things we do and things we won't, and which is which doesn't always make a lot of sense. I pulled the letter out of my pocket—it was the copy I got from Mam Kelsey back in Shanuga—and started to move toward the door, but Berry took it from my hand, carried it the rest of the way, and tossed it through the bars with a quick little motion that didn't get any part of him close enough to the bars to be in range of whatever the man might do.

The man didn't do much of anything, except reach a hand up so fast I couldn't follow the motion and catch the letter as it flew. He unfolded it, angled it to catch the light, and read it. After a good long moment I said, "Make much sense?"

He glanced up at me again. "I assume it does to you."

"I've got some guesses. But I've also got some questions."

"Of course." He folded the letter again and with a snap of his wrist sent it flying back out through the bars, where Berry caught it. "I will answer any question you ask except one."

"Who are you?"

That got me just the faintest bit of a smile. "That is the one."

One of Ran's prentices started laughing, a sudden loud laugh like a donkey braying, and stopped all at once when Ran gave him a hard look. I wasn't too surprised, though. "Who paid you to get the letter from me?"

The thought seemed to startle him. "No one paid me."

"Why did you want the letter, then?"

"To find Star's Reach, of course."

"Why?"

He looked at me for a long moment. "If it exists," he said then, "and if the stories about it are true, and if the people there did manage to speak to beings from some other world—so many ifs. Grant that it is all true. If the beings from some other world told them some way to do the same things to this world that our ancestors did in the past, that knowledge must be destroyed."

"And you want to go there to destroy it."

"Tell me this." He leaned forward and stared at me, as though he was the one on the outside of the bars. "If you discover Star's Reach, and you find knowledge of that kind, what will you do?"

"Hand it over to the priestesses," I told him.

He considered that. "And those with you?"

"It's the ruinmen's way," I said, but of course he had a point, and I knew it. That's one of the things ruinmen ought to think about more than they usually do, because we deal with what's left over from the old world. The priestesses say that the old world couldn't survive once it burnt through most of Mam Gaia's oil and coal and gas, and it's going to be millions and millions of years before she can store enough carbon underground to let anyone do anything like that again. Still, nobody knows that for sure, and the idea that the aliens might have passed on something that would give people too much energy again, and do the same kind of harm to Mam Gaia a second time, hadn't occurred to me.

The man who'd tried to kill me was still watching me. "I hope it is so. If you find something of the sort I have named, you may have a fight with those whose ways are different."

"I think we can handle that," I told him, but there again he had a point, one that I hadn't considered anything like enough.

"Perhaps so. I grant that you were better with that iron bar than I expected."

That startled me. "I couldn't land a solid hit on you for anything."

"You did so several times. I am—" He shrugged. "—difficult to hurt."

All at once Berry let out a long low whistle. "Sir and Mister," he said to me, "I know who he is." I nodded, answering the question he hadn't said out loud, and Berry turned to the man on the other side of the bars. "You're Thu," he said. "You're the last king of Yami. Am I right?"

Ran's prentice laughed his donkey-laugh again, and stopped when Ran glanced at him.

The man gave Berry a long slow look, and then nodded once. "That is correct."

Ran blinked, and muttered a bit of hot language under his breath. I stared at Berry, then back at the man who'd tried to kill me. "That explains a few things," I said, for want of anything better.

"I suppose it does." There was something new in his voice, an edge that hadn't been there before. I could guess why: if he was who he said he was, there were a lot of people in Meriga, Meyco and the coastal allegiancies who wanted his guts in a bucket and would pay good money for the chance to see them there.

Ran cleared his throat then. "Mister's lodge is going to have to sort this out," he said. "Unless there's something else you want to ask him?"

There wasn't, so we left him there in the little room with the barred door. Ran turned off the light and locked the door to the basement behind us. As we started up the stairs, he asked Berry, "How did you guess that, prentice?"

"I've heard a lot of stories about him, Sir and Mister. There really wasn't anybody else he could be."

Ran gave him a long steady look, and then nodded. "Clever."

Of course there was a lot more to it than that, more even than Berry explained to me once we got back up to my room. Still, I wasn't paying too much attention. Part of me was trying to figure out what to say to the mister's lodge when it met, and part of me was more or less stumbling around in shock that somebody who was nearly as much of a legend as Star's Reach had come jumping out of the shadows on a Memfis street and tried to gut me, but a good part had something else to think about.

I knew I was stupid even to consider it. I knew that the man had done his best to kill me and that the misters would be making a good choice if they either killed him or sold him to somebody who wanted to kill him, but damn if I wanted the last king of Yami to die because of me. As we climbed the stair—slowly, because the cut in my side wasn't too happy just then—I started trying to figure out if there was a way I could get him out of there.

There was a reason for that, and most people in Meriga could probably guess it. Still, as I wrote a while back, the next person who comes here to Star's Reach might be from the Neeyonjin country over on the far side of the dead lands, and won't have the least idea of how things are over on this side of the dead lands. If you grew up in Meriga any time in the last thirty years or so, it's a safe bet that you've heard of the last king of Yami, and before then it was his father or his grandfather or someone else in his family, back to the days when Yami was drowned by the rising oceans, but nobody from Meriga has gone to the Neeyonjin country since before that happened. I probably need to tell Thu's story, then, and it so happens that I got to hear Thu tell his story himself.

That happened about a week before we got to Star's Reach, on the road west out of Cansiddi. We left the last few scraggly trees behind us by the time we were out of sight of the Suri River, and from then on it was grass: tall grass at first, tall as I am, whipping in the wind off the desert, and then shorter and shorter as you go further west, until finally it's low and sparse and as brown as the ground itself, just before the grass goes away and you're in the desert. We weren't that far, but the grass was no taller than my knees and the wind muttered and wheezed through it like an old man who's drunk too much whiskey for too many years. We found a place where a building had been in the old world, and part of a concrete wall still stood shoulder-high at the right angle to screen us from the wind; it was late enough in the day to camp, and our chances of finding anything better up ahead didn't look too good, so we staked the pack horses where the grass looked decent and settled in for the night.

There were eight of us, me and Berry and Eleen, Tashel Ban and Thu, Anna, Jennel Cobey, and his man Banyon; eight when we left Cansiddi and eight when we got to the door of Star's Reach, though there were just six left not too many minutes after that. Once we got a fire going and some food cooked, we sat and talked, as we usually did, and somehow the talk wound its way around to Thu and the lost kingdom of Yami, and he told his story.

"It began with the three voyages," he said in that deep musical voice of his, motioning with his hands; the firelight turned their shadows into big looming shapes on the crumbling wall behind him. "First, the voyage of grief, from Affiga across the sea to Meriga. That was long ago, when men were first beginning to dig their way into Mam Gaia's flesh to get the fossil fuels they craved. They still needed strong muscles in those days, and so the people of Meriga enslaved my people and brought them here to labor for them.

"Then there was war, and my people won their freedom. Many stayed here in Meriga, but some took ship back to Affiga, to a country whose name meant the place of freedom. That was the second voyage, the voyage of hope from Meriga back across the sea to Affiga, though the hope was a long time seeking its fulfillment. It was not in Affiga as it was in Meriga; the power and the wealth and the technologies were here and not there. There, there was bitter poverty and much war, until the old world began to break apart.

"It happened then that a strong ruler took power in the country called the place of freedom, and seized countries near it to make a larger kingdom, and because the land was rich and had things the rest of the world needed, the kingdom grew strong as the old world grew weak. He lived long and left behind two sons, and when he died there was war between them. The younger had not so many followers as the elder, and when he knew he could not win he and his followers took ships and sailed west across the ocean, to Meriga. That was the third voyage, the voyage of power, from Affiga back across the sea to Meriga again.

"Meriga the rich, Meriga that had ruled the world, was then torn by war, crushed by drought, and broken into many quarreling parts, and an army that was not strong enough to win a kingdom in Affiga was still strong enough to take what it wanted here. So the prince of the place of freedom landed in a country that is now beneath the ocean, the country called Florda, and took it for his own, and much of the country along the shores of the Lannic that the allegiancies now hold, and many other lands that now lie under the waves.

"Those became his kingdom, and he ruled it from the city of Yami; and because he was heedless, and did not learn from the mistakes that brought Meriga and the old world low, he gathered as many of the old technologies as he could and made use of them to add to his power. That was when he and all his line lost the need for sleep; it was something that could be done with the old technologies, some trick of genetic engineering that someone still remembered; it was one of many things he claimed for himself out of the heritage of old Meriga.

"What he did not remember, and should have remembered, is that Mam Gaia does not care why we do what we do. The best of reasons and the worst are all one to her. All that matters to her is what we do, and all that mattered to her just then was that the king of Yami gathered and used the old technologies, and burnt what fuel he could find to power them, and the smoke added carbon to the carbon that had already been sent up into the sky in years past—just enough, or more than enough, to stir her to wrath. So the high cliffs of ice in the place called Nardiga broke and plunged into the sea, and the seas rose.

"Mam Gaia's wrath is not quick. It was in the time of the third king of Yami that the cliffs of ice fell and the seas began to rise, and it was most of a lifetime before the seas reached where they are today. Long before they stopped, though, Yami was deep below the waves. Many died and many more lost all they had, and even though the king of Yami tried to rescue as much as he could, a crowd came upon him and tore his body to pieces with their hands.

"That was long ago. He who would have been the fourth king was taken by friends to a place of safety in the mountains of Joja, and when he came to manhood he swore a great oath, that he and his sons and his son's sons until the ending of his line would make amends for what had been done. Since then it has been our purpose to make it so that the technologies that ravaged this world shall not do so a second time. I say we, for I am the heir of Yami, the eleventh king of the kingdom that is gone; the eleventh and the last, for Mam Gaia has not chosen to give me a son."

He shrugged, and the shadows on the wall behind him rose and fell like waves. "So that is my story, or part of it. If you want to know every place I have gone and everything I have done since I first went out to fight with those who would reawaken those technologies that should sleep forever, well, we will be here a long time."

That got a laugh, not least because he was right and we knew it. As I wrote a bit earlier, most people in Meriga know about Thu, and a fair number of them can tell stories about some of the things he's done. The priestesses don't like to hear people tell those stories, because they think we ought to keep clear of the bad old technologies because they're bad, not because someone who never sleeps and can't be bribed or bullied will come out of nowhere and mess with anybody who dabbles in them; and they don't like fighting for any reason, and of course Thu has done a lot of that. Still, the stories get told, because most people in Meriga have their own reasons to want the old technologies to stay buried, and because someone who never sleeps and can't be bribed or bullied is better than most of us at doing things that make for good stories.

"It seems almost unfair," said Eleen then. She hadn't laughed with the rest of us. "The first king of Yami simply did what most rulers in those days were doing, salvaging whatever technologies they could find, and if I recall right, his grandson didn't even do that much."

"That is true," said Thu. "By then the last of the fossil fuels in the kingdom were gone, and so were the technologies they used to find more underground. Still, that is the way of it."

"Very much so," Jennel Cobey said. He was sitting next to me, with Banyon behind him like a shadow, and he'd spent the whole story with his chin on his hands, watching Thu. "The balance of the world is always exact but it's never fair. That's true in politics, in war—" He shrugged, glanced at me. "Anything else you care to name. One person gets the benefit, another pays the price, and there's no justice to who does which—but the price still gets paid."

There was a little more talk, I forget about what, and then all of us but Thu wrapped ourselves in our blankets and went to sleep, or tried to. It took me a while, because I was thinking about what the jennel said. It wasn't until we got to Star's Reach that I realized that he was giving me a warning, and by then it was too late for things to end any other way but the way they did. Looking back on it now, though, I'm sure it was a warning, and not the only one he gave me, either. That was his way, because I was a friend, or as near to a friend as a jennel with ambitions can let himself have.

I began to find out just how near to a friend he considered me when we were at Memfis, right after I met Thu for the first time. I think it was the next afternoon, when I was going over the contracts I'd drafted with the misters of the Memfis ruinmen, that a prentice I didn't know came pelting into the room, out of breath. "Mister Trey," he said, "it's the jennel—Jennel Cobey. He's here—"

Up the stairs behind him came quick footsteps, and then Jennel Cobey was there in the room. I got up, partly because that's what you do when a jennel comes into the room, and partly because I was about as surprised as you can get. I was expecting a letter from him, and maybe a visit from one of his men, but not the man himself.

His face lit up when he saw me. "On your feet already! That's a welcome thing. The reports I got made me think you were badly hurt."

"More or less, Sir and Jennel," I said. "Still, it's mostly healed. I hope you didn't come all the way down here just to check on me, though."

"I have business in Memfis that has to be done before the rains." A little fast gesture brushed them aside. "I also wanted to talk to you and find out how your plans are shaping up."

I knew him well enough already to know that he meant I should tell him that right away, in detail, so I sent the prentice down to get him some wine, and started handing the jennel contracts and papers, explaining what was what as he peppered me with questions. By the time the prentice got back with the wine we were deep into the details: which misters and their prentices would be working for him, which provision merchants would be selling us the food and gear we'd need, plans for the first year's digging, and the rest. He wanted to know all of it; that was his way, then and always. I don't think I've ever met a man who was curious about so many things so much of the time.

So we went over all the preparations I'd made, and he nodded, said he'd have the money to me in two weeks, and started to get up. Then he stopped and sat back down. "I was told the ruinmen caught the man who attacked you. What happened to him?"

"He's in the basement," I said.

He gave me a startled look. "Alive or—"

"Alive."

"Why?"

I hadn't wanted to tell him, but I knew by that point that he'd get the whole story out of me or someone else quickly enough. "Because of who he is, Sir and Jennel. You've heard of Thu, the king of Yami."

He took that in, and whistled after a long moment. "Plenty of people would pay good money to have him in their hands."

"I know." Then, though I hadn't meant to say anything of the kind: "But damn if it's going to be me who puts an end to all those stories."

The jennel just stopped, stared at me for a while, and then started laughing: a quiet unwilling laugh like nothing I'd ever heard from him before. "Good," he said. "Very good. You want to see him go free, even though he tried to rob and kill you."

"I've been trying to figure out how to do it for a couple of days now," I admitted. "Haven't been able to come up with a plan."

"Very good," he said again. "I may be able to arrange something. No promises, you understand."

I heard later that he went to the misters the next day and asked them how much they wanted for Thu. They set a good high price, though to be fair to them it was no higher than they could have gotten from some of the dons from Meyco who wanted him dead. Jennel Cobey paid it, and a bunch of his soldiers came over at night and hauled Thu away, took him out of the city, and let him go. I never did hear the details. Still, about a month later, when I was doing the rounds of the provision merchants again one evening, a shadow moved in the shadows of an alley and said, "Ruinman Trey."

I would have recognized the voice anywhere. I stopped and turned to face him, and Berry backed away in case he had to run for the guild hall again.

"Your prentice need not worry," said Thu. "I owe your friend the jennel a great favor, and you a greater one. What I wish to say, though, is this. When you find Star's Reach—for I think you will find it—consider sending for me. I may be useful to you."

That startled me, but I had enough of my wits about me to think of the obvious problem. "If I want to do that, how do I send for you?"

His laugh set echoes running down the alley. "Speak to the night air," he said. "I will hear of it." Then he was gone.

The odd thing was, that's pretty much what happened. After I found my way back to Sisnaddi with the secret I learned in the ruins of Deesee, if that's really where I learned it, I got to thinking about who I wanted with me when I went to Star's Reach. I knew Berry had to be there, and Eleen would be our scholar, and I wrote to Tashel Ban because I knew we'd need a radioman and to Jennel Cobey because he was the one person who never stopped trusting in me to find it; and then one night I stood at the narrow little window of the rickety little room Eleen and I shared during those weeks, and called out into the darkness, "Thu, I'm going to Star's Reach and I want you in the party."

It was the only thing I could think of to do, and I felt about as stupid as you can imagine when I did it, but a week later a knock rattled our door and there he was. The three of us, Thu and Eleen and me, sat up late into the night talking about the journey. We all agreed that if there was anything at Star's Reach that would put Mam Gaia at risk, we would destroy it or put it in the hands of the priestesses, but that nobody was going to destroy anything until all of us agreed to it. Once he agreed to that, I was glad to have him, since I knew we might have to fight, and of course I was right about that.

Still, the one thing I never did learn was how he knew to come looking for me. Did some friend of his outside the gates of Sisnaddi hear a rumor from the ruinmen and send for him, or did the night air actually tell him somehow? If it was anyone else, I'd laugh at that last notion, but Thu is, well, Thu, and I'd have laughed at the notion that somebody could have had his genes changed so he never has to sleep again, if I hadn't seen the results. It's easy enough to say that this belongs to stories and that belongs to everyday life, but what do you say when you're washing dishes in Star's Reach and the person who's drying them has more stories about him than a dog has fleas?

CHAPTER 22

MEMFIS NIGHTS, ARKSA DAYS

We got bad news over the radio tonight. I mentioned earlier that we agreed to let Tashel Ban get his radio receiver working so we could start listening to broadcasts from the station in Sanloo. He spent that evening getting the thing working and hooking it up to one of the big radio antennas built into the roof of Star's Reach, and at least one of us listens to it every night once radio waves start bouncing off whatever it is that bounces them back from the high thin air.

Until now, we could have spared ourselves the trouble. All we got was the same things I used to hear when I listened to the little crystal radio my father had, the one that could pick up signals from Sisnaddi sometimes: an hour of music, though it wasn't always the patriotic stuff they always play on the Sisnaddi station, and a few minutes of news. The one thing we got from that was that nobody had started fighting yet, but then we all knew that nobody would, not so long as Sheren still lived.

That was before tonight. Most of the news bulletins were the usual stuff, a band of Jinya raiders caught and driven off by our soldiers in Wesfa Jinya, a namee that washed away parts of three towns in Nuwinga, negotiations with Meyco over a trade treaty, that sort of thing. Then, at the end: "The presden's staff in Sisnaddi said yesterday that because of the presden's illness, this year's meeting of Congrus has been called off. We don't have any other details at this time."

Tashel Ban and I were in the radio room—that's what we call the little room, probably somebody's sleeping room back before Star's Reach was abandoned, where he set up the receiver—when that came over the loudspeaker. When we heard the last little bit of music the Sanloo station plays before it goes off the air, Tashel Ban let out a whistle. "Cancelled," he said. "Not postponed. That's bad."

"I heard she was sick again," I said; people had been talking about it in Sanloo.

"It's been on and off for years. Cancer, or that's what they say in Lebnan."

That was no surprise—that she had cancer, I mean, and also that Tashel Ban's family in the Nuwinga capital would know about it. Something like half the people in Meriga who live past childhood die of it. You can be as careful as you want, but there are so many poisons still left over from the old world that the odds are pretty good that sooner or later you'll get enough in you to start something growing that shouldn't. Ruinmen know a lot about that, more than most people, because if you're a ruinman and the ruins don't take you, it's a pretty safe bet that that's how you're going to get reborn.

We'll tell the others tomorrow morning, but Berry was another matter. I went and tapped on his door as soon as the radio was shut down. He was still awake, doing something that left paper scattered all over the table in his room; I told him about the bulletin and what Tashel Ban said, and he gave me a dismayed look and thanked me in a way that told me he really didn't want to talk. I wished him good dreams, and came back here to the room Eleen and I share.

I'd be lying if I said I wasn't worried about that will happen once Sheren is gone, but that's not what I want to write about, not tonight. We've still got enough food left to stay here for a month, or maybe a little longer. Eleen and Tashel Ban are chasing down everything the people here found out during the last years before they killed themselves, and that probably won't take all of a month; then we have some decisions to make, and so do I, and one way or another I'll have plenty to do after that. That means I have a month or less to finish writing down my story, or as much of it as I have time to tell.

Most of what's left to tell happened in Memfis, or on the dig just west of it near Wanrij in Arksa. I spent the better part of three years going back and forth between those two places, and a lot of things happened there—a lot of things in one sense, and not much in another, since most of it was just doing what ruinmen do when they have a ruin to dig up. Thinking about my story today, while I sprayed resin over another alien-book, I spent a while wishing I could write about everything that happened in those two and a half years, day by day, and then half decided to skip the whole thing and pick up the day I left Memfis, walking alone up the road beside the Misipi, knowing right down to my bones that I'd failed and been an utter fool besides.

Still, now that the pen's in my hand, I know that neither of those is really what I want to do, or maybe it's that neither of them is how the story wants to be told. What I want, or the story wants, is to write about Memfis, because that's where the trip that brought me to Star's Reach swung around the way a door swings on its hinges, where I could have succeeded and lost any chance of getting here, and failed instead in the one way that got me where I needed to be.

I've written already about how I got to Memfis and what happened right after I got there. I haven't written much about Memfis itself, though, and that's something that needs doing, because Memfis is the biggest city in Meriga and one of the biggest in the world, and it's not like anywhere else. By that I don't just mean that it's not like anywhere else I've ever been, though that's true enough; it's got fifteen neighborhoods by most counts, though some people say seventeen, every one of them bigger than Shanuga and as different from the next one as Shanuga is from Troy or Cago. What I mean is that people who've sailed around the world and visited a hundred ports—and I met some of those in Memfis—will tell you that Memfis isn't like any other place they've ever been, either.

Part of it is the river trade, which I wrote about earlier, and which runs through Genda and Meyco but doesn't stop on either end. The Meycan Empire goes a long ways south, but there are other countries even further south, all the way down to Nardiga, which used to be covered with ice and now is all trees and grass and cattle. Genda goes up to the North Ocean, and on the far side of that there's a bunch of countries, Norj and Rosh and half a dozen others, that didn't fall to the Arabs when so many countries on that side of the Lannic did.

You can sail from Nardiga straight up the Lannic to the North Ocean and get to Rosh that way, but as Slane said on board the *Jennel Mornay*, you'll have to take your chances with Jinya pirates on our side of the ocean and Arab pirates on the other. Since the Arabs are still fighting with Norj and Rosh and the others over who's going to follow what religion, and Jinya pirates are, well, Jinya pirates, your chances of getting through into the North Ocean that way aren't so good. That's why, after our Third Civil War was over and the river trade started up, so much freight started coming up from the South to Memfis along routes Meyco's navy keeps good and safe, and so much started coming across the North Ocean under the guns of Genda's navy, and then down through Genda to Cago. Memfis was already a big city by then, but it was the river trade that turned it into one of Mam Gaia's biggest.

It was already a big city because there aren't many places anywhere in the world that you can get so much to eat out of the water. That's one of the first things I learned once Berry and I got there. From Memfis south for well over a hundred kloms, the Misipi widens out into something that's almost ocean but not quite, wide enough from east to west that when you stand on one shore you can't see to the other. The priestesses call it an estuary; people in Memfis just call it Banroo Bay, after a city that's down under the water toward the mouth of it, and depend on it for a good half or more of what they eat.

Back before the Third Civil War there were still places in Banroo Bay where there were too many poisons left over from the old world to risk eating anything. Now you can just about dip a net into the water anywhere and pull up something good. There are villages and towns all around Banroo Bay where people keep themselves fed and make their money doing something not too different from that, and a lot of people in Memfis make their living from the water the same way. I used to look out from my window high up in the Memfis guild hall toward the end of the rains, when it was safe to sail but the roads weren't dry yet, and watch the little boats heading out before dawn to bing back fish, crabs, shrimp, seaweed, and just about anything else that lives in the water and is good to eat.

They don't bring back whales, of course, nor seals or porps or any of the other mammals, who are too high on the food chain. The priestesses say the mouth of the Misipi is probably clean now, but nobody really wants to find out the hard way that it's not quite clean enough. Go to the markets in Memfis, though, and you can get just about anything else that anybody on Mam Gaia's round belly likes to eat, and some things I'm amazed that anybody eats at all, but most of the time when you sit down to dinner at a Memfis table you're going to get rice, which grows like weeds in the low country to either side of the Misipi's mouth, and fruit, which grows in the hill country further back so well it puts weeds to shame, but also a mother of a lot of seafood.

Well, really, there's a mother of a lot of everything, because Memfis is rich—rich from the river trade, rich from the ships that come there from all over Mam Gaia's round belly, rich from the seafood out of Banroo Bay, rich from the farms and orchards, and rich from plenty of other things, too, including good unstripped ruins within reach of the Memfis ruinmen. It's rich even compared to other rich towns in Meriga, and let's not even talk about what it looks like to a farmer's child like me from the Tenisi hill country. I figured out pretty soon after Berry and I got to Memfis that it was a good long ways past anything I was used to, but I didn't realize just how far until the rains came rolling up off the Gulf of Meyco.

That was after I finished healing up from the knife wound Thu gave me, and after I finished making all the arrangements with Jennel Cobey and the Memfis ruinmen for the next season's dig. That took a lot of time and a lot of work, and I spent more days than I like to remember going over the papers and making sure nothing got missed. Then I took them to a couple of misters from the Memfis guild who were making a point of helping me out and had them go over the same papers with me. All of that paid off when we started digging, but I didn't know that at the time; all I knew when the clouds started piling up blue-black in the southern sky was that I was tired of all the papers and negotiations, really tired, and wanted to relax for a bit.

Then the rains started, and I got my wish and then some.

The rains in Memfis aren't like the rains we get inland in Shanuga or Melumi. There you get plain heavy rain, enough to soak you to your skin if you stay out in it for a while, and boats have to pull up to the shore and get covered with tarps or they end up flooded after a bit. In Memfis the rain comes down like an ocean that somebody poured on your head. The clouds aren't just the blue-black you get elsewhere, they're literally dark as night, and if you're caught out on the water in a boat you might as well just start swimming because the boat's going to be full of water and heading toward the bottom long before you have any chance to get it to land. The small boats they use to bring in fish and everything else get hauled out of the water as soon as the clouds come in sight, and get stacked upside down in the big indoor fish markets close to the water; the riverboats take their smokestacks down and go into big sheds; and any sailing vessels that get caught in Memfis by the rains—most of them are far away over the ocean by the time the rains come—batten down their hatches and hope for the best.

You don't just go anywhere when the rains come, though, the way you do in most other places. Every one of Memfis' fifteen or seventeen neighborhoods has its own way of dividing itself up and its own rules about who goes where; none of it's written down or official, but you can end up dead in a gutter if you ignore it and somebody decides to get upset. The ruinmen at the Memfis guild hall explained all of that to Berry and me, and once the clouds started rolling in I made some plans about where to go once the rains started.

It turned out that I could have spared the trouble, because I'd made some good friends among the youngest Memfis misters by the time that happened, and the evening that the thunder rolled and the lightning snaked across the black sky, a couple of them came pelting up the stairs, laughing, and pulled me with them back down the stairs and out into the street.

That was my first time meeting the Memfis rains, and I gasped and spluttered and laughed pretty much the way I would have if they'd tossed me into Banroo Bay, which couldn't have made me any wetter. The two misters who'd come to get me were as drenched as I was, of course, and so were all the other misters and prentices who were spilling out of the guild hall and the tall narrow houses on either side. Everyone was laughing and whooping and splashing each other with water, but they were also drifting down the street toward the big covered market where the ruinmen and the chemists and a few other guilds buy their groceries. Light was pouring out of the market's windows and doors, and a kind of music I'd never heard before was blaring out over the pounding rain.

Inside all the stalls had been cleared away from the middle, leaving plenty of bare tile floor. The musicians were up at one end on a platform, with instruments you don't see in other towns. The kind of music they play in Memfis isn't something you hear in most other parts of Meriga, either, though I've heard that Sanloo and some of the other river towns have bands that play it too. It's got its own rhythms and notes that bend and slide and wail, and a lot of it gets played on horns, which nobody else but the army uses these days. I never did learn much about it, other than that it's what Dizzy played when he was on his way home to Nyork after the fight over Troy, and that it's the best dancing music I've ever heard, but most people in Memfis know a lot about it, and there must be more than a hundred bands that play it there.

So the musicians had their place, and they were starting to play. Around the other three sides of the building, all the stalls had their usual signs taken down. The ruinmen had most of one side, the chemists had half of another, and each of the other guilds had their places, which I learned later they'd had since the market was built more than a hundred years ago. There were big fancy banners hanging from the ceiling where the signs for the stalls usually go, and down below on the tables was more food and drink than I've ever seen in one place at one time. Prentices from all the guilds were hauling in covered pans and kettles and barrels and tarp-covered boxes, and when they ran out of room to put anything more on the tables they stacked things up in the spaces behind. I'd already figured out that there was going to be a mother of a party, a mother with babies and a grandchild or two, but it was when one of the misters I was with told me that all the food and drink was free that I started to realize just how rich Memfis is.

I was right, though; it was a mother of a party. There must have been more than a thousand people inside the market by the time the dancing started, and we were all wet and happy and, before long, pretty thoroughly drunk as well. Most of the women were wearing thin little dresses that didn't hide much at the best of times, and given a good dousing with rain—well, let's just say you didn't have to wonder what they'd look like if things got friendly enough that the dresses came off. Me, I did my share of dancing and drinking, and I must have had something to eat, though I don't remember the details too clearly, and I ended the night by stumbling back out into the rain with a couple of women from the picker's guild, laughing and kissing all the way to the place where they lived, which might have been all of six doors down from the market. Things were very friendly by then, and the dresses came off pretty quick once we got someplace private; from the sounds I heard through the walls to either side, we weren't the only people being friendly there, either.

I woke up with the kind of pounding head that's practically welcome, since it reminds you of what kind of night you had the night before. Things got lively again, and finally I kissed them both and stumbled back to the ruinmen's guild hall. I bathed and got something to eat and slept for a while, and then damn if we didn't head on down to the market and do it all again.

That's Memfis in the season of the rains, one party after another, night after night, until the skies dry out and everyone gets back to doing the work that pays for all that food and drink. By the time a couple of weeks have gone by it's not quite so crowded or so wild as it is when the rain first comes down, but every night until the rain stops there's food and drink and music for everyone who happens to come by, so long as they're where they should be. That's Memfis, too; the burners and smelters and a couple of other guilds have their own parties in another covered market about a klom from the ruinmen's guild hall, and ruinmen don't go there if they don't want to get beaten or worse, and of course nobody from the guilds outside the Memfis city walls is going to get past the guards and wander into one of the parties inside the walls.

I didn't mind that the first year, when I was half drunk on Memfis and the other half on pretty Memfis women. I minded it even less the second year, when I was more than half drunk on running my own dig for a successful season, and still thought that Star's Reach might be one shovelful of dirt away. The third year, when I knew for certain that the dig was a failure, dancing and drinking and spending the nights with pretty Memfis women beat the stuffing out of sitting in my little room in the Memfis guildhall, and facing the fact that everything I'd done since I fell through the floor in Shanuga and found the dead man's letter had brought me to a bare blank wall with no way forward. Not that sitting in the little room would have gotten me any closer to Star's Reach, or to anything else but misery. There are times when getting drunk and falling into bed with someone you've just met is as reasonable as anything else you can do.

But the other side of my story, or this part of my story, is the two seasons I spent digging in the Arksa jungle, hoping that I was going to find Star's Reach or at least some clue of how to get there. If I had all the time in the world I could tell that in some kind of order, from the day we first broke ground a month after the rains to the day we packed up the last of the tools and went back to Memfis, but we're not that many weeks from running out of food, and I still have other things I want to write down for—well, for whoever reads this, if anyone ever does. It's my part of the one big story Plummer talked about all those days and kloms ago on the road to Sisnaddi, and if nobody ever reads it, at least I had the chance to tell it.

The Arksa jungle—that's part of the story the way Memfis is, and for most of the same reasons. The Tenisi hill country where I grew up has woodland here and there, but it's too far inland, too high up, and too dry in the dry season to get the kind of jungle you get down close to the Gulf of Meyco. There are parts of Arksa that are like the Tenisi hills, or so I was told, but the part where we were digging was close enough to

Banroo Bay that the best way to get there from Memfis was to hire one of the steamboats that work up and down the bay and go across to a little town on the far side of the Misipi called Url, and then hire wagons and go from there. The old Walnut Ridge Telecommunications Facility was a couple of days north and west of there.

The first time I went there was a few weeks before the rains set in, that first year I was in Memfis, a week or so after Jennel Cobey's men took Thu and let him go. We took a boat across to Url, hired some horses with the jennel's money, and took the main road up out of the soggy land near the river to Josbro. That's a fair sized town, and if you go past it a ways you get to Wanrij, which is just a road house, a shrine, and a once a week market. We stayed the night at the road house, and then hired a guide and went into the jungle to find the place called WRTF.

It might as well have been any other patch of jungle, green and dark, full of huge tree trunks rising up from the ground, birds yelling at each other up where you can't see them, and a million different bugs flying around, most of which took at least one nip out of me. We did some searching, and found what was left of concrete walls here and there, overgrown with tree roots or sticking out of the undergrowth all anyhow like an old man's teeth. We poked the ground with metal rods here and there, and got a rough sense of how far the buildings went, then tied red cords around the trees that would have to go.

That's something I'd never done before, since the ruins in Shanuga had been cleared long before I was born, and it's something most people in Meriga won't do at all, since cutting down trees is one sure way to get Mam Gaia good and mad at you. Still, ruinmen do it when they have to, and we had to. That meant getting priestesses to come out and do the ceremony, paying to have ten times as many trees planted and tended somewhere else, and dealing with lumbermen, which nobody wants to do.

As soon as the rains were over and the ground was dry enough, we were back with the priestesses, and we stood around and looked respectful as the priestesses asked forgiveness for each of the trees that had to come down. They finished around noon, and the lumbermen came about an hour later, men with big dirty beards and shabby leather clothes and old rattletrap wagons drawn by oxen. Most of the ruinmen made themselves scarce, but I was in charge and that meant I had to go around with them and make sure they knew which trees to take.

You don't pay lumbermen. They mill the trees they take, sell the useful wood to carpenters and turn the rest into charcoal for the blacksmiths, and they'll take more than they're supposed to if they can make it look like a mistake, or at least that's what people say. When I got back to the site after they finished, the only trees they had taken out were the ones we'd marked, but maybe that was because they knew we were keeping track. Still, the site was cleared and ready to dig, and that was what mattered.

We used to joke back in Shanuga about the old habit of calling a place where ruinmen work a dig, because the Shanuga ruins don't take much digging. The Wanrij dig, which is what everyone ended up calling ours, was another matter. The whole thing was covered with four hundred years of fallen leaves and mud, and that had to be dug up and hauled away before we could get to the ruins themselves. It was a big installation, big as a town, and before long we found mud-filled stairs heading downward, rough concrete poured into gaps in good concrete, and all the other signs that tell you that somewhere down below are underground shelters from the last days of the old world.

That was an exciting time, and it took some work to keep everyone working in their own sections when somebody found a promising stairway, but I wanted the dig to be done right. That was partly because I knew Jennel Cobey was paying good money for it, and partly because I knew that the Memfis misters were watching me to see what kind of ruinman I was, but more than anything else it was because this was my dig, my very first dig, and damn if I was going to let anyone mess it up. So all the misters and prentices kept busy in their own sections, and we got it cleared one shovel of mud at a time.

I didn't get to do much of the shoveling, though. Back when I was Gray Garman's senior prentice, I did a lot of the work of running his section of each year's dig in the Shanuga ruins, but I'd never had charge of a dig, much less a brand new dig in a ruin that nobody had touched since the old world ended. That meant a lot of time in my tent over to one side of the ruin, ordering supplies and tools, coping with squabbles, settling accounts with the metal merchants who came out to buy scrap once we started turning it up, and much more. Berry was my senior prentice—well, of course, he was my only prentice, but the custom still held, and that meant that he ran a mother of a lot of errands for me, and sat in at the end of each day when all the misters and their senior prentices met to discuss how things were going and what needed to be done.

That usually happened in my tent, but not always. Once a week we had a mister's lodge, the way ruinmen always do, and of course Berry couldn't come to that. Once or twice a week we'd walk up the rough little road we'd made through the jungle from Wanrij to the roadhouse, and the misters and senior prentices would meet there.

The cook at the roadhouse was named Maddy, and she was a failed scholar, though we didn't know that at first. She'd come out with our meals when we met there, and ask how the dig was going; we didn't find out that she'd been to Melumi until the failed scholar we had at the dig happened to mention that the two of them had been friends at the Versty. We teased Maddy about that afterwards, but we also asked her advice when it came to the kind of questions scholars can answer, and we all got along wonderfully after that.

I just never knew what was going to happen. One morning the prentices started yelling over on the eastern side of the dig, and it turned out that a snake had come crawling out of the jungle during the night and was sleeping in one of the old stairwells. It was a big one, almost ten meedas long, which is bigger than they usually get even in the jungle. I asked the Memfis misters what they did with snakes like that, and that's how we ended up having snake chops for dinner the next two nights, which saved a good bit of money on our food that month. One week it was a fever that came through and put half the misters and prentices flat on their backs, another week it was a shipment of tools I ordered back before the rains that didn't arrive on time—it never did show up, in fact—and the next week it was something else again.

One week, it was Jennel Cobey. He came to see the site late in the first season, on his way from Memfis to Sanloo: political business, he told me, so I didn't ask any more questions. He was as curious as always, wanting to know everything we were doing at the dig, and the prentices stared and whispered as I took him all over the site and he talked to me as though I was a jennel too. He stayed for three days and then rode away with his soldiers and servants first thing in the morning.

When the misters and I met at the roadhouse in Wanrij that night, some of them talked about other jennels who were hurrying around the country with their soldiers. There was a cold feeling down in the pit of my stomach as we talked. I knew, we all knew, that all those jennels and soldiers meant six kinds of trouble sometime soon.

By the end of that first season, we'd cleared the whole site and gotten down to the first basement level of all the buildings. We had to stop there, because we were too far from Memfis to risk staying at the dig until just before the rains; instead, tools and gear had to be packed up and hauled back down the road to Url, and parties of prentices went with them, heading home to Memfis. By the time everything was shut down, clouds were rolling in from the Gulf, and we left the site in a hurry and beat the rains by two days. Then it was Memfis parties and pretty Memfis women, and days spent at the ruinmen's guild hall sleeping off rum and whiskey and planning the next season's work. We knew by then where there were stairways going further down and where the underground shelters probably were, and if Star's Reach or anything connected to it was still at WRTF, that's where it would be.

Finally the rain stopped, and the parties stopped, and as soon as the roads were dry I was on my way to Wanrij with Berry and the first party of misters and prentices. A mother of a lot of mud had washed into the ruins during the rainy season, and once we had the camp up and running again, that had to be dug out again. There were snakes—no more of the really big ones, luckily—and other things that thought the ruins we'd dug up made good homes, and they had to be chased back out into the jungle.

Then there was a little lake not far away from the dig, where we sent prentices to get water the year before, and it somehow got a resident gator, a big one. You don't kill gators unless you have to, and we didn't have to, so the prentices hauled water from a different lake that second year, and we got used to the way our gator would roar most evenings, calling for a mate or just letting everybody else on that part of Mam Gaia's round belly know that he was alive and minded to stay that way.

Since we'd cleared the site and knew where to look, the work went faster that season. One shovelful of mud and basket of concrete chips at a time, we got the deep stairways cleared and the rough concrete broken, and started getting into underground places where nobody had been since the old world ended. One afternoon, I was in my tent writing out orders for the next month's food, and Berry came at a run: they'd smelled the sour lightning smell deep in the ruin, behind a concrete plug that had just been cleared away. The orders could wait. I went back with him, fast.

It was two levels down, and would have been dark as midnight except that we'd spent the extra money to get plenty of electric lamps. As it was, the prentices and misters were a crowd of shadows around a rough doorway in the concrete. Beyond the doorway was darkness, and a very faint point of red light off in the middle distance. I knew exactly what I was seeing, and so did everyone there, even though none of them had nearly fallen onto a trapped floor the way I did.

There was some talking, and then the senior prentice of one of the Memfis misters walked into the room. He knew what he was doing, too; he stepped from safe spot to safe spot all the way to the little red dot, found the switch, and turned it green. The rest of us followed, and for a moment I was sure that the door on the other side of the room was going to lead us straight into Star's Reach.

It didn't. What was on the other side was a shelter, pretty much like the one I'd found in the Shanuga ruins. It had plenty of metal in it, a radio, and some guns, and that was all. The prentice who'd crossed the floor was made a mister on the spot, and we all cheered and congratulated him, but all the same it was a bleak moment, and not just for me.

The days and weeks and months went on. W found and emptied every underground room in the ruin; we found nearly enough metal to make the dig pay for itself even if it hadn't been a contract dig, and a few real prizes like the radio; we even found a room with a row of old metal filing cabinets in it, full of the moldering scraps of what used to be paper, just enough of it still readable that the failed scholar I'd hired for the dig was able to tell us that it was what the ancients called "human resources records," which was their phrase for all the papers they needed to tell them who got hired and who got fired from a job.

What we didn't find was one single scrap of anything that had to do with Star's Reach or with messages from other worlds. If it had been any other dig, it would have been a success, but it wasn't any other dig, and as the season wound up and the ruin was stripped down to the rebar in the concrete, I couldn't shake the feeling that I had wasted years of my life on a daydream.

We finished the dig a month before the rains came. The prentices and the misters packed everything up, one party at a time, and hauled tools and tents and cooking pots back home to Memfis. The last wagon from the metal merchants came and went. We filled in all the holes we'd dug and sent a letter to the priestesses, letting them know the site was clean and that we'd be most grateful if they could tell people who wanted to get right with Mam Gaia that they could come plant trees there. Then, last of all, I sat down in my tent and wrote a letter to Jennel Cobey, telling him that we hadn't found Star's Reach.

That kept me busy until late that night. The next morning Berry and a few of the other prentices folded and packed my tent and the few other things that were left at the dig, and loaded them on a wagon. I took one more walk around the site, made sure everything was in order, and then went to join them. We hadn't hired any horses this time, since it was clear that the jennel wasn't going to get what he hoped he was paying for. The teamster tapped the oxen with his stick, the wagon started to roll, and the rest of us—me and Berry and half a dozen prentices who were more or less friends of his, and had been lent to me by their misters—started walking up the dusty road to Wanrij.

CHAPTER 23

THE THING THAT MATTERS

You never know where you're going to find the thing that matters. That's one bit of wisdom I learned on the long road from Shanuga to Star's Reach, and if it hadn't gotten through my skull already, this morning would have pounded it in nicely.

Anna and I were about to put breakfast on the table, Thu and Berry were talking politics over in the corner, and Eleen and Tashel Ban were bent over something they found in the computer yesterday. It was just an ordinary morning at Star's Reach, and then Tashel Ban let out a bit of hot language I don't think I've ever heard him use before. Thu and Berry looked up from their conversation; I set down the plate I was carrying; Eleen stared at him; only Anna kept on with what she was doing, spooning soup into bowls as though no one had said a thing.

"Well," Tashel Ban said after a bit. "I think you're all going to want to look at this."

"This" was something the people at Star's Reach before us had mostly translated out of the code they and the Cetans worked out to talk to each other. Close to half the words had little curves around them (like this), which I already knew meant that nobody was sure if that was the right word or not, and here and there were little curves with a line of dots between them like this (.....), which meant that nobody had the least idea what word ought to go there. It was a mess to read, no question, but it seemed to be telling a story about someone going someplace on a boat. The place the boat was going, it said, was a place where a long time ago (.....) to the third planet.

Right after that was one of the little stars they used in the old world to mark where somebody wanted to put a note, and the note was down at the bottom of the page. What it said was this: *ref. to precollapse space travel—see briefing paper 223.*

It took a moment for that to sink in, and then I said a bit of language even hotter than the one Tashel Ban used. We were all staring at the thing by then. Even Anna came over, read the paper over my shoulder, and nodded, as though she expected it.

"How easy will it be to find that briefing paper?" This was from Thu.

"I'm about to find out," said Tashel Ban, and started to get up, but I said, "After breakfast, I hope." He gave me one of his owlish looks and nodded, and so we all sat down and had one of the fastest meals I've ever eaten. As soon as he was done with his soup, Tashel Ban was on his way to the computer, and Eleen and Berry were right there with him, while Thu and Anna and I did the dishes.

They found it before noon, and Tashel Ban managed to get the printer to behave and give us each a copy. It's sitting on the desk next to me right now, answering a question so big I don't think any of us dared to ask it before now.

"They did the same thing we did." That's what Tashel Ban said, as the printer grunted and whirred behind him. "They figured out how to use the concentrated energy sources on their planet, and used them up so fast and so carelessly that they ran out of energy and messed up their climate around the same time. They had droughts, the way we did, but much worse. There was no rain worth mentioning on their islands for something like two thousand of our years."

Berry caught what that meant a moment before I did. "Without rain—"

"Exactly," said Tashel Ban. "The Cetans' intelligent phase can't stay together for more than a few hours. So that was the end of their old world, and even when the droughts started to break, there would be a while when some of the islands would get regular rains, and then the rains would go away and whatever got started on those islands went away too.

"That went on for another few hundred of our years. Finally the rains lasted long enough on one set of islands that the Cetans there figured out how to build catchment basins and cisterns, and finally solar stills that would make artificial rain right through the drought periods. So their culture survived, and they built boats and spread the skills they had from island to island right around their world. That was something like a thousand years ago."

"What sort of space travel did they manage beforehand?" Thu asked.

"About as much as we did," Tashel Ban told him. "Some satellites, some probes out to other worlds, and a few trips that put a couple of Cetans on the surface of Tau Ceti III for a day or two and got them back alive. That much they've been able to figure out from the old records, now that they can read them again. That took a long time—the way their old world ended, the languages were completely lost, and all they had to start from were ruins and records that nobody could understand."

I thought about that this evening as the three of us who know how to work on the computer kept chasing after the last things the people at Star's Reach learned, and the three of us who don't cleaned up after dinner and got a pot of beans soaking and some sourdough rising for the next day's meals. When people talk about the end of the old world—our old world—they talk about how hard it was, how many people died and how much got lost. I don't remember anybody saying "You know, it could have been a lot worse," but it was a mother of a lot worse for the Cetans than it was for us. I imagined what it might have been like if there wasn't a living person in Meriga for two thousand years, and then a trickle of people coming in from somewhere else who didn't know the first thing about where all the ruins came from.

But that wasn't what I wanted to write about when I sat down here at the desk tonight. I wanted to write about what happened after we finished up the dig at Wanrij and went back to Memfis for the rains, and I spent a couple of months drinking myself stupid and tumbling into bed with pretty Memfis women. That's what all the other ruinmen were doing, of course, but I had a better reason for it than they did, or at least that's what I thought at the time. They knew that as soon as the rains ended, they'd be back to work on some other dig. I knew that as soon as the rains ended, I'd have to face up to the fact that my search for Star's Reach had run up against a blank wall and there was no way forward.

Then, about the time the rains started slackening off, a couple of the senior misters of the Memfis guild came looking for me. It was late afternoon, about an hour before the music started up at the big covered market down the street, and the rain was drumming against the one little window of my room in the guild hall. I welcomed them and found them a couple of chairs, and we chatted about nothing much for a few minutes before they got to the point of their visit.

"That was a well run dig you did up at Wanrij," one of them told me; his name was Orin, a gruff gray-haired mister from the hill country down by the Meycan border. "Nice and orderly, and everyone got paid on time. Doesn't always happen the first time somebody runs a site."

I thanked him, and wondered where the conversation was going to go. The other mister, who was lean and bald and had little bright eyes like a sparrow, answered that question soon enough. "We've talked to the misters, and if you're minded to stay here in Memfis—of course you might have other plans—if you're so minded, anyway, we'd be willing to see you have a place in the guild here."

I'm not sure how I kept my mouth from falling open. That sort of thing happens sometimes, when a mister from one town gets involved in a dig somewhere else and everyone gets along well, but I hadn't even thought about the chance that it might happen to me. I managed to stammer out something like a thank you, and then remembered that I had to get things settled with Jennel Cobey and tried to say something about that; I was pretty much babbling nonsense, or at least that's the way I remember it, but the two misters were as professional as you can get. They let me know that I had plenty of time to sort things out and make up my mind, said a few more things I don't remember at all, and left.

I told Berry that evening before we went down to the market. His eyes got big and then narrowed a bit. He was weighing the thought of staying in Memfis against the hope we'd had of finding Star's Reach, I knew, the same way I was. We partied that night, and the next, and the next, and with every day that passed I got more perplexed and more upset about it all. I knew that staying in Memfis was the only choice that made any kind of sense at all, but something in that choice just didn't sit well with me.

One evening about a week later, we were alone in the room, taking care of some of the last work on the Wanrij dig—bills that still had to be paid, money from metal sales that had to be accounted for and paid out, all the little things that keep misters busy the last few weeks of the rains. As we got to the end of the paper, Berry sat back and looked at me. "Sir and Mister?"

I think I mentioned a while back that he never used my title except when it was something really important. I set down the bill I was reading and nodded for him to go on.

"What do you think now about finding Star's Reach?"

"I wish I knew," I said. "What do you think?"

"I think..." He got silent for a long moment, then: "I wonder if maybe we've done as much as anybody could have done."

I gave him a look, and didn't say anything. I couldn't think of anything to say, because everything else seemed to be saying that he was right, except for that little cold feeling in the pit of my stomach that said he was wrong.

The rains end in Memfis a week or two after they've gone away everywhere further north, and so as soon as the rains slacken off in Memfis, the riverboats come down the Misipi to dock at the Memfis levee. That was how a letter from Jennel Cobey got to the Memfis guild hall when the last scant rain was falling, long before the roads were dry enough for traveling. I'd been worrying about what that letter would say, because I'd spent a lot of the jennel's money and come up with nothing. Still, that just showed how much I still had to learn about the man. What the letter said was this:

> To Mister Trey son of Gwen, at the Memphis Ruinmen's Hall, my greetings. The money's not an issue; I'm sorry to hear that nothing concerning Star's Reach turned up after all, but it was always a gamble. Have you considered searching the archives at Cincinnati? If you're minded to keep looking, that might be the best of the remaining options.
>
> —General Cobey Taggart

I thought about that for the rest of the day, and it kept coming to mind that evening while I danced and drank and tried to pretend to myself that I didn't have to make a choice by the time the sun came out for good. One more pretty Memfis woman put it out of my head for a little while, but after we'd finished what we were doing and fallen asleep in her bed, I started dreaming, and there it was again.

It was another of my Deesee dreams, with the wide streets and the silvery sky up above that was the surface of the sea. I found my way to the Spire, the way I usually did, and there was the man in the old world clothing, the one we found long dead in the Shanuga ruins, standing there waiting for me.

I hurried up the grassy slope toward him, and then I saw his face, tense, almost pleading, waiting for me to do or say something.

Then I knew what he wanted, and I must have cried out, because all of a sudden I was awake, light was coming in through the window next to me, and the woman I was with was bending over me, soft and sweet and brown, asking if I was all right. I lied and said yes, and kissed her, and things pretty much went from there, but all the while I knew what the dead man wanted from me and what I had to do.

When I told Orin, the Memfis mister, I made it sound as though Jennel Cobey had asked me to go to Sisnaddi and the archives there. He nodded, frowned, and said, "I can't promise that there'll still be a place for you when you're done, you know." I told him I knew that, and I did, but it didn't keep me from feeling like the number one fool on Mam Gaia's round belly when he went his way and I went mine.

A little later that day I told Berry. I expected him to argue, but he didn't. He gave me a look I didn't expect at all, wary and guarded. "Trey, I can't go to Sisnaddi," he said. Before I could say anything: "I can't tell you why, but it's worth my life. Probably yours too."

I looked at him for a long moment, and then said, "Do you want to stay in Memfis?"

"Well—" He paused, then: "I was thinking about Cob's site in Tucki, the empty nuke."

That sounded like a good idea to me. "That ought to work. I could get you a message fast if anything turns up in the archives."

"And I can save up some money for whatever's next. It's too easy to spend money here."

"True enough," I said, and we agreed that he'd go to Tucki as soon as the roads were open, and I'd head for Sisnaddi as soon after that as the last of the paperwork for the Wanrij dig was finished. We probably could have gone together, but

I figured the sooner he got there and earned some money, the better, and I knew myself well enough to know that I could use the time alone. It didn't occur to me that Berry might have his own reason for wanting to go back to that corner of Tucki, but then I had plenty of other things on my mind just then.

As soon as the roads were open, I sent a letter to Cob to let him know there was a spare prentice on the way, and a couple of days later Berry went with a crew of metal traders who had business in Tucki. Most of the Memfis ruinmen headed out to digs of their own. All around me, Memfis got busy making money, and I sat in my little room in the Memfis guild hall with nothing to do but wait for the last bills to come in, feeling more and more like a fool with every day that passed. The music and the dancing were over and the pretty Memfis women had other things to do with their time, and a dream, a jennel's good wishes, and a letter from a dead man were the only things I had to show for more than three years of my life.

I got the last of the bills paid on the last day of Oggis, and left the Memfis guildhall the next morning. It was a bright clear day, with salt air sweeping in from the Gulf of Meyco and high billowing clouds drifting here and there. I said my goodbyes at the guildhall, walked past the big covered market, and kept on going. Just the part of Memfis outside the gate where the ruinmen live is as big as all of Shanuga, but I knew where to go and where not to go, and so nobody gave me trouble on the way. By noon I was walking past the little farms that keep the city markets in greens and garden truck.

Off to the left, riverboats were churning up the water; off to the right everything was green and growing. All in all, it was as nice a day as you could ask for, but for all I cared just then it might as well have been some day in the drought years with dust falling from the sky onto bare gray dirt. I missed Berry, and I missed the friends I'd made among the Memfis ruinmen, but I was glad to be alone, so that nobody else had to put up with my mood.

Still, life on the road is life on the road, and I'd learned to like it well enough during the time Berry and I spent wandering the long way around from Shanuga to Memfis. Before too many days were past, Memfis was far enough behind that the sour taste of my failure there was starting to fade from my mind. It still hurt to think about it, but it was a mother of a lot easier not to think about it, and that helped. The river road along the Misipi isn't as busy as some others, since anyone who can afford a ticket takes a riverboat, but there were plenty who couldn't or who, like me, didn't want to spend the money they had, or who had business that took them to the little towns and villages along the way.

Before long I was walking with a bunch of actors who made their living going from town to town, putting on the same play wherever they went. It was good enough that I'd have paid money to see it, but since we were on the road together I just gave them a hand setting things up and packing up again afterwards. It was about an old man who lived on an island off in the Gulf of Meyco, with nobody but his daughter and a couple of robots to keep him company—this was a long time ago and he knew all about technology, you see, and so he had robots. Then there was a big storm, and the old man's brother, who was a jennel and who'd chased him out of Memfis and sent him to the island, gets blown ashore, along with a bunch of friends, and the presden and her son: they were all on a ship together, you see. It's all a merry romp from there, until the old man triumphs, the jennel's humbled, the presden's son falls in love with the old man's daughter, and they all go sailing back to Memfis.

The actors were good company, and I traveled with them all the way north to where the Hiyo River flows into the Misipi. They were going to Sanloo and I wasn't, so we said our goodbyes one bright morning and they got a ferry over to the Misipi's west bank. I went east along the Hiyo toward Dooca, crossed on the ferry at Troplis, and followed the road that ran along the northern bank from there. I could just as well have stayed in Tucki, but I didn't, and it was because I didn't that two important things happened to me.

The first was at a town called Conda, a couple of days walking past the ferry. The road north of the river doesn't get much travel along that stretch, and since there are faster ways to get from Dooca to places further east, I had the road to myself most of the time. Conda's a little place, not much more than a weekly market and a levee where riverboats tie up; it had one tavern, with a sign that said they had rooms for the night, so I went in. I was just about the only person there, except for the barmaid and a woman maybe ten years older than I was, who was sitting at the bar nursing a drink.

I figured out right away that she was a harlot; it didn't take her much longer to figure out that I wasn't looking for a harlot; once that got settled, since neither of us had anywhere else to go, we sat there at the bar and talked, while the barmaid did her chores and kept our glasses from getting dry. The harlot's name was Lu, and she was on her way from Naplis to Sanloo, where she hoped she could get a place at one of the big houses and put some money aside before she got too old for her trade. I told her a little about where I'd been and where I was going; I didn't say a word about why, but damn if she didn't suddenly turn and stare at me for a good long minute, and say, "You're the one who's looking for Star's Reach."

So I asked how she'd figured that out, and she turned back to her drink and started to cry. That's when it came out that she'd been a scholar at Melumi, and got sent away the way Eleen was. She ended up in a brothel in Naplis, because she was pretty and good in bed, and not too proud to make old men think they were twenty again. She still had a few books from her Versty days, but she kept them tucked away where they couldn't be seen; a lot of men like a harlot to pretend to be this or that, but nobody I ever heard of has a thing for scholars.

I ended up buying her dinner, because I had the money and she didn't, and over the food we talked about Star's Reach, and what I found and didn't find. After that we had a few more drinks, and after that she took my hands and let me know that if I was minded to share a bed she had one upstairs, and I was young and nice and just because she made her living that way didn't mean it was all about money.

That was how I ended up in a cramped little room on the upper floor of a little tavern in Conda, in a cramped little bed that wasn't quite long enough for one person or wide enough for two, in that warm quiet place you get to sometimes after you've tumbled somebody. She felt like talking, which isn't something a harlot can do very often in that sort of situation, so I nestled up to her and listened, and that's when she told me about the place on the Lannic shore by Deesee where every question has an answer.

She didn't know much about it, just that the road west from Pisba through the burning land leads there, and that there were stories about people who went there and asked questions nobody else could answer, and got the answer. I wondered at first if there was supposed to be a robot there, or something else from the old world that could answer questions, and then if it was like a Dell's bargain; she laughed and said no, it was just a place where questions got answered, or that's what the stories said. You crossed the burning land and went to the Lannic shore along the road west from Pisba, and there by the water, where the Spire rose out of the waves, you could find the answer to anything.

"Maybe," she said in a drowsy voice. "Maybe if you don't find what you need at Sisnaddi, you should try going there. Better than nothing, maybe."

"Maybe," I said. I didn't feel like arguing, or doing much besides being there next to her; neither of us said anything for a while, and then she mumbled something I couldn't make sense of, and pretty clearly fell asleep.

I didn't stay awake much longer, but somewhere in the middle of the night I woke up cold out of a dream about Deesee. I'd been walking through the wide streets with fish swimming past me and the water a silvery sky up above, and I couldn't find my way to the Spire. I needed to know how to get there, and I couldn't find the way. Then I was awake, and off past Lu's shoulder a little window let in a flurry of stars.

It was almost a year later, when I'd followed every last lead in the Sisnaddi archives out to a dead end, that I followed the hint I'd gotten in a harlot's bed in a little Ilanoy town in the middle of nowhere. Maybe the stars that night knew enough to tell me to follow it sooner, but if they did know, they weren't telling that either.

I still had some long roads ahead of me, from there along the Hiyo to Sisnaddi by way of an empty nuke in the northern part of Tucki, from Sisnaddi east across the burning land to the beach where the Spire rises up out of the distant waves, and then back to Sisnaddi again with the thing I'd been trying to find all along, and then from Sisnaddi by way of Sanloo and Cansiddi and the desert to Star's Reach, where I sit in a little pool of light with a pen in my hand and an old notebook on the desk in front of me. Getting here has been close to the only thing on my mind all that way—well, other than what's going to happen between Eleen and me, and what's going to happen to Meriga when the presden dies, and a few other things like that.

Still, I got here, and pretty soon I'll be finding out whether that was a good idea or not. Tashel Ban thinks he's found the last thing the people at Star's Reach put on the computer before they died.

CHAPTER 24

WHEN THE DOOR OPENED

The presden died today. We heard this evening when Tashel Ban tuned up the receiver and caught the broadcast from Sanloo. I was in the radio room with him, along with Eleen and Thu, when the loudspeaker crackled and hissed and started playing music. It wasn't the music the Sanloo station usually plays, the lively sort of tune on tars and drums you hear all over Meriga; it was the slow sad old-fashioned music that always comes ahead of bad news.

I guessed right away what it meant, went to the door, and shouted down the hall, since there was one person at Star's Reach who wasn't in the radio room just then and needed to be. Plates rattled in the kitchen, footsteps rang down the hall, and Berry came in just as the music stopped and the radio, or the man on the other end of it, started talking.

The announcement was all in the sort of formal language you never hear unless the presden's court is involved somehow, and I won't try to repeat all of that word for word. The important thing was that Sheren darra Emeli, Presden of Meriga, died this morning of having too much cancer in her. Now of course he said some other things, mostly that there will be a funeral in a week to send her back into the circle, and that the Baspresden, who usually just bangs the gavel when Congrus meets and whose name I can't even remember, will run the country until the succession gets sorted out. All that is probably important for people who live in Sisnaddi or have to deal with the government. What matters for most of us here at Star's Reach and across most of Meriga, though, is that for more than forty years the country's been mostly at peace and mostly prosperous, and all of that could stop between now and the next rains.

That matters for Berry, too, but he had something else to think about as well. He stood there in the doorway, listening, not saying anything at all. I thought just then of the child who'd helped me stagger to my tent in Shanuga after I became a mister, but he didn't look like a child any more, and the look on his face wasn't a child's look, not by a good long walk. The announcer went on for a while, talking about what there was in the way of other news, and then he stopped talking, the slow sad music started again, and Berry turned without saying a thing and went back to the kitchen.

I think everyone else was looking at him by the time he left, and then they were all looking at me. I couldn't think of anything to say, so I followed Berry down the hall to the kitchen. He'd gone back to washing the dishes, though his face was all twisted up trying not to cry, and his eyes weren't looking at anything at all. I found a towel, stood next to him and started drying the plates as he washed them.

"My mother died about six months after Gray Garman took me as a prentice," I said after a little while. "So I know there's nothing anybody can say."

He stopped, and looked at me for a long moment. Finally: "When did you find out?"

He wasn't talking about my mother, of course. "I started wondering after you said you couldn't go to Sisnaddi, but Jennel Cobey took me to see her in Sisnaddi. That did it."

Berry started washing again. "Do you suppose Jennel Cobey knew?"

"I'm pretty sure of it."

"And the others here?"

"If they didn't, they do now." I took the last plate from him, dried it.

"I suppose it was stupid to think nobody would ever figure it out." He started in on the bowls. "I hope they keep their mouths shut, or I'll end up dead in a ditch somewhere."

"Or Presden," I said.

He snorted. "Not as a tween. If I'd been born one way or the other I'd be in Sisnaddi right now taking the oath of office, but—" He handed me a bowl. "She couldn't even admit I existed. Can you imagine what the Circle elders would have said? No, I'll get offered the presdency the day after a dozen false stars turn up drunk in a Memfis whorehouse."

I couldn't think of an answer to that, and he didn't say anything else for a while. We finished up the dishes, and then he said, "Trey—thank you."

"Sure."

He nodded, and then turned and went to his room. I knew better than to follow.

I've been thinking since then of the one time I saw the presden. It was a little more complicated than I told Berry, because Jennel Cobey didn't just up and decide to take me to see her. What happened was that Sheren found out about his plans to go looking for Star's Reach, and whoever told her about it gave her more details than the jennel wanted her to know.

This was after I'd come back from Deesee and started making arrangements for the journey here. Everyone in our party but Berry, who was still in Tucki, and Anna, who we didn't know about yet, was already there, and in the middle of everything one of the jennel's servants brought a note telling me to dress up as well as a ruinman could and meet him that evening at the presden's palace inside the walls in Sisnaddi.

The jennel sent somebody to get me through the city gates, and so I turned up at the palace doors all scrubbed and in the nicest clothes I could find. I was as nervous as I've ever been, and it didn't help any to see that Cobey looked nearly as nervous as I felt. "Trey," he said in a low voice, "Don't say any more than you have to. I don't know what this is about." That was all the time he had to talk, since the guards in their fancy uniforms came out of the big front door of the palace just then, and I followed him in the door and through more huge rooms and long corridors than I've seen anywhere this side of a really big ruin. At first there were people everywhere, guards and courtiers and servants all bustling about, but the further we went the more the crowd thinned, until finally we came to a door with two guards standing outside it and no one else anywhere in sight except the servant who was guiding us.

The door opened, we went through, and the guards and the servant stayed outside. Inside were shelves of books and a big map on the wall, ancient or copied from some ancient book, showing Meriga as it was before the old world ended. That caught my eye, and so it was a moment or two before I noticed the woman over in one corner, facing mostly away from us, turning the pages of a book.

She was smaller than I expected, and she didn't look well; her face was drawn and her hair was mostly gray, though you could see traces of the red it had been when I was still a boy. She looked up after a moment, glanced at the two of us, and then put down the book and came over and started peppering the two of us with questions: where we thought Star's Reach was and how long the jennel thought he'd be gone and who we'd be taking with us, and other things like that. All the while I was looking at her and wondering why it seemed like I knew her from somewhere, because something in her face and voice reminded me of somebody, but I couldn't think of who it was.

We were probably there for half an hour before she thanked us and turned back to her book, and we went to the door to find the servant opening it for us. So we went back the way we came, following the servant, and my thoughts wouldn't stop circling around why the presden made me think of someone and who that someone might be. I barely noticed all the other people around me, I was that deep in thought, but just before we got to the big room just inside the outer doors of the palace I happened to see someone I knew.

I have no idea to this day why I looked up just then. All I know is that there was a man walking toward me, and I recognized him at once. This time he was dressed in the loose jacket and tight trousers and boots that people at the presden's court wear these days, rather than the traveler's clothes he'd had on before, but that bland face was one I wasn't likely to forget. It was the man who had followed Berry and me all the way from Troy to Cago.

I don't think he saw me. If he did, his face didn't show it. A moment later he was past me, and I was following Jennel Cobey out the doors, and that was when I realized whose face the presden's kept almost calling to mind. It was Berry's, of course.

It all made plenty of sense once I thought of it—the way Berry talked, the things he knew, the way Jennel Cobey reacted the first time he saw Berry, all of it, except for the simple fact that a ruinman from Shanuga ended up with a presden's child as his prentice. Of course then I remembered that it was Berry who chose me, not the other way around, and gambling everything on the chance of finding Star's Reach was pretty much what you might expect from someone who had a presden's blood and instincts but no chance at the succession.

To this day I remember only one thing about the rest of that evening. I must have said my goodbyes to Cobey, gone back to the cheap little room I shared with Eleen, told her everything about what had happened except the one thing that mattered, and gone to bed with her, but none of that left the least trace in my mind. All I recall now is lying awake late at night next to Eleen, watching the stars through the one little window we had next to our bed and wondering what a farm boy from the Tenisi hills like me was doing, getting ready to go to Star's Reach with a jennel, a king, and the presden's secret child. If the stars knew, they weren't telling.

I didn't even know that much when I was doing what I want to write about next, which was walking up the long slow road from Memfis to Sisnaddi more than a year before. I left Conda, where I left off telling my story earlier, after saying good-bye to Lu and promising that I'd look her up if I ever got to Sanloo. The last stars were setting as I got up; it was a clear cool morning, but there were clouds coming out of the south that promised rain within a few days, the sort of thing you get now and then during the otherwise dry months. Farmers cheer when they see those clouds, and ruinmen groan; me, I just kept walking.

I had plenty of thinking to do, and plenty of time to do it. Further east, when you get into Inyana and Hiyo, the roads along the north shore of the Hiyo River are as busy as anything, but there on the bottom end of Ilanoy it's mostly forest with a few scattered farms, and here and there a levee on the bank where one of the smaller riverboats will stop if somebody flags it down. I watched more than a few of them heading the same I was, but I didn't want to spend money if I didn't have to, so I didn't stand there and wave. That meant there were nights I spent in taverns in little towns, and nights I spent in barns and farmhouses, and now and then nights where the sun went down and there wasn't anybody or anything in sight, and I found a place to curl up under a tree and slept there.

One way or another it must have taken me most of two weeks to get to Ensul, which is the first town of any size north of the river as you go upstream from Dooca. That was partly because I had to go almost a day's walk north to find a ferry across the Wobbish, where Ilanoy and Inyana come together. It was also because the rain I'd seen coming showed up more than once, and a muddy road's a lot slower going than a dry one, even when part of the road's still paved with old chunks of concrete. Still, the rain stopped the day I crossed the Wobbish, the road on the other side was well tended and mostly dry, and two days after I got off the ferry I was in Ensul.

Like every other town in Meriga, Ensul used to be much bigger than it is now. If you have a ruinman's eyes, you can see where the old streets and buildings used to run long before you get to the town. There used to be a ruinmen's hall there, years back, but they ran out of ruins and sold the hall for scrap metal before heading elsewhere. Now it's just another market town with riverboats at the levee, three or four streets full of shops, and a big open space where farmers and crafters and traveling shows set up and sell whatever it is they have to sell.

The way the road comes into Ensul, the marketplace is to your left and a row of taverns to your right. I probably would have headed straight for the nearest tavern, since I'd been on the road since first light and was thinking comfortable thoughts about a meal and a bed, but it was late afternoon, the market was winding down, and through a pause in the noise and talking came a voice I knew. I almost stopped right there in the middle of the street, which would have been a bad idea, since there was an oxcart not too far behind me and I wouldn't want to risk my life on the common sense of a couple of oxen. Instead, I got over to the side of the street closest to the market, and looked, and there he was.

He was up on a wooden platform, the sort of thing that players and actors use when there aren't too many of them, and a cloth banner along the front of it yelled GENUINE HERBAL MEDICINE in bright red letters. He had a black coat and a black hat and a bottle of something black and more or less liquid in one hand, but I wouldn't have mistaken the voice or the face or the round glasses like moons in a thousand years of trying. It was Plummer, all right.

So I walked over toward the platform, toward the outer edge of the small crowd he had around him. Of course he spotted me well before I got there. "Here," he said, "is one who could benefit from the very best of my medicines. A ruinman,

mams and misters, no doubt come straight from some dangerous ruin, where he has been risking his life to keep the rest of
us safe from toxic wastes and well supplied with metals. Come
up here, sir and mister."

The crowd made room for me, and I went to the platform
and climbed up the three creaking steps onto it, doing my
level best not to grin. Plummer checked my pulse and whispered to me, "Pretend to pay me when I ask for money." Then,
in a voice they could probably hear in the taverns across the
way: "A slow and heavy pulse. Aching muscles?" I nodded.
"Unusual thirst?" I nodded again. "I thought as much," he
said, and rattled off a string of words that probably meant
something, though I don't pretend to know what. He asked
some other questions, and I guessed at the right answers, and
before he'd finished everyone there, including me, was half
convinced that I must be six senamees from death on a slick
muddy slope.

Then, of course, he sold me the medicine, and I reached
into my pocket and pretended to hand him a coin. He took it,
checked it, and pocketed it so convincingly that I just about
saw the thing glint in the sunlight. By then, of course, half the
people in the crowd had noticed that their muscles were aching and they were pretty thirsty, too, and he got busy answering their questions and selling bottles: this one for tiredness
and that one for colds, and this other one if your gums bleed
and your teeth get loose. He had at least a dozen different
medicines for sale, and by the time he was finished most of the
people in the crowd had at least one bottle to take home.

"A profitable day," he said later on. We were facing each
other across a table in one of the taverns, with a big glass of
beer on my side of the table and a smaller glass of Tucki whiskey on his. "And partly your doing. Something about an earnest young ruinman inspires confidence. And particularly—"
He leaned forward, considered me. "An earnest young ruinman who looks rather the worse for wear. I gather the site near
Memfis didn't fulfill your hopes."

I met his look, shook my head. "It was worth a try."

"Of course. And your prentice—I trust nothing untoward..."

"Berry? He's fine—I sent him to work on a dig in Tucki to make some money while I search the archives at Sisnaddi. I figure that's the last chance I've got."

He considered that. "An interesting coincidence, and possibly a useful one. I'm also headed east, though not quite to Sisnaddi. It also occurs to me that we may have some things to talk about."

That's how it happened that we left Ensul the next morning on the road east toward Luwul. I was in good spirits for the first time in longer than I wanted to think about. That was partly because I knew Plummer would be good company on the road, partly because wondering about him spared me from wondering about whether Star's Reach was ever going to be more than a dream for me, and partly—well, I was no more sure what Plummer had been not-quite-offering me, there on the riverboat just upstream from Altan, than I'd been the morning I went and found him gone, and I wanted to know. Not that I was going to push the issue; I knew Plummer well enough already to be certain that he'd talk about that when he chose to, and not a heartbeat sooner.

So we took the road, or maybe the road took us, and pretty soon it was as if we'd been traveling together since the first time we'd met back there in the ruin in Tucki. He didn't have much medicine left to sell after Ensul, but a little ways upstream was a little town named Nuber, and he had a friend there—it was another one of his nameless friends—who kept plenty of it stored in bottles down in the cellar. After that, he worked every town we passed.

We still made fairly good time up the north bank of the Hiyo until we got past Nuwabnee, which is right across the river from Luwul and brought back some memories. While we were there, the clouds started coming up out of the south again, and a few days later the rain came following it. It was good and heavy, too, and we ended up finding a ruin with a bit of roof left to it and waiting it out. That's where we were when Plummer started talking about stories, and that's when he said the thing I wrote back at the beginning of this, about how all stories were scraps of one big story, and I decided he was drunk. Looking back on it, I think he was, but that doesn't mean he was wrong. It's occurred to me more than once since then that he may have been so fond of whiskey because he was right.

But the clouds finally cleared away, and on we went. It wasn't more than a few days after that when we went through a little place called Bellem—not big enough to be a town, really, just a couple of buildings and a levee for the boats—and there on the side of one of the buildings was a big poster. You don't see those too often, because there aren't that many trades that have need of them, but this was the exception: it said, in big fancy red and black letters, that the Baraboo Sirk was going to be twenty kloms up the river in Madsen for a couple of days, which happened to be that day and the next.

I laughed, remembering all the times I'd wanted to see a sirk back when I was a boy, and we didn't have the money. Plummer, though, stopped and considered the poster and said, "Excellent. We'll have to stop for that."

I closed my mouth after a moment, and then said, "Friends of yours?"

"Exactly." He gave me the look I've mentioned before, the one that made me think I'd said the right thing or something close to it. Then, without another word, he turned and set off along the road, and I followed.

We got to Madsen late the next afternoon, which was soon enough for the evening show. I honestly can't say I remember the town at all, just the big tent off in a big pasture just outside of town, red and white in stripes, with big solar panels on the grass nearby to power the lights and a couple of smaller tents close by. There were oxen grazing not far away, and wagons painted in bright colors, red and blue and green, with BARABOO SIRK on them in big gold letters. People were already lining up in front of the tent, and a man in fancy clothes outside the tent was telling everyone about the show in a voice I bet they heard on the other side of the river.

I should probably say something about sirks, just in case whoever reads this is from the Neeonjin country or somewhere else that doesn't have them. A sirk is a show in a tent, or rather it's a whole bunch of shows one after the other in the same tent, and it's not like any other show there is. Part of it's people doing things nobody else can do, like eating fire and lifting big weights and dancing on a rope way up in the air, and part of it's clowns making fun of everything and everybody, and there's music and all kinds of other things jumbled in together with it. There are, I think, three of them now, though the Baraboo Sirk is the oldest of them, the only one that's been around since before the old world ended, and not that long ago there was just the one.

So I was almost as excited as I'd been when I was six or seven years old and would have gladly sold my teeth for a ticket. Plummer paid for both our tickets, if he paid anything at all. He said something in a low voice to the woman at the ticket booth, and I wouldn't be too shocked to find out that the coin he gave her was every bit as real as the one I gave him in Ensul. Then there we were, inside the tent, going up the wooden steps to seats where we could see the whole thing.

It was as good as I hoped. We bought hoddogs—I don't know anywhere they sell those now but sirks; it's a little loaf of bread slit open the long way, with a sausage plopped down inside—and cups of pink lemonade, and then waited while the lights changed and the ringmaster came out. He had old world clothes on, a big fancy coat and a hat that looked like somebody took a piece of stovepipe, put a brim on it and fancied it up in green and gold, and a voice that covered even more ground than the man outside the tent could manage. He welcomed everyone and called out the first act, and from then on it was one thing after another.

There was a strongman who had the six heaviest men in the place pile onto a table, then hefted the thing onto his back and walked it around the ring. There were a couple of jugglers who tossed cavalry swords back and forth between them so fast you were sure somebody was going to get split open like a hoddog loaf, but they never missed a one. There were people who climbed on top of each other into a triangle—four on the ground, three on their shoulders, two on theirs and one on top—and then did it the other way, with only one on the ground and four up at the top with their arms thrown out at the sides. There was a woman who did rope dancing, way up in the air, without a safety net to catch her if she fell. I'm used to high places, being a ruinman, but the thought of trying to walk along that rope, much less dancing out there in the middle, was enough to make my blood run cold.

All the while, of course, there were clowns scampering around. One of them, toward the later part of the show, was a ruinman clown. He had a pick that was bigger than he was, and was trying to crack open this big concrete box that seemed to be half buried in the ground and had old world writing on it, but every time he tried to take a swing at it, it moved away from him. Finally, when he was winding up for one more swing, it sneaked up behind him and pushed him over. I laughed so hard I had tears running down my face. The words on the box didn't say STAR'S REACH, but they might as well have.

There was a pause not long after that, while the rope dancer was climbing the ladder, and right then Plummer leaned over to me and whispered, "There was a time when sirks had animal acts. People would make animals do any number of surprising things."

I gave him a startled look. The first thing that went through my mind was why anybody would want to watch people bullying animals; then I noticed that he was watching me the way he did, waiting to see what I would say; and then I realized what he was trying to tell me. "Back in the old world,"

I whispered back, "didn't they like to think they could make everything do what people wanted?"

He smiled. It wasn't just his you-said-the-right-thing look, either; it looked like a door swinging open. "Exactly," he said. "Exactly."

Then the rope dancer started out onto the rope, and we were both staring upwards, like everyone else in the tent. That was the big act, and after that things wound up pretty quickly; a few more clowns, someone who could eat fire, and then all the performers and the clowns and all were out in the middle of the ring, bowing, as we roared and clapped and let them know how much fun we had.

Then the lights went down, the performers left, and the audience started filing out. Plummer motioned me to follow him, though, and zigzagged down through the crowds to the edge of the ring. The ringmaster spotted him and came right over, and before long I was being introduced. The man's name was Ellis, and his voice sounded like anybody else's when he wasn't out there being the ringmaster. He and Plummer knew each other from a long time back, or so I gathered, and the outcome of it all was that the two of us got invited back to another, smaller tent back behind the big tent, where everybody in the sirk was having a late meal.

There were about fifty of them all told, from the ringmaster and the rope dancer down to the big burly men who handled the oxcarts and hauled things around. We got introduced and then sat down at the one big plank table with everybody else. They were tired, all of them; there were two shows that day, and two the day before, and the next morning they'd be packing everything up and heading on to the next town they were going to play, a place called Clums that was about halfway between Madsen and Naplis; so they were friendly enough but not too talkative. I was fine with that. I was still trying to figure out why Plummer said what he did, and what the door was that had just opened for me, if I wasn't just imagining it.

I wasn't. After the meal was over, Plummer and Ellis talked for a bit, while everyone else headed off to the wagons or wherever else they were sleeping that night, which for most of them was a couple of blankets and a straw pallet on the ground right there in the tent where we were sitting. Then Ellis got up, made a tired little gesture that said "blessings on your dreams" better than words could have done, and headed out into the night. Plummer came over, gave me one of his long considering looks, and said, "Are you possibly still up for conversation? There are, I think, some things we should talk about."

"I'm still awake," I said. "Here, or—"

"A little more privacy would be useful." He motioned toward the tent door.

Outside it was a clear cool night, with stars splashed across the sky and the lights of Madsen flickering off one by one not far away. A few quiet sounds came from the circus tents and wagons, and I could hear night birds calling from the banks of the river close by. We walked far enough from the tents that nobody could hear us, and then Plummer motioned: here?

I sat down, and so did he; he pulled out his bottle of whiskey and took a drink from it, then offered it to me, and I took it and downed a swallow before handing it back. Then, there under the stars, he started to talk.

"Do you recall," Plummer asked me, "the children's book we talked about that evening at Altan, the one about the little toy boat that the boy sent all the way to the Lannic?"

I did, and said so.

"That was written most of a century before the end of the old world, and there were hundreds of thousands of copies printed, maybe more, before things got so bad that books stopped being printed at all. As far as we can tell, only three copies survived. Two were in Meriga and one in Nuwinga, all three in our collections."

Plummer paused then, watching me, waiting for a question. What I wanted to know most just then was who "we" and "our" meant, but I knew him well enough to guess that that wasn't the question I needed to ask. "Did they get there before the old world ended?"

It must have been the right question; I could barely see his face in the darkness, but the stars mirrored in his glasses shifted in the way they did when he smiled. "We don't know. The collections existed in the drought years, that much we know, and there were people keeping them in much the same way we do now. They had the three copies, and a decision was made just over a hundred years ago to take one copy out of the collections and put it back into circulation." He gestured, palms up. "A simple thing, really. A farmer found it in an old chest in the attic, and brought it to the local priestess, who saw nothing harmful in it and much that was good. Word got to the printer's guild in a town not far away, and the printers bought it from the farmer, set it in type and made woodcuts of the pictures. Copies found their way to a Circle elder here, a priestess there, always to those who could see to it that the book would find its way to children. It made the printers a very nice sum of money in the end, and so people went searching in their attics and basements and found four more books, one of which was unknown to us."

"And all of that was planned," I said.

"Except for the four books. That was a happy accident."

He waited again, and after a moment I asked, "Why that book, just then?"

Again the glasses moved, echoing the smile I couldn't see. "Good. The Third Civil War was past, and we wanted something that would remind people in Meriga and elsewhere that their lives are woven together by something more than muskets and cavalry swords."

"How often do you put a book—" I had to pause to remember the words. "Back into circulation."

"It varies," Plummer said. "Once in ten years, maybe. Some of us would like it to happen more often, others are worried that too much might be given out too fast. There are risks either way."

Another silence went by. The night birds were calling to each other down by the river. I tried to think of any other way to find out what I most wanted to know, and couldn't, so finally I asked, "You say we and us and our. Does that mean your friends with no names?"

That got me one of his dry soft laughs. "You've met a few of us, but only a few."

"How many are there?"

"No one knows," Plummer said. "It would be far too great a risk for any one person to know more than a small number of us—or more than a few of the collections."

"Or how many collections there are?"

"Exactly. Or where they are, or what is in them, or who tends them and guards them."

That made sudden sense to me. "Of course. They'd have to be guarded."

"Guarded, studied, tended, and hidden, by Swords, Rods, Cups, and Shields respectively; and then the Cords link circle to circle and tie the whole together. It's an old symbolism, useful for our purposes."

"You're a Cord," I said.

"The Cord of the eastern Hiyo valley."

"Do you know other Cords?"

"No, though I have my suspicions about a couple of travelers I've met."

I thought about that for another long moment. "What would happen if the priestesses found out about all of this?"

"Oh, they know that we exist." Even in the darkness, he must have been able to see my face, because he laughed his dry laugh again. "We have, shall we say, a working agreement. That's why the farmer took the book he found straight to the local priestess. Who was, I might add, expecting something of the kind. Part of the agreement is that we don't surprise them."

"There are stories," I told him. "Stories and rumors about people who have books they shouldn't have. That's the way people say it, you know."

"Of course. The rumors are deliberate, some of them, and some of them are a side effect of the way we recruit new members."

That was when it finally dawned on me why Plummer was telling me all of this. Maybe I'm just slow to catch on, but I stared at him for what seemed like a long time.

"It's a lengthy process," he said then, looking off toward the river. "Sometimes it starts by chance, when it's necessary to allow someone from outside the circles to know a secret of ours, such as where a safe place happens to be hidden. Sometimes it's more deliberate. In either case, a Cord begins the process, and then Shields listen for any evidence that the potential candidate has betrayed the secret."

"You said something about throats being cut," I reminded him. "The Swords do that?"

"It's one of their skills." The way he said it, as though he was talking about any other trade, put a cold wind down my back. "That's rarely necessary, though it does happen. If the candidate keeps silence, there will be another conversation later on, and another, and still another, while Shields wait and watch. Rods make the final decision, but the Cord must concur, and it's the Cord's task to choose the right time for the conversation in which the point of the process will be discussed, and an offer made."

"Like this one."

"Like this one." Stars shifted in his glasses.

My mouth was dry, and my tongue felt like it was two sizes too big for my mouth. I knew what I wanted to say, and I knew what I had to say, and it was a good long moment before I managed to force out, "There's a job I have to finish first."

"Of course there is. That's part of the process."

He was waiting for a question again, but I thought I already knew the answer. "You wait until the candidate has something else to do, so nothing happens in a rush."

"And so any final risk of betrayal can be forestalled." He turned to face me. "Everything I've told you so far is already known to the priestesses, and to a few other people outside the circles. You could tell it to anyone, and we would be in no more danger than we were before. I would be at some risk, to be sure, but that could be managed easily enough by my disappearance or my death, and once my time as a Cord is over, it's simply another story. You could tell it to anyone, but we require you not to do so—not to speak a word of this to anyone for any reason, until and unless your Cord or the senior Rod of your circle gives you permission to do so."

"Ruinman's bond," I said then, and he laughed again. "Good," he said, "very good. We have people in a number of guilds, and for good reason. Prentices and misters alike, they know how to keep secrets. We may be a guild ourselves someday, for that matter." I stared at him for another long moment, and he said, "The Rememberers' Guild."

I don't think I'll ever forget those words, or the way he said them. His voice had barely changed enough to notice, but all at once I could feel right down in my belly what it was like to have all those books from the old world hidden away, some that might bring good things to our world and some that might bring more evil than I want to think about; and to wish that the work of guarding and studying and tending and hiding them could be done the way the scholars at Melumi take care of the books they have, out there in front of everybody; and to know that it couldn't be that way, and why it couldn't be that way, not now, not until our world changes into something else and people don't have to think every day about the time when the wrong knowledge used for the wrong things in the wrong ways left poisons and ruins and heaps of dead bodies all over Mam Gaia's round belly.

We sat there saying nothing for a while as the stars wheeled and the river birds talked about whatever river birds talk about when the moon's coming up out of the mist in the east. "That," Plummer said finally, "was what I wanted to talk about. I suspect you have some idea of what comes next."

"You won't be here when I wake up in the morning," I told him.

"Exactly," he replied, and we both laughed. "You have, as you said, a job to finish first. When that's done, we'll meet again, and then you'll have a decision to make."

I nodded, though I don't think he could have seen me. Then, because I'd been wondering: "Why did you decide to talk about this tonight?"

"Good," he said, and I realized I'd asked another question he wanted me to ask. "It's a very easy thing to pass judgment on the old world and call it evil, the way the priestesses do: easy, and not wholly unmerited. It's a much more difficult thing to understand it, to grasp some part of why people then did what they did. The former isn't of use to us. The latter is."

He stood up then. "In your place," he told me, "I would go back to the big tent. There's loose straw there, and that's noticeably more comfortable to sleep on than the bare ground will be. Breakfast will be at dawn or close to it, so I won't keep you longer." I looked toward the tent, and when I looked back at where Plummer had been, he was gone. I laughed again, got up, and crossed the field to the big tent.

The next morning I woke up early and lay there in the darkness for a moment before I remembered where I was and what I was doing there. I stretched and brushed bits of straw off me and went outside. The sun hadn't quite gotten around to peeking around Mam Gaia's belly; there were a few pale stars still shining overhead and more of them off to the west. More to the point, there were clattering sounds and just a bit of smoke coming from the smaller tent where Plummer and I had dinner the night before, and if there's one thing you learn when you're on the road, it's that a good hot meal comes way up on the list of things to look for.

So that's where I headed. Ellis was already there, and so were a bunch of other people from the sirk, and they waved me over as soon as they saw me; we all said our good mornings, and then I said I'd be glad to help get things loaded up if there was anything I could do, which is how you ask for breakfast on the road. That got me a big plate full of bacon and hotcakes and a mug of chicory brew, and I sat with them and mostly listened as they talked about the day ahead and the trip up to Clums. It was like having a meal with ruinmen or members of any other guild; Ellis was the mister, the performers were the senior prentices, and the others had their place, right down to the big men who hauled things and handled the oxen. They were as friendly as you could ask, but there was never any question who was in the guild and who wasn't.

Afterwards, I paid for my breakfast by hauling on ropes and carrying rolls of canvas tenting over to the wagons. That was hard work, but it's nothing I hadn't done plenty of times already as prentice and ruinman, so I didn't mind. Once everything was done and the first of the wagons was rolling out of the field, Ellis thanked me and told me that any time I happened by where they were, I was welcome to a couple of meals and a free show. He didn't have to say that I could pay for it with a few hours of work, but again, that's the way you do things on the road. So I thanked him and said I'd keep an eye out for their posters, and he gave me a big grin and climbed aboard the last wagon. I waved as they headed north, and only then realized that nobody all morning had so much as mentioned Plummer's existence.

I spent a good part of that day thinking about that, and about the people Plummer talked about the night before, his guild of rememberers. It was a good day for thinking. The weather was clear and not too warm, the road dry but not yet dusty, and there weren't that many people traveling the way I was going, which was across the Hiyo and down into Tucki. That was out of my way, strictly speaking; Sisnaddi was only another couple of days ahead if I kept going along the north banks of the Hiyo; but I wasn't in all that much of a hurry to get there, and I wanted to visit Berry and make sure everything was working out between him and Cob.

There used to be a bridge across the Hiyo at Madsen. Of course it's gone now, but there's a ferry there, a big one, that goes back and forth across the river. I paid the two bits it cost to get on, and sat next to the water as the engine groaned and puffed and burned peanut oil and the Hiyo rushed past. Then I was in Tucki again, heading south on roads that weren't much more than cart tracks, past farms and fields and big patches of forest.

It all reminded me of the country Berry and I walked through, back at the very beginning of our search for Star's Reach; and that reminded me of how far I'd traveled and how many things had happened since then. If I'd been on one of the busier roads, with plenty of people to talk with and everything, that wouldn't have been a problem, but I was alone a lot of the time, and that meant I didn't have anything to do but think, and wonder what was going to happen when I finally admitted to myself that the whole business had been a waste of time.

I was pretty much convinced by then that that's how things would turn out. Now and then I tried to talk myself into believing that I could find something in the archives at Sisnaddi, some piece of paper with the letters WRTF on it that would point me to the place I needed to go, but the further I went south into Tucki the less likely that seemed. I walked past old bits of ruin here and there, rounded chunks of concrete rising up a little ways out of the grass, and it occurred to me more than once that they were telling me that what was left over from the old world didn't really matter any more. Another hundred years or so of rains pounding down on the concrete, wearing it away a bit at a time; another hundred years or so of ruinmen stripping metal out of anything that might pay for another day's room and board; another hundred years or so of people in Meriga and all over Mam Gaia's round belly living their lives in ways that made sense, instead of chasing some wild dream of talking with creatures from some distant world—what would be left after that, but a few old stories about a time when we tried to touch the stars and almost killed Mam Gaia and ourselves doing it?

So that's what I was thinking as I walked south day after day from Madsen to Lebna. From there the empty nuke was only a few hours more south and east. I left Lebna after noon, saw the gray towers looming up within an hour or so, and got to the place where the trail led down off the road well before sunset. I could hear voices down below, and followed them down to Cob's camp.

Cob and Berry and Cob's prentice Sam were busy hauling chunks of metal out of a half-stripped building when I got there. Berry saw me first, let out a whoop, and came pelting over to throw his arms around me; Cob and Sam were less excited but not a bit less welcoming, and so we stood there and talked for a bit, and then I helped with the hauling until we'd carried as much out as was ready to move. By then it was getting on for time to eat, so we all went into the main building, and Cob and I talked while Berry and Sam got dinner ready.

Not much had changed since we'd been by. The ruin still had plenty of metal in it, and Cob was doing well enough that he had money put aside in the guild at Lekstun for when he got too old to work. He'd thought about getting another prentice or two, but never quite gotten around to it, so it was no trouble at all to have Berry there, quite the contrary. "You got yourself a good one," he told me more than once. "Prentices like that aren't so easy to find."

Then dinner was ready, and we ate bean soup and bread, just as if I was back at the Shanuga ruins, and talked the way ruinmen do. I was watching Berry and Sam, though, and after dinner was over and the two of them had hauled the dishes off and were washing them and chattering in one of the other rooms, I turned to Cob and said, "Those two look like they've gotten pretty close."

He snorted. "You could say that."

I'd pretty much figured out already what he was hinting at, though it surprised me more than a little. "You know Berry's a tween?"

"So's Sam," said Cob.

"I didn't know," I managed to say then

"Well, there you have it," said Cob. "I figure, Mam Gaia bless 'em, it's not as if they've got lots of other people to pick from, and as long as it doesn't keep 'em from doing their work, it's not exactly any of my business."

I nodded, and we talked about something else after that. Still, that night when we'd all wished blessings on each other's dreams and the rest of them were asleep, I lay on my pallet and thought about that. Of course Cob was right. I don't know of any reason why a tween couldn't get as friendly as he wanted with a man or a woman, take your pick, but it's not something that happens, or at least if it happens nobody talks about it. The priestesses like to say that it's nobody's fault but the ancients' that some poison from the old world got into somebody's insides and messed with their children's children, and of course they're right, but some people still aren't comfortable around tweens at all, and let's not even talk about sharing a bed.

The next morning I woke up early. Cob was still snoring, though the other two pallets were empty, and I slipped outside and stretched and decided to go down to the creek at the bottom of the little valley to wash up. I got most of the way there before I heard water splash, and then Berry's voice, low enough that I couldn't make out what he was saying. I looked around, and saw Berry and Sam sitting on the bank not ten meedas from where I was.

They were paying too much attention to each other to notice me, which is just as well, because it didn't take much work to figure out what they'd been doing, and what they were probably going to do again before long. I backed away fast and quiet, and went to a different part of the creek, on the other side of the ruins. By the time I finished and came back to the main building, Cob was awake and breakfast was cooking. The way Berry and Sam said their good mornings to me, I don't think either one had the least idea I'd seen them.

So I ate my breakfast and thanked Cob for his hospitality, said my goodbyes to Berry, and loaded up my bags and left. I could have stayed. The whole time I was there, I knew that if I asked Cob if he wanted another pair of hands to help with the ruins, he'd welcome me, and I could get back to the work I knew how to do, breaking down a ruin bit by bit and selling the metal. I could have stayed, and left dreams about Star's Reach to somebody else.

That's not what I did, though. I climbed back up the trail to the road, and started walking toward Lebna. The journey wasn't over, I knew that right down in my bones, and I had to follow it out to the end even if there was nothing at all waiting for me there.

The funny thing was, I wasn't brooding over it, not any more. When I was walking from Memfis up to Ensul, before I met Plummer again, I couldn't keep my mind on anything but what I was going to do if nothing turned up at Sisnaddi, and then on the way from Madsen to Cob's camp I didn't think of much else, either. Now that Sisnaddi was just a few days away, it was like the last few days at a ruin before the rains come in or the work runs out. You don't worry or argue or complain, you just figure out the thing that still needs doing, and then you do it.

So I walked north and a little east, following the roads through farm country that got richer and more thickly settled the further I went. The fifth day after I left Cob's ruin, toward the middle of the afternoon, the road I was on bent around a low hill, and ahead of me I could see the gray and brown patchwork of a city, a big one, off at the edge of the northern sky. It was a clear day, and if I'd known what I was looking for I could have made out the presden's palace and the big gray building of the archives next to it, but I didn't know that yet. I drew in a breath, and started down the last part of my journey to Sisnaddi.

CHAPTER *25*

AT A TABLE OF STARS

Berry and I were in the radio room last night, listening to the broadcast from Sanloo. There wasn't much new, just a speech by somebody important in Congrus who said nothing at all in the most graceful way you can imagine, and some guessing about how soon the funeral's going to be. Berry was there because Tashel Ban taught him how to run the radio, and because he had even more reason to listen than the rest of us. I was there with him partly because I wanted to know what was happening back home in Meriga, partly because Berry's my prentice and my friend and I figured he could use the company. Tashel Ban and Eleen were still working on the computer, trying to get the last file on it to make some kind of sense; Anna never listened to the radio, and I have no idea where Thu was just then.

So it was Berry and I, sitting there listening. He didn't say a thing until the broadcast was over and the last of the music faded back into hisses and crackles. Then, suddenly, he turned toward me. "Trey," he said, "do you know the thing I'm sorriest about? It's all the nonsense I told you about who I am and why I ended up as a ruinman's prentice."

It took me a moment to remember what he was talking about. "The business about your mother being an Old Believer and all that."

341

"Yes."

"Well, you had to say something."

He tilted his head, considered that. "You're probably right. Still ..."

"Did you really grow up in Nashul?"

A quick shake of his head denied it. "I spent some time there, so I could make the story believable if anybody who knew the place asked questions. No, I grew up in Sisnaddi, inside the walls. My mother wanted me close, so she could visit me sometimes, and one of her servants came to check on me pretty often."

"So there are people in Sisnaddi who know about you."

His face tensed. "Some. Not many, and I hope they keep their mouths shut."

We talked a little more, I forget about what, and then he turned off the radio and said goodnight and went back to his room. I watched him go, and then went back to the main room, where Tashel Ban was hammering at the keyboard as though he meant to keep at it all night, and Thu was sitting over in the opposite corner doing one of his meditations, and Anna was finishing up the dishes. She saw me come in, gave me and Tashel Ban her sidelong look, and then smiled to herself. She doesn't smile often, and I'm just as happy for that. This one was worse than usual; it curved like the blade of a knife.

So I went back to the room Eleen and I share, made sure she was sound asleep, and started writing. Well, to be honest, I sat here thinking for a long while, and then finally picked up the pen. Ever since I wrote about the conversation Plummer and I had in the field outside the tents of the Baraboo Sirk, I've been thinking about what we're going to do once we finish up here, and especially what I'm going to do.

Partly, of course, I'm wondering about what's going to happen to Meriga, and whether there's going to be any safe place at all, even for a ruinman, if we get a fourth civil war. Partly, there's Plummer's offer. Partly, there's what happened to Jennel Cobey, and I still don't know what's going to happen because of that. Partly, there are all the places I passed on my travels where every scrap of ruin was stripped bare by ruinmen long before I was born, and wondering what's going to happen to the guild when there aren't enough ruins left for us to work; and of course partly I'm thinking about the fact that I managed, by sheer dumb luck and a lot of wandering, to find the place that everybody's been looking for since the old world came crashing down, and what do you do after you've done that?

At any rate, I wasn't ready to sleep yet and couldn't make myself write, and so I slipped out of the little room Eleen and I share and went into the big space where the people who were here before us used to grow their vegetables. The glass block skylights up above were pure black, no trace of starlight in them at all, though I was pretty sure it was a clear desert night and plenty of stars were looking down on this side of Mam Gaia's round belly. I sat on the edge of one of the concrete tubs full of dirt where the vegetables used to be, and looked back up at them.

I was pretty sure that something was going to happen the next day, something big. Eleen went to bed with a look on her face that wasn't the one I expected. Ruinmen talk about trying to get through a concrete wall by pounding your head against it, and I'm sure the scholars in Melumi have a more elegant way of saying the same thing; I know the look Eleen gets when that's what she's been doing, but that wasn't the way she looked.

She looked frightened. Not frightened as though something's come lunging out of the darkness at you, the way Thu came at me on that night in Memfis; frightened as though everything you thought you could trust just dropped from beneath your feet, the way—I was about to write "the way the floor dropped from beneath my feet in the Shanuga ruins," but I knew better, any ruinman's prentice past his first season knows better, than to think you can ever trust an old concrete floor. I sat there and stared up at the night, and thought about the frightened look on Eleen's face, and all the things we'd learned about the Cetans, and the night stared down at me and didn't say a thing. Finally I got tired enough to sleep, and went to bed.

The next morning I was up before it was light. It was my turn and Anna's to make breakfast, and so I washed and dressed and headed for the kitchen. She was already there, which was unusual. We didn't see her much before breakfast unless it was her turn to help with the cooking, and even then she'd get to the kitchen when things were well along and do most of the serving to make up for it. This time she was waiting. She didn't say much most mornings, and this morning she smiled her knife-curved smile, and watched me out of the corners of her eyes, and didn't say a word.

I don't think any of us said a dozen words during breakfast. Everyone knew that something was about to happen. People don't live together as long as we have, here at Star's Reach, without getting to sense when a discovery's been made or a problem's come up. The longer breakfast went on, the thicker the silence got, until finally Tashel Ban drained his cup of chicory brew and said, "When the rest of you are finished, there's something Eleen and I have found that we all need to talk about."

The rest of us were finished. Berry and Thu took a couple of minutes to clear the table, but nobody even thought about washing the dishes. Tashel Ban waited until they were back at their places, then leaned forward onto his elbows and said, "We've recovered the last thing that was put on the computers before the people here died."

He stopped there, and after a moment I said, "And?"

"I have no idea what to make of it. It's not a document. It's a program, a huge one, and we can't figure out what it is or what it's supposed to do. It's—" He gave us all his owlish look. "I'm not at all sure how much of an explanation you would prefer."

"Details," said Thu, "are more useful than generalities. Please go on."

Tashel Ban sat back in his chair. "I don't claim to know everything about the way computer programs were put together back in the old world, but I know a fair amount, probably as much as anybody does nowadays. The Nuwingan government has a few computers that are still in working order—I'm pretty sure the Merigan government has some, too—and I've worked on ours. I've learned enough to look at a program written for the kind of computer they put here at Star's Reach, and know what to expect, what the files look like, and so on.

"The program we've found is gibberish. Or it looks like gibberish. It's got things stuck into it that are ordinary pieces of programming code, but I think they were lifted out of other programs that were already in the computer, and they do things with those other programs or the operating system that runs the computer. The rest of it is nonsense, letters and numbers and other things all jumbled together without any structure I recognize at all. But—" Here he leaned forward again. "I don't think it's actually nonsense. There are patterns in it. I just can't figure out the first thing about them.

"So we tried to figure out where it came from and when it was used—you can find that out from inside the computer if you know how—and that's when things got truly puzzling. The program ran just once, a few hours before the people here tried to delete all their files and then shut everything down. It was downloaded onto the computer a day before, by another program, an even bigger one. This other program was downloaded onto the system four days before that, spent all four of those days doing something I can't figure out, and then deleted itself.

"Then we tried to find out where the first program came from, and that's what kept us busy most of yesterday. It looked as though it just popped up out of nowhere, until we thought of checking the logs for the main radio receivers. That's where it came from. There was a radio message, a long one, that repeated itself over and over again—" He moved his hands in a circle. "And somehow that set up a repeating pattern all through the communications and computer system here, and the big program somehow unpacked itself from that. I don't know how to do that. I don't think anyone anywhere knows how to do that."

"Clearly someone did," Thu pointed out. "I wonder if it came from Sisnaddi."

"Not those receivers," Tashel Ban said.

It took just a moment for that to sink in. When it did, Thu's eyes narrowed. "You are saying that the program came from—" A motion of his chin pointed upwards. "Out there."

"As best we can tell, yes."

I thought I understood then. "So it's something from the Cetans?"

"That's the question we asked," Tashel Ban said. "But the program doesn't look anything like what the Cetans send, and it doesn't correspond at all to what the people here before us were able to learn about Cetan computing."

I was still trying to get my head around that when Berry spoke. "That message," he said. "The one that brought the program. When did it arrive?"

"That was the next question we asked," Tashel Ban told him. "I gather you've guessed the answer." Then, because Thu and I were both looking puzzled: "The main antennas point whichever way this part of Mam Gaia's belly is facing. Right now, they're facing Tau Ceti in the morning hours. More than a few hours to either side, and—" He shrugged. "They're pointing to another part of the sky."

That's when I realized what he was saying. "So it's— someone else."

"Apparently so," said Tashel Ban. "And I have no idea what to make of that."

We all stared at him, and then someone laughed. It was a dry, harsh laugh like paper tearing, and it took me a good long moment before I realized that it was coming from Anna.

"Forgive me," she said, still laughing. "Of course you don't know what to make of that. You haven't been looking in the right place." She looked straight at me, then. "You understand. Or you should. You're the only one who read the books they left for us—the only one but me."

I knew right away what she meant, but before I could think of any way to answer, Tashel Ban said to her, "Perhaps you can explain it to the rest of us, then."

"If you wish." She looked at him, and then at the rest of us. "The Cetans aren't the reason all of this is here. They were the one species who answered the radio messages we sent, because they're at about the same level of technology we are, and they haven't been contacted yet by the Others." The way she said that last word, you could tell she would have written it with the capital letter. "The Others are the reason Star's Reach was built."

"Another species." This from Thu.

She gave him something I'd have called a pitying look from anybody else. "Thousands of other species," she said. "Millions of years more technologically advanced than we are. They have ships that can travel from star to star in less time than it took us to walk here from Cansiddi. They have answers to all the questions human beings tried and failed to find back in the old world. They were already visiting this planet before the old world went away. One of their ships crashed here, at a place called Roswell, off in the desert, and that's when the government back then started building Star's Reach, to make contact with them, to talk to them and get the technologies that would keep the old world from ending the way it did.

"But they wouldn't answer. We weren't ready for first contact, not then, not for a long time afterwards. They knew that if they landed, if they even communicated with us openly, people couldn't stand knowing that we're nothing more than a backward species on a backward planet that needs all the help the Others can give us." She gestured outwards, the movement sharp as broken metal. "Think of all the people in Meriga who spend their days praying to Mam Gaia. What would they do if they suddenly found out that their Mam Gaia is nothing more than a grain of dust spinning around an ordinary star in an out of the way corner of the galaxy?

"So the Others didn't contact us. They didn't think we were ready. They didn't contact the Cetans, either, and so we and the Cetans made contact with each other, and spent a couple of hundred years talking back and forth by radio. And maybe it was that—" She stopped, and shook her head. "Maybe it was that, that we were able to communicate with an alien species and bear it, that convinced the Others that we were ready to be contacted. And when they contacted us, we still weren't ready."

"You think that's why the people here killed themselves," said Eleen.

"I don't know," Anna admitted. "I've told you already most of what I remember; it was a long time ago, and I was very young. Still, once I got here and started reading the books they left for us, it all made sense. And—" She gestured again, palms up. "They left the books about the Others here for us to find, when they burned so much else. Why?"

"Tell us," said Eleen.

"To give us the chance to figure out ahead of time that the Others are out there. I don't think they expected anyone to be able to read the computer files, the way you have, but they probably guessed that when Star's Reach was found, we'd start talking to the Cetans again, and sooner or later the Others would try to contact us a second time. That's what the program's for, I'm sure of it—a way to contact them, or a message from them. They're still waiting out there with their advanced technology—waiting for us to be ready to welcome them, waiting until they can make this world even better than it was before the old world ended. Waiting to come down and take humanity to the stars."

There was a light in her eyes like nothing I ever saw there before. All at once I remembered the books we'd both read, the alien-books and the make-believe stories set in space, and I knew what was in her mind. I'd read the books and scratched my head and wondered, but she'd read them and believed all of it, and I thought I could guess why. "Anna," I asked her, "did your parents tell you any of this?"

She turned to face me then. "A little," she said. "My mother told me about the Others just before she died. I didn't know what to make of it. Now I do."

No one else said anything. I glanced around the table. Tashel Ban had his owl-look on; Berry was pale and distant, Thu still as an old stone. It was Eleen's face that caught my eye, though; she was watching Anna with an odd, sad look. It took me a moment to realize what it meant: Eleen knew something about all this, something she wasn't saying. What?

I didn't know, and there was something that had to be settled right away. "Tashel Ban," I said. "Can you make the program run?"

He nodded. "All I have to do is type in the command."

"Thu?"

He was the one who mattered most, just at that moment. If he decided it was time, we'd clear a space for a circle, he and Tashel Ban would go at each other with knives, and if it was Tashel Ban's time to bleed out his life there on the floor, I'd have Berry or Eleen delete the program and that would be the end of it, until whoever sent it decided to try again. That was the agreement we had, and if that was the way things had to go, I knew it would be better to get it over with at once.

Thu thought about it for a moment, then shook his head. "The program ran once before, and it did not bring spaceships down from the skies. I will not invoke our agreement on the mere possibility that this thing would violate it. If it proves to be a message or gives access to a technology, then it may be necessary to settle the matter in the circle. Not until then."

"I think," I said then, "we need to run the program, and find out what it is."

"Even though the last people who ran it killed themselves?" Berry asked.

"We have to know," I said, and after a moment, he nodded.

So we all got up and went over to the computer. Tashel Ban typed at the keyboard for a bit, and then glanced back at me. I nodded, and he hit the enter button.

I realized over the next few minutes that there's more than one kind of silence. There's ordinary silence, and there's deep silence, and then there's the sort of silence that you get when everything seems to stop, just like that, and hang there in the stillness until the silence breaks. That last kind is how silent it was there in Star's Reach as we stood around the computer and watched the screen go black. After a while, some words appeared in the middle of the screen:

```
please wait
```

So that's what we did. Lights down on the body of the computer flashed and flickered as though they were frantic about something. Around the time I was wondering if the thing was calling home to somewhere off past Tau Ceti II and waiting for the answer, a red point appeared at the center of the screen, and then grew into a ball that turned slowly. More words appeared:

```
Is something visible on the screen? y/n
```

Tashel Ban tapped the Y key. I swear the sound echoed off the walls of the room.

```
Is it a sphere? y/n
```

He tapped it again.

```
Is it red? y/n
```

Another tap. A moment later, a sound like a flute playing one note came out of the computer.

```
Can you hear the sound? y/n
```

Tashel Ban tapped the same key.

"Can you hear this voice?" It was the computer, no question, talking out of the little holes on both sides of the screen, but it sounded like a woman's voice, cool and calm and not quite saying the words the way they're supposed to be said.

"Yes," said Tashel Ban.

"Is it speaking the English language?"

"Yes."

"Is it clear and understandable to you?"

"Close enough."

"I don't know what that means."

I think we all looked at each other just then. "Yes," Tashel Ban said after a moment.

"Thank you," said the voice. The red ball vanished, and the screen stayed black for another longish time while the little lights on the computer body went frantic again. Then stars appeared, coming out slowly the way they do after sunset, and in the middle of them something that nobody in Meriga has ever seen in person and everybody in Meriga knows at a glance: what Mam Gaia looks like from space.

"This is your world," said the same voice. All at once, Mam Gaia shot away into distance, as though the screen had turned into a window on a spaceship like the ones in all those stories I read. After a bit you could see the sun and the other planets scattered around it, and then everything else fell into the sun and the sun turned into a little white star out there among all the other stars, and then you could hardly see the sun at all.

The spaceship, if that's what it was, slowed down; another sun came past on one side, and then another world came into view, big and pale green and covered with swirls and stripes.

"This is ours," the voice said. "You would call it the fourth planet of the star Delta Pavonis."

The screen turned and plunged down toward the planet. Green swirls filled it, and then all at once we were in among the swirls, in a place where the sky was pale green and big white clumps of something else that might have been clouds drifted past, and there was no ground at all, just green sky above and below and as far as you could see in every direction. Something drifted into sight, something that looked a little like a clump of soap bubbles with a lot of thin feathers dangling down from it, but the feathers were moving and the soap bubbles got bigger and smaller as it drifted on by.

"That's one of them," Eleen said in a whisper.

She was right, too. Two others came into the screen, and the voice said, "You cannot visit our world and meet us, but if you could, this is what you would see."

The image drew back, so we could see hundreds of the bubbles-and-feathers things, drifting around in the green sky. "More than four million of your years ago," the voice said, "our species reached the stage of complex technology." Something like a vast heap of soap bubbles and spiderwebs came into sight, glowing with points of light; I guessed it was a city, or something like one. "We made the usual mistakes, and suffered the usual consequences." The image changed; the sky turned brown and murky, and another of the city-things came into sight, torn, lightless, empty. "Our recovery was long and difficult. Afterwards, we began reaching out, as you have, to try to contact other species on other worlds.

"We succeeded." Another of the city-things appeared, tiny compared to the first, but with something I guessed was an antenna spread out over what must have been a huge piece of green sky. "Other worlds had already contacted one another by radio, beginning almost twenty-two million of your years ago. There are thirty-eight species currently in contact with one another. If you and the species you call Cetans both choose to open radio contact with us, you will be the thirty-ninth and fortieth. Our world is closer to your world and the Cetans' world than any of the others, and we have been listening to your radio communications for many of your years now, so it is our place to invite you both to enter into communication with us. Here are the other species who are waiting for your answer."

One at a time, as the voice went on, pictures appeared on the screen. Every one of them had something toward the middle that must have been an alien, and something behind it that must have been an alien world, but that's about all that I can say about most of them. As I write this, I'm remembering one of them, a little like an upside-down flower with seven long fleshy petals, or maybe they were feet. The petal-feet were orange and so was the body of the flower, where the petal-feet came together in a spray of long thin drooping spines. Around the top of the body, where the stem would be, were a couple of dozen stalks with bright blue cones on the end of them; I guessed they were eyes. The alien stood on what looked like blue sand, or maybe it was snow, and something like blue fog swirled around it. The reason I remember that alien is that it looked more like a human being than any of the others did.

"Your messages to the Cetans, and theirs to you, have taught us much about how you communicate and how you understand the universe," said the voice, as the aliens appeared and disappeared. "The message you received from us was designed to launch a set of self-replicating patterns that can adapt themselves to any information technology. Those patterns analyzed your technology and your means of communication so that this message could be given to you in a form you will understand. If you choose to accept our invitation, the analysis will be sent to us by radio, and we will be better able to understand what you say to us thereafter. If you accept our invitation, we know that you will have many questions. We can anticipate certain of these questions and will answer them now.

"Most species, when first contacted by one of the worlds already conversing with one another, want to know if we can travel to their world, or bring them to one of ours. We cannot. Most of the technological species we have contacted have attempted space travel, and made, as you did, short trips to nearby moons and worlds. That much can be done, at a great cost in energy and resources. To travel from star to star, however, involves a cost in energy and resources that no species known to us has ever been able to meet, and technological challenges that no species known to us has ever succeeded in overcoming. You are free to make the attempt, and other species will gladly teach you what they have learned from their failures, but we cannot offer you any hope of success.

"Most species want to know if we can help them repair the damage to their world that they caused when they first reached the stage of complex technology. We cannot. We can share our own experiences with you, and other species can do the same, but each world that supports life has its own unique patterns and problems, and the experiences of other species on other worlds may be of little help to you. At best, principles learned from those experiences may be of use to you, if it happens that you have not yet learned them yourselves.

"Most species want to know if we can teach them sciences and technologies they have not already learned for themselves. We can try, but this is less easy than you may yet realize. You will already have learned from your communications with the Cetans that different species understand the universe in very different ways, that many of the things you think are true about the universe are actually reflections of the deep structures of your own organisms, and that many more depend on conditions on your world that are not found elsewhere.

We encourage you to tell us about your technology and the ways in which you understand the universe, and we will gladly try to share our knowledge with you. We will marvel at what we learn from you, but much of what you share with us, we will never fully understand; and you will find the same experience waiting for you."

The parade of aliens finished, and then the screen showed the green sky of Delta Pavonis IV and the bubble-and-feather things floating in it.

"When our species first reached out to find other beings on other worlds, we expected to find beings much like us, living on worlds that were much like ours. We found ourselves instead communicating with beings we can scarcely imagine, living on worlds we will never fully comprehend. You will find the same thing.

"Thus we cannot solve your problems; we cannot come to you or take you to some other world; we cannot teach you anything you are not ready to learn. All we can offer is the chance to communicate with other intelligent beings, to try to grasp something of the way we and other species experience our worlds, to share your own experiences with others who are eager to learn about them, and to know that you are not alone in the universe. If that is enough, we welcome you to the conversation between worlds.

"Please communicate this message to the appropriate members of your species and make the decision according to your ways. We await your reply."

The screen went black again, and words appeared a moment later:

```
You may repeat the message at any time.
After each repetition, this device will ask
if a decision has been made, and if the deci-
sion is favorable, you will receive instruc-
tions on how to proceed.
```

I have no idea how long it was after the words appeared that anyone talked or moved. I know that I spent a good long time staring at the screen, thinking about the green skies and bubble-and-feather creatures of Delta Pavonis IV and the other aliens, scattered across who knows how much of space, talking to each other since long before our first ancestors followed whatever hint Mam Gaia gave them and climbed down out of the trees in Affiga, if the priestesses are right and that's where it happened. I thought of the blobby yellow Cetans, who practically seem like friends and neighbors to me, and wondered what they thought when they got the same message, the same offer to sit down and talk around a table made of stars, knowing that whole lives would pass by between asking a question and getting an answer.

"The usual mistakes," said Thu. It was a moment before I realized he was quoting the voice. "And the usual consequences."

"I was thinking about that, too," Tashel Ban replied. "Also about what it means that they can send a program to a computer they know nothing about, and still get results like the ones we've seen. That shouldn't be possible."

"With four million years of practice?" Eleen pointed out.

"Twenty-two million years," said Thu, "if they learned the trick from others."

That brought another long silence. I don't know for sure that everyone else was thinking about what that much time means, but I certainly was.

"There was a debate," Eleen said then, "in the old world, about technology. Almost everyone back then thought that technology could just keep on progressing forever, becoming more and more powerful, until human beings could do anything they could imagine. There were a few scholars who pointed out that everything else follows what's called the law of diminishing returns. Trey, if you're digging for metal in a ruin, the longer you keep digging, the harder it gets to find metal, am I right?"

"True enough," I said.

"What these scholars were saying is that knowledge works the same way, and technology works the same way. So the kind of thing that Anna—"

Her voice trailed off. After a moment I realized why. Anna was nowhere in the room, and from the blank looks on everyone's faces, nobody had seen her go. A cold thought stirred, and I thought I knew where she would be; I turned away from the computer and headed at a run to the room where the old alien-books were.

I was wrong, but as I got there I heard something hit the floor in the kitchen. I sprinted that way, and there she was, lying in a puddle of blood with her hands on a knife and the knife in her chest. Her eyes were already staring up at nothing as the last color drained out of her.

CHAPTER 26

WAITING FOR THE THUNDER

"She was almost right," Eleen said.

We were outside, not far from where we'd taken the bodies of the ones who died at Star's Reach before we came. There wasn't much left of them, a few odd scraps of bone here and there in the dust, but they had company now. We did our best to save her, but Anna knew exactly what she was doing when she turned the knife on herself.

So we found an old table and hauled her outside on it, the way we hauled what was left of the people her parents knew, to send her back into the circle. Eleen said the litany for her, we stood there for a while, and then we walked a little ways off, over to one of the big angular lumps of concrete that hid the antenna elements from the wind and sand. After a while, the silence got too heavy to bear any longer, and we started talking, quietly, about what had just happened.

"When I was going through the files we'd reconstructed, I found messages among the people who ran things here, talking about the same things Anna mentioned," Eleen said. "From the very beginning, there were always a few people who worked here who thought that aliens were already visiting Mam Gaia in flying saucers, and would come down and rescue humanity someday. As long as they did their jobs, the others didn't concern themselves, just as they didn't worry

359

about the few who were Old Believers and wanted time off one day out of every seven to talk to their god.

"As the years went by, though, more and more people here came to believe in the flying saucers. The others worried about that, but the believers couldn't be spared—Star's Reach had mostly shut itself off from the rest of Meriga by then, because of the troubles that led up to the Third Civil War, and even if they'd gone looking for help there was nobody else in Meriga or anywhere else who knew how to do the things they needed to get done.

"So the people in charge worried but didn't do anything, and the number of believers grew, until finally everyone at Star's Reach either believed in the flying saucers, or shared the same hope that a more advanced civilization would contact them and help humanity if they just kept working on the project. I can't fault them for talking themselves into that belief. They needed some reason to keep on, some way to convince themselves that what they were doing mattered to anybody but themselves. So they traded messages with the Cetans and waited for someone else to contact them. And—" She spread her hands, palm up, and let them drop.

"You didn't say anything about this before," I said then.

"I didn't think it was important. There were many other documents; I could have bored you all for hours every evening, talking about everything we found. It never occurred to me that those messages would explain why they killed themselves."

"I'm not sure I understand," Berry said. "They got the message they were waiting for."

"Except it wasn't what they were waiting for," Eleen pointed out. "Like Anna, they believed, or hoped, that the aliens who contacted them would be so far ahead of us that they could come here, give us back the kind of energy sources we had in the old world, fix everything we did to Mam Gaia—all that, and more. They wanted the old world back again, and they thought the aliens would give it to them. And what they got instead was what we just heard."

None of us said anything for a little while, and then Thu spoke. "The question that occurs to me is whether the message was telling the truth."

"I don't know," Eleen admitted. "I don't know of any way we could know."

"One part of the message is certainly true," said Tashel Ban. "Delta Pavonis IV is a gas giant with an atmosphere that looks green to us. Scientists discovered that before the old world ended—and as far as I know, that information isn't in the computers here at Star's Reach."

Thu nodded. "But that does not tell us whether the beings who sent the message might respond to a reply with something more than a radio message."

"Like a spacecraft?"

"Or a great many spacecraft."

Tashel Ban shook his head. "If they could do that, they wouldn't have had to send a message and wait for a reply. They could have sent a spacecraft as soon as they detected our signals, found out whatever they wanted to know, and followed up with a fleet, if that's what they had in mind. But—" He held up one finger. "If they could do that, we'd have been visited a long time ago; Delta Pavonis is only twenty light years away." He held up a second finger. "And we've been receiving messages from the Cetans all along. They apparently got the same message we did; I don't know whether they answered or not—we haven't taken the time to decode the messages from them that are stored in the main computers down below—but they've been trying to talk to us ever since, and waiting for a reply. If somebody came calling from Delta Pavonis IV, that didn't disrupt the Cetans' transmissions at all."

"There's one thing more," said Eleen then. "I mentioned the debate about whether progress could go on forever. There was one argument against that theory that nobody ever managed to push aside. It's called Fermi's paradox, after the scholar who first thought of it."

"I have heard of it," said Thu.

"I haven't," I said.

Thu nodded, and Eleen went on. "Even when scholars still believed in the Big Bang, they knew the universe had been around for at least thirteen billion years, and there had been plenty of stars with planets long before Mam Gaia was formed. If other intelligent species evolved during those thirteen billion years, and interstellar travel is possible, then they would have been all over the galaxy long before our time, leaving traces we couldn't miss. There are no such traces. The most likely reasons for that are either that we're the first intelligent species to evolve in this galaxy, or that interstellar travel isn't possible. Once we contacted the Cetans, the first reason stopped being a possibility—two intelligent species less than eleven light years apart means that intelligent species are fairly common. That leaves the other, which most scholars back then didn't want to think about."

"None of that is conclusive," said Thu.

"True," said Tashel Ban. "If you want conclusive proof, though, it's twenty light years away."

"Or ten," said Berry.

"True enough," Tashel Ban replied. "The Cetans probably know one way or another by now. I wish we could ask them."

"Actually," said Berry then, "we can." The pale tense look he'd had since we heard about his mother wasn't exactly gone, but there was something past it, something that flickered and glowed like a flame.

"In theory, yes," said Eleen. "But we'd have to finish working out the code—"

"Not just in theory." He glanced from Eleen to me to Tashel Ban to Thu. "Let me show you."

So we left Anna to the wind and the blowing sand, and went down into Star's Reach again. Berry led the way to his room, opened the door, waved us in. The stacks of paper were still scattered all over every flat surface but the floor. He went straight to one stack on his desk, took a sheet of paper off the top, and handed it to Eleen. "I think you can read this."

She glanced over it, then stopped, read it over again with eyes going wide. "Yes."

"If you're willing," Berry said.

She nodded, considered the paper for a moment longer. "There's a center from which movement radiates outward, linked to radio frequency and to this end of the communication—oh, of course. 'Our radio station.' Then there's a reference to a previous state of flow, but the flow drops away to nothing—'stopped transmitting to you.' A spatial-subset indicator, and then interference patterns—'because of local troubles.' I think I can read the rest: 'and was abandoned for a time. The troubles have ended, the sphere—no, the planet, our planet, is unharmed, and we have reoccupied the station. We will resume regular communication once we review past messages and finish learning how to send new ones.'"

We were all staring by the time she finished. "Berry," I said then, "you worked that out yourself?"

"I kept wondering about the Cetans, what they must have been thinking after our transmissions stopped. It seemed only fair to let them know that our species is still here." With a little shrug: "And I didn't have much else to do, other than wash dishes and help with the computers when I could. So I started printing out messages and translations at night, and tried to figure out how the code worked."

Tashel Ban had taken the paper from Eleen, and was reading over it. "The syntax is correct," he said. "If we sent this, I'm quite sure the Cetans could read it."

I was looking at Berry when I realized what had to happen next. "That's not prentice work," I said. "Give me your pry bar."

He stared at me, then without a word went to his work belt, got the bar, and handed it to me. I hefted it, then flicked out the sharp end good and fast, catching him on the face just under the cheekbone. I heard Eleen gasp, but by then I was holding out the pry bar for Berry. "Take it, ruinman," I told him.

He took it, and his face lit up the way mine must have, deep down in the Shanuga ruins where Gray Garman made me a mister. For a moment he looked as though he was about to say something, and then gave it up and flung his arms around me. I patted his back and looked past him at the others. As he drew away, I said, "Eleen, Thu, Tashel Ban, I'd like to introduce Sir and Mister Berry of the ruinmen's guild of—well, of Star's Reach, for now."

So of course they all congratulated him. While Tashel Ban was doing that, though, Thu turned to me. "For now," he said. "It seems to me that certain decisions need to be made."

"I know," I told him, and he nodded, once, as though that settled something.

I waited until the congratulations were over and Berry was dabbing something on the cut I left on his face, and then said, "Well. We know as much as we're going to know about what's here, and you know as well as I do how much food we've got left. We've got some choices to make—but I'm going to need a little time first, to think about everything that's happened."

Nobody argued.

"An hour, perhaps?" This from Thu.

Nobody argued about that, either, and so I turned and went out into the hallway.

I knew where I needed to go, though I didn't know why, not at first. The metal stair boomed beneath my footsteps, and the door groaned open, letting in a spray of dust and sand. A moment later I was outside, underneath the empty desert sky, with the concrete antenna housings stretching away into the distance on all sides and the low dark shape that used to be Anna, lying there where we'd left her.

I thought about what little I knew about her and her life, the circle through time that brought her back here to the death her parents managed to escape. I thought about the things she'd said about the false stars and the priestesses; I thought about the alien-books we both read, and the promises that sounded so true to her and so false to me, and where the difference was; and I stared past her, back eastwards to the place where the ground pretends to meet the sky. That's when I figured out why she died, and why the people who were here at Star's Reach before us died, and maybe, just maybe, why all those billions of people died when the old world ended: their universe was too small.

I don't know if that will make the least bit of sense to anyone else who reads this, if anyone ever does. After I wrote those five words, I sat at the desk here in the little bare room I share with Eleen, with the point of my pen not quite touching the paper, for something like a quarter of an hour. I must have decided half a dozen times to scratch the words out, and half a dozen more times to spend the next half dozen pages trying to explain what I meant, and changed my mind each time.

Still, it's simple enough. The people who wrote the alien-books, and most of the stories that were in the shelves with them, had all kinds of notions about what might be waiting out there between the stars, but they never dreamed that the universe was big enough to hold distances that couldn't be crossed or problems that couldn't be solved. It wasn't that people back then were just plain wicked, the way the priestesses say. They really believed the universe was small enough that they could make it behave, the way Plummer says they used to make animals behave in sirks. That's why they ignored so many of their problems until it was too late to do anything about them, and why they told themselves stories about flying saucers and space travel and how we were all going to go to the stars someday, where we'd find lots of people like us and lots of planets like Mam Gaia, because they never imagined the universe was big enough to hold anything else.

That's what I figured out, as I stood there looking east across the desert. I figured out something else, too, which is that we've learned something now that they didn't know, back in

the old world. That was when I knew what I was going to say
to the others.

I left Anna's body to the wind and the dust, then, and went
back down into Star's Reach. I wasn't the first one in the main
room, though that was only because Thu was sitting in his usual
chair at the table, where he'd probably been the whole time.
He nodded to me; I nodded back, walked over to the table, and
stood there waiting, because I couldn't think of anything else.
Everything I'd done and tried to do during the five years since
I found the dead man's letter in the Shanuga ruins came down
to one decision we were going to have to make then and there.
That two of the people I liked best on Mam Gaia's round belly
might have to go into the circle with knives to settle the thing
didn't help at all.

A door opened and closed down the hall, and Berry came
in next, with the kind of brittle calm on his face you see when
people are ready for a fight they don't want but know they
can't get out of. He nodded to me and Thu, took his seat at the
table, folded his hands and waited. About the time he settled
into place, another door opened and closed, and Eleen came in;
her eyes were red, as though she'd been crying, but she greeted
everybody by name, went to her place at the table across from
Berry's and sat.

A good long minute went by, and then boots sounded on
the stairway down to the rest of Star's Reach. Tashel Ban came
up them, his face grim. He didn't say anything to anyone, just
walked over to his chair, pulled it out, plopped down into it
and sat there with his chin propped on his hands and his eyes
staring at nothing in particular.

I sat down then, and looked from face to face, remembering
all the roads we'd walked together in one way or another, and
also remembering the others who walked part of them with us
and weren't there for one reason or another.

"The way I see it," I said then, "we've got three decisions to
make. The first is what to do about Star's Reach, the second is

what to do about the messages from the Cetans, and the third is what to do about this last message."

"What to do about Star's Reach?" This from Tashel Ban. "I don't see much that we can do about that."

"Turn it over to the ruinmen to break apart for scrap," said Thu at once. "Find some way to preserve it in its current condition, so the conversation with the Cetans can continue. Abandon it, claim that we found nothing, and leave it for someone else to find."

"More or less," I said. "There's also Anna's choice, I suppose, but I don't see much point in that."

That got a moment of silence, then: "No," Tashel Ban said. "I don't see a point to the last of your three choices, either, and which of the first two we choose depends on what we decide about the Cetans and the others. That's the real question, as I see it: do we tell the priestesses, your government, and mine what we've found about the Cetans and the others, or do we destroy the computer up here, erase the data from the mainframes down below, and hand the site over to the ruinmen?"

"How hard would it be to do that?" I asked.

"The second choice? Stripping the data from the mainframes would be very slow—my guess is that that's why the people who were here before us didn't do it. Destroying the computers up here? As long as it would take to toss each one of them down the stairwell."

Eleen drew in a sharp breath and closed her eyes, but said nothing.

"Does anyone disagree that those are our choices?" I asked then. Nobody did, and after a moment I nodded. "Then I want to hear what everyone thinks we should do. Tashel Ban, maybe you can go first."

"If I must." He didn't say anything for a while. Finally: "When I offered to come with you here, Trey, I had hopes: not Anna's hopes, but closer to them than I like to recall. I hoped that if we could get here, find messages from some other world, and figure out how to read them, that might teach us how to live on this planet without damaging it, and still have some of the things they had in the old world. Not all of them, not even most of them, and not in our lifetimes—but some of them, someday.

"Maybe we will, even so, but there's nothing here that helps with that, and much that speaks against it. Do you remember what the message from Delta Pavonis IV said, about how they can't teach us anything we aren't ready to learn? That's something I had learned already from the Cetan messages. Even something as simple as their way of turning sunlight into electricity—and that's a very simple thing, something we could have figured out long ago if we happened to be looking in the right place—even that took most of a hundred years of work by people here at Star's Reach to understand, because Cetans don't think like us or build things the way we do. Maybe some of the other aliens out there think a little more like human beings, but I wouldn't put money on it.

"I still think it's worth saving what we've found, and sharing it. Those solar spheres the people here worked out from the Cetan formula would be worth having, and we might be able to figure out a few more tricks like that, given enough time. But—" He leaned back, and let his hands fall into his lap. "If the rest of you think that it's too dangerous, for whatever reason, I'm not going to fight for it. I've read messages from aliens, and seen a little of what they and their worlds look like. Maybe that's enough."

The room was silent again for a while, and then Thu laughed his deep ringing laugh.

"This is a rich irony," he said. "Shall I speak next?" I nodded, and he went on. "You will all no doubt remember our arguments in Sanloo, where Tashel Ban spoke of the hope he has just described, and I spoke of my fear of what human beings might do with any equivalent of the old world's technologies. He says that what we have found here has betrayed his hopes. Equally, it has betrayed my fears.

"He has reminded us of one part of the message from Delta Pavonis. I will remind you of another part, the part that spoke of making the usual mistakes and suffering the usual consequences. If so many species have done to their own worlds what we did to ours, and struggled back from the results of that folly the way we are doing, then who can pretend that it was merely bad luck that brought the old world down in flames? Who can ever claim again that we can repeat the same stupidities and avoid the same results? And especially—" He tapped the table with one finger. "—especially when some of those others, such as the Cetans, suffered much more than we did.

"I distrust the technologies that can be found here at Star's Reach, and what human beings might do with those in the future. I know that some message from another species might someday teach human beings something far less harmless than the solar spheres you have mentioned. I know, for that matter, that it is possible that the message from Delta Pavonis is filled with lies, and the beings who sent it intend some harm by it. Even so, if the rest of you decide that it will be best to share what we have found with the priestesses, the government of Meriga, and the world, I will not demand that the matter be settled in the circle."

Something like a knot came undone inside me then. "Eleen?" I asked.

"I don't want the knowledge to be destroyed," she said simply. "If everything we've gotten from the Cetans has to be printed out, bundled up, sent to Melumi and locked in a vault for a thousand years, I won't object, but I don't want it destroyed. Maybe it's just because I was trained as a scholar, but the thought of seeing all that knowledge lost isn't something I can face. If the rest of you decide that that's what has to be done—" She closed her eyes. "I don't know what I'll do." Opening them again: "But there are places such things could be kept safely for a very long time, if that's what it comes to."

"Do you think they need to go someplace like that?" I asked her.

"No," she said at once. "No, I think it would be better if everyone in Meriga knew about the Cetans and what happened to them, and about the others—the ones from Delta Pavonis, and all the rest. I think—I think it would be better if we could keep on communicating with the Cetans, and take up the others on their offer, but I know the rest of you may not agree with that. I'll yield on that if I have to, but I want to see the knowledge preserved."

"Berry?" I asked.

He looked up from the table. "I'm thinking about what will happen when word gets out. Whatever we decide, once people learn where Star's Reach is, they're going to start heading this way. Some of them will just want to see it, the way people want to see Melumi or Troy, but some of them may have other plans, and the men and guns to put those plans into action."

"We came too close to that already," said Tashel Ban, "with Jennel Cobey."

"Exactly," said Berry. "So whatever decision we make, we need to keep that in mind, and do something to make our decision more than empty wind."

"That said," I asked him then, "what do you think we should do?"

"I don't know," he admitted. "I don't want to see the messages from the Cetans destroyed. I'm not at all sure I want to see everything handed out all anyhow to the world. If my mother was still alive, I'd say we should contact the government and the priestesses and let them deal with it, but right now? Until a new presden gets chosen, it's up to Congrus to decide, and I don't even want to think about the kind of mess they'd make of it. So I don't know."

Another silence came and went. "Trey," Eleen asked then, "what do you think?"

I looked from face to face. "I think," I said then, "that we're asking questions that are too big for five people to answer. I've got my own preferences—I'd like it if more people found out about the Cetans and the others, I'd like to see those solar spheres turning sunlight into electricity all over Meriga and the rest of Mam Gaia; I'd like to have people keep talking with the Cetans, and take the others up on their offer to talk—but are those the right choices? I don't have any idea. If there are answers here at Star's Reach, it's going to take a lot of people a lot of time and work to figure them out. That's more than we can do.

"I think that what we need is to get more people here. We need ruinmen, scholars, and priestesses, to start with, because they're used to ruins and things left over from the old world, but sooner or later there need to be people who are trained to do the work that needs doing here, and can keep it going for a good long time."

Eleen was staring at me by then. "What you're suggesting," she said, "is a guild."

I hadn't thought of the word, but the moment she said it I knew it was the right one. "Yes," I said. "Not like the group that was here in the time of Anna's parents, closed off from the rest of Meriga, but something like the ruinmen, the radiomen, the scholars—" Plummer's guild of rememberers, I wanted to say, but didn't. "A guild that can work with the priestesses and the government to make sure that what happens here doesn't do anything wrong or illegal, and still keep the conversations going with the Cetans and the others."

"You'll need scholars," she said, "and I don't know how many of those you can get to leave Melumi."

That's when I figured out the last part of it. "We'll just ask the ones that aren't at Melumi any more." I could see their faces: Mam Kelsey at the Shanuga camp, Maddy the cook at the Wanrij roadhouse, Lu the harlot, others I'd met along the way. "The failed scholars. How many of them get turned away from Melumi every year?"

"Anything up to a dozen," she said. I don't think she was seeing the same faces I was, but she was looking past me then, at something I couldn't see.

"That might work," said Tashel Ban. Then: "It would take money, quite a bit of it."

"There's a lot of metal here that isn't needed any more and could be sold for scrap," I told him. "That'll be enough to make a good start. After that—well, how much do you think the chemists would pay to know how to make those solar spheres?"

Tashel Ban whistled. "A very pretty figure."

"I bet plenty of people would pay a couple of marks to have a picture from Tau Ceti II to hang on the wall, too," I said. "The money won't be a problem."

"As Berry has said," said Thu then, "your guild will need to be armed, especially at first."

"That's why the first thing I think we should do is get a bunch of ruinmen out here," I said. "Not to strip the place—I have finder's rights on it, and they'll honor that—but to make sure that nobody else will try to take it. People don't often mess with us."

"I well remember," Thu said, with a slight smile.

"Time might be an issue there," said Eleen. "One of you would have to go back to Cansiddi, talk with the guild there, get enough ruinmen together—"

I shook my head. "I left notes on how to get here at the Cansiddi guild hall, in case we didn't come back. They're sealed and locked away, but all it would take is one radio message from me to get them to open it. And if I know ruinmen at all, once word got around that I went west from Cansiddi into the desert, dozens of young misters with no other call on their time headed for Cansiddi on the off chance that they might be able to get in on the dig."

They were all looking at me by then, Berry nodding, Eleen still staring at something none of us could see, Tashel Ban giving me his owlish look, Thu unreadable as always.

"It would be a gamble," Thu said finally.

"If you've got a better idea," I told him, "I'd be happy to hear it."

He allowed a smile, said nothing. I glanced at the others. Berry was still nodding; Eleen had stopped looking past me at whatever it was, and had begun to smile; Tashel Ban frowned, and then said, "It's a gamble, no question. Shall we cast the bones?"

So that's what we did. It took the rest of the day for Tashel Ban to get his transmitter put together, tested, and hooked up to an antenna that could toss signals toward Cansiddi and the rest of Meriga. Thu sat in the room with him, watchful and quiet as a hawk in the air, and the rest of us tried to find other things to do and mostly didn't manage it. Finally, about the time the sun threw its last red light into the glass skylights where the people here before us grew their vegetables, Tashel Ban came out blinking from the radio room and called us all in.

The transmitter and receiver were sitting side by side, two metal boxes with dials on them, on an old metal table. A low hiss came out of the receiver. We stood around them, looked at each other.

"If anybody has second thoughts," I said, "now's the time to say something."

Nobody did. Tashel Ban looked at each of us, sat down on a metal chair in front of the radio gear, turned some switches, picked up the microphone and talked into it: "Cansiddi station. Cansiddi station. Message traffic. Am I clear?"

The hiss turned into a voice. "This is Cansiddi station. You're clear. Go ahead."

"Message for the Cansiddi ruinmen's guild from the misters at the Curtis dig."

"Copied," said the voice.

"They're going to need more help here. Contract terms are on file at Cansiddi. Let us know how many misters and prentices are available."

"Copied," the voice repeated. "Anything else?"

"No. Curtis station out."

"Cansiddi station out and waiting," said the voice.

Tashel Ban turned some switches again, and set the microphone down. "That's all. They'll have a prentice run the message to the Cansiddi ruinmen tomorrow, and we'll probably get an answer this time tomorrow evening." He looked at me. "If they're ready to answer."

"They will be," I told him. I hadn't talked to the misters at the Cansiddi guildhall about Star's Reach, much less told them what was in the packet of papers they locked up. All I did was tell them to wait for a message from a dig at Curtis, or if they didn't get one in two years, open the packet anyway. Still, ruinmen are ruinmen, and I knew it was a safe bet that rumors spread all through the guild by the time we were out of sight of Cansiddi on the road west.

"I hope they will be armed," Thu said then.

"For a dig this far out from settled country," I said, "of course."

The news from Sanloo always starts a little after full dark, and Tashel Ban was already twisting the dial on the receiver, past louder and softer hisses and something that was probably a voice too soft and blurred to hear, some other message going to some other radiomen's guildhall a long ways off. Most nights I listened, but just then I wanted to be alone for a little while. I'd walked a long hard road from the underplaces of the Shanuga ruins to Star's Reach and the things we'd found there, and now it was over, or close enough that the last few steps were hardly worth counting. Pretty soon there would be work to do and choices to make, but before that happened I wanted to sit for a while and look at nothing much, and let everything that happened along the way sink in for a time.

So I left the room. Eleen left with me, and put her arms around me for a while; when she looked up again her face was wet, but the look on her face told me she was relieved, not sad. She kissed me, and then she smiled, let go of me, and without a word went off somewhere else. I watched her go, and wondered again whether the two of us loved each other or not. Then, though part of me wanted to follow her, I went to the room where the alien-books and the stories were sitting in their boxes, next to the bare bookshelf, and stood there for a long moment.

That's where I was when I heard Berry shout: *"What?"*

Things were very quiet for a while, and then footsteps came down the hall. I went to the door in time to see him go past. His face was hard and closed, and I don't think he saw anything in front of him; he certainly didn't see me. I waited until he was past, then went out into the hall. Half of me wanted to go back to the radio room and find out what happened, but the wiser half said to go after Berry, and so I turned to follow him as the door to his room shut with a slam.

There's a fine art to figuring out what to do when that happens, and it has a lot to do with the person. The very few times that Gray Garman slammed the door to his room, the senior prentices made good and sure that nobody made the least bit of noise for the rest of the night, and right about dawn one of them would open the door, find Garman slumped in his chair, dead drunk and passed out, and get him into bed. Then everything would be all right. Conn, who became Garman's senior prentice when I found the letter in the ruins, was just the opposite; somebody had to knock on the door right after he slammed it and go talk him down, or he'd decide that none of us liked him and stay in a foul mood for days.

I'd never heard Berry slam a door before, but I knew him well enough to guess how long to wait. I stood at his door for what seemed like a good long while, then tapped on it.

"Please go away." His voice was muffled by the door.

"Berry," I said, "it's Trey."

A silence came, sat there for a while, and went somewhere else, and then the door opened.

I stepped in, and Berry pushed the door shut. "There's nothing you can say," he told me.

"I didn't plan on saying much," I said. "Not least because I don't know what happened."

He considered that. Then: "They had a formal viewing of my mother's body today. There were questions in Congrus about what killed her—the usual political thing. What they didn't know until they had the viewing is that my mother was a tween."

I'm not sure how long I stared at him before I realized that my mouth was open, and closed it.

Berry turned away from me, faced the bare concrete wall. "And so none of it had to happen." His voice was shaking. "She—he—didn't have to pretend I didn't exist, send me off to the ruinmen—all of that. She could have done what her mother must have done. I—" In a whisper: "I could have been Presden. If she could pretend, so could I."

Maybe it was his voice, or the way his shoulders tensed and rose, but all at once I thought of the time Jennel Cobey and I went to see the Presden in Sisnaddi, and the gray, gaunt, guarded old woman who was waiting for us in the room full of books. "Maybe she didn't want you to have to live like that," I said. "I can't imagine what it would have been like to have to hide something like that for a whole lifetime."

"I would have done it," Berry said.

"Knowing that you couldn't ever have a lover like Sam."

His head snapped around, and he stared at me. After a moment: "I didn't think you knew about me and Sam."

"I just about tripped over the two of you when I was visiting Cob's dig, before I went to Sisnaddi." He blushed, and I went on: "How your mother—" I was going to say *got pregnant with you*, but stopped, because I'd thought of one way that might have happened and didn't want to mention it.

Berry laughed, though, a short hard laugh like a dog barking. "I already thought of that," he said. "Yes, my mother may also have been my father."

"I didn't know tweens could do that," I said, for want of anything better.

"Some can have babies, some can father them. Some can do both. Some can't do either one. What I heard from older tweens is that you just never know." The hard bright brittle tone was slipping away from his voice. All at once, he turned and sat down on his bed as though all the strength had gone from his legs. "Trey," he said then, "it's not just that. Someone in Sisnaddi talked. The news bulletin said that there were rumors that there was a child, a tween. Rumors." Another laugh, desperate. "With the right year and my real name attached. Every jennel in Meriga with an eye on the succession will have soldiers hunting for me by now."

"What's your real name?"

He stared up at me, and I could see the lump in his throat go up and down. "Sharl. Sharl sunna Sheren." Then: "Mother of Life. You have no idea how long it's been since the last time I said that aloud."

I thought about that, and thought about him. "What are you going to do?"

"I don't know." He bent over, face in hands. "I just don't know."

It's a funny thing, but when he said those words, I knew he had to say them, and I knew what I had to say in response. Thinking back on it a moment ago, as I sat here and listened to Eleen's soft breathing and tried to think of what to write next, I wondered for a moment if I was remembering something out of the stories that were left here among the alien-books, or something from the stories my father used to tell when I was a child and he hadn't yet been called away to the war that killed him. Then I thought of what Plummer said, about the one big story, and realized that he was right: there is only one story, and there was only one way it could go right then and there, in Berry's bare little room in the ruins of Star's Reach.

"I do," I said. "You're going to declare yourself a candidate." Before he could answer: "If you're going to say a tween can't be Presden, you're wrong. We just had one for more than forty years, and everyone knows it now."

He stared up at me for a long moment, then said, "They'll kill me."

"They're going to kill you anyway," I reminded him. "What have you got to lose?"

Another moment, then: "I'd have to figure out how to go about it . . ."

"Tashel Ban will know."

"That's true," he said. "That's true." He drew in a ragged breath, and just for a moment I could see the child he'd been back at Shanuga, all those years and kloms ago. "Trey—will you come with me?"

"Let's go," I said, and motioned toward the door.

A better storyteller than I am could probably make something out of what happened after that; what comes to mind now, thinking back on it, are little bright images like scraps of broken glass. I remember Tashel Ban's hands moving in a pool of lamplight as he explained how presdens are chosen and how Berry—Sharl, I should probably say now, though it doesn't come easily after this long—could proclaim himself and get the process going. I remember the table in the main room, all five of us sitting around it, while Berry told us what he meant to do and the rest of us listened and agreed. Then we were all in the radio room, with Tashel Ban turning switches on the transmitter, making sure a message would get bounced back off the high thin air to stations all over this end of Meriga, and handing the microphone to the thin red-haired ruinman who'd been my prentice not so long ago, and would probably be either Presden of Meriga or a corpse before much more time went past.

"My name is Sharl sunna Sheren." His voice was calm, there at the last, as though he knew all along what he was going to do. "I meant to announce myself later on, after my mother's funeral, but the news that came out today changed that. Unless there's someone with a better claim, I am my mother's heir and a candidate for the Presdency.

"You've heard the rumors; they're true. I was born eighteen years ago and raised secretly in Sisnaddi. My mother didn't want me to have to live the kind of lifelong lie she did, so as soon as I was old enough, I was prenticed out to the ruinmen. I'm a mister in the ruinmen's guild now, and was working at a ruin when the news came about my mother.

"I'm not going to say where I am, for two reasons. One should be obvious. The other one—that'll be known soon enough. Since as far as I know, there are no other heirs or candidates, I'm calling a meeting of the council of electors in Sanloo on the twentieth of Febry, a month and a half from now. I'll present proofs of my identity and ancestry there, so the electors can decide on my candidacy."

The words he'd rehearsed with Tashel Ban a few minutes earlier ended there, but he held onto the microphone, and after a moment went on. "One other thing. There have been a lot of rumors about this jennel and that one, about soldiers—about war. I want to ask everyone to put those rumors aside. We have laws in Meriga to decide who will be Presden, and whether or not the electors accept me, those laws need to be followed. The three civil wars we've had in this country should have taught us that there's nothing good to be gained from a fourth. On the twentieth of Febry I'll make my case before the electors in Sanloo; if any other candidates want to be considered, they can do the same; whatever the electors decide, I'll accept it, and everyone else needs to do the same thing. That's all. Thank you."

He handed the microphone back to Tashel Ban. A moment later, the hiss from the receiver turned into a voice: "Copied."

Then it was over, and we went one at a time back to our rooms. Eleen fell asleep almost at once, but it's taken me a good couple of hours of writing to feel sleepy at all, and I don't imagine that Berry will get any more sleep tonight than Thu ever does. When I was a prentice working in the Shanuga ruins and Gray Garman would set gunpowder charges to bring down a building, we'd see the flare of the fuse being lit, and then wait in a safe place until the charges boomed like thunder and the building came down. We lit the fuse on a mother of a charge tonight, a mother with babies and grandbabies all around, and there's no safe place anywhere in Meriga or around it; all we can do now is wait for the thunder.

CHAPTER *27*

WHEN THE SPIRE FELL

The first night after our messages went out we were all in the radio room early, waiting for whatever it is after sunset that makes the high thin air start bouncing radio waves back to the ground. Tashel Ban had the receiver on by the time I got there. Berry and Thu were in the room already, and Eleen arrived not long after I did, while the loudspeaker was still hissing to itself. After another few moments Tashel Ban, who was sitting at the table, nodded to himself, glanced back over his shoulder and said, "Any time now."

He must have heard something in the hiss that the rest of us didn't. Before he could turn back to the receiver, a voice came through: "Curtis dig. Curtis dig. Message traffic. Am I clear?"

Tashel Ban had the microphone in his hand before the voice was finished talking. "This is the Curtis dig, and you're clear. Go ahead."

"Message from the Cansiddi ruinmen's lodge for the misters at the Curtis dig."

"Copied," Tashel Ban said. "Go on."

"Contract terms are acceptable. Misters Cooper and Damey are on their way with prentices and gear. Prices for most metals are up, so there should be no trouble getting more help if you need it. That's all."

"Copied and out," said Tashel Ban. "Thank you."

"Cansiddi out," said the loudspeaker.

As soon as Tashel Ban had the transmitter off, I let out a whistle. "That's better than I was expecting."

All the others but Berry gave me the sort of look you get when you're talking nonsense. "Two misters?" Thu asked. "That seems—inadequate."

"One hundred forty-three misters and senior prentices," Berry corrected him. "They should be here in two weeks or a little less."

It was Tashel Ban who caught on first. "Good," he said. "Do ruinmen often use code?"

I grinned and said, "When there's need."

"That's a better response than I expected, too," Berry said then. "There must have been a crowd of them waiting at Cansiddi."

I thought about the places I'd seen where every last scrap of metal had been broken out of concrete and hauled away before I was born; I thought about the places where the guild's closed and new misters have to leave town and find somewhere else to work, because there aren't enough ruins left to support more than the misters who are already there; and I figured I could guess why a hundred forty-three misters and senior prentices had been waiting around the Cansiddi guildhall on the off chance they might have a shot at helping dig up Star's Reach. I could see from the look on Berry's face that he was thinking about the same thing. It's something that most ruinmen think about these days.

By then, though, Tashel Ban was turning knobs on the receiver again, because it was almost time for the news broadcast from Sanloo. I shut up and listened with everyone else.

The broadcast came through the hissing a little while after that. Most of it was the same thing as usual. Sheren's funeral had finally been scheduled, and the presden of Nuwinga and the meer of Genda were both going to be there. The emperor of Meyco wasn't, but he was sending one of his younger brothers, which is more than Meyco usually does. Some Jinya pirates got caught raiding merchant ships in the waters south of Memfis, there was a sharp little sea battle the pirates lost, and the lot of them got hauled ashore to a navy base in Banroo Bay whose name I almost remember, where they're going to be tried and hanged over the next few days. There were bits of news out of the government in Sisnaddi and the army along the border with the coastal allegiancies, nothing important.

Then, at the end: "Last night's radio message from Sharl sunna Sheren, who claims to be the late presden's heir, seems to have taken everyone by surprise." A scratchy recording of Berry's voice followed: "I'm calling a meeting of the council of electors in Sanloo on the twentieth of Febry, a month and a half from now. I'll present proofs of my identity and ancestry there, so the electors can decide on my candidacy." After a few clicks and pops, the announcer went on. "There's been no word yet from the electors about whether they'll consider the claim."

That was all, and then the broadcast ended. We all looked at each other. "At least," Tashel Ban said, "it's being discussed." With that not very comforting reflection, we wished blessings on each other's dreams and headed off to bed.

We spent the next day figuring out where to put a hundred forty-three ruinmen, and starting to get the rooms ready for them: a mother of a lot of work, and I was tired enough that I crawled into bed with Eleen without taking the time to write anything. That night, there wasn't anything at all in the news bulletin, not even a mention of Berry. The next night, though, after another day of hard work, we listened to one of the important jennels say that Meriga had enough good candidates for presden, and didn't have to go looking for them among tweens and ruinmen. Eleen spat a piece of hot language at the radio when that came through, which startled me, but Tashel Ban shook his head.

"Not at all," he said. "Jennels aren't fool enough to say whatever comes into their heads. If he's that worried about Berry's case, the wind's blowing the right way."

The evening after that, there was news. Half a dozen of the less important jennels, I think it was, sent an open letter to Congrus saying that Berry's claim should be considered. None of them were electors, and the electors could ignore them if they wanted, but they were still jennels, and that counted for something. What they said was simple enough: by law, one of a presden's children became the next presden unless there was some good reason to do something else; being a tween would probably be good reason, but there weren't any other candidates in the direct line, and being a tween hadn't stopped Sheren herself from being one of the best presdens we'd had since the old world ended, so if this Sharl sunna Sheren was who he claimed to be, his claim ought to be taken seriously.

That was promising, but the next two evenings went by without any news about Berry's candidacy at all—not surprising, because those were the days set aside for Sheren's funeral, and the news didn't talk about anything else. Not that long ago, Berry would have spent those days jittering like a drop of water on a hot griddle, but not any more. I could just about hear him telling himself, no, a presden doesn't do that. Still, it was probably just as well that the two of us spent those days finding a couple of disused kitchens down in the deep levels of Star's Reach; hauling the pots and pans back up all those stairs didn't leave him enough strength left to jitter.

It was the following evening that things changed, hard. Tashel Ban got the receiver working and then sat there, staring at it, as though he expected something to happen, and he wasn't disappointed. After some final news from the funeral, the announcer said, "Meanwhile, the succession is on a lot of minds. Odry darra Beth of Sisnaddi Circle had this to say." Pops and crackles, and then an old woman's voice: "It was always a disappointment that Sheren was never able to become one of us, though of course now we know why. Circle had an excellent working relationship with her, and if her child is cut from the same cloth, I can't imagine anyone in Circle objecting if the electors favor his claim."

Tashel Ban let out a long low whistle. I didn't know who Odry darra Beth was, but he did, and I could guess. The old women in red hats who run Circle don't just do things on their own; you won't hear one of them make an announcement unless the rest of them are pretty much in agreement with it. With the power that Circle has in Meriga, if the Circle elders were willing to accept Berry's candidacy, he was past one big hurdle.

The announcer wasn't done yet, though. "And this from Jor sunna Kelli, of the Sisnaddi ruinmen." Berry and I gave each other startled looks as the radio crackled and popped; that was a name we both knew. "Mister Sharl is one of ours," he said, in the kind of voice that sounds like gravel getting crushed, and warns you not to mess with the person who's attached to it. "Whether he ends up presden or not is up to the electors. That's the law in Meriga, and we'll abide by it, but if anybody tries to make that decision for them, they're going to answer to us."

More crackles, then the announcer: "Still no word from the electors, but word is expected in the next day or so. This is Sanloo station, with this evening's news."

The music started to play, and we all looked at Berry, who mostly looked dazed. "I take it," said Tashel Ban, "that Mister Jor is important."

"Senior mister at Sisnaddi," I told him. "Ruinmen don't have a chief over them all, but if they did, it would be him."

"So the threat is credible," said Thu. "That may be helpful."

"The Circle elder's the one that interests me more," Tashel Ban said. "They rarely involve themselves in the succession this early on. Well, we'll see what happens."

Berry shook his head, then, as though he was shaking himself awake, and said, "Well." It seemed like a reasonable thing to say, and none of us had anything to add to it.

So we went to our rooms, and I kissed Eleen and watched her fall asleep, and then pulled out this notebook and sat here for a while deciding what I still have time to write. I'm not going to say much about the time I spent in the archives in Sisnaddi. Not much happened there, other than day after day with the archivists, trying to find something that would turn WRTF from a jumble of letters to a place I could find, and night after night in a little room in the ruinmen's guild hall outside Sisnaddi, wondering how soon I would have to give the whole thing up.

I don't even remember what day it was when I finally ran out of places to look in the archives. It was just before lunch, I remember that, and I sat there at the little desk where I worked, staring at the bare metal, trying to think, and failing, until the soft bell sounded to let everyone in the archives know that lunch was ready. I went and sat with the archivists, ate bread and soup, and tried not to think about the years I'd spent and the chances I'd thrown away chasing what looked just then like an empty dream. I really was up against the bare walls just then, and that's probably why I thought about the place Lu the harlot told me about, the place at the Lannic shore by Deesee where every question has an answer.

If I'd been able to think of anything else to do, I wouldn't have given it a second thought. Still, as I walked back to the guildhall and slumped in the hard metal chair in my room, the thought wouldn't leave me alone. I pushed it away a dozen times, and tried to be reasonable and figure out what I was going to do now that Star's Reach was just a story again, and a dozen times it came whispering back to me that I had one more chance to find the thing.

So I had my dinner and went to bed. I wasn't expecting to sleep at all, but I dropped off after an hour or two of lying awake and staring into the darkness, and damn if I didn't slip right away into one of my Deesee dreams.

It wasn't much different from the others I had down through the years, except this time there were lots of people in drowned

Deesee with me, walking the wide streets and going into and out of the big white buildings where all the windows looked the same. Gray Garman went past me, nodding a greeting the way he did, and then all of a sudden Tam ran up to me, gave me a kiss, and hurried away. Slane the riverboat trader was there, and Cash the elwus and his motor Morey, and a lot of ruinmen I knew from Memfis and Shanuga, and scholars from Melumi and traveling folk from the roads I'd walked and, well, just about everyone I'd ever met on my search for Star's Reach. They were all going different places, but somehow they were all walking with me, too, down the street to the place where the hill rose up, green and smooth and grassy, to the foot of the Spire.

I stopped there, and they stopped, too. They were waiting for me, I knew, and there was someone else waiting for me, up there at the foot of the Spire. I was scared, more scared than I've ever been in a dream or waking life, of taking that first step onto the grass. I looked around, trying to find some other way I could go, but the people who were with me pressed right up close behind me, and the only way I could go was straight ahead, up the grassy slope, to where a dead man was waiting.

That's when I woke up. I was shaking like a leaf in a windstorm, and my heart was pounding, but I knew what I had to do. The sky was just starting to lighten up; I packed my gear, got breakfast, let the prentice who had charge of the rooms that day know that I wouldn't be needing my room that night, and walked out the door before I had time to have second thoughts.

There's a lot more of Meriga west of Sisnaddi than east of it, but you wouldn't know that from the countryside close by. Hiyo's green and prosperous, and it has more towns than empty ruins, which is something you can't say of most other parts of the country. I didn't have a lot of money left, so inns were out of the question, but there were plenty of farms where a traveler can get a night's sleep in the barn and a breakfast on the kitchen steps for a couple of bits.

There weren't any guildhalls where I could stay, though. Even where there were big towns, and there were some good-sized ones, there were no ruinmen. All that country had every scrap of metal and everything else worth taking stripped from the ground a long time before I was born.

It took me a good while to cross Hiyo, and then cut through the little neck of Wesfa Jinya that you go through before you get to Wes Pen, and Pisba. Pisba's in a valley where two rivers come together to make the Hiyo River, and it's shaped like a wedge. It's also full of soldiers, because Pisba is about as far east as you can go and still be in Meriga.

There's a ruinmen's lodge in Pisba, and it's the only ruinmen's lodge anywhere I know of that's inside the city walls. Everything in Pisba is inside the city walls. Even the farmers who work the fields around Pisba live inside, because raiders come from further east so often. The guards on the bridge I crossed seemed to be used to traveling ruinmen, and let me past with only a couple of questions; the ruinmen in the guildhall were friendly as ruinmen usually are, but they wanted to know where I was headed, and when I told them—I didn't say anything about the place where every question has an answer, just that I wanted to go look at Deesee and the Spire—they got very quiet.

"You ever been out east of here?" one of the misters asked me, and when I said I hadn't, he gave me a long look and said, "Let me show you something."

He was back a moment later with a paper map. "You see this highway? You keep on it and you might just stay alive. You know what's out there?"

I did, or at least I'd heard stories about it. "That's the burning land, isn't it?"

He nodded. "That's right."

It was evening when I got to Pisba, and I planned on leaving the next morning, so I talked with him and some of the misters after dinner, and found out everything I could about the road east and south toward Deesee. Still, when I left the next morning, it wasn't too hard to figure out that the ruinmen there didn't expect to see me again.

I bought a bunch of food at a shop before I went out through the gates of the city, and it was a good thing, because nobody lives further east, not until you get to the coastal allegiancies. Everything was green and quiet at first. I think it was three days out of Pisba when I saw the first plume of smoke coming out of a hill off to one side, and not much more than a day after that it was all over the place, filling the air with haze and the stink of sulfur.

Everyone in Meriga knows about the burning land, but not too many of them know what happened and why. I didn't, not until I went that way. This is the way the ruinmen in the Pisba guild hall explained it to me.

Wes Pen used to be just Pen, and it was a big state running east almost all the way to the Lannic. It had a lot of coal, oil, and gas under it, and since it was close to the big cities of the Lannic shore, all of those got dug up pretty thoroughly. First they put in mines and dug as much coal out of them as they could, until that ran out, then they drilled for oil and pumped it until that ran out, and then they drilled some more and pumped chemicals down into the ground to get more of the oil and gas, until those ran out.

Then somebody figured out how to pump more chemicals into the coal, down where the mines couldn't get, to turn the coal into gas they could pump out. This was toward the end of the old world, when they were desperate for fossil fuels even though the weather was going crazy from all the fossil fuels they'd already burned, and seemingly nobody asked enough hard questions. Different parts of the country had different laws about what you could pump into the ground, and the laws in Pen basically didn't stop anybody from doing anything, so people started drilling wells and pumping the chemicals down and pumping gas out. For a while they were happy, or as happy as you can get when the weather's going crazy and everything around you is right on the edge of falling apart.

Then the coal down underground started catching fire. Nobody's quite sure why, but something happened whenever the chemicals in the coal got to old mine tunnels that brought them into contact with air, and the coal underground started burning. At first they tried to hush it up, and then they claimed that it was just some kind of rare accident, but eventually every place they put those chemicals down wells caught fire, because the chemicals spread in the groundwater until they got to an old mine shaft and started another fire. Of course then they had to stop the drilling, but before then they'd drilled a lot of holes all over Pen and pumped a lot of the chemicals down them.

So there were underground fires burning under most of Pen. They're still burning today, and they'll still be burning for a long time to come, because there's a lot of coal down there still, and you've got sinkholes opening up here and there to let more air get down and keep the fires going. If you want to get through the burning land, you've got to know where the fires are and where the smoke collects, and that changes from one year from the next. If you want to get metal from ruins there, you can do it, but it's risky, because you never know when the place where you are will suddenly start smoking under your feet. If you want to live there or farm there, you're just plain out of luck.

I just wanted to get through, and enough other people want to get through for one reason or another that the ruinmen in Pisba and a few other places keep track of which roads might be safe. Even so, you never know when the ground's suddenly going to start smoking under the road, or just collapse from a sinkhole without any warning at all. If you're lucky, that doesn't happen; if you're not, nobody ever hears from you again, and that's the end of it.

I was lucky. There were times the highway I was on had sinkholes and smoking ground close by, and there was one long stretch where the smoke was so thick that I just had to keep walking, a day and a night and most of the next day, because I knew if I lay down and tried to sleep it was a pretty safe bet I'd never wake up again. Still, there were other parts of the countryside that were green and beautiful, with the last scraps of ruined farms and farm towns here and there to remind you what it was like before people got greedy and careless and messed it up for hundreds of years to come.

Finally I came down out of the hills and saw the bright silver line of a river looping and curving through woodland. From the map I saw in Pisba, I knew that it was the Tomic, the river that ran by Deesee in the old world.

I knew something else, too, from the ruins down by the river. Even from there I could see that they'd been shoveled up all anyhow by people who didn't know how to do a proper dig, and just wanted whatever metal they could get. I was outside of Meriga, and if I met anyone at all between there and Deesee, it would be Jinyans—the people who killed my father. I drew in a breath, and started down the road.

The days I spent after that, walking along the Tomic, were the strangest part of the whole strange journey that brought me here to Star's Reach. I had no idea what I was looking for or where I might find it, and it was sinking in by then that following a story I heard from a harlot in a little town in Ilanoy might not be the brightest idea, especially since it took me all the way outside of Meriga and into the nobody's-land between us and the coastal allegiancies. Still, it felt like walking over the trapped floor in the Shanuga ruins, where the whole journey started: not something you necessarily want to do, but once you start, there's nothing to do but finish.

So I followed the old crumbling road alongside the Tomic, watched the water rush past me toward the Lannic, and got used to water in the river, wind in the leaves, and my own boots crunching on the old road being the only sounds there were. I've been in plenty of places where you could walk for a day and not see any sign that people had been there since the old world ended, but this seemed emptier still, and of course I knew why. Every few years raiders from the coastal allegiancies come through here trying to push their way into Wesfa Jinya. Every few years the Merigan army marches the other way to return the favor, and there are plenty of safer places to start a farm if you want to do that or, well, anything else. It must have been full of towns and farms before the old world ended, and maybe someday it will be full of both again, but as long as we're at war with the allegiancies, the Tomic valley is going to stay empty.

Day followed day, and I followed the river. After I forget how long—it must have been a week or so, maybe a little more—the mountains turned into hills and the hills spread out and hid their feet in the forest, and when the breeze blew in my face I started to catch a hint of the salt smell I'd gotten to know so well when I was living in Memfis. That's the way the breeze was blowing one sunny morning when I heard hooves on the road ahead.

That was in a place where the road ran straight for a while, and by the time I'd thought of running into the woods to hide, the riders were in sight. There were four of them, coming straight up the road, and I knew that if I tried to run they'd chase me down like a deer, so I just kept walking.

They slowed their horses and stopped maybe twenty paces ahead, waited while I walked up: four men, three of them younger than I was and the fourth a good bit older. They were wearing brown homespun clothes and big floppy hats, and they all had long hair, long beards, and a couple of pistols each stuck into leather holsters that had seen a lot of hard wear. Their horses, though, were big and strong and skittish, the kind that jennels and cunnels ride in Meriga.

I walked up to within a couple of paces of them and stopped. They looked at me, and I looked at them, and the oldest one finally said, "Who the hell are you?"

I told him my name.

"You out of Meriga?"

"Yes."

"Ruinman?"

"Yes."

"What the hell you doin' here?"

I knew that if they thought I was lying they'd kill me without a second thought, and I couldn't think of anything to say that wouldn't sound like a lie, except the truth. "I've been looking for Star's Reach for getting on five years now," I told them. "I hear there's a place down by the Deesee ruins where—where every question has an answer. Nothing else worked, so I figured I'd try that."

They looked at each other, then back at me. "Where'd you hear that?" the oldest one asked.

"From a harlot in Ilanoy," I told him.

They looked at each other again, this time for a good long while. Finally the oldest one leaned forward in his saddle. "There's a place like that," he said. "You go straight down this road all the way to the sea, and then turn to your left hand and walk along the water a good bit until you see a chair made of chunks of concrete. That's where it is; you sit down there before the sun sets and you don't get up again until it rises. Got that?"

"Yes," I said.

"Good." He leaned forward a little more. "Now if you go straight there and come straight back and go home, and don't stick your nose into anyplace it shouldn't get, you're gonna be okay. And if you don't—well, then you better pray real hard, because you're gonna wish you never got born. Got that?"

"Yessir," I said, the way that soldiers do, and he nodded, and the four of them snapped their reins and rode right past me at a trot, two on each side. When they were past, one of the younger ones turned around in the saddle and called back, "You find Star's Reach, you tell the aliens hi for us, you hear?"

I promised I would, and they trotted on up the road. After a bit, I turned and started walking the other way. For a while

I wondered if they would come back after me and see where I went, but the hoofbeats faded out and from then on it was just my boots crunching on what was left of the road, and the sounds of the river and the wind. The sun rose up in the sky ahead of me, and moved past to my right side, and sank toward the hills behind me, and all the while the salt smell on the wind became stronger and stronger, until finally the forest fell away into scrub pines and beachgrass, sand and pieces of driftwood covered what was left of the old road, and I went up and over a dune and stood looking out at the sea.

There were waves rolling up to the beach in lines of foam and sweeping out again in flat sheets of water, and big gray masses of concrete rising up here and there, with waves crashing into them and seaweed and things growing all over them. It was a long moment before I noticed them, though, because I was looking at the Spire. It was just like the pictures I saw when I was little, a tall white shape rising up straight out of the water well out to sea, and the light of the afternoon sun shone on it and made it blaze like a still and silent flame.

I have no idea how long I stood there looking at it. Finally, though, I remembered the directions I'd been given, turned left, and walked north along the beach.

I've written more than once about the times along the way from Shanuga to Star's Reach when I saw how much bigger and more crowded everything was in the old world, and how small and sparsely peopled Meriga is nowadays. As I write this, I'm thinking of the ruins of Cago, and how they stretch for kloms and kloms along the shores of Lake Mishga. I'm thinking of the towns and cities that used to be on the banks of the Ilanoy and Misipi Rivers and aren't there any more. I'm thinking of the view from Troy Tower—and none of them, not even all of them put together, were like walking along that beach.

Ahead there were rounded masses of concrete rising up out of the water and the sand as far as I could see, and further, and I knew that the same thing went pretty much without a break all the way up into Nuwinga, and I also knew that all of that was just the western edge of the drowned cities of the coast, which used to go a hundred kloms or more further east before the sea rose up and swallowed them all. I thought of the millions and millions of people who used to live there, more people than there are in all of Meriga nowadays, and now there was just one stray ruinman a long way from home, wandering past the little that was left of it all. The wind went whispering past me, picking up sand and tossing it against my boots and my legs, and I wondered whether the dust of old bones was mixed in with it.

That's what I was thinking as I walked north along the shore, and the waves rolled and splashed, and the sun sank closer to the western hills. I started to wonder after a while if I'd walked right past the chair made of concrete the man from Jinya mentioned, and what would happen if they found me a couple of kloms past the place I was looking for. About the time I was starting to get really worried, though, I walked up most of the way into the dunes to get around a big ragged mass of concrete, and saw not too far ahead a clear space and something that might be a chair. I kept going along the beach, and after a while, I got to it.

I really had no idea what to expect when I got there. Back when Lu the harlot first told me about the place where every question has an answer, I'd wondered if it was some kind of installation from the old world, with computers, maybe, that would take your question, check it against data that got lost everywhere else in the world, and give you the answer in glowing letters on a screen. Later on, I'd made any number of guesses about it, but all of them were wrong.

There was a rough chair made of big chunks of concrete half buried in the sand, and a circle made of more chunks of concrete, not much more than knee-high, rising out of the sand like an old woman's teeth. Here and there people had taken sticks and driven one end into the sand, and tied strips of cloth to the upper end, so that the cloth fluttered in the wind. That was all. There were some big masses of concrete further south, and much more to the north, but right there the beach was flat empty sand and the sea stretched out into the east, unbroken except for the Spire, a little south of straight ahead.

I stood there for a long moment, looking at the chair, and felt like a complete fool. I couldn't think of any way a chair of salvaged concrete in the middle of nowhere was going to answer the question I came to ask. Since there wasn't anywhere else for me to go, and the sun was maybe an hour from setting, I sat down on one of the chunks of concrete in the circle, and ate some bread and sausage and dried fruit I bought in Pisba. The sun got low, and the wind turned cool and then cold, and finally I laughed out loud and got up and went over to the chair. The seat and the back were both flat smooth pieces of concrete, which was better than I'd been expecting. After a long moment, I sat down.

Nothing happened right at first, or nothing that I noticed. I settled back and looked out at the Spire as the setting sun turned it gold, and then orange, and then the color of blood. Then, finally, night closed in, and I waited.

To this day I have no idea what actually happened then. I know what I saw. Even here in Star's Reach, sitting at this desk in a little pool of light and listening to Eleen's breathing, I can close my eyes and remember every bit of it, but I'm pretty sure that some of it couldn't have happened at all, and I have no idea whether the things that could have happened actually did.

At any rate, this is what I remember.

I sat there for a while, waiting for I didn't know what. The sun went down behind me, the stars came out ahead, and the wind along the beach blew cold. Then there was a flash of orange light out to sea, right along the horizon, and I stared at it for a long moment before I realized that the moon was rising. It was a few days past the full, big and golden. As it rose, the light shining from it seemed to make a path across the sea right up to where the waves were splashing a couple of meedas from my feet.

That's when everything went silent. All at once the wind stopped, and the waves weren't moving any more. The moon stood there, right on the horizon, and as the path of light stretched across the ocean, wherever the moonlight touched the water, it started flowing away, back out from the beach toward the deep places of the Lannic. I know perfectly well that water doesn't do that, but that's what I saw: the water drawing back, forming a path of wet sand just as wide as the light from the moon. On both sides of the path, the sea stood black like a wall.

I don't remember thinking that any of this was out of the ordinary. I don't remember thinking anything at all. I simply got up from my chair and started walking across the bare wet sands ahead of me, following the path down into drowned Deesee.

It wasn't anything like my dreams, though. In my dreams the water is like air and the sun is shining on the top of it, turning the surface of the water to silver, and the buildings are all just the way they were when Deesee was above water and the presden and her jennels ruled half the countries on Mam Gaia's belly. The path I followed, though, was all sand and stones and seaweed, with crabs scuttling around, and fish lying there gasping in pools of salt water. There wasn't much left of the buildings close to the beach, just low masses of concrete hammered to roundness by hundreds of years of waves and tides, but as I went further and the sand turned to mud, I passed ruins covered with barnacles and mussels and sea anemones, with roofs fallen in and every bit of metal corroded by the salt water, but still looking like buildings. I passed the hulks of old cars, stepped over poles that used to hold lights up so they could shine on the streets.

I have no idea how long I walked down between the black walls of water into the heart of Deesee. Finally, though, I got in among the part of it I remember from my dreams, with the big white buildings with windows lined up like soldiers on parade, except that the buildings were half-fallen and stained with mud, and draped all over with great blades of kelp. Still, I knew what came next, and I wasn't wrong. I passed what was left of the buildings and reached the big open space with the hill in the middle of it, and the Spire rising up above all. The top of it was above the water, glowing in the moonlight; all around it the sea rose up black and motionless, and there was nowhere else to go.

Up at the foot of the Spire, someone was waiting for me.

I saw him as soon as I got to the base of the hill. The light was dim and I couldn't make out anything but a human shape at first, but I knew who it was. As I climbed the hill, the details came clear one by one: the stiff heavy clothing that soldiers used to wear in the old world; the funny broad hat, flat on the top, with a bill in front and a bit of flashy metal above that; more bits of metal here and there on the clothing, especially on the shoulders and right above where his heart was; the face, lean as a hawk's, looking toward me with a look I couldn't read, not yet. The face was only familiar from my dreams, but I knew the rest of him well enough, since the day I found his corpse sprawled on the table next to the letter about Star's Reach, down there in the underplaces of the Shanuga ruins.

I was within a few steps of reaching him when I saw that he had the letter in one hand. He held it out to me so that I could see it, and read the words on it. I looked at it, at him, and that's when I knew that he wanted me to understand it. He wanted me or somebody to find Star's Reach. His face didn't change at all, but I could see hope and longing in his eyes. He waited until he knew I'd recognized the letter, and then turned it over so that I could see the single word *Curtis* written in gray on the back.

Yes, I wanted to say, I know. That was you. That was your name back then. For some reason or other I couldn't speak, but I think he must have heard me anyway, for he shook his head, a sudden brisk move, and pointed at the word again with one finger.

I didn't see his lips move and I didn't hear anything, but all at once I knew what he was trying to tell me. Not my name, he was saying, and not any other person's name, either—it was the name of a place.

All at once I could see him, huddled in the shelter down under some government building in Shanuga when it was still called Chattanooga and the ruins weren't ruins yet. He was listening to the radio we'd found, waiting for a message, and when it came he copied something down on a sheet of paper, looked something up in a book, and then copied down one word onto the back of the letter. They'd told him the name of the town where he was going to go once it was safe, once they could get him out of Chattanooga and send him to Star's Reach, and he'd written down the name of the town on the back of the original message so he wouldn't lose it. Then things went wrong, and it never got safe enough to get him out of there, and the food ran out and he died. I saw all of that in less time than it takes to blink.

Then we were standing there under the Spire again, facing each other, him in his stiff old world clothes and me in my dusty ruinman's leathers, and suddenly the ground beneath my feet began to shake. He looked up at the Spire with fear in his face. I looked up too, and damn if the Spire wasn't swaying back and forth above us, moving in wider and wider arcs.

All of a sudden I wasn't in Deesee any more. I was sitting in the chair made of concrete slabs by the beach, in the place where every question has an answer, and it felt as though I was being shaken awake. I looked around, but there was nobody shaking me. The moon was high in the south, and it no longer made a path across the sea in front of me, but the ground shook again, and the sea began to draw away, just as it did earlier, except this time it was all drawing back, as far as I could see to either side.

Back when I was writing about my first dream of Deesee, I must have mentioned the old strange stories about the Spire. When I was a child, people used to say that as long as it still stood tall above the sea, out there beyond the breakers, the drowned city at its feet might just rise up out of the waters someday, and if it did, the old world and all its treasures would come back again. Just for a moment, as I sat there and stared, I wondered if that was what was happening, if somehow learning the key to Star's Reach was bringing something even more wonderful.

Then the ground beneath my feet shook again, and I knew what I was seeing.

There's a place called Greenlun I've mentioned before, off to the east of Genda, between the Lannic and the North Ocean. It's covered with trees now, but in the old world it was covered with a layer of ice a couple of kloms thick, and when they messed up the climate in the last years of the old world, all the ice broke up and melted, and the meltwater flowed into the sea. That's part of why Deesee is underwater now. The priestesses say, though, that when the ice melted, the land started to rise because all that weight was off it, and ever since they've had big earthquakes all along the eastern coasts of Genda and Nuwinga and the coastal allegiancies—earthquakes and namees. A namee's a really big wave that's stirred up by an earthquake, and you know one is coming because the sea draws back from the land.

The moon gave enough light that I could just about see the land around me. Back behind the dunes and maybe half a klom further inland, there was a hill with trees on top of it—not much of a hill, and maybe not high enough, but it was the only high ground in sight. I knew there wasn't a lot of time, so I got up and grabbed my pack and ran for the hill. It wasn't an easy run, since there was driftwood back behind the dunes that I had to dodge, and once I got to the hill the brush clawed at me and scratched my face as I ran. I was panting and bleeding by the time I got well up the hill, and I stopped for a moment to catch my breath, and turned around and looked back toward the sea.

There before me was Deesee. I could see all of it, the Spire rising up above the half-fallen buildings caked with mud and seaweed, reaching north and south as far as I could see and east to a blackness that had to be the ocean. I stood there, forgetting everything else, and as I watched, the ground shook again, hard. Then the Spire began to lean toward me: slow at first, then faster and faster, until finally it crashed to ruin in the black mud.

Then the sea rose up and came rushing back into its place.

I turned and sprinted the rest of the way to the top of the hill, found the tallest and stoutest tree that I could, and scrambled up it. By the time I got up as high as I thought I could safely go, Deesee was drowned again. I read once about somebody who got through a namee alive by clinging to the top of a tree, so I found a good sturdy branch high up. By then I could hear the water boiling and surging, and I looked and saw it rushing up the slope toward me, black as the walls of the sea on either side of the path I'd followed to the Spire. I sucked in one last breath and put my arms and legs around the branch as tight as they'd go and prayed to Mam Gaia, the way you're supposed to do when you're about to get reborn.

The wave covered the hill and rose about halfway up the tree, but it never quite got up to me. A moment later the crest was past, and the tree hadn't given way. I clung to the branch for I don't know how long, shivering with the cold and certain that I was about to die.

All around me, the only things I could see were the tops of trees on the hill, and black water all around. After a while, the water stopped moving inland and started moving back out to sea, until it was back where it belonged; a second wave came rushing in a little after that, but that one only got about halfway up the hill, and I think there was a third and a fourth wave, too, but I'm not sure. I'm not sure about much of what happened during the last part of that night.

The next thing I remember for certain is waking up a little after dawn, still up there in the tree, still clinging to the branch, cold as old concrete and aching from head to foot, but more or less alive. I blinked and shook myself. Slowly, because my muscles didn't want to move, I clambered down to the ground and stood there, trying to get my thoughts to do something other than circle around and around the fact that I probably should have been fish food just then.

I don't know how long it was before I finally walked over to the brow of the hill and looked east. The Lannic was blue and mostly calm, with long rolling breakers coming in from the far horizon to crash over masses of weathered concrete or rush landwards across the beach. I stood there looking out to sea for a long time, and finally realized what was missing.

The Spire was gone. Either I watched it fall, or Mam Gaia sent me a true dream. I still don't know which.

I walked down to the beach then. I'm not sure if the chair and the ring of concrete chunks around it were gone, or if I somehow ended up at a different part of the beach. There was sand and seaweed and driftwood all over, but then there had been sand and seaweed and driftwood all over when I came there the day before. Still, whether the namee was a vision or a real wave, I had an answer to my question, and I also had a good long way to walk. I stood there looking out to sea for a while, seeing the smooth line of the horizon where the Spire used to be, and thinking about what it meant that it was gone.

After a bit, I turned and walked south again, looking for the road back inland, up the Tomic valley. There was a big mass of weathered concrete right where I'd come down to the beach—not even a namee is powerful enough to wash those away—and I recognized it and turned, and headed back inland until I found the road back home to Meriga. Once I found it I sat down and ate some of the food I'd brought from Pisba, and finally got up and started west toward the mountains and the burning land.

I didn't see another human face until I was a day out of Pisba. I don't know what happened to the Jinya horsemen I met on the way to Deesee, but I didn't see them again. I don't know how many days it took me, either, though I know I ran out of food halfway through the burning land and didn't get another meal until I showed up at the ruinmen's guild hall in Pisba and startled the stuffing out of the guild misters, who hadn't expected me to make it back alive.

All the way along the road, as I followed the Tomic as far as I could and then climbed up into the hills and started across the burning land, I had nothing to do but think. I'm not sure why, but I didn't think much about Star's Reach, or about whether or not I would be able to track down the place called Curtis once I got back to the archives in Sisnaddi. Mostly I thought about the Spire and the stories I mentioned, the ones that said that the old world might come back someday, so long as the Spire still rose out of the Lannic over drowned Deesee.

I'm not sure that people really know what they believe until something comes along that makes it come true or makes it go away forever. All along the winding road from Shanuga to here, I believed I was going to find Star's Reach. If somebody had asked me whether I believed that in Melumi or Memfis or Sisnaddi, or anywhere else along the way, I probably would have said no, but when we got within sight of the antenna housings and Star's Reach stopped being a dream and turned into the place where I'm sitting now, it didn't feel like a surprise, it felt like something that was always going to happen and just finally got around to it.

Before I left Sisnaddi to find the place where every question has an answer, if anyone had asked me whether I believed the old stories about Deesee rising back up out of the sea, I'd have laughed and said no. On the road back through the burning lands, though, my thoughts kept circling back around to the

Spire toppling in the moonlight, and the flat blue horizon I'd seen the next morning, standing there on the beach, and every time I thought of those what passed through my mind next was that now the old world was never coming back.

Later on, when I was back in Sisnaddi getting ready for the trip out here, I heard more about the Spire, and that's when I was finally sure that what I saw wasn't just a dream. Word trickled back from the coastal allegiancies that the Spire was gone, just rumors at first, then messages passed from their priestesses to ours, and a few weeks before we set out for Star's Reach some scholars who crossed over into Nuwinga from Nyork and negotiated some kind of deal with the Jinyans came back with pictures. Once that happened, in Sisnaddi and Sanloo and Cansiddi, I heard a lot of people talk about how the old world was finally gone forever, now that the Spire wasn't there any more, and that's when I knew that I wasn't the only one who believed the old stories.

Still, I'm not at all sure they're right. So much of what we do in Meriga today is about the old world even more than it's about ours. We plant trees and have laws against fossil fuels because of what happened in the old world, and we have a presden and jennels because they had those in the old world, and when a priestess wants to make sure people live the way they're supposed to, the way that keeps Mam Gaia happy with us, she just has to remind them about how they did things in the old world and what happened because of that.

It's no wonder that people used to tell stories about Deesee rising back up above the water and bringing the old world with it, because the old world may be dead but it's still here, sprawled over Meriga the way the man I found under the Shanuga ruins was sprawled over the table. I wonder how many more years will have to slip past before it finally goes away.

CHAPTER 28

A STEP TOO FAR

Berry and I spent today getting the last of the rooms ready for the ruinmen from Cansiddi, talking and joking as we worked, and right as we were finishing it sank in that in a few more days it won't just be the five of us here any more. It was Berry's turn to cook, so he went off to the kitchen, and once he was gone I went to the room with the alien-books and sat there for a while, remembering the time we've been here and everything that's happened, and I didn't leave until Eleen came looking for me to tell me that dinner was ready.

After dinner we all went to the radio room to find out if there was any more news about Berry. It's been most of a week now since the Circle elder and the Sisnaddi ruinman added their bit to the talk about the succession, and I'm sure we haven't been the only ones listening one evening after another to find out if the electors have anything to say. Until tonight, they didn't, but tonight the announcer started off the news broadcast saying that Jennel Risher Macallun had made a statement.

That had all of us listening, because Risher's not just an elector, he's also as important a jennel as you'll find in Meriga. His family owns a mother of a lot of land in Inyana, and he's been with the army since before he inherited the jennelship. When we lost at Durrem, in the war with the coastal allegiancies that killed my father, it was Jennel Risher who pulled what was left of the Merigan army together and got it back safe across the border in the teeth of everything the Jinyans and Cairlines could throw at him. I never heard anyone name him as a candidate for the presdency, so it's a safe bet that he didn't want it for himself, but no one was ever going to get it without Jennel Risher having a say in the matter.

The radio crackled and spat, and started talking in the sort of growling voice you get when you've spent years downing way too much of the cheap whiskey that soldiers drink. "The electors have been talking about this Sharl sunna Sheren," the voice said. "Informally, you understand. We were as surprised as everyone else. I won't say all of us are pleased by some of the details, but the law is what it is, and the college agreed to meet him in Sanloo on the twentieth of Febry to consider his claim."

The announcer went on to say something else, but I don't remember a word of it. I was looking at Berry. The rest of us had pulled chairs over to the radio and sat down, but he hadn't, and so he was standing, staring at the radio with an expression on his face that I've never seen there before or since, strange and quiet and very far away. Looking at him, I knew down in my belly that he was going to become presden, and I knew that he knew it too. I had the oddest feeling just then, as though I was in two places at once, there in the radio room and somewhere else, reading about the scene in the radio room in a history book a long time from now.

I think Tashel Ban felt the same thing. He got up and left the room without saying a word, while the radio chattered on about something else I don't remember. I heard him rummaging around in his room close by, then the clink and clatter of glasses down in the kitchen, and then came back with a bottle of Genda whiskey and glasses for everyone, and poured us all a good solid drink. Nobody said anything. He raised his glass to Berry; Berry raised his in answer, we all did the same, and then drank it down.

"Some of the details," Eleen said then, sourly. "I suppose that means that the electors are grumbling because they have to talk to a tween."

"Or a ruinman," I said, grinning. "At least he's not a lumberman. Can you imagine how they'd have carried on if that was how things had turned out?"

That chased the strange look off Berry's face, and he laughed and aimed a swat at me, which I ducked. All of us laughed, and for a moment it was just the five of us again, instead of four of us and the next presden of Meriga and a mother of a lot of people reading about it all in some history book that hasn't even been written yet. Tashel Ban offered everyone another drink, I took him up on it, and so did Berry, and then the announcer finished saying whatever it was that he was saying, and we went off to our rooms and I sat at my desk and thought about jennels.

Most ruinmen never get to meet one, and even though things turned out the way they did, I'm not sorry that I knew Jennel Cobey. That's partly, well, because most ruinmen never get to meet one, but it's also because Cobey Taggart was one of the most likeable people I've ever known. He never forgot for a moment that he came from an old proud Tucki family that was some kind of relation to the presden, but he didn't go around expecting everyone else to remember that all the time, the way some jennels and cunnels do. When he talked with me, it felt like I had every bit of his attention for that moment, and it didn't matter that I was a ruinman with dirt on my leathers and he might just become the next presden.

That was true all through the time I knew him, but it was even more true while we were traveling out here to Star's Reach. On that trip he wasn't surrounded by soldiers and servants, the way he usually was. He had his man Banyon with him, but that was all, and the two of them ate the same food and sat at the same campfire as the rest of us, and kept watch at night over the horses and the camp when their turns came; and we talked about everything and nothing, not just as travelers do but as friends.

That's the way it was, all along the journey from Cansiddi west to here. It was a special time, too, though there again I didn't recognize that until we were almost to Star's Reach, where it ended. I wonder to this day if it was a special time for him, or for that matter if he had any idea how it was about to end.

I've written already about how we found the two fences and then came in sight of the low blunt concrete shapes of the antenna housings, and found the door half buried in the sand. There were high thin clouds overhead and gray sandy desert all around us, and the sun was well over to the western side of the sky. If we'd gone walking into the antenna housings for another couple of kloms we would have found the door to the living quarters where we're staying now and spared ourselves some searching, though of course we didn't know that yet. We got to work right away with shovels and cleared the sand away from the door, and I got the lock picked, and finally hauled the thing open despite the shriek of the hinges.

Inside was darkness, and a smell I more than half expected and recognized at once, the lightning-smell you get when there's a mother of a lot of electricity flowing very close by. As my eyes got used to the dim light inside, I could see the thin lines of metal crossing the floor, full of current.

"Trapped," I said.

"Can you turn it off?" Jennel Cobey asked, looking past me into Star's Reach.

"If it's a standard trap, I think so." Then, staring into the darkness, I saw the little red light on the far side of the room. "Yes," I said. "I'll need to get my tools."

"Do it," he said, in a different voice. I turned away from the door, startled, and only then saw that he had drawn his gun. Back behind him, Banyon had another gun out, and moved away from the door to cover everyone else in the group.

"I'm sorry to say there's been a change of plans," Jennel Cobey said then, to all of us. "Don't move or say anything, and there won't be any trouble. Otherwise—well, Banyon and

I will both start shooting, and the rest of my people will be here in a few minutes once they hear the shots. Yes, there's been a party following us the whole way. All of you—" He motioned to everyone but Banyon and me. "Get over there, away from the door. Trey, you'll get your tools and disarm the trap now."

He followed me as I went to the horse that had my gear in its pack, got the things I needed, and went back to the door. I could feel the gun pointed at me the whole way.

While I did that I was trying to think, trying to figure out why he was doing what he was, and what he was going to do next, and a thought I didn't like at all was settling in somewhere in my belly, cold and heavy as old metal. If he wanted a contract dig, he didn't need the guns. He didn't need them if he meant to do anything the laws allowed, and if he planned on doing something else, it was pretty clear what his next step would have to be, once he'd gotten me to open the door to Star's Reach.

There was a metal panel in the concrete wall next to the door, with some buttons on it and some slots in the metal, mostly choked with dust. I popped the panel off with the pry bar, found the wiring behind it, and took a good long time figuring out which wires to snip. "There," I said finally. "That should do it."

He gave me a long steady look, and motioned toward the door. "Go in."

I went to the door and stepped inside, into the darkness and the lightning-scented air.

"Keep going," Jennel Cobey said.

I shrugged, and started walking. There was a door at the far end of the room; I could just barely see it in the faint light. I got maybe halfway to it when Cobey called out, "Stop there." He stepped through the door, considered me, and said, "I'm sorry, Trey," as he took another step and raised the gun.

His first step had been lucky. The second one wasn't.

As his foot touched the floor, the electricity discharged with a crack and a blinding flash. I hunched down where I stood, hoping I could dodge the bullet, but I needn't have bothered;

the shock threw him forward, and though the gun went off, the bullet didn't go anywhere near me. For just a moment as he fell, I could see his face, pale and contorted with an expression I didn't recognize at first, and then he landed hard, full length on the floor, with something like a dozen of the metal strips beneath him. The current surged again with a series of flashes and bangs, and his body jerked and twisted and started to smoke.

"So am I," I answered him, though I knew that only his ghost could have heard me.

Then I walked the rest of the way across the trapped floor, the way I'd done in the hidden place in the Shanuga ruins, to the little red light beside the door on the other side of the room. As I started, I heard another shot, outside, and then silence. I didn't let myself think about what that might mean. All that mattered was stepping in the right places and getting to the door and the switch on the other side of it.

I got there, opened the door, reached through and flipped the switch. The light went from red to green, and Cobey's corpse went limp. Just then, Thu's deep voice echoed in the empty room. "Trey? Are you there?"

"Yes," I called back. If it had been anyone else, I might have wondered if Banyon had a gun against somebody's head, but nothing on Mam Gaia's round belly can make Thu say something he doesn't want to say.

"Banyon's dead," he called out. "The rest of us are unhurt."

A wave of panic I hadn't let myself feel broke and flowed back to wherever fears go when you don't need them. I crossed the floor, going around what was left of Jennel Cobey, and got to the door.

For a moment, while my eyes got used to the sunlight, I couldn't see anything. The very first thing I saw was Banyon; he was sprawled across the ground with his neck at a funny angle and one side of his head caved in. He still had his gun in his hand, but I gathered he hadn't had time for more than one shot before he died, and that didn't hit anything but sand.

"When the trap went off," Thu said, "he was startled, and turned toward the door. Not a wise thing to do in the presence of enemies."

"I don't believe," said Tashel Ban, "that he thought you could react that quickly, and jump that far, that fast. I certainly didn't."

Thu shrugged. "It seemed like the appropriate thing to do." Then, to me: "You will need to get more training for Berry. A blind man could have told that he was about to rush Banyon."

I turned to Berry. "I figured I could distract him so that Thu or Tashel Ban could kill him," he told me.

"You would have gotten yourself reborn," I said.

"It would have been worth it," Berry said. His face was pale and he was still breathing big ragged breaths, but I didn't doubt for a moment that he meant it.

Then I turned toward Eleen. She was pale and trembling. Scholars don't see violence very often, and she hadn't been a failed scholar long enough for that to change. She didn't say a word; she came to me, put her arms around me and stayed there for a good long moment, shaking like a leaf in a wind. I held her. After a moment, Berry came and put his arms around us both, and I shifted one arm and gave him a squeeze to let him know he was welcome. Thu and Tashel Ban stood close; only Anna remained off by herself, silent as usual, watching us all out of the corners of her eyes.

"We need to get inside," said Tashel Ban. "If he had people following him—"

That was all the reminder any of us needed. We were all pretty shaky, except for Thu, but we got the packs off the horses and hauled them inside. Tashel Ban, who's good with horses, muttered something in their ears and then slapped them across the hindquarters, and they went galloping off eastward, back the way we'd come.

"What should we do with that?" Tashel Ban asked, gesturing at what was left of Cobey.

"Haul it outside," Thu said. "Pour oil over both corpses and light them on fire. If his people find a sealed door with two burnt corpses outside, I doubt they will try to get in."

So that's what we did. Thu and I used shovels to haul what was left of the jennel out into the open air, and splashed some of our cooking oil over him and Banyon, enough to get the clothes burning. While Thu lit them, I got the door back in working order, and once he was done and followed the others inside I locked the door, went to the far side of the room and turned the switch so the light went red again.

Just beyond the trapped room was a corridor leading further into Star's Reach. Berry had a lamp going, but the little spot of light it cast was all but drowned by the darkness of the ruin. He'd already found a stairway going down; I got a second lamp, and we shouldered our gear and started down the stairway. We didn't say much. The thought that Cobey's people might find some way into Star's Reach was on all our minds, and so was getting some distance and a lockable door or two between us and them.

Two floors down, we found the rooms I've already mentioned, dry and not too dusty, with big metal doors that could be closed and locked. We put our gear there, found a few pieces of furniture, and sat there for what seemed like half of forever, listening for any sound that might mean that Cobey's people had followed us. Thu went back up the stair; I sat close to the door in a metal chair that didn't look like anyone had used it since the old world ended, and stared out into the darkness of the corridor and the stairwell beyond it. I probably should have been thinking about the fact that I was at Star's Reach, that all the long years of traveling and working had finally gotten me to the place every ruinman had dreamed of reaching for all those years, but that wasn't what I was thinking about. I was thinking about Jennel Cobey, of course.

I thought then, and still think now, that he meant what he said when he raised the gun and pointed it at me. I was his friend, or as near to a friend as a jennel with ambitions can let himself have, and even though whatever plans he'd made meant that he had to shoot me dead, I don't doubt for a moment that he felt sorry that he had to do it.

That much made sense to me. What I didn't understand, though, was the expression on his face as he fell, when he understood the trick I played on him, and realized he was about to get reborn. For what felt like hours, and probably was, I couldn't read what it was that showed in his expression right then. So I wondered about that and waited, while afternoon turned to evening and evening to night; and then Thu and I left the others and went back up the stair.

He'd found another door to the outside, a good half-klom away from the one where we entered; it was trapped, too, but a flick of the switch took care of that. Outside it was as dark as a desert night can get, with the stars blazing overhead and the moon low in the east. Thu vanished into the night, and came back maybe a quarter hour later with word that Cobey's people had come and gone. I followed him to the place where we'd left Cobey and Banyon, and we risked a lamp. The bodies were gone, and there were plenty of bootprints and hoofprints in the sand, but that's all we ever saw of his people, then or later.

We went back inside, I locked the door and reset the trap, and then the two of us went back down the stair. As we walked, I wondered again about the look on Cobey's face, and all at once I knew that it was ordinary surprise. I think it never occurred to him that he might lose.

That's when I understood something about him, and something about the old world as well, that I never really understood before. The people in the old world never thought they could lose, either. They played with the thought now and then, or so Eleen told me once, but they never believed that anything could stop them from doing what they wanted. That's why they kept on burning fossil fuels and all the rest of it, until they took that one step too far, the way Cobey did, and found out what was really going on just a little too late to do anything about it. I still wonder now and then how many people when the old world was coming apart had the same expression on their faces as Cobey did, the moment or so before they died.

CHAPTER 29

THE SPACES BETWEEN THE STARS

This afternoon I was sitting in our common room here at Star's Reach. The table we use for meals made a good place to spread out papers, and I was sitting at one end reading back through some of the things Tashel Ban and Eleen printed out earlier, mostly papers about the Cetans. Berry was at the other end, writing out the rules of how to say things in the language the people here and the Cetans worked out to communicate with each other, so someone else can do that once he goes to Sanloo and the meeting with the college of electors. Eleen and Tashel Ban were working at the computer, getting it to print out something else that the Cetans sent us.

Everything's ready for the ruinmen. I don't think any of us were sure that we could get it all done before they arrived, but yesterday toward dinner Berry and I went over everything one last time, and couldn't find anything else that needed doing. In the evening, after dinner, we all sat around the table until late, talking as friends will, about the times we've spent together and the long road here. There won't be many more times like that, not for the five of us, and I think that was on all our minds. Certainly it was on mine, and damn if I didn't keep thinking of that night in the Shanuga ruins when I'd just made mister, and the prentices and I sat and drank small beer and talked about the same things, the good times and bad ones that we'd spent together, and the people who weren't there to remember them with us.

This morning we were all pretty much at loose ends, since there was nothing left to do but wait for the ruinmen to show up. I went back to the room with the bookshelf and unpacked all the stories I'd boxed up, and put them back in their places on the shelf. I considered doing the same thing with the alien-books, but didn't; whenever I look at them I think of the bodies we found lying here with dried poison on their lips, and Anna falling over with a knife in her chest. I think I'm going to try to get Eleen to have those sent to Melumi, where the scholars can keep them safe and people aren't going to talk themselves into believing them.

So I unpacked the stories and read bits from some of the ones I'd already read, and by then it was time for lunch. After that, as I said, I was sitting at the table reading about the Cetans when Thu came down the hall from the stair to the surface. "Riders," he said. "Not many, but more than one, coming from the east. I saw the dust they raised. We have maybe half an hour before they arrive."

That had all of us on our feet at once. The one thing we still had to worry about, and all of us knew it, was some jennel or cunnel sending soldiers to find Sharl sunna Sheren before he could get to Sanloo.

"If they find the door here, we could be in trouble," I said, meaning the door Thu had just used to go outside.

"Exactly," said Thu. "My advice? You three—" His nod took in everyone but him and me. "—take what can't be spared, and bar yourselves in a safe room in one of the deep levels. Trey, you and I will go to the east entrance and see who it is that comes. There are ways to spy on the door."

"What about the room where we first stayed?" Eleen said. "It's close to the entrance, but those doors were solid, and there's been enough going up and down the stairs that our tracks won't be visible in the dust."

That seemed like a good idea to all of us, so Tashel Ban pulled a couple of things out of his radio gear to keep it from working, Berry and Eleen packed up the papers from the Cetans into a couple of boxes, and we all hurried down the stair and through the belly of Star's Reach to the eastern end, where we'd first come in all those weeks ago. Once we had the other three safe in a room where they wouldn't be found and couldn't be gotten at, and we'd settled on a signal we could to let them know that it was safe to come out, Thu and I went up the stair to the rooms just behind the eastern entrance. I could smell the lightning-smell in the air from the trap long before I got close to the room where Jennel Cobey died.

We didn't go there, though. Thu led me off to one side, down a narrow corridor, and into an even narrower room. There was a metal fitting on the far wall at eye level; Thu motioned to me to look into it, and when I did, I found myself looking through a narrow slit at the area outside the door.

"I found this more than a month ago," said Thu in a low voice. "There are two of them by each of the original entrances—there were machines here at first to watch the doors, but those must have been stripped for parts after the old world ended."

Outside was the same sandy desert I remembered, with the hollow descending toward the door. After a moment I caught sight of the dust cloud Thu mentioned, close by, and after another moment what looked like two tiny dark shapes just this side of the dust.

I stepped back, let Thu look. "Two of them," he said after a moment. "That might be a good sign. Anyone planning violence would have sent more."

"Might be a scouting party," I said.

"True." He watched for a while longer, then moved away and let me look again. The two dark shapes had become men on horseback. I watched them pass the first fence and then the second, and then, riding more slowly, come toward Star's Reach. By the time they reined in by the second fence, I knew that they didn't look like soldiers and didn't really know how to ride. By the time they dismounted and separated, one of them holding the horses' reins and the other walking toward us, I realized they were wearing what looked like ruinmen's leathers, but it wasn't until the one who came forward got within sight of the hollow in front of the door that I broke into a big grin and stepped back from the slit.

"We're safe," I said to Thu. "Ruinmen—I know one of them."

We left the little room, and while he went down the stairs to let the others know, I turned off the switch in the trapped room, waited until the current went away, crossed the floor, and unlocked and opened the door. "Conn!" I shouted. "Right over here."

He turned—he'd been looking at the antenna housings, kloms and kloms of them reaching west toward the afternoon sun—let out a whoop, pelted over and threw his arms around me, then drew back a bit. "And damn if you aren't waiting here. Trey, you rascal! Did you know we were coming?"

"We saw the dust cloud most of an hour ago."

"And—"

I could see a hundred questions in his eyes. "It's Star's Reach," I told him. "There are messages from aliens. Pictures of aliens. All kinds of things."

His eyes and his mouth both went round, and he let out a piece of hot language that just about blistered the air. He turned, then: "Dannel! Get over here."

The other rider turned out to be another young ruinman, one I didn't recognize. He was already on his way, leading the horses, who didn't like the look of the hollow or the antenna housings and were lettng him know that. "What I want to know," I said to Conn, "is what you were doing in Cansiddi."

The astonishment on Conn's face went somewhere else. "I made mister a year after you did," he said, "and by then they'd closed the guild. Not enough metal in the ruins to keep new misters in work, they said, and of course they're right.

So I went to Cago and worked there for a few years, met Dannel there, and when word got to us from Cansiddi that there might be something big in the desert west of town, we up and headed this way."

Dannel got the horses calmed down enough to finish walking over. "And when the Cansiddi misters opened your message, well, we weren't first in line, but close. You're Trey? Pleased to meet you. Everybody else is about a day and a half further back—we offered to ride ahead and make sure you and everyone else here knew—"

His voice trailed off, and I realized about then that he was looking past me at the door to Star's Reach. Conn was staring the same direction, too, and if a bright yellow Cetan had come squishing out the door to offer them each a drink of nice cold gasoline, I don't think they could have looked any more surprised.

I looked back that way, and of course it wasn't a Cetan. "Hello, Conn," Berry said. He had just come out through the door.

Conn closed his mouth, swallowed, and said, "So that was you—Sharl sunna Sheren?"

It's a funny thing, but the people you spend the most time with are the ones who can change the most without you noticing. The moment I saw Conn through the slit in the wall, I saw how much five years had done to him, but it wasn't until I looked back over my shoulder and saw Berry there that it finally sank in how much he'd changed during the same five years. He'd always looked like his mother, though it took me a good long time to realize that, but now it wasn't something you might notice if you took the time to think about it. It was something you'd notice at a glance if you passed him in the street.

I don't even remember what Berry said in answer. "Damn," said Conn, and a moment later: "Well, damn." Then: "If I'd had any idea who you were, I wouldn't have had the guts to thrash you that time you got careless up in the tower we were stripping."

"I'm glad you didn't know, then," said Berry. "That probably kept me from getting reborn later on."

"True enough," said Conn. Dannel, who had been watching the whole time with his mouth open, shook his head and said, "There's a lot of people who are going to want to see you in Sanloo."

"I know," Berry said, a little grimly.

Dannel shook his head again, sharply. "No, I mean it. We were in Cansiddi when the radio broadcast what you said, and the next day that's all anybody was talking about. Not just ruinmen—we were out buying food and gear during the day, and the people you'd least expect were talking about it, asking every ruinman they met if we knew you, that sort of thing. And talking about going to Sanloo, to see you—and to make sure that nobody tried anything stupid."

"It was something," said Conn. "When's the last time you heard a barmaid say she was going to walk to Sanloo for something like that? Two of 'em told me that, and both of 'em said that anybody who gave you any trouble was going to get his whatnots cut off. You should have seen their faces. I honestly think they'd do it themselves, with the dullest knife they could find."

"The thing you said about civil war," said Dannel. "A lot of people were talking about that before then, but they were saying, well, what can you do? Now they've got another choice, and I wouldn't want to be the jennel who tries to take it away from them."

I looked at Berry, and he looked at me, and then at them. "That's good to hear," he said. "Still, I'm going to need to talk to some of the younger misters and senior prentices about the trip to Sanloo. I wouldn't put it past some jennels to send some soldiers looking for me."

"Easy," said Conn. "We can get more people from Cansiddi if they're needed, too. And more guns."

"I hope it doesn't come to that," said Berry. "Do you think those horses of yours want some water?"

They did, of course—we were standing in the middle of a desert, after all—and so I went and got a couple of pans of water for the horses and a bottle for the two of them, while Conn and Dannel peppered Berry with questions, some of them about himself and some of them about Star's Reach. We talked a little more while the horses drank, and then it was time for them to head back to the rest of the ruinmen and let them know that we were ready for them. "We'll be back with everyone day after tomorrow," Conn said, swinging up into the saddle. "And I want to see those pictures of aliens."

"I'll have 'em waiting," I promised.

He laughed, and the two of them rode off. Berry and I looked at each other again. "Well," he said. "That's not something I expected."

I couldn't think of anything to say in response that didn't sound stupid, so I simply clapped him on the shoulder, and we turned and went back into Star's Reach.

It wasn't until we were going back through the trapped room, with the lightning-smell lingering in the air and the black marks on the floor where Jennel Cobey died, that it struck me all at once that one way or another, the next presden after Sheren was always going to come riding out of Star's Reach. The only question was whether the presden was going to be Cobey Taggart or Sharl sunna Sheren, a jennel from a rich old Tucki family or a ruinman who happened to be a presden's secret child, someone who was going to start the Fourth Civil War or someone who might just stop it before it could get going.

One way or another, I had to be around to make that happen. If Cobey had been a little smarter than I was, the day we first got here, my part in it would have ended with me bleeding to death from a bullet hole, and Berry's story would have never have gotten past might-have-beens. Instead, it was Cobey's story that never went any further, and I had to stay around so I could talk Berry into announcing himself as a candidate. Once that happened, my part in his story might as well have been over, and when he goes riding off toward Sanloo with a guard of young ruinmen around him, my part is over for good. I've learned and done a mother of a lot of things over the last five years, and I'm sure there are other things I can learn and do that I haven't tried yet, but a farmer's child from the Tenisi hills isn't suited to anything they do in a presden's court.

So that's what I was thinking about as we went to get the others and then walked through half of Star's Reach. By the time we were back in the common room, it was evening. Thu and Berry got to work on dinner, Eleen and Tashel Ban went back to trying to coax the computer into giving up another paper on the Cetans, and I sat back down at the table and tried to read the papers I'd been reading when Thu came to warn us about the riders. It was the long paper full of brackets and dots, the one that seemed to be talking about a sea voyage to a place a little like Star's Reach, and first told us that the Cetans traveled to other planets in their system the way we did in ours, back before the old world ended.

I hadn't read it since Tashel Ban first printed copies for all of us and handed them around, and any other time I'm sure I would have been lost in it within a page or two, but just then it might as well still be a bunch of Cetan magnetic pulses for all I got out of it. I kept on trying to read it, though, since the alternative was to talk about the decisions we'd have to make before the ruinmen arrived. I didn't want to do that yet, and I don't think anyone else did either.

So I stared at the pages until it was time for dinner, we all sat and ate as though it was just one more evening at Star's Reach, and Tashel Ban and I washed up the dishes afterwards. We all gathered in the radio room to listen to the broadcast from Sanloo—there was nothing about Berry this time, just bits of news that didn't seem to mean much—and then called blessings on each other's dreams and went our ways. I sat up reading for a while, and once Eleen was asleep I wrote for a while and went to bed.

The next morning we'd all pretty much run out of other things to do, and were close to running out of time as well. After the breakfast dishes were cleared away, everyone stood around the common room, not quite getting to anything else, waiting for someone to say something. Finally I went to the table, sat down in my chair, and said, "Well."

That was all it took, of course. The others came over and took their seats. I looked at each of them and tried to think of something to say.

Thu, the four free winds bless him, made that unnecessary. "Tomorrow," he said, "or shortly thereafter, we will each have to decide where we will be going. Those of us who will be going, that is."

"I plan on staying here for another week," Berry said at once. "That ought to be enough time to arrange to leave safely and get to Sanloo."

Thu nodded. "If you wish," he said, "I would welcome the opportunity to go with you."

Berry's eyebrows went up. "That would be—very welcome." He opened his mouth as if he meant to say something else, and stopped.

Thu laughed his deep laugh. "You are too polite to ask why. It is really quite simple, though. My work here is done, or nearly so, and Sanloo is convenient. And there is the matter of your safety, which—" He shrugged. "—for wholly personal reasons, is important to me."

"Thank you," Berry said, meaning it.

"My work here," Tashel Ban said then, "isn't done, or anything close to it, and I don't expect to leave for a good many years, if ever. We've only succeeded in getting maybe a tenth of the papers on the Cetans out of the computer. All the raw communications are still in there, and there's the matter of resuming contact with them—and beginning contact with the others, if it's decided that that should happen. This is Meriga's territory, so it occurs to me that the Merigan government should probably make that decision."

He said it with a perfectly bland face, but Berry grinned and said, "If everything goes well, I think that can be arranged."

"If everything goes well," Eleen asked, "what will you do?"

"Ask Congrus to charter the guild that Trey proposed," Berry said at once. "Once that's done, nobody can challenge its right to be here and take care of communications with the Cetans and the others. After that, have the guild start sending messages to the Cetans right away, send a 'yes' to Delta Pavonis IV, and see about getting the Cetan solar power technology to the guilds that can start putting it to work."

Eleen blinked. "I gather you've been making plans."

"It seemed like a good idea," said Berry.

"In any case," said Tashel Ban, "my future is settled for the time being."

"And mine," Eleen said then. "The guild will need plenty of trained scholars, and it's not as though there are many other places a scholar can find work."

That left me, and I drew in a breath and said what I had to say. "I won't be staying. I don't know yet where I'll go, but I expect to leave within a few days."

They were all looking at me then, and I made myself go on. "Partly, my work's done. I'm not a scholar or a radioman, and I don't plan on becoming either—and once the extra metal here is hauled off, there won't be much for ruinmen to do. Mostly, though, it's Jennel Cobey."

"It would surprise me," said Thu, "if there was no trouble over that."

"Trouble for me," I said, "I can handle. I don't want it to become trouble for the rest of you, for the guild we've talked about, or for Star's Reach—and the Taggart family is important enough to make a lot of trouble for everyone, unless we all agree that I'm the one who killed him, and leave it at that."

Nobody said anything for a while. "There's got to be a better option," said Berry. "I'm not willing to see you have to run for your life—not when it's because you saved ours. If you can lie low here for a while, and everything goes well, I can protect you from the Taggarts once I'm inaugurated."

"Maybe," said Tashel Ban. "It depends on politics—which of the important families support you, how your allies and enemies sort themselves out in Congrus. They or one of their allies might also decide to take the risk of killing him, and pay whatever price they have to pay."

I raised my hands. "It's not worth risking. I've got some ideas in mind for what to do, but you don't need to know those. As far as you know, I just up and vanished as soon as the ruinmen got here, and nobody saw which way I went."

Berry didn't like it, I could see that on his face, but he said nothing more. I happened just then to look at Eleen, just as she looked at Tashel Ban. She didn't say anything, either, but the look told me something I'd been wondering about for a while.

We ended up talking about other things, mostly the guild that would be set up here at Star's Reach and what Berry could and couldn't do to help it along if he becomes presden, and before long it was time to cook another meal; we kept on talking straight through cooking the meal and eating it and washing up afterwards, too. We had a lot to talk about, no question, but there was more to it than that. Tomorrow the ruinmen will be here, and once that happens, this time will be over for good. We'll all remember it until we get reborn, but it's like the time I was together with Tam, or the two years I spent digging in the Arksa jungle through the dry season and partying in Memfis through the rains: when it's over, it's over, and no doubt there'll be plenty of good times later on but it won't ever be the same.

We ended up talking straight through until dinner. Afterwards we all went to the radio room to listen to the broadcast from Sanloo, which didn't have anything much to say but took the usual time to say it anyway. After that, we went our own ways, or mostly.

I started for the room where the alien-books were, and got about halfway there when Berry called my name from behind. I turned, and he walked up and took hold of my wrists and looked at me for a long moment with his face tight and unhappy.

"Trey," he said, "if there's ever anything you need—anything at all—get word to me and you'll have it. No questions, just— you'll have it. Understood?"

I nodded and thanked him, and he managed a smile, let go of me, and turned and went back toward his room. I knew when I thanked him that I wasn't ever going to take him up on that offer, no matter what, and I think he knew it, too, but he had to make the offer and I had to accept it, because we're ruinmen, and because we're friends.

So I went the rest of the way to the room with the alien-books, and stood there for a while. I'd had some thought or other about reading a bit from one or another of the stories, but when it came down to it I wasn't in the mood for that, or much of anything else. After a while I left, and went back to the room I've been sharing with Eleen. I didn't expect to find her there, but there she was, sitting on the bed and looking miserable.

"Trey," she said, "I told you back in Sisnaddi that I'd go anywhere with you. I meant that, and it still stands. I'll go with you when you leave, if you'll have me."

I blinked, sat down on the bed next to her, and said, "No you won't. You belong here at Star's Reach."

"Trey," she said again, and then started crying. I'm not going to try to write out how the conversation went from there, because she cried for a good long while, and when one person's crying and the other's trying to calm her down, the words that get said don't make a lot of sense when they're written out on paper. After that, I kissed her, and she kissed me back, and things more or less went from there, which doesn't make things any easier to write down. What it amounted to, though, is that she tried to convince me that she wanted to go with me, when we both knew that the one thing on Mam Gaia's round belly she wanted more than anything else was to stay at Star's Reach and spend the rest of her life studying the messages from the Cetans and the other aliens, and I had to find some way to get her to do the thing she wanted to do without making her feel that I didn't want her. Of course it didn't help that it was starting to sink in that I probably wouldn't ever see her again, and that wasn't an easy thing.

Still, it wasn't as though I had a choice. Though I hadn't whispered a word of it to any of them, of course, I already knew exactly what I'm going to do as soon as I shoulder my pack and head back east toward the settled country along the Suri River. I'm going to get rid of my ruinman's leathers as quick as I can and get some ordinary clothes, then head as fast as country roads will take me to the Hiyo valley, and find Plummer or get found by him, I don't care which. That's not just because I need to drop out of sight for a while, though of course that's part of it.

I don't know if anyone who's not a ruinman will understand the rest of it. A lot of what ruinmen do is dangerous, more of it is boring, and nearly all of it is hard work, as hard as anything anybody does in Meriga nowadays. Even when we're breaking concrete to get at the metal inside or doing some other chore that isn't exactly a bubbling mug of fun, there's always the hope that next day or the next season might just bring something wonderful. That's not always the easiest thing to believe, especially since so many ruins have gotten stripped clean and it's getting harder for new misters to find anything that will even so much as earn them a living, but the hope's there, and it's a lot of what keeps ruinmen going.

When we left Jennel Cobey and his man Banyon burning on the sand and came down the stairs into Star's Reach, though, I found the thing that every ruinman in Meriga used to dream of finding, the biggest and richest ruin of them all. If I'm lucky and a building doesn't flapjack on top of me or something, I could work as a ruinman for twenty or thirty or forty more years, but there's nothing I could find, not even if I found every one of the lost cities of the dead lands out west, that would be worth mentioning in the same breath as what's around me right now. That's why, or a good bit of why, I plan on taking Plummer up on his offer—and whatever path might be on the other side of the door he opened for me that night at the sirk in Madsen, it's a path I know I have to walk alone.

So Eleen and I talked, when we weren't doing other things, and somewhere in the middle of it all she agreed that she was going to stay and I wasn't, though I was a little preoccupied at the time and don't remember exactly when that got settled. Finally, though, we were lying there in bed; I was on my back and she had her head on my shoulder and the rest of her about half draped over me, and after a bit she started crying again, very quietly, and I lay there and stroked her hair and felt the empty aching space that was going to be part of my life once I started walking again.

That's when I decided that we really did love each other. It's a funny thing, for we both spent a lot of time wondering about that, and talked about it now and then. I also knew, from the look she'd given Tashel Ban earlier when I'd said I planned on leaving, that the two of them would probably end up in bed together not too long after I was gone, if they hadn't done it already. Still, love is like that. As Plummer said, human beings don't have to make sense, and when love sits on one side of the balance and everything else you ever wanted is on the other, love doesn't necessarily come out ahead.

She cried for a long while, then lay there quietly with me for a longer one, and then all of a sudden propped herself up on one arm and said, "There's one thing more we need to settle. The Cetan paper you were reading this morning—do you remember it?"

The change of subject left me blinking for a moment, but then I got my head clear enough to answer. "The story about the sea voyage?"

"Yes. It's their account of how they first got to the place where spaceships used to take off, before their old world ended. They sent that to the people here maybe twenty years before the message from Delta Pavonis IV came through, and they wanted the people here to send them something like that from our world. There's some discussion of that in the records we've found, but the people here hadn't settled anything when communication stopped."

I nodded. "And?"

"Tashel Ban and I were talking about that the other day, and we both remembered that there's a story right here very much along the lines of the one the Cetans sent us. So we wanted to know if you'd be willing to leave the notebook you've written here, so we can translate your story into the language we use to talk to the Cetans, and send it to them."

I gaped at her for a good long moment and then said, "Can you do that? Translate it?"

"Yes. Berry showed me how he put together his message, and we've also got computer programs that are set up to handle the translation, so it shouldn't even be that difficult."

I stared at her for another long while, thinking of blobby yellow Cetans sitting in pools of gasoline rain, reading all the things I've written since we came to Star's Reach. I know that it'll be whatever they use instead of computer printouts, and in their language of magnetic fields, but damn if I didn't keep on imagining them turning the pages of my notebook, looking at the ink and the paper.

"If you think they'll be able to make any sense of it," I told her finally, "yes, you can have the notebook."

She thanked me, and I kissed her, and before long we were going at it again, long and slow and gentle this time, because we both knew that this was pretty much certain to be our last time together. Afterwards, we lay close, and when I was sure she had gone to sleep I got up, went to my desk, turned on the little light there, and sat there staring at my notebook for a good long time before opening it and starting to write. I've thought more than once about what it would be like if someone from the Neeonjin country were to come here and read this, but the Neeonjin country might as well be one room over compared to where it's going to go.

I wonder what the Cetans will think of it. Will they ever really know what a ruinman is, or what jennels are, or what Shanuga or Memfis or drowned Deesee look like? They don't have parents or children or lovers, they don't make babies, they just crawl up out of the gasoline ocean in little pieces and come together, and go back to it again and fall apart. Will they even be able to figure out what Eleen and I were just doing, or why?

I think of that, and then I wonder just how much we'll ever know about the Cetans and their world, and let's not even talk about the thirty-eight other intelligent species out there who are waiting to hear from us. It's a big universe, and it shows just how little of the universe I can know that right now, the couple of meedas between me and Eleen feel as wide and cold as the spaces between the stars.

CHAPTER *30*

HOW THE OLD WORLD ENDED

This morning I woke up in a cold sweat, and as soon as I was washed and dressed, while Thu and Berry got breakfast made and Eleen and Tashel Ban printed out papers for the ruinmen, I read back over the story I've written in this notebook. I realized, somewhere in the middle of the night, that some of what I've written down mentions things I promised Plummer I wouldn't tell anyone, and flipping through the pages first thing, I found myself reading what I'd written about the talk we had in the field in Madsen, with the river on one side of us and the big tent of the Baraboo Sirk on the other.

I had no idea what to do. If I hadn't promised Eleen to leave the notebook with her, I could just have taken it with me when I left, but I didn't want to break my promise to Eleen any more than I wanted to break my promise to Plummer—well, and in the latter case there were the Swords to think about, and the very calm way he'd talked about throats getting cut. So I was paging through the notebook, trying to figure out if I could tear out just the pages that mattered or something, and then breakfast was ready. I stuffed the notebook in one of the drawers of the old metal desk and left it at that.

All through breakfast I was thinking about that. Back when I was writing most of it, though I wondered now and then whether anyone else would ever read the notebook, I couldn't ever quite make the thought look real. We were in Star's Reach, after all, and the rest of Meriga and everything else seemed very far away. Now that the rest of Meriga was about to come knocking on our door, I wondered how on Mam Gaia's round belly I could have been such an idiot, but the morning didn't have any answers for me.

About the time we got things cleaned up, Thu came down the stair from outside to announce that he could see a dust cloud off to the east. We'd decided the day before what to do, so as soon as the last copies of the papers were printed out, Berry and I went down the stair and set out for the old east entrance where the trapped room was, while the others went to the big room with the printers and notebooks down below the living quarters, and started getting things set up for the newcomers.

It was a strange journey, going along the big corridor on fourth level through the middle of Star's Reach. Berry didn't say much, and I said less. Pretty soon, I thought, I was going to be walking back to Cansiddi all alone with a pack on my back, and a while later, he would be riding to Sanloo with Thu and a guard of young ruinmen, and nothing would ever bring back the time we'd spent wandering around Meriga or digging up the jungle outside of Wanrij or trying to figure out what was hidden here at Star's Reach. So we walked together, the way we'd walked down that road north from Shanuga the day we started this long journey of ours, and got to the trapped room a lot sooner than I wanted to.

I turned off the trap, we both waited the couple of heartbeats it takes for the charge to go away, and then we crossed the floor where Jennel Cobey died, unlocked the door at the far end of it, and walked out into the sand and the pale sunlight of my last day at Star's Reach.

The dust cloud looked a lot bigger, but it was still just a dust cloud, with no sign yet of the people who were making it.

We walked up out of the hollow and went to the closest antenna housing; it was flat on top and low enough that you could climb up and sit, and that's what we did. The wind blew by, spraying sand against my back and whipping around us on its way toward the Suri River and the green and settled lands off beyond.

"You know what I'm thinking about?" Berry asked all of a sudden.

"Nope. Tell me," I said.

"The way I talked you into picking me as your prentice, back in Shanuga. You have no idea how glad I am that it worked."

"Maybe not," I told him. "But I know how glad I am."

He grinned and put an arm around me, and I put one around him, and we sat there and waited until the first dark shapes of people and horses came into sight in the distance. One hundred forty-three misters and senior prentices make a mother of a lot of dust, and when they've got horses loaded up with enough food and gear to keep going through the rains and out the other side, it's a mother with babies. I was glad that the wind was blowing toward them and not toward us.

Not too long after that, they were close enough to see us. We got off the antenna housing, stood there and waved, they waved back, and a little later one of them broke from the front of the column and came running forward. It was Conn; he came up to us, panting, gave Berry a mock-serious bow, and then threw his arms around me. "Here we are!" he said. "Everything's fine?"

"Ready and waiting," I told him, and he laughed. "Star's Reach," he said. "I slapped myself this morning, just to make sure I wasn't dreaming all this."

Then the others came up, and damn if one of them wasn't Orin, the mister who'd offered me a chance to join the Memfis guild. He hadn't forgotten, either, and after he'd given me a big backslapping hug, he said, "Well, Sir and Mister Trey, you seem to have done pretty good for yourself after all."

I laughed and said, "Put it down to plain pigheaded stubbornness."

There was dust and shouting and horses whinnying and jostling all around us. Berry was talking to Conn, and then all of a sudden he heard something off in the middle of the noise that jerked him around as though somebody had a string tied to his nose. A moment later he was running through the crowd of ruinmen and horses. Orin turned to look, blinked, and after a moment said, "Is that who I think it is?"

I just nodded. Orin's eyes widened, and he shook his head. "Of all things."

Then Berry was back, and somebody else was with him. It took me a moment to recognize the other person as Sam, Cob's prentice from the empty nuke in Tucki. It took me longer still to notice that Sam had a bundle wrapped in cloth cradled in one arm. While I was figuring all this out, Berry walked straight up to Conn and said, in an outraged voice, "You didn't tell me!"

"Sam made us promise," Conn said. Berry glared at him and walked right past him to me. "Trey," he said, "you remember Sam, don't you?"

"Of course." To Sam: "Glad to see you here. I hope Cob's all right?"

"More or less," said Sam. "He fell off a ladder and I had to get him to the guild hall at Lekstun—it was pretty bad. I don't think he'll work again, though he's got enough money to be fine. So I came west. Is this really Star's Reach?"

The last part of that more or less slipped by me, because I'd finally figured out what the bundle was that Sam was carrying. I looked at Berry, who was beaming, and then back at the bundle, and Sam noticed and pulled back the cloth a little. Yes, it was a baby, with a little lick of red hair on its forehead just to tell you whose grandchild it was.

Orin was staring past me by then. He turned to face Berry. "Yours?"

"Yeah."

"So you've already got yourself an heir."

You could just about watch Berry the ruinman turn into Sharl sunna Sheren the next presden of Meriga as the question sank in. "Yes."

"Well, damn. A lot of people are going to be happy if we won't have to go through this same nonsense again. Any chance you can get yourself a couple more, just to be sure?"

Sam turned bright red, but managed to say, "We'll do our best."

Everybody laughed at that. "Trey," Berry said to me, "we'd settled that if this happened, we'd name him after you—if you don't mind."

I'm not exactly sure what words I used to tell him I didn't mind at all, because I had my arms around both of them and my face was wet. Still, we got that sorted out, and Berry went off with Sam and the baby, and that left me to get the ruinmen, the four failed scholars they'd brought, and all the horses and gear and everything inside. The horses didn't like the smell of the trapped room at all, but there was a big room close to the eastern door that made a pretty good stable; and once they were settled and a few of the prentices got talked into staying to take care of them, the rest of us went on into Star's Reach.

If I needed a reminder of how big and dark and silent Star's Reach seemed when we first arrived here, that would have done it. As we went down the stair to fourth level and along the big central corridor to the room below our living quarters, everyone but me was staring this way and that, talking only in low voices and not much even then. I got them to the room with the printers and the books of numbers; Tashel Ban was there and so was Eleen. With their help I got everyone up the stair to the living quarters, and we spent the next hour or so getting the newcomers settled into the rooms we'd cleared for them. Some of the prentices got working on a meal, and then the failed scholars gathered in the common room to talk with

Eleen, while the rest of us went back down the stairs to the room below.

We'd hauled all the desks and low dividing walls out of the way and brought in chairs for everyone, so the ruinmen sat down and Tashel Ban stood in front and started talking. He'd figured out a way to get pictures from the computer up onto a big white screen, so I got to see it all again, and watched Conn and the others get told in a couple of hours everything we'd learned since we got here. I heard some pretty hot language, but toward the end I don't think anyone said a word; they were all staring with round eyes as Tashel Ban talked about the message from Delta Pavonis IV.

Then it was over. Tashel Ban had the briefing documents he'd printed out all stacked on a table, and made sure all the misters got a copy of everything, and then we all went back up the stairs for lunch. I spent the meal and a good while after it talking with some of the senior misters about how much metal there was that could be salvaged and sold, and what had to be left. I had my finder's rights to sell off, and that's a complicated thing when the money to pay for it will be coming in a bunch at a time for years. Meanwhile some of the prentices who'd heard Tashel Ban got sent to take care of the horses and wash the dishes, and the ones who hadn't went back down the stair so that Tashel Ban could say the whole thing over again for them.

By the time we'd finished sorting out the metal, the money, and the rest of it, I was ready to go hide in my room or something. Until the ruinmen arrived, I hadn't noticed just how used I'd gotten to the quiet of a big empty site with only five people in it. Now that it was as loud and busy as a ruinmen's camp always is, well, let's just say I didn't have much trouble telling the difference. When I got up from the table, though, Orin said, "One other thing. A few of us need to talk to you about something private."

I could see from his face that he meant really, really private. "Sure," I said. "Down below, maybe?"

The "few of us" amounted to Orin and two other misters, one from western Tucki and the other from Sanloo, I forget their names. We went down the stair and crossed the room behind the prentices, who were staring with wide eyes at something Tashel Ban had up on his screen, then ducked into the empty parts of Star's Reach. Two levels down another stair and along a corridor was a meeting room, or something like one, with chairs in it and a big black table and a white board up on the wall with marks on it none of us had been able to read.

We sat down. I thought I could guess what this was about, and I wasn't wrong. "We need to know what happened to Jennel Cobey Taggart," Orin said.

I nodded. "I'm wondering how much you already know."

Orin looked at the other two, who nodded, and then turned back to me. "Here's what happened. About two months ago, the ruinmen's hall in Luwul got contacted by the Taggart family. They knew he'd gotten himself reborn, and they knew that old world technology had something to do with it. They wouldn't say a lot else, but they wanted to know if we'd heard anything about him messing with the kind of thing, well, that you don't mess with."

I took that in. "Nobody in the Luwul guild knew anything about that," Orin went on, "but they did some checking around, and contacted ruinmen in other cities. That's when I got involved. We decided we needed to find out what happened to the jennel, and why the family was being so tight-lipped about it all. We called in quite a few favors with the other guilds, and—well, I won't go into it.

"We found out." He leaned forward. "He'd been dabbling in the worst sort of old world technology. One of his servants tipped off the family. He had plans for an airplane, one that burned alcohol in its engine and could carry guns and bombs. He had some other things—I'm not even going to go into them, they're that bad. He was—" I could see the bump on Orin's throat go up and down. "He was planning on using those if the electors didn't give him the presdency and it came to civil war. And he was planning on starting that here, where it could be done out of sight of anybody, and where there's an old airfield close by. He knew that; he had some maps of this facility in his private papers."

I closed my mouth after a moment.

"So we need to know what happened to him," Orin said. "The Taggarts want to know—and so do the priestesses. This is not a small thing."

I nodded, drew in a breath, and told them what happened. When I was done, Orin looked at the mister from Tucki, who nodded and said, "That matches what we got from the family."

Orin turned to me and said, "That was a good piece of work. Still—" He leaned forward again. "The family's trying to keep things quiet, for obvious reasons. The priestesses are willing to let them, so long as it doesn't become a public scandal—then they'd have to call in the government, and there would be trials and a mother of a lot of very ugly things aired for everyone to see."

"What Orin is trying to say," said the mister from Sanloo, "is that some very important people would be glad if nobody ever hears what happened—and it would probably be a good idea for you to make yourself good and scarce for a while. Maybe a long while."

We talked a while longer before we went upstairs, but I don't remember more of it than a stray word here and there. I was trying to fit my mind around what I'd just heard. It all made sense in the worst possible way. I could imagine Cobey Taggart watching the plan come together, and realizing that if he just let me keep on blundering ahead, he could get rid of two dangers, Sheren's heir and Thu, and take over a place where he could build his airplanes without anyone knowing about it. When they came buzzing out of the western sky to fire bullets and drop bombs on his rivals, who could be sure that they hadn't been waiting at Star's Reach?

All I had to do was find out where Star's Reach was, and if I'd failed, he could have brought out his maps, handed them to me, and claimed that his people had found them in some unlikely place. All he had to do to fool me and make it work was to take a few risks, and he'd succeeded so often I don't think it ever occurred to him that he might fail.

It was when we were going back up the stairs to the living quarters that I realized that I finally knew when the old world ended. Not that long ago, I thought like everyone else that it ended four and a half centuries ago. After I watched the Spire fall, if I really did see that, I wondered if the old world had ever ended at all. Both times, I was wrong, because the old world ended in the trapped room by the east entrance of Star's Reach, when Cobey Taggart took his last step and his foot came down on metal. He couldn't have brought the old world all the way back, not really, but he could have tried, and if he'd gotten far enough, he might have convinced other people to think the same way he did, and brought one last round of Mam Gaia's fury down on all our heads.

Instead, he got himself reborn, and it'll be Berry who comes riding out of Star's Reach to become presden. I don't think I'll ever rest easy thinking about how little it would have taken to make things go the other way.

So that's what I was thinking when we got back to the living quarters. Orin and the other two misters thanked me and went off to make sure their prentices were settled in, everyone else was somewhere or other besides the common room, and I stood there for a good long moment wondering what I was going to do.

Then I heard footsteps whispering down the stair to the surface. I turned just as Thu came down them. He stopped, motioned to me to come over, and very quietly said, "A friend of yours is waiting above."

I stared at him for a moment, and all at once realized who it had to be. He put his finger to his lips. I managed a nod somehow;

he stepped out of the way, and I went up the stair and out the door into the afternoon sunlight with my head spinning. There was someone sitting on one of the antenna housings close by, and he turned as I stepped out onto the sand. I didn't need to see the round eyeglasses glint like moons to know that it was Plummer.

"Allow me to congratulate you," he said, after we'd greeted each other. "For this very remarkable find, and—" He gave me one of his considering looks. "—for the details of your arrival, shall we say. Thu told me what happened, though of course I'll want to hear your account as well."

"You know," I said, "I never would have guessed that he was a friend of yours."

"Thu? If you mean a member of our guild, no, not at all. We have an arrangement with him, as we do with the priestesses and some others; with his family, I should say, for it was originally made with his great-great-grandfather. We have him review any book on technology before we put it back into circulation, and he does occasional work for us, when that's needed."

"As a Sword?"

"Essentially, yes." He motioned for me to join him, and I climbed up and sat next to him on the antenna housing. Wind whipped sand around us, and the sun sank toward the haze in the western sky.

"I'm honored," I said.

Plummer chuckled at that. "I hope I won't disappoint you by saying that you weren't the main reason he was here. No, that was your young prentice—I'm by no means certain what to call him now."

"Sharl sunna Sheren. I'll always think of him as Berry, but—"

"Understood. Thu believed he needed protection, and of course he was quite correct—and we were mistaken. Since Cobey Taggart had ample opportunity to kill young Sharl if he'd wished to do so, and since he'd also spared Thu's life when killing him and throwing the body into Banroo Bay would have been the simplest option, we didn't treat the rumors about his intentions as seriously as we should have. Things could have ended so badly."

I thought about that for a while. "I wonder if anyone knows why Cobey didn't kill Thu."

"As it happens, yes." Plummer shook his head, and chuckled again. "It's quite funny, really. We found out from the Taggart family, who got it from some of the jennel's servants after his death. He didn't believe that the man who assaulted you was actually the last king of Yami. He found it highly amusing that some ordinary Memfis street criminal had convinced you of something so very unlikely, and would laugh about it when he'd been drinking."

I thought about that, too. "And Berry?"

"That was considerably more complicated. Did you ever find out who it was that was following you along the back roads of Tucki, when we first met?"

"If it was the same person who was following us in Inyana, yes."

Plummer nodded. "Sheren kept watch over her child. If anything had happened to Sharl, and she had any reason to think that Cobey Taggart was involved, he would have died in some very unpleasant manner, and I'm sure that he knew it. He couldn't act until he was certain she was dying, and not even then unless he was far enough from settled country that he could keep word from getting back to her while she still lived. We failed to take that into account."

"And I helped the whole thing along," I said, shaking my head.

Plummer looked at me for a long moment. "He would have come here one way or another, you know," he said. "With you or without you. Because it was the first of those, and not the second, there won't be a Fourth Civil War in our lifetimes. The gains of the last hundred years or so have the chance to become the foundation of something lasting, and not just one more of history's might-have-beens."

The wind rushed past us on its way to the green hills beyond the Suri. "Meriga is healing now," Plummer said. "Not healed—it won't be healed for many centuries to come, not fully—but it's healing. There's strength and hope and a sense of possibility that might be turned to good purposes, or bad ones. All things considered, the country could benefit just now from a presden who's earned his living with his own hands, who's traveled from one end of it to the other on his own feet, who's learned what it means to be disliked and distrusted for no better reason than the prejudices of the thoughtless. That might spare us some mistakes, and put some high hopes in reach." He glanced at me. "Or not. There are no guarantees."

"I suppose there never are," I said.

Plummer nodded. "At the same time," he said, "your find here may have quite some impact of its own. Thu told me some of what turned up here; I admit to a great deal of curiosity about the details."

"I have a copy of everything we printed out. It's down below, but I can get it for you."

"Many thanks. And of course that brings up another matter we should discuss."

"Your offer."

"Precisely. Have you considered it?"

"Over and over again." I drew in a breath. "I'd like to take you up on that—but there's a problem, or might be." I swallowed, then, and told him about this notebook, about the account I'd written of my journey here, and where Eleen and Tashel Ban wanted to send it.

He took that in, then: "Are you willing to place yourself under my authority as Cord?"

"Yes."

"Even if that means that I tell you to destroy the manuscript?"

I'd already thought about that. "Yes."

"That won't be necessary," he said at once. "Can you arrange for it to be hidden once the translation has been made and sent to the Cetans?"

I thought of what Eleen said, when we were discussing the message from Delta Pavonis IV, about hiding everything we'd found for a thousand years, and nodded. "The scholar we have here is a good friend. She'll do that if I ask her."

"That will be quite adequate." He paused, then went on. "Perhaps we can arrange with her to have the manuscript placed in one of our collections, once she's finished with it. Fifty years from now, anyone could read it without danger. It's simply the interval between then and now that's at issue." With another of his little smiles: "And I confess to a certain degree of vanity. It would be pleasant to know that beings on another planet will have heard of me. More to the point, of the work in which I'm engaged."

"I wonder what they'll think about that," I said. All at once I could imagine a bunch of blobby yellow Cetans sitting in a pool of gasoline in some tilted-bowl building of theirs, under the golden sky of Tau Ceti II, talking to each other in their magnetic-field voices and trying to figure out who this Plummer person was in the strange story they'd gotten by radio from Mam Gaia all those light-years away. I grinned and said, "For all we know, some of them might be doing the same work."

"An enticing thought." Plummer looked at me for a moment, then said, "How soon would it be convenient for you to leave?"

I'd been wondering all along how soon he would ask that question, or one close enough to it that the difference wasn't worth worrying about. "Whenever you like. Well, I'll need to see to the notebook and get my things packed, but that's all."

"Excellent. It would be best if we could leave before nightfall."

I got off the antenna housing. "So long as you won't disappear when I turn my back."

That got me a broad smile. "I can certainly promise that," he said. "In fact, one of the first things you need to learn is how that's done."

"I'd like to know that," I told him.

"We can begin as soon as you return," he said.

There are voices outside in the hallway now, prentices talking with each other as they head for the kitchen and the evening's chores. In a little while, when they're gone, I'll shoulder my pack and head up the stair and leave Star's Reach behind, and Plummer and I will be on our way—where, I have no idea, and I'm not at all sure it matters to me just at the moment. The note for Eleen is on the bed we've shared. I'd be lying if I said the note was just about this notebook and what to do with it, but that's one of the things I wrote about.

I wondered for a while if I should take something from Star's Reach to carry with me wherever I go next, the way I've carried Tam's yellow metal butterfly, the ring that used to be my mother's, the star they sent her after my father died, and the few other things I've got in the little bag of keepsakes down at the bottom of my pack. Still, I decided against it, and I think that was the best choice. I'll be carrying plenty with me anyway: the view from Troy Tower, the nights with Eleen and those other nights in Memfis during the rains, the lazy days on the canal boat and the riverboat, the stories I heard when we were camping at night with travelers on a dozen different roads, the slow arc the Spire made as it fell and the expression on Jennel Cobey's face as he fell, too. It's more than enough.

I asked Plummer about that, in a way, before I came back down into Star's Reach. I'd just about turned to go, and then stopped and said, "One other thing," and reminded him about what he'd said about the one big and nameless story that has all other stories in it.

He blinked. "I said that?"

"I think you were drunk."

"That's certainly possible," he admitted.

"The thing I'm wondering is this," I said. "If I've finally gotten out of the one big story, what do I do now?"

He thought about that for a moment. "If it's true," he said, "that all stories belong to that one story, you can't leave it, because whatever you do is a story—whatever any of us do is a story, and part of other stories. As long as the end of the story you're in isn't the end of you as well, I suppose you find a new story that the rest of your life can tell."

He paused, then, and glanced up at me. "In a way, you know, that's what Meriga has been doing for the last four hundred years. The old world had its own favorite story, which said that we owned Mam Gaia and everything else and could make them all do whatever we wanted"—he gave me a little smile—"like animals in a sirk. That story didn't have a happy ending, quite the contrary, and since then, we've been looking for another story to tell."

"Well, most of us," I said.

"True enough. Cobey Taggart wanted to go back to the old story, and look how his story ended." He shrugged. "But most people know better now. It might just be possible now for us to find out what our new story should be, and get to work telling it."

I thought about that as I came down the stair into Star's Reach, walked down the corridor to this bare little room, turned on the lamp and got out this notebook as I've done so many times over the time I spent here. Plummer's right, and not just about Meriga. Nuwinga and Genda and the coastal allegiancies are looking for new stories, if they haven't found them already, and other people all over Mam Gaia's round belly are busy looking for their own new stories—and they'll find them.

I'm sure of that because there are others who've already done it. The Cetans might still be figuring out their new story, but the bubble-and-feather things from Delta Pavonis IV figured out theirs back before the first of Mam Gaia's human children climbed down out of the trees in Affiga, and I don't even want to think about how long ago some of those other species made—what was it the message said?—the usual mistakes and suffered the usual consequences, picked themselves up again and found some new story to tell with their lives and their worlds. If they could do it, I'm pretty sure we can.

And you know, I think I probably can, too.

* * *

There are three pieces of paper pasted on the inside back cover of the original notebook. The first is a handwritten note, which seems originally to have been pinned to the outside of the front cover:

My dear Lissa,

This is the manuscript I told you about. You may read it
if you wish, but please don't make a copy of it or show it
to anyone else in the guild, and give it to *(a word or name
carefully blotted out with ink)* as soon as possible. She'll see
to it that it gets to the place it needs to be.

With all my thanks and gratitude,
Eleen darra Sofee

Below this is a handwritten label:

Manuscript #338
Received into this collection on 14 Janwer,
24th year of Sharl sunna Sheren's Presdency

Below this is a printed label:

This manuscript, accession number 2878,
has been placed in the special collections
of the Central Archive of the Guild of Rememberers
on the occasion of its public dedication
on the twenty-second day of Toba
in the sixteenth year of Trey VII,
Presden of the Union of Great Meriga
being in the ancient calendar
October 22, 2821 AD.